Forbidden Fantasies

forbidden fantasies

JAID BLACK, JACI BURTON,
ANN JACOBS, SAHARA KELLY,
SHERRI L. KING, CHEYENNE McCRAY,
LORIE O'CLARE, & JORY STRONG

Pocket Books

New York   London   Toronto   Sydney

Pocket Books
A Division of Simon & Schuster, Inc.
1230 Avenue of the Americas
New York, NY 10020

First Pocket Books hardcover edition October 2008

POCKET and colophon are registered trademarks of Simon & Schuster, Inc.

For information about special discounts for bulk purchases,
please contact Simon & Schuster Special Sales at 1-800-456-6798
or business@simonandschuster.com.

Designed by Marie d'Augustine

Manufactured in the United States of America

10 9 8 7 6 5 4 3 2 1

Library of Congress Cataloging-in-Publication Data
Forbidden Fantasies / Jaid Black . . . [et al.] — 1st Pocket Books hardcover ed.
    p.   cm. – (Ellora's Cave anthologies)
1. Erotica stories, American. I. Black, Jaid.
  PS648.E7F66 2008
   813'.60803538—dc22   2008002777

ISBN-13: 978-1-4165-7869-7
ISBN-10:   1-4165-7869-2

Contents

forbidden fantasies

Bossy & Clyde

JAID BLACK

Chapter One

"I'm afraid this simply won't do."

"I don't understand."

"What's not to understand, sir? It's ugly. I hate it."

Damon Clyde ran a hand over his five o'clock shadow as he tried to make sense of the tiny, odd creature standing next to him. Tan, blonde, blue-eyed and full-figured, she was a beautiful woman from an aesthetic standpoint. Not a conventional looker by any means, but provocative in an earthy way.

He knew all kinds of females—from dancers to accountants, actresses to schoolteachers—but he could honestly say he'd never met, let alone lusted after, a woman quite like Kandy Kane, a self-proclaimed psychic artiste with an I-just-escaped-from-the-nuthouse air about her. He couldn't understand why his dick got rock hard every time he so much as caught a whiff of her scent.

Her name was actually Kandrea Kane and, from what he'd been warned, she hated it when people took the liberty of shortening her name to Kandy. Damon made a mental note to make use of that torture tactic very soon if she didn't quit frustrating the shit out of him.

Kandrea had hired his firm, Clyde & Masterson, to renovate her newly purchased one-bedroom Manhattan apartment. She wanted her home to be "the perfect little aura retreat" and had used her so-called psychic ability to decide on which of New York City's umpteen builders she would hire. He had found himself wishing more than a few times this past week that her premonitions, or more likely the Yellow Pages, hadn't led her to him.

"Ms. Kane . . ." Damon inhaled deeply and exhaled slowly. She would not, under any circumstances, get to him. "I'm trying to understand what exactly it is you find ugly about this wall, but seeing as how my crew hasn't even built it yet, I'm somewhat puzzled."

He forced a smile, pleased that he managed to spit that sentence out calmly, if a bit gruffly. He could almost understand her taking a disliking to a wall that actually existed, but an imaginary one?

Holy shit, the woman was a kook.

"But you're *going to* build it," Kandrea said crisply. "And then you're going to paint it."

"You said you wanted it painted."

"Yes. But I didn't say I wanted it to be canary yellow! Good grief. My alcoholic aunt vomits up bile more attractive than that color."

"It will *not* be painted yellow. It'll be the *exact* shade of violet-blue you asked for."

"That's not what I saw in the vision I had this morning."

"Oh for cripes' sake—"

"I distinctly saw a member of your crew paint my wall an ungodly yellow hue!"

Her nostrils flared as though this had all really happened. Damon didn't know whether to laugh, cry, bellow at her to find another builder, fuck her until she shut up or all of the above. He slapped a palm to his forehead. The woman was driving him into the same psychotic mental state she called home.

Nothing and no one got to him. Ever. He didn't want her to be the first.

And just what was it about her that was so damn alluring anyway? Damon was the sort of man whose nature was ruled by logic and science. He didn't deal well with feminine feelings, let alone cuckoo psychic ones. He was stoic and in control, sturdy and concrete. He didn't raise his voice or use his physical strength to make others cower. He never lost his cool.

And then came Kandy Kane.

He could feel the need to shout, possibly hit someone or something, boiling dangerously below his typically collected exterior. She was getting under his skin and making a mess of his well-ordered world.

"My sensitive aura," Kandrea said crisply, "cannot *and will not* tolerate the putrid color of stomach bile coating my wall."

Damon's fists balled at his sides. It was either that or punch a hole through the nonexistent wall in question.

Kandrea Kane was crazier than bat shit. And his dick was so hard it ached. He didn't know whether he was angry at her for being a first-rate nutjob or at himself for being attracted to a woman who made Sybil seem lucid by comparison.

He waved the work order in her face. "I have it written right here—F4, which is as violet-blue as you can get. The wall will be painted that color per your instructions." His jaw clenched. Sweet God, even he could take but so much. Back in his Army days, Damon had survived two wars and ten enemy ambushes without falling apart, but this short, bizarre woman might take him down yet. "It will be built by the end of the week. It will be painted to your damn aura's liking by the weekend! Are you satisfied, *Mizzz* Kane?"

Her hands were challengingly planted on her hips, but she said nothing. Their gazes locked in a war of wills, her wolflike blue eyes narrowed. The silence stretched out between them.

He had shouted at her. The burst of passion had left his heart racing, his nostrils flaring and his chest heaving. He had learned long ago never to let his emotions get the better of him. Such displays worried people.

Damon was well aware of the fact that his size and muscular build were intimidating to men and women alike. He had stood a solid and powerful six feet, six inches since the ninth grade. In thirty-eight years of living, nobody had ever been stupid enough to pick a fight with him. People were instinctively wary of men sporting his mass and brawn. Yet Kandrea Kane stared at him as though she'd killed gnats more worrisome than he was. He wasn't certain if he should be impressed or irritated.

Apparently his dick thought he should be aroused. The damn thing was pressing hard against his jeans, pre-cum leaking out. The kook and her aura were driving him insane.

She turned with a whoosh of her wispy skirt and eyed the invisible wall. She always dressed like a gypsy vampire, a look that suited her perfectly. She unfailingly wore head-to-toe black clothing, her fingers and wrists decorated with bejeweled rings and arm bangles in every color under the sun.

"Yes," Kandrea finally said, ending the long, tense silence. She whirled around, showing him a hint of ankle and a wisp of blonde curls. He'd seen more skin on a nun, yet his cock seemed to think they were at a strip club. "I am satisfied."

If only *he* was. Damon frowned severely. He feared he'd spontaneously combust if he didn't get out of the apartment soon. Enough was enough.

"Good," he grunted. "I'll be back tomorrow."

• • •

"Breathtaking!"

"Haunting!"

"Pure genius!"

Kandrea recalled the enthusiastic compliments Olivia and Andie had showered her with an hour ago regarding her latest artistic endeavor. Were it not for Kandrea's tendency toward self-criticism, she would have dared to call the vivid emotional rendering a masterpiece. It was definitely the best thing she'd ever painted.

She knew her two best friends had meant every word of their praise. For starters, they were both fellow artistes and recognized the need their kind harbored for brutal honesty. And being the sensitive empath that she was . . . well, it was difficult if not impossible to fool Kandrea with false, empty words. There had been many times throughout the years when she'd wished things were normal—that *she* was normal—but such wasn't the hand life had dealt her.

Kandrea had become self-aware at the tender age of five. She had always known she was unlike other kids her own age, but until kindergarten hadn't understood just how different she was. Her mom had referred to her as "special" and called her "gifted." The children at school had teased her mercilessly, opting for "freak" over "special" and "possessed" over "gifted."

While the neighborhood girls played outside, jumping rope and enjoying hopscotch, she drew and painted pictures of events that had taken place anywhere from the day before to thousands of years ago. She usually didn't know who the characters in her sketches and paintings were, but had long ago accepted that, for whatever reason, the ghosts of the deceased wanted their stories told.

And so Kandrea told them—in honest, sometimes heart-breaking, detail.

Her latest painting was probably the most haunting re-creation of past events she'd ever put to canvas. She couldn't say why because it certainly wasn't the saddest thing she'd ever painted, yet something about the three-panel objet d'art wrenched her heart.

The first panel showed a boy, barely an adolescent, being teased mercilessly by other kids. Freakishly tall for his age, the boy stood out like a sore thumb at school. His mother looked on, heartbroken, wanting to shield her son from the pain, yet knowing when the cancer that was eating her alive worked its course, her child would need to be strong and able to fend for himself.

The second panel flashed forward a few years, to the mother's funeral. The giant of a boy was weeping quietly as he stared down at what was left of his mother's frail body. He had wanted so much to be accepted by the other kids before she passed on so she'd know he would be all right, but that had never come to be. His peers no longer picked on him—they'd be fools to—but they ignored him as though he wasn't even there.

The final panel of the painting showed the mother's ghost in vivid blue and poignant purple swirling above her casket. She reached down to the son who could no longer see her, trying to tell him that she knew he would grow up to become an extraordinary man. The height and brawn considered beastly by high school standards would be seen as an attribute by women and a point of envy by other men when he was an adult. She ached to hold her son, to reassure him that her love would always be with him, but she dwelled in a different world from the boy now and couldn't breach the portal that separated them.

Kandrea's eyes grew misty as she stared at the painting. She wished she knew who the boy was so she could give him the painting. She sighed, realizing that such luck rarely happened. The only thing she could do now was sell it, hoping it ended up in the right person's hands. Over the years she had learned to console herself this way, knowing there was little else she could do.

She had been tempted to keep this particular painting, for it called to her on so many levels. She too had lost her mother at a young age—and she definitely knew what it felt like to be branded a freak. But, reclusive and possessing all of two friends, Kandrea knew that more people were likely to see a sold painting than one that stayed in her studio. She had no choice but to put the work of psychic art up for sale in her next collection.

Turning away from the painting with a whoosh of black skirt, Kandrea walked to the window and peered across the narrow Manhattan street. The contracting company she had hired,

Clyde & Masterson, would be done refurbishing her new home in roughly two weeks. She couldn't wait to move into the much bigger apartment. Plus, living where she worked was becoming psychically exhausting.

As she recalled her earlier conversation with the construction company's owner, her lips pinched together and she turned away from the window and crossed the tiny studio to her even tinier kitchen.

She didn't know what it was about the large, brooding man that she found so handsome, but her attraction to him was undeniable. He frowned more than smiled, grunted rather than laughing. He was prickly and pompous and quite obviously didn't believe that true empaths existed—not her type by a long shot. Nevertheless, the desire to have a torrid affair with the stuffy lout pounded through her libido as acutely as the recollections tore through her psyche.

"I must be losing it," she muttered, clanging dishes around as she searched for her favorite teacup. "Damon Clyde is *not* my type."

Turning off the kettle and popping a bag of herbal tea into the retrieved cup, Kandrea consoled herself with the notion that the attraction she felt was purely physical and no doubt one-sided. He was so tall as to make her feel tiny, though in reality she stood five feet, six inches and weighed in the vicinity of one hundred fifty pounds on a good day. He was dark-haired and dark-eyed, and just as muscular as he was tall. He was . . .

Oh, forget it! She never had to worry that he would find out about her bizarre attraction to him, for a man such as himself, a man who could have any woman he wanted, would never even notice the likes of her other than to gawk at her. His type never did.

Irritated, she violently strained the hot tea bag in her hand over the cup, causing it to burst apart and spray her with herbal leaves. "Damn it!" Kandrea swore as she wiped up the mess. She had given up her precious caffeinated coffee for decaffeinated tea a week ago and found herself, not for the first time, lamenting that decision.

Her teeth gritted as her gaze flicked over to the window. She prayed that Damon finished her new apartment soon so she wouldn't be obliged to deal with him ever again.

And preferably before he drove her entirely bonkers.

Chapter Two

*W*e should be done with the Kane place ahead of schedule," Damon's business partner, Mathias Masterson, predicted over pizza and beer. "Then we can move on to that singer's apartment down in Soho."

"Supermodel," Damon corrected.

"Huh?"

"She's a supermodel, not a singer."

"Oh. Well, whatever. The point is we are running ahead of schedule."

Damon watched from across the table as Mathias brushed what he supposed was a microscopic piece of lint off the jacket sleeve of an expensive designer suit. He sighed, suppressing the need to roll his eyes. He loved his partner like a brother, but the man put the *A* in *Anal*. After Mathias finished arranging his pizza symmetrical to the fork and knife on either side of his plate, Damon put a question to him.

"Have you met Kandrea Kane yet?"

"Yes," Mathias confirmed. He picked up his mug of beer and inspected it for any hint of dead gnats, parasites, crusty food the dishwasher had overlooked—and God knows what else—before taking a swallow and setting the mug down. "A strange lady, if you ask me."

"That's kind of like the pot calling the kettle black," Damon said drolly.

"I am *not* strange," Mathias shot back. "I'm fastidious."

"All right. Fastidious and strange, then."

His partner frowned. "Ghosts don't talk to me. I don't paint portraits of imaginary dead people for a living." Another infinitesimal piece of lint was plucked from his sleeve and brushed to the floor. "I just prefer for my life to be a clean, well-oiled machine. There's not a damn thing strange about striving to be your best."

Damon sighed. "I didn't mean to insult you. Listen, buddy, let's just eat, all right? I'm in a pisser of a mood."

"Why? Something happen between you and Ms. Kane today?"

"You could say that."

"How intriguing." Mathias flashed him a grin. "She might be bizarre, but she's not exactly hard on the eyes."

"Nothing like that happened. And she's not bizarre!" Damon snapped.

He glanced away for a moment, trying to make sense of his outburst. For some reason he didn't like it when his best friend insulted Kandrea. It was one thing for Damon to think she was nutty—it was another thing for Mathias to verbalize it. "I meant that nothing sexual went on."

"What happened, then?"

Mathias stared at Damon in bewilderment as he told him the story about the nonexistent canary yellow wall. "She was really angry. Like this whole imaginary incident had actually happened. It was weird, man."

"She's crazier than a three-dollar bill. Too bad the Creator wasted a face and body like that on someone obviously not taking her medicine."

Damon's jaw tightened. "Anyway," he ground out, trying to ignore that second jab at Kandrea, "it's been a long day."

"I'd say it's about to get longer."

"Huh?"

Mathias's eyebrows rose as he gazed across the small pub. "She just walked in. You might want to run before she accuses you of some other future misdeed you haven't committed."

Damon's head slowly cocked to the left, his dark gaze finding Kandrea and homing in on her. Her fingers and arms sparkled in a plethora of contrasting, vibrant colors, so she wasn't difficult to find. Her gypsy skirt and shirt were black, as always, but the outfit made him do a double take nevertheless.

Tonight, Ms. Kane was wearing a tight, spaghetti-strapped camisole that ended well above her navel, showcasing a jeweled belly ring. Her long golden ringlets had been swept up into a loose bun, two soft tendrils cascading down to either side of her neck. Her large breasts were unbound, no bra to cover up her stiff nipples which poked against the fabric. Those soft globes of flesh jiggled a bit when she walked, but not much, making him wonder if she'd had breast augmentation surgery. He'd never met a woman in her thirties whose breasts were still that naturally firm.

Damon swallowed roughly. His cock didn't seem to care whether those tits were real or fake. It was throbbing in agony, forcing him to shift uncomfortably in his seat.

Holy shit. Kandy Kane might be insane, but she was a damn beautiful nutjob.

Taking a deep breath, Damon tried to stave off his rapidly growing arousal. He hoped Mathias hadn't noticed his intense reaction to Kandrea. He couldn't understand it himself so explaining it to someone else was mission: impossible. She was fine as hell, but their personalities were day and night. Damon's world was a concrete and earthy one, while Kandrea's existence was smoky and ethereal.

"Wow." Mathias whistled under his breath. "Not bad, eh?"

Damon attempted to show no reaction whatsoever to his best friend's vocal admiration of Kandrea. He failed miserably.

"She's mine," Damon growled, his gaze still trained on Kandrea. "So back off."

"Whoa!" Damon glanced at his partner in time to see him

almost choke on his beer. "*Yours?* What are you talking about?" Mathias stilled. "You don't mean . . ."

"I don't know what the fuck I mean." Damon ran a beleaguered hand over his jaw and sighed. Conflicting emotions battled inside him. "The woman is crazy and she's trying to take me with her."

Mathias's soft chuckle made Damon frown.

"I'm not laughing," Damon mumbled.

"I am."

"So I see."

"I don't think Ms. Kane sees things your way, Damon. Look who she's taking a seat next to." Mathias's smile was huge. He wanted to smack it off him.

Damon's head slowly turned, his dark eyes narrowing at the couple seated on the opposite side of the Italian bistro. The twosome was holding hands, talking quietly to each other from across the table they shared. His jaw tightened.

Of all the men to date in New York City, Kandrea Kane was being courted by none other than Damon's lifelong nemesis. Tyler Thomas. Son of a bitch.

Tyler had seen to it that Damon's childhood and adolescent years had been filled with teasing, angst and torment. As quarterback of the high school football team, Tyler and his goon squad pals had taken great delight in publicly humiliating Damon at every given opportunity. From getting tripped in the cafeteria to repeatedly getting his head forced into a toilet, Damon had endured it all.

It wasn't until after graduation, when Tyler went off to college in Boston and Damon studied on a full scholarship at NYU, that the ghosts of childhood past had weakened their grip on Damon's self-esteem. Once gangly, awkward and bespectacled, he traded his glasses for contact lenses and his physique evolved into solid, unforgiving muscle. He excelled in his studies, took up sports and enjoyed every moment of college life.

According to rumor, Tyler was now a third-rate lawyer in a third-rate law firm in Queens. He had a hell of a reputation for ambulance-chasing and taking advantage of his ill and injured clients. *Once an asshole, always an asshole,* as Mathias often said of him. Damon just wished the fact that he'd triumphed both professionally and monetarily over Tyler Thomas made him feel better about the fact that the prick was currently holding Kandrea's hands.

"I need some sleep," Damon muttered, standing. "It's been a long day. I'll see you tomorrow."

• • •

A faint bell rang, announcing that a patron was either entering or exiting the eatery, but she was too focused on the appalling situation at hand to notice much else. Kandrea's nostrils flared as she tried to pull her hands away from Tyler's grasp. She didn't enjoy making a scene, but if he didn't let go of her soon she would do just that.

And to think he had lured her to the bistro under the guise of being worried about her best friend—his *girlfriend.* Insofar as she could tell, Tyler's only concern was getting into Kandrea's pants. What a schmuck.

"Listen!" she snapped, irritated. "You have to the count of three to remove your cheating hands from over mine or I'll scream loud enough to shatter glass."

"Kandy, come on—"

"*Kandrea,*" she ground out. "And I've had enough." She had nicely asked him to let go of her at least three times now. The politesse was over. *"One. Two. Thr—"*

He quickly snatched back his hands. She smiled sardonically.

"Are you going to say something to Olivia?" Tyler frowned. "Because I don't think you should."

"Of course you don't."

"I don't know what came over me. It'll never happen again."

"That much is true at least."

He sighed and rolled his eyes. "Grow up. All you'd do is hurt her. She's in love with me."

Thankfully, Kandrea knew that Olivia was already growing tired of Tyler Thomas and his reputation for being quite the lecher. What Livi had seen in him to begin with remained an enigma. His aura was more repugnant than the cheap cologne he wore.

"I don't hurt people I care about," Kandrea said pointedly as she stood up. "On the other hand, I have no qualms whatsoever about obliterating those I loathe." Her smile dared him to so much as think about her again. "You'd do well to remember that."

One grand exit later, Kandrea made her way along the sidewalk and down a narrow stairwell that led to the subway station below. Her mood was blacker than midnight, so she was happy to be engulfed by the dense sea of nameless, faceless people hurrying to meet their desired trains. Some people disliked the anonymity of big-city life, but Kandrea basked in it. Having spent her entire childhood sticking out like a sore thumb, she relished the fact that in Manhattan she was just another artsy type on an island already teeming with them.

Men.

She wasn't certain if she should confide in Olivia about Tyler's behavior. While her mind screamed to tell Livi all, her intuition insisted it wasn't necessary. If Kandrea's sixth sense was to be believed, Livi would ditch the loser sooner rather than later anyway.

The train came to a grinding halt, its doors automatically opening. Kandrea pushed her way through the crowd on the platform, ensuring she wouldn't have to wait for the next departure. She sighed as she grabbed the overhead bar, wishing the train was empty so she could plop her butt down on one of the seats. *Not at this hour.*

Kandrea was exhausted, both physically and spiritually. She had her own man problems to contend with—namely the inexplicable attraction she felt toward a certain Neanderthal contractor. Dealing with Livi's faithless whore of a boyfriend was tonight's icing on the woe-is-me man cake.

"Hurry up, train," she mumbled under her breath. "There's no place like home."

Chapter Three

Damon was in a foul mood when he got up to go to work the next morning. Despite the fact that Kandrea was dating his mortal enemy, he had masturbated to forbidden images of Sybil at least four times last night. And his dick was still harder than a damn rock when he woke up.

Prowling around the apartment he hoped to finish remodeling in record time, he undertook a thorough look-around. Damon grunted with delight as he inspected the impressive work his crew was busily submerged in. As usual, his men were right on target.

There was the small platform Kandrea had requested for meditation and yoga. The extended window bench where she would drink her tea in the mornings. The freshly tiled floors. The newly built wall that one of his men had started painting canary yel—

He did a double take. And a triple take. He'd have done a quadruple take, but there was no mistaking the color coming off that brush and affixing itself to that wall. It just couldn't be . . .

"Oh fuck," Damon growled. Blinking, he quickly came to his senses. "What the hell are you doing?" he bellowed, scaring the painter into almost dropping his brush. "Stop painting that wall yellow!"

"I-I'm sorry, Mr. Clyde," the young worker squeaked. He held up a piece of paper. "The order you wrote out says color E4—that's canary yellow."

Damon snatched the piece of paper from the kid's hand. He took a calming breath as he scanned the work order. It didn't say

E4—it said F4—but he couldn't blame the boy for not being able to read his chicken scratch. Hell, most days he could barely read his own handwriting. "It's all right, kid." He sighed. "I shouldn't have yelled. This was just a simple misunderstanding."

He went on to explain to the kid—Ben, he was pretty sure his name was—that the wall was supposed to be violet-blue. The instructions came out of Damon's mouth, but his mind was elsewhere so he quickly brought the worker up to speed and shoved off to the kitchen for a moment of peace and quiet.

There had to be an explanation. There was always an explanation.

But how could Kandrea have known?

As dumbfounded as Alice must have been in Wonderland, Damon was no longer certain of what was real and what was fantasy. He didn't believe in fortune-telling, psychics or any ethereal things of that nature. He never had. And yet he also knew that the chances of Kandrea having been able to accurately *guess* what happened today were slim to none.

Damon ran a hand over his face, rough with two days' worth of stubble. This was just too weird.

"*Holy shit!*" a female voice shrieked from another room. "I was promised that this would never happen!"

He stilled.

"This is giving me a headache! Oh my *God,* this is the ugliest color I've ever seen in my entire life!"

Uh-oh. If poor Ben had been shaken by Damon's yelling, he could well imagine how the kid was taking Kandrea's tirade. She could make a monk break a vow of silence in order to spare himself from her wrath.

"Where is your boss? I *demand* to speak to him *immediately!*"

Damon's nostrils flared. Lust, confusion, anger and defensiveness formed a knot of chaos inside him. He prowled out of the kitchen and into the next room, coming face-to-face with the tiny woman, who could give the most seasoned of truckers a few lessons in cursing.

"I'm here," he bit out, his eyes narrowing. She was angry. Very angry. Good. At least he wasn't the only one being driven insane. "I believe you wanted to speak with me."

• • •

Kandrea fell uncharacteristically silent as she stood before Damon Clyde. Good lord above, he was a handsome man. Not the sissy *GQ* type by a long shot, but rugged and earthy. The kind of man who, had he lived back in the Stone Age, would have had no trouble hunting meat for the clan and dispatching predators from the cave.

She swallowed a bit roughly, the dry lump in her throat feeling the size of a softball. He looked especially good today in a pair of jeans and a basic black T-shirt. She could easily see the delineation of his honed biceps rippling beneath the cotton fabric. He was a tall, solid, reassuring presence in a world that was anything but.

She could sense that, despite Damon's glowering, the magnetism that drew her to him like a moth to a flame wasn't one-sided. There was a burning in his eyes, a desire that was at odds with his gruff stance and surly frown.

Kandrea glanced away, doing her best to shrug off the odd attraction. They were an unlikely match. Too dissimilar. While opposites may attract, she supposed they rarely stayed together.

She forced herself to resume eye contact, though the yearning to bolt away was fairly overwhelming. "You promised me this wouldn't happen," she said crisply.

He opened his mouth to speak, but nothing came out. He stared at her for a suspended moment, then shook his head and looked away.

She was accustomed to this sort of thing, to people not knowing how to react when confronted with the truth of her psychic abilities. For some reason her lack of normalcy embarrassed her this time, a small part of her having hoped that Damon Clyde would react differently than the average joe.

"How did you know?" he asked softly, surprising her.

"I—"

She tried to respond, but the next thing Kandrea knew, she was being led by the elbow into the kitchen. Damon pulled her alongside him, then twirled her around to look at him as soon as they reached his destination. His face was gruff, his stance like a caged panther. She wasn't certain what to make of his contradictory behavior and, unfortunately, her intuition wasn't talking.

"You're driving me crazy," Damon gritted out, his jaw tense.

She was driving *him* crazy? Because she had been able to accurately predict the future, she supposed. Disappointed in him, whether or not she had a right to be, she snatched her arm from his grasp and turned on her heel to leave. Large, strong hands seized her from behind and pulled her back.

"Let go of me!" Kandrea fumed, spinning around to face him. "What the hell do you want from me? An apology for who I am?" She realized how vulnerable she sounded and hated herself for it. Forcing the helpless girl inside her at bay, the tough woman she was took over. "It isn't going to happen."

"Kandrea—"

"Let. Me. Go."

"No."

"Then I'll fire you."

"I don't care."

One second she was on the ground antagonistically staring up at him, and a heartbeat later she was plucked from her feet and pressed hard against him. His rough hands seized her buttocks and held on as his mouth covered hers.

Damon thrust his tongue inside her, his breathing labored.

Kandrea responded in kind, letting go of her inhibitions and kissing him with matched passion. She ground her hips into him, rubbing her pussy against his sizable erection. He moaned into her mouth and grabbed her buttocks tighter. They kissed as though neither could ever get enough of the other, all of their pent-up sexual frustration bursting at the seams.

An uncomfortable cough broke the spell. Their mouths ripped apart.

"Uh, sorry to interrupt, boss," an embarrassed worker mumbled. "I'll come back."

"No," Kandrea breathed out. She had no idea what had come over her, but she couldn't recall ever behaving so brazenly toward any other man. Crimson stained her cheeks as Damon gently put her down. "I'll go," she instructed the worker. "You stay."

"Kandrea," Damon bit out, "we need to talk."

It was too late. The strong woman had fled and the scared child had taken over.

Kandrea ran out of the kitchen and from her soon-to-be apartment faster than she'd ever moved in her life. "Kandrea!" she heard him bellow, unmistakable warning in his tone. She didn't care. Her breathing came out in gasps as she darted down the stairs, flung open the door and dodged bumper-to-bumper Manhattan traffic to get across the street.

She had never—ever—felt such a powerful need to be with a man as she had just experienced with Damon. For a person who had erected walls around her heart many years ago to avoid the hurt that being different invariably brought, the emotions were simply overwhelming.

By the time she reached her building and took the elevator up to her apartment, she was a mess. Kandrea slammed the door behind her, then did something else she hadn't allowed herself to indulge in for years.

She fell onto her bed and cried like a baby.

Chapter Four

A cathartic cry and a three-hour nap later, Kandrea sat up in her bed and stretched her arms with a yawn. The passionate kiss she'd shared with Damon Clyde instantly rushed back to her memory, sending her cheeks up in flames. She didn't behave like that. Ever.

"I wish I was a lesbian," Kandrea mumbled under her breath. She threw the covers off and stood up.

Well, minus the whole pussy-eating thing. She wished that particular aspect of being with a woman held some allure, but it didn't. The only tuna going in her mouth would be straight out of a can and on some crackers. Too bad. She would have made for a great lesbian otherwise.

"No men to deal with," she harrumphed. "They have it made."

Making her way into her studio, she decided to clean it up rather than contemplate the scene she'd made with Damon that morning. Washing paintbrushes bored her to tears, but today it seemed much safer to the psyche. Tedious and monotonous perhaps, but safe.

The portrait she'd painted a few weeks ago, the one of the gangly boy whose mother died of cancer, snagged her attention. Her heartstrings tugging, she walked over to the easel it was set on and stared at it. The painting had dried long ago so she gently lifted her hand to the weeping boy. She ran a consoling finger across his image, ending at his shadowy face. "I wish I could find you," she murmured. "I don't know why, but I find myself obsessed with you."

"What the hell?" a male voice growled, making her jump. Her hand dropped as she spun around to face the intruder. "What the hell is this?"

Kandrea's nostrils flared as she narrowed her gaze at Damon Clyde. Her heart was pounding from the shock he'd given her. She opened her mouth to blister him with a tongue-lashing for entering her apartment uninvited, but stopped when she realized he wasn't paying her any attention. His dark eyes were haunted, his total awareness fixated on one thing and one thing only.

Goose bumps worked up and down Kandrea's spine as she watched Damon slowly walk closer to the painting.

Could it be? Is it remotely possible that . . .

The realization of who the boy she felt so much profound sorrow for was hit her hard in the stomach. She couldn't believe it, but nothing had ever felt so true. He *did* understand what it felt like to be different. He'd suffered that wretched teasing from other kids while enduring the slow, painful death of his mother—just like Kandrea had.

Somehow this made everything different—and clear. A spirit had never acted directly in her life before, but there it was. Damon's mother had led Kandrea to her son.

Kandrea gently cleared her throat. "Your mother wants you to know how proud of you she is," she said softly. "And that she knows you overcame all the torment that was unfairly inflicted upon you."

She could see him still, his back rigid with tension.

"I-I'm so sorry," she whispered. "If I had known the painting was about you, I would have given it to you long ago. But it doesn't work like that. I never know who the paintings are about. I can only hope they end up in the proper hands when I sell them."

He slowly turned to look at her. His facial expression was unreadable.

"I'm sorry," she dumbly repeated, not knowing what else to say.

Damon stared at her, his gaze working its way up and down her body. "Is . . . my mother here now?" he asked.

"No." She shrugged. "The ghosts—spirits—whatever you wish to call them, they tend to leave me and go to wherever it is they need to be once the paintings are done."

A spark of defensiveness ignited inside Kandrea. Even after being presented with the proof of her ability, he still thought to mock her? To not believe that her otherworldly experiences were genuine?

"That's probably for the best," Damon said. His gaze pierced hers. "Because I could never do any of the nasty things I want to do to you in front of my mother."

Her breath caught in the back of her throat. She was torn between sheer nerves, the elation of knowing someone other than Olivia and Andie believed in her and the hedonistic pleasure of realizing Damon Clyde wanted her so badly. Kandrea anxiously brushed a long blonde curl behind her ear and bit her lip.

"What kind of nasty things?" she squeaked.

Idiot! What a dumb thing to say!

Obviously she would never possess the sophistication of Lauren Bacall. It was too bad, Kandrea thought. She should be smoking a cigarette from one of those long sticklike holders and daring him with beguiling eyes. Instead she was behaving, well, like a dweeb. She continued to mentally chastise herself even while entertaining all the wicked possibilities his words brought to mind.

"How about," Damon murmured as he edged his way toward her, "I show you instead of tell you?"

Her blue eyes widened. She tried to swallow, but her throat had gone dry. Kandrea blew out a none-too-subtle breath. Her breasts heaved in time with her shallow breathing as her heart rate went into overdrive. She supposed she should be afraid of a man his size prowling toward her with such obvious intentions . . .

Kandrea enthusiastically leapt into his strong, demanding arms as Damon plucked her from the ground and carried her to the nearest chair. She grabbed the back of his head and clung to him fiercely, their mouths colliding as their tongues sought each other out. They collapsed as one onto the oversized chair.

"I need to be inside you," Damon told her hoarsely, pulling his mouth from hers. His breathing grew increasingly heavy as he tugged at the black gypsy skirt she wore. "I can't wait anymore."

She pulled her skirt over her head and flung it to the floor. Damon grabbed at her top and helped her quickly discard it. Straddling his lap, Kandrea's nipples hardened as she watched him stare at her large breasts intensely enough to brand them.

Damon palmed her breasts, his dark eyes heavy-lidded. His thumbs began playing with her nipples, massaging them. Kandrea gasped, her body on fire.

"Suck on them," she breathed out.

"Not until I'm inside you."

"But they *ache*."

His thumbs grew more demanding. "Good."

Oh, he was evil. Evil and sexy as hell.

Her legs shaky, Kandrea managed to stand up on the chair and pull off her panties. His giant's hands easily followed her, never leaving her breasts as he moaned in appreciation of the new view.

"You've got a beautiful pussy," Damon rumbled. His tongue flicked at her navel ring.

Kandrea blushed despite herself. Her two-year dry spell in the sex department had often made her wonder just why she took the time to keep herself trimmed and well-groomed downstairs. Suddenly she was thankful that she had.

She would have responded, but his tongue shot up and

brushed her clit. She groaned, her already trembling legs feeling as steady as overcooked spaghetti noodles. He must have realized as much because his hands let go of her breasts and palmed her buttocks. Letting his head fall back, he pulled her down on top of his mouth and frenziedly sucked on her pussy.

"Oh my God," Kandrea gasped. Her nipples were painfully stiff. "Oh yes! Oh God."

She rode Damon's face, grinding her aroused flesh into his mouth. He moaned against her pussy, sucking on her clit and opening harder and with more urgency.

"*Mmmmmm*," he purred. "*Mm mm mmmmmmm.*"

Damon sucked harder. And harder and harder and—

The coil of tension in her stomach sprang loose. Blood heated her face and nipples as she came loudly.

"Oh. My. Fucking. Gaaaaaaaawd!"

Damon growled as he lapped up her juices, his calloused hands roughly squeezing her soft buttocks. Kandrea's fingers clung to the head of the chair, her hips wriggled, forcing her pussy as close to his mouth as humanly possible. Her panting reached a crescendo as she came again, unable to stop the strong climax.

By the time she finished coming, Kandrea's body had turned into that of a limp rag doll. A happy kind of sleepiness fell over her, drugging her. She pulled herself up from Damon's face and collapsed into his lap, straddling him once again.

"No rest for the weary," Damon murmured.

She could feel his steel-hard erection poking against his jeans, demanding her undivided attention. It didn't matter how exhausted she was. He'd made it clear that the evening had just begun.

Thank God.

Kandrea hoisted up the black T-shirt Damon wore, lifting it over his head and flinging it away. Her blue eyes narrowed with desire at the sight of his naked, chiseled torso. Damon Clyde was all muscle and zero fat. His body was hard and masculine, and in total contrast to her soft, womanly one.

"You are so beautiful," she whispered, her fingers gliding through his black chest hair. "So manly and beautiful."

"Take off my jeans," Damon instructed hoarsely.

She unbuttoned them and slid down the zipper. He pulled himself up from the chair a little bit, just enough to allow Kandrea to slide his jeans off his buttocks and past his knees. His thick, rigid cock sprang free, his chest working up and down in rhythm with his labored breathing. She wasted no more time, grabbing his penis by the root and settling it at the entrance to her pussy.

"That's it, Kandy," Damon groaned. "Sit on him, baby."

Kandy. Ordinarily she detested it when people called her by that nickname. When Damon said it though, all male possessiveness and arousal, it had a sexy ring to it.

He kneaded her buttocks, drawing her closer. "Put him inside you, Kandy. I need to fuck you, sweetheart."

His words were intoxicating. Rough, dirty and, oh, so stimulating.

Holding his cock with one hand, she used her other to spread apart her pussy lips. She slid down onto his shaft, impaling herself with a groan.

"Damn, you're tight," he gritted out. *"Shit."*

"You're huge," she gasped.

Kandrea placed her palms against his chest for support and began to ride him. Her breasts jiggled as she picked up the pace, her nipples stiff. Damon's tongue darted out. He curled it around one aching nipple and forced it into his mouth. She moaned as he feverishly sucked on it, instinctively riding him faster, spearing herself harder.

"You're mine now," he growled, releasing her nipple with a popping sound. "All mine."

She rode him faster, his big cock feeling so damn good inside her. She wanted to come but staved it off, afraid it would make her too sleepy far too soon.

"Harder," Damon groaned. *"Fuck me harder."*

She rode him without inhibition, reveling in his desire for her. Her blonde curls bounced as she fucked him long and hard, never wanting the moment to end.

"My sweet Kandy Kane," Damon ground out. "All mine."

The possessive words were her undoing. Kandrea sank down onto his cock once, twice, three times more, then came so loudly and violently she thought she might pass out.

"Yessssss!" she wailed. "Oh Damon! Oh *yes!*"

He grabbed her roughly by the hips and pounded his cock up inside her. His eyes closed as his entire body tensed, preparing to come.

"Kandrea," he gasped. *"Shit."*

Damon came inside her, his hot cum shooting up to fill her pussy. Kandrea rode him hard, milking his cock for everything he had to give.

"You're so sexy," Damon said hoarsely. He kissed her nipples as she brought the pace to a slowing halt. "So perfect."

Perfect? Her?

Her heart swelling, Kandrea collapsed against his chest, her energy depleted. She supposed three huge orgasms outside of thirty minutes could do that to a woman. Being told she was sexy and perfect by the world's most handsome man was icing on the cake. She smiled as she snuggled close, hoping that the night never came to an end.

• • •

Damon had never even thought about wanting a woman more than he wanted Kandrea. She was a study in contradictions. Innocent and sexual, naïve and worldly, forbidding and tempting. She was everything he wanted and more.

"I need to be inside you again," Damon rasped. "Now."

Her blue eyes widened—naïveté. Her hard nipples poked against his chest—worldly.

She was a paradox.

He had to fuck her again before his cock exploded.

Apparently, she had other intentions.

Kandrea wound her way down his body and slid onto the floor between his legs. He watched with hunger as her full, puffy lips opened up and wrapped around his stiff cock. Damon groaned, as turned on by the visual as he was by the physical sensation.

"That's it, baby," he hissed, his eyelids heavy. "Suck on him."

He slid his fingers through her long blonde hair and held on to the back of her head. Kandrea's mouth worked up and down the length of his shaft, her blue eyes staring up at him as she sucked on his dick like a favorite lollipop.

"Faster," Damon ground out. "Harder."

She eagerly complied, giving him the blow job of all blow jobs. She sucked him harder and faster, her lips and tongue making smacking sounds. "Mmm," she purred from around his dick. *"Mmmmmmm."*

Damon bellowed in response, hot cum threatening to squirt out as Kandrea continued to suck him off. His toes curled as a hard orgasm tore through him, semen shooting out in streams. She drank all of him, not missing a drop.

"Holy shit," Damon panted, his chest heaving up and down. "Damn."

He didn't want her to ever leave him.

There was no way to make sense of their instant, mutual attraction, but he didn't care to anyway. It went so much deeper, as if they'd known each other all of their lives, as if they had been made for each other.

All Damon knew for certain was that, for whatever reason, Kandrea Kane had come into his life wanting an apartment and had managed to get under his skin and make him feel again. Feel in a way he'd never let his guard down long enough to feel before. It was at once a wonderful and terrifying realization.

Not one to self-contemplate, Damon pulled Kandrea up onto his lap and held her tightly. If she got away, it wouldn't be because he had let go.

Chapter Five

Kandrea awoke the next morning in her bed, Damon's body possessively wrapped around her. The bed— they had made it to the bed! She smiled softly as she recalled the prior night's events.

They had *tried* to make it to the bedroom countless times, but couldn't stay away from each other long enough to get there. In the chair, on the floor, in the hallway . . . everywhere but in the kitchen sink. And, of course, the bed. Maybe they would remedy that situation today.

"Good morning," a gravelly voice murmured. "You sleep well?"

"Like a baby."

"Me too."

"I know. I woke up because of your snoring."

He grinned. Damon let go of her long enough to stretch and yawn, then resumed holding her close to him. She could feel his morning erection poking against her belly, demanding attention. Kandrea reached down and grabbed his penis by the root, her belly clenching at his groan.

She wanted him. Yesterday, today . . . always. The realization was sobering. Her hand fell away as the walls around her heart tried to shove Damon out. What if he didn't feel the same way? What if she was just another notch in the bedpost, or chair, as it were?

"Listen, Kandy," Damon said, propping himself on one elbow, "we've got to talk."

Kandrea sighed. No good had ever come from those particular words.

"You don't like to talk?" he growled. "I thought chicks dug that kind of shit."

She frowned as she sat up in the bed and glared at him. The teasing light in his eyes played havoc on her defenses. She smiled. "I think we both know I'm not your average chick."

"You're much better," he said seriously. "You're a keeper."

A keeper? Not exactly a Hallmark card, but it made her heart go flippity-flop nevertheless.

"So are you." She grinned.

"I'm glad you feel that way, sweetheart. But I have to set the record straight here."

Her smile faded. Here it came. The I-like-you-a-lot-but-I'm-not-ready-for-a-commitment speech, she supposed.

"I don't share," Damon said gruffly. His eyes pierced hers. "Tyler has got to go."

Kandrea stilled. "Tyler?"

"I saw you two together."

She couldn't help herself. She had to laugh.

"I'm dead-ass serious, Kandrea." His face was a scowl. "I don't share with anybody, let alone with a prick like that."

She brought her laughter under control and explained to him what had happened that night at the bistro. She was as attracted to Tyler Thomas as a fly was to a swatter.

"Thank God," Damon said, bemused. "I was afraid for a minute there that I was going to have to go beat the shit out of him."

"I like you," Kandrea said, her expression sobering. "And only you."

His dark gaze found hers. "And I like you. Only you," he said softly.

A premonition of things to come seized Kandrea hard, forcing her to see the future. She hated it when this happened. Inevitably, she ended up breaking things off when shown that the man in question wasn't the one.

An image formed, crystal-clear in her mind. She was walking down the street holding hands with two small children, a beautiful blonde-headed girl and a cute-as-a-button dark-headed boy. Twins. Her twins. She gasped as she saw their father.

It was Damon. Strong and handsome Damon, as gorgeous as ever. He picked their children up, mouthed the words "I love you" to Kandrea and the foursome made their way into the very bistro they had just discussed.

A soft smile curved her lips. "I'm glad I'm the only one you like, Damon Clyde." She grabbed his cock again and resumed massaging it. "Because I'm never letting go. Of you—or this!" She laughed.

Jaid Black

USA Today bestselling author Jaid Black is the owner and founder of Ellora's Cave Publishing/Jasmine-Jade Enterprises. Recognizing and legitimizing female sexuality as an entity unique from male sexuality is her passion. Jaid has been featured in every available media, from major newspapers like the *Cleveland Plain Dealer,* to various radio programs, to an appearance on *The Montel Williams Show.* Her books have received numerous distinctions, including a nomination for *Nerve* magazine's Henry Miller award for the best literary sex scene published in the English language.

Legend's Passion

JACI BURTON

Chapter One

Dylan Maxwell prowled Golden Gate Park in San Francisco, waiting for his contact.

Some woman with dark hair. Yeah, great description. That told him a lot.

Then again, at two in the morning, he didn't expect to find a lot of females wandering the depths of the park. In fact, with the recent killings it was damned dangerous for a woman to wander alone in one of these parks in the middle of the night. He wondered if she was planning to bring someone along to protect her.

Zipping his jacket closed, he leaned against the thick tree and tried to discern which direction the infernal wind was coming from. He finally gave up, deciding it was swirling in off the bay and hitting from all sides. There was no hope of getting warm. He was just going to be cold.

It was freakin' July, for the love of God. How could it possibly be so cold in California in July? It was supposed to be summer here. Home in Oklahoma he'd be sweltering, the air conditioner cranked. Not that he got home that often anymore. Working for the National Crime Agency kept him on the road nearly all the time. He couldn't remember the last time he'd either had a vacation or been home.

Damn good thing he liked to travel.

And now he was loitering in a park, skulking behind a tree like a pervert. He was really going to have to get better info out of the NCA analysts. This was a big case. The murders were grisly, all having occurred in parks in the middle of the night, and the bodies—well, what had been left of the bodies anyway—hadn't given them much information. And they were similar to killings that had occurred in other West Coast states a couple years ago, which was why the NCA had been called in.

They'd been following this case for months, with very few leads and really messy evidence. The crime scenes had been grisly as hell; bodies completely torn apart.

Animal attacks, they had thought at first. Bite marks and hair had suggested a wild pack of wolves, but that made no sense at all. Wolves would have been easily spotted and captured, and so far animal control and wildlife authorities hadn't tracked a single wolf, much less a pack of them.

Then again, nothing much about this case made sense. Because saliva tests indicated human.

Fucking weirdo cult no doubt. And now they'd received an anonymous lead from a woman who said she had vital information on the case. Which was probably a false lead, but just in case it wasn't, they had to follow up. This woman had way too much detailed information about the case to be a fluke. Maybe, just maybe, it would be the break they needed.

So here he was. Waiting. And freezing his fucking ass off. Maybe he'd get lucky, and instead of the informant, the actual killer would decide to show up. He could solve this case and go home for a little R & R.

Where it was warm.

• • •

Chantal Devlin closed her laptop and stretched, then stood, looking out the window of her office at the gorgeous view of San Francisco spread out before her.

She wrinkled her nose, then yawned.

God, she was bored. And tense. And frustrated. And horny. And so ready for a little action. Buried at her desk for the past

three months, she was relieved to finally put the last filing toget
on this case. Long, tedious and dull, dull, dull.

What she needed right now was action. A little run.

And a lot of fucking.

Pent-up anxiety and need sizzled through her nerve endings. She hadn't shifted and had some fun in far too long. Work had kept her tied up and in human form for months now.

She was ready to play. Her pack contact had set her up with a guy for tonight. An out-of-towner from the South, because she refused to fuck anyone within the pack. And of course she would never, ever, fuck a human. The risk of accidentally turning one was too great. She wasn't anywhere near ready to mate with another pack wolf and the pack liaison knew that, so this guy coming in from out of town was perfect. No strings, no requirements for relationship or mate choice. She was more than ready for a romp in the park and a little anonymous sex to ease the tension. By tomorrow morning she'd be back to normal and in prime form to get back to work.

No rest for the wicked, she thought with a chuckle. Or for the nonwicked, because she sure as hell hadn't been wicked enough lately.

She hustled down to the parking garage and drove the short distance to Golden Gate Park. Her juices were already flowing and she hadn't even met the guy yet. She didn't know anything about him other than that he was tall, built, with blue eyes and a Southern drawl. Maia, the pack liaison, said this guy was hot. And when Maia said a guy was hot, he was *hot*.

Good enough. Her nipples tightened, her breasts warming. How long had it been since she'd had a good fuck? Too damn long. She should know better than to go so long without sex. Tonight was going to be rough. She hoped this guy had stamina because she intended to screw his brains out.

She pulled into the parking lot, climbed out, and headed

toward the designated meeting area. The cool wind bit at her skin, offering blessed relief to the heat boiling inside her. She'd worn a stretchy casual skirt, a tank top and sandals to work tonight since it was a Saturday, so stripping would be easy. But first she had to find her partner.

The breeze blew tendrils of hair free from the clip, but she didn't care. Her blood was boiling in anticipation. She snaked her way through the path, then headed into a dense copse of trees and bushes where she couldn't be seen by security, the thick area of the park where no one traveled.

She spotted him huddled against a tree. Tall, broad-shouldered, watching her approach. Her skin tingled with the need to shift. But she wanted this in human form.

At least at first.

He was gorgeous. Thick dark hair, stunning blue eyes, sharp brows arched in a frown.

"Took you long enough to get here," he said in a sexy Southern drawl that made her toes curl.

"I was working. Trust me, I'll make the wait worth it."

"I hope so. So what have you got for me?"

"A little impatient?"

"I've been waiting awhile for this. I want it now."

Oh, man, he was hot. Her nipples nearly broke through her top, her pussy swelled. A trickle of moisture wet her panties.

"You want it, take it." She trailed her fingernails between her breasts, enticing him, then circled around him so she was pressed against the trunk of the tree.

He moved with her like a predator, as if he was stalking her. "You'd better show me what you're offering. I'm not into playing games."

Yes, he was. A game she was thoroughly enjoying.

"Show you, huh? Sure, I'll show you." She grasped the hem of her skirt and slipped her fingers upward, sliding her fingers underneath the straps of her panties. She gasped as she tucked one finger into her pussy, felt the cream pouring onto it. So wet, her cunt quivered as she touched it. She withdrew, scenting her own arousal as she held her finger out for him. "It's right here. Taste me."

Dylan's knees damn near buckled as the raven-haired seductress held out her wet fingers in front of him. Her scent traveled on the breeze, intoxicating his senses. Like a drug had been shot into him, he found himself rooted to the spot, unable to move, but dying to grab her hand and suck her soaked finger into his mouth.

What the fuck was going on here? He felt dizzy, disoriented. Something wasn't right. Whatever she was offering, he wanted it. And it wasn't the information he sought, but he didn't give a shit about the informant anymore. This stranger had bewitched him, put him under some kind of spell. He couldn't even remember why he was here. His cock twitched, lengthening, hardening, his balls drawing up with a throbbing ache of desperate need.

He didn't know her.

He wanted to fuck her. No, that wasn't right. He *needed* to fuck her.

Up against the tree.

Right now.

He grabbed her wrist. Hard. She gasped, but her green-eyed gaze lit up and sparkled. She smiled when he took her finger and licked it.

Goddamn, she tasted good. He covered her finger with his lips and sucked. Every last drop of her honeyed cream. And he wanted more.

"Shit," she whispered. "More."

He pulled her finger out of his mouth. "Yeah, baby. More." He pushed her against the tree and dropped to his knees, grasping her ankles. Her skin was utter silk, trembling under his fingers as he wove a trail with his hands up her calves, her thighs, sliding under her sexy, tight little skirt, pushing it up with his hands until he revealed little white lace panties.

"Sexy little things," he said, leaning in to breathe the scent of her cunt. The more he inhaled, the more fogged his brain became. And the harder his cock got. He looked up at her. She was watching him, her lips parted, her breathing ragged as he dragged her panties over her hips and down her legs.

Her pussy was so pretty, with a little thatch of raven hair just at the top of her sex. The rest of her was bare. He reached out to smooth his fingers over the swollen lips, bringing away more of her sweet honey. He licked it from his fingers like candy.

"Eat me," she begged, spreading her legs wider. "Please lick my pussy."

With a growl he reached up and grabbed her ass, digging his fingers into her soft flesh as he pulled her cunt toward his face and buried his tongue in her sex.

"Ohhh God," she cried, tangling her fingers in his hair and thrusting her hips forward to undulate against his questing tongue.

He sucked her clit, ravenous for the taste of her. Damn, he couldn't get enough, swallowing her cream, licking her up and dipping his tongue into her pussy. Her little moans only made him want more, made him want to take her over the edge. He wanted her to come in his mouth, wanted to possess her completely. He wanted her screaming and writhing against him, to give her a climax like no man had ever given her.

He didn't know why he wanted it like that, he just did.

Relentless, he assaulted her clit, swirling his tongue over the distended pearl until she was shrieking, pulling at his hair. She came apart then, flooding his tongue with her cream. He drank every bit of her juice and continued to lick her until her legs were trembling uncontrollably.

Then he rose and covered her mouth with his, needing the taste of her lips.

She devoured him like a hungry animal, wrapping her leg around his waist to hold him in place.

As if he had any intention of leaving. Not until he'd filled her with his cock; his cum.

Not until he made her his.

Chantal was quivering. Every damn part of her body. She didn't know who this man was, but she wanted him. All of him. Inside her.

God, he had a talented mouth. No man had ever made her come like that. Shrieking like a goddamn banshee. Her clit still tremored with the aftereffects of her climax.

And the way he kissed her, it was as if he'd possessed her, his tongue mastering hers with velvety strokes that made her belly tighten. She was past the point of clear reason. Chantal Devlin, who never lost control with a man, who was always so clearheaded, even with sex, had totally and completely gone over the edge with this guy.

And she still didn't even know his name.

She tore her mouth from his, the mating call reaching desperate proportions now.

She searched his face, lost in the depth of his steely blue eyes. "I'm Chantal. Tell me your name."

"Dylan."

She palmed his chest. Steely hard, just like his abs as she trailed her fingers down to his crotch. She popped the jeans button, then drew the zipper down, shuddering as her knuckles brushed his hard-on. It was thick, long—she couldn't resist dipping her hand inside his jeans to encircle his flesh.

"Christ," he said on a harsh breath, surging against her hand. His breath was hot against her cheek.

With each stroke she felt his pulse pounding in his cock, felt her own blood rampantly racing throughout her veins. The need to shift, to run wild, was strong. The need to tear into this man was even stronger. The animal within her was dying to break free.

She leaned her head back to gaze into the dark intensity of his eyes.

"Fuck me, Dylan."

His nostrils flared, his gaze narrowing as he palmed the tree trunk next to her head with one hand, jerking his cock out with the other. She stared down at it, thick and pulsing in his hand, and licked her lips, swallowing past the dry lump in her throat.

She'd never wanted a fuck so desperately before.

"You want it here? Against the tree? My cock ramming into your hot cunt?"

"Yes!" His voice made her insane. "Fuck me now, dammit!"

He lifted her with one arm and she wrapped her legs around his waist while he placed his cock at the entrance to her pussy. She surged against him, engulfing his shaft between her pussy lips, gripping him like a vise as she slid all the way down until he was buried deep.

She could come right now, the contractions were so strong inside her. But she wanted to wait, to enjoy every blissful moment of this mating frenzy. He lifted her higher, then slammed her against the trunk of the tree.

Oh, it hurt. So damn good she cried out, then growled, letting the animal within her partially loose. He wanted it hard, she'd give everything he gave. She unleashed her claws, raking them down his back, lifting his shirt to draw her nails along his skin. He grunted, thrusting his cock deeper.

"Fuck, baby" was all he said in reply.

She snarled in protest when he didn't drive hard enough, no longer conscious of the human side of her. She couldn't speak, could only give him nonverbal signals to slam into her, to give her every stroke. Deeper, harder, to make it hurt. She needed this, wanted the fury, the passion, everything he had and then some.

When she felt it spiraling inside her, she let her canines burst forth and buried her face in his neck, clamping down on the flesh between his neck and shoulder as the first wave of her climax sent her careening into oblivion.

He shuddered and groaned, spurting his hot cum inside her as he, too, rode an orgasm that sent her crashing again. His fingers dug into her buttocks as he slammed her forward into the tree.

Shaking all over, Chantal was exhilarated. What an orgasm! Or orgasms, to be precise. She released her hold on his skin and let the human side of her regain control, resuming her normal breathing patterns.

She stroked his hair, kissed his sweat-soaked neck then pushed against him.

Dead weight.

"Hey."

No response. She frowned.

"Dylan?"

Again. Nothing. He lay slumped against her. She pushed again, and he fell to the ground.

Oh shit. Something wasn't right. She smoothed her skirt down over her hips and bent over him.

He was pale, blood pouring from the wound in his skin where she'd bitten him.

A cold chill passed over her.

Uh-oh. This couldn't be. Stepping over him, she lifted his shirt, wincing at the bloody claw marks on his back.

If he was a werewolf, the bite and claw marks would have healed over immediately.

This guy wasn't a werewolf.

"Oh crap."

She'd just made a huge error. No, a catastrophical mistake.

She'd just fucked a human.

She sank to the ground as the realization hit.

It was even worse than that.

She'd just *bitten* a human.

Okay. Don't panic.

She really wanted to panic. She rose and ran to her car, grabbed her purse, then headed back to Dylan, not wanting to leave him alone. She dialed her pack leader and gave him her location.

He was going to be so pissed. But she couldn't leave Dylan out here alone.

The second call she made was even more important. Family was needed during a crisis and she really needed family right now.

"What?"

Even though the one word was curt and irritated, she melted in relief at the sound of her brother's voice. "Noah. I need you out here right now. I have just screwed up so fucking bad and I need your help."

"I'm on a plane in an hour."

She clicked off the phone, closed her eyes and batted back tears. He didn't even ask what she'd done. God, she loved her family.

How was she going to repair this damage?

She looked down at Dylan, at the man whose life she had just irrevocably altered. She didn't know. She thought he was her tryst, that he was sent here. She hadn't thought anyone human would be out this time of night, in this location.

Goddamn, she didn't know.

Brushing her fingers over the dark locks that fell over his forehead, she whispered, "I'm so sorry."

Chapter Two

Chantal paced while Noah was in the bedroom with Dylan.

That's all she knew about him. His first name. Dylan. The pack had retrieved him from the park, brought him to the main house and closeted him in one of the upstairs bedrooms, refusing to allow her access. She'd been cooling her heels for the past six hours, going without sleep. She looked a wreck and felt even worse.

Guilt tightened her stomach. She felt sick. What if he died? Did humans die from wolf bites? Hell, she didn't know the physiology. She'd never done this before.

Stupid thing to do, Chantal. Where had her head been?

Easy. She hadn't been using it at the time. She'd been thinking with her pussy.

Noah had arrived, true to his word, about four hours after she'd called him. Thank God he'd been in the States instead of out of the country and had been able to hop on one of the Devlin jets immediately. She'd given him a quick, utterly embarrassing recap of events. After hugging her and telling her everything would be all right, he'd marched upstairs and muscled his way into the bedroom where Dylan was being held, despite the two vicious guard-hounds at the door.

Like anyone would get in Noah Devlin's way when he wanted in somewhere.

But he'd been in there an hour.

And hadn't come out.

She chewed on a fingernail and loitered in the hallway.

Finally, the door opened and Noah walked out, his brows knit together in a very tight frown.

Oh shit. That so wasn't good.

"What?"

"Let's go talk somewhere."

She led him to the room she stayed in when she visited pack headquarters, shutting the door behind her and resting her head against it. "How bad is it?"

Noah dragged his hand through his hair and sat on the bed, looking up at her through half-lidded eyes. "I know him."

"You do?"

"He's NCA, Chantal."

"Oh God." She wanted to sink to the floor and cry. "Government employee?"

"He's an agent. On assignment, working on the wolf attacks."

"What wolf attacks?"

"Don't you watch the news or read the paper? Jesus, Chantal, it's happening right in your own fucking backyard."

Lifting her chin, she stalked to the wet bar and poured a glass of water. "I've been kind of busy, Noah." She took a long swallow and turned back to him. "What wolf attacks?"

Noah sighed. "They've been going on in four West Coast states for the past year. Grisly dismemberments. Mostly park attacks that the Feds and local police at first attributed to wild animals. Until forensics found human saliva in the wounds."

"Shit. Weres?"

"Probably. But rogues. Or someone who's gone off the deep end. We don't attack humans, not for food or sport."

"Of course not. Jesus, that's disgusting." She wrapped her arms around herself. "And Dylan's an agent?"

"Yeah."

"Damn." She crossed the room and sat next to him. "I didn't know. I didn't know he was human. I was supposed to meet an out-of-town werewolf in the park. I just assumed . . ."

"I know, honey. It's okay." He slipped his arm around her shoulder.

She laid her head against him, needing that few minutes of comfort before she looked up at him. "Is he going to be all right?"

He nodded. "His wounds are already healing. He's in prime shape. The change will happen soon, though."

She sank into the chair next to the wet bar. "Oh God, Noah. I've never turned a human before."

"You'll have to be there for him now. He'll need you to see him through this."

Damn. This was going to be so complicated. They were bound now, through blood. She was responsible for him. She didn't want to be. But she had no choice.

"I can't believe I did this."

Noah shrugged. "You're not the first wolf to inadvertently change a human. You'll do the right thing."

Whatever that was. "So now what do we do?"

"He has to be told. And knowing Dylan, he isn't gonna like it."

She swallowed. "I guess I should tell him."

He nodded. "I'll be with you. I can handle him."

Somehow that didn't sound encouraging. She had her own brand of strength, but one riled newly turned werewolf could be formidable. And Dylan was big.

What exactly would his strengths be? His powers? "Do you know anything about a newly turned wolf's powers?"

"Yeah."

She stood and walked over to face him. "Tell me everything. Forewarned is forearmed."

His brows lifted. "Nervous? You? The great Chantal Devlin, fierce litigator, who eats prominent judges for breakfast, who fears nothing and no one?"

She shoved him. "Shut up already. This is new territory for me."

He grinned. "That's what you get for not keeping your panties on."

"Jerk." How utterly mortifying. "Now tell me what happens."

"He'll wake up confused and not remember what happened. Except the sex, of course. But he'll be hungry. And really full of energy. And his sex drive will be through the roof. You'll have to . . . uhhh . . . take care of that for him, because under no circumstances is he to be allowed to go off and fuck his brains out with the human female population. So feed him, fuck him, then tell him what you did to him and how it's going to affect the rest of his life."

She chewed an errant hangnail. "How soon will he make the change?"

"Full moon is in three days. You'll have to prepare him for the physiology. The first change isn't going to be easy on him. It's not like us. It's going to hurt. Bad. The more you keep him fucked down and relaxed, the easier it'll be. In fact, if you're having sex with him when the change occurs, even better."

She groaned. "I don't think he's going to want to have anything at all to do with me, let alone sex." God, the sex had been phenomenal though. She wouldn't mind a repeat performance. Or ten or twenty. And he'd been human at the time? God almighty. His sexual prowess would only increase as a wolf. She might not live through it.

What a way to go.

"Then I guess you'll have to use your powers of . . . persuasion to convince him, won't you?"

"You want me to chain him up in the dungeon and hold his dick hostage until he turns?"

Noah laughed. "Not a bad idea."

"Asshole. You're not helping."

He held out his hand. "Come on. Time to face your destiny. He should be waking up soon."

Why were her knees knocking? Noah was right. She wasn't afraid of anything or anyone, had faced formidable opponents without batting an eyelash.

What she'd done to Dylan was unforgivable. How was she going to explain it to him, to get him through this? She wasn't sure she could handle his change, let alone help him get past the next few days.

But she didn't really have a choice, did she? She took Noah's hand and allowed him to lead her back down the corridor, past the gargoyles protecting Dylan.

He was alone in the semidarkened room. The shades were closed, a white sheet drawn up to his chest. Naked, his skin was tan against the bright sheets. Noah stayed near the door. Chantal moved forward and slid into a chair next to the head of the bed.

At least he wasn't pale. There was color in his face, and now that the frenzy to screw his brains out had passed, she had a chance to study him.

He was gorgeous. Thick, dark hair that he wore a little long in back, with a tiny bit of curl at the ends. She slid her fingers through his hair and brushed a lock off his forehead.

His lips were full, his nose a bit crooked, which she found charming. It made him a little less than perfect. He had sharp cheekbones and a square jaw, which was covered with dark stubble. She brushed her palm across it and shuddered at the sensual scraping of her skin, then gasped when his hand shot up and grabbed her wrist.

She found herself staring down into steely blue eyes.

"Where the hell am I?"

Chantal looked to Noah, who stepped forward to the side of the bed. "Hey, Legend."

Dylan frowned. "Devlin?"

"Yeah."

"What are you doing here? Where's here?"

"You're safe, so don't worry. And this is my sister, Chantal."

He looked to Chantal, then back at Noah. "She's your sister?"

Noah nodded.

"I need to sit up." He pushed off the bed and struggled. Chantal started to help him, but Noah shook his head. She kept her hands at her sides. When Dylan managed to rise to a sitting position and push the pillow behind his back, he looked to Noah. "I feel like shit. What happened?"

"Long story. Long, really fucking complicated story. And you aren't going to like the outcome."

"I already figured that."

The sheet had dropped down to his waist, leaving his chest and abdomen bare. Chantal couldn't help admiring his broad shoulders, sculpted pecs and well-toned abs.

Now is not the time, Chantal. You can fuck him later.

"So which one of you is going to break the bad news?"

"I will," she said. "Since I caused this problem."

He crossed his arms.

She inhaled. "Last night, you and I had sex."

He looked to Noah and back at her. "You sure you want to discuss this in front of your brother?"

"He already knows anyway."

Shrugging, he said, "Whatever. It's your story."

"Anyway, it wasn't exactly normal sex."

"Really."

"Really. There was a small added component at the end." She looked down at her nails. God she needed a manicure.

"You care to elaborate on the added component at the end?"

Not really. She wanted to go back to last night and change her mind about meeting a stranger in the park. She wanted to go home instead. She wanted to erase everything. She looked at him, holding his gaze. "I bit you."

"You did?" He felt his neck. "I don't feel anything."

"The wound is already healing. Anyway, it wasn't an ordinary bite."

Dylan looked at Noah. "Does this have anything to do with what I'm investigating?"

"Yes and no. Let her finish first and we can talk about your case after that."

Dylan turned a now-sharp gaze to Chantal. "Go on."

"We're not human," she blurted, then winced. Okay, so she probably could have finessed that a little better.

"Excuse me?"

"We're werewolves."

Noah leaned against the wall and crossed his arms. "Way to throw it out there, Chantal."

She half turned to shoot Noah a scathing look. "Well, there is no easy way to say it, is there?"

"Werewolves." Dylan shook his head. "You can do better than that."

"She's not lying, man," Noah said. "We're wolves. Shapeshifters."

"Uh-huh. Come on, Noah. We've known each other a long time. What's really going on here?"

"Chantal bit you during sex. She changed you."

"Changed me . . . how?"

"When I met you in the park," Chantal started, "I thought you were another wolf, like me. I had made an arrangement to meet with someone . . . an out-of-town sexual arrangement. I thought you were him. I didn't know you were human when we had sex. I didn't know you were human when I bit you, otherwise I'd have never touched you. But because I did, you've been infected with werewolf blood. You're going to become what we are."

"You people really believe this?" He tossed off the sheet and swung his legs over the bed, heedless of his nudity. "You're both fucking insane and I've got a job to do."

Noah rushed him, growling and partially shifting. His voice became dark and menacing as he pushed Dylan back onto the mattress with his forearm across Dylan's throat. "Stay put!"

Dylan's eyes widened as he took in Noah's changed features. The eyes turning yellow, fangs where his teeth were, his voice now more of a growling snarl than a human's voice.

Holy shit. Was he hallucinating? Had they fed him drugs or something? Noah backed off and Dylan watched him change back to human, his features softening.

"Sonofabitch," he whispered.

"Sorry, man," Noah said. "Had to show you we weren't making this up."

"I still don't believe it."

"It's true, Dylan," Chantal said.

He looked at her, his memories flooding back from last night. The woman with dark hair he'd thought was his contact. The sex. God, the sex—how could he forget that? She was still as beautiful in the daylight as she'd been in the park last night. He couldn't believe what had happened between them. It wasn't like him at all to forget his job and have sex with a stranger. "I don't fuck women I don't know."

She nodded and dropped her gaze to her lap. "It's in my pheromones. When I'm in heat like that it's irresistible to human males. It's like a drug, an aphrodisiac. It makes you drunk with desire." She looked up at him. "I didn't know you were a human. I never would have come near you had I known."

He rubbed his forehead where a headache was starting. "This is all a lot to process. And still damned hard to believe. Werewolves only exist in the movies and in books."

Noah smirked. "Apparently not."

"And you say I'm going to change now, become like you?"

"Yes. But it's not so bad. We lead normal lives. We belong to packs and we guard and take care of one another. You just have to be careful around humans."

"Obviously," Dylan deadpanned. "This is real, huh?"

"Yup."

Dylan dragged his hand through his hair. "Holy fucking shit. Okay, I need to get up. I'd like to get dressed. Where are my clothes?"

Noah opened the closet door. "These have all been brought from your hotel. The dresser has the rest of your things. Your toiletries are in the bathroom."

All his stuff. "Where exactly am I?"

"This is the San Francisco pack leader's mansion," Chantal said. "You're safe here among your own kind."

"Werewolves aren't my own kind."

"They are now," she said in a low voice that spoke of embarrassment. She could barely meet his gaze.

God, she was beautiful. And every time he looked at her he was reminded of the wild, animalistic sex they'd shared last night. And his dick was getting hard. So not a wise thing to let happen in front of her brother. He grabbed the sheet and bunched it up over his crotch. "I need a shower and to get dressed. And I'm starving. And I have a million questions."

Noah nodded. "Take your time. One of the guards will escort you downstairs when you're finished. We'll meet you there."

"Fine." *Just get the fuck out of my room.* Christ, this was confusing.

Chantal stood, opened her mouth as if she wanted to say something, then clamped it shut and followed her brother out the door. He locked it, walked into the bathroom and turned on the shower. He tried to relax under the hot, steamy spray. When he was finished he stared at his reflection in the mirror, checking his neck and shoulder for marks.

Other than a faint hickey-looking mark where Chantal said she had bit him, he didn't see anything that resembled the vicious bite marks similar to the ones on the bodies from the case he was investigating.

And obviously the victims had been torn apart and killed, not transformed into werewolves.

So what was the connection between Chantal and Noah and this case?

Was he really going to turn into a werewolf? And what the fuck did that mean? For him, for his career, his future? Was all this real? He'd seen Noah partly change from human to beast. That had been no illusion.

Goddamn.

He'd sure as hell had one life-changing fuck last night, hadn't he?

Chapter Three

Chantal sighed as Lamont Burkhart, the pack leader, read her the riot act.

"What were you thinking?"

"I thought he was the man Maia set me up with."

"Didn't you smell the human on him, for Christ's sake?"

"No, I was too busy fucking him to think about his scent, Lamont." And that was the truth. She hadn't bothered to track his scent. And even if she had, all she would have scented was human. Even werewolves smelled human unless they changed or were releasing pheromones, and only the females did that. Smelling wolf on him wasn't her primary objective last night. Getting his cock inside her was.

Lamont paced, his hands clasped behind his back. He was over six and a half feet tall and had to nearly double himself over to get in her face. "If you would mate with someone in our pack we wouldn't have had this problem."

"I'm not ready to mate—"

He held up his hand as he straightened. "Spare me the same bullshit you've been spouting for the past two years. I don't want to hear it. Turning humans is frowned upon and you know it. It's hard enough to keep our identities secret without bringing in outsiders. What is it with you Devlins and your predilection toward mating with humans?"

He was referring to her brothers, Jason and Max, both of whom had fallen in love with human females. But her situation was different. "I'm not the least bit interested in mating with a human or any man right now."

"A little late for that given the situation, don't you think?"

"It's my fault, Lamont. I should have been more specific in my description of the were I set her up with. I should have gone with her."

Chantal looked with fondness toward her friend Maia. "It's certainly not your fault, Maia. I take full responsibility."

"As you well should," Lamont said. "Though Maia bears some blame in this too. We hardly run an escort service here, Maia. And you know how I feel about pack members mating with outsiders."

Maia nodded. "My humble apologies, Lamont."

"Leave us," Lamont said.

Maia turned away, smiling and winking a violet eye at Chantal on her way out. She was one of the few friends Chantal had made since being assigned to this pack two years ago, and Chantal refused to allow Maia to take the blame for her own error. Chantal had been the one to approach Maia about needing a man and not wanting to mate with a pack member. Maia didn't mate with anyone inside the pack either. As a flight attendant, she had plenty of contacts in other packs and had offered to make arrangements.

No one else was going to suffer for Chantal's mistake. It was bad enough that Dylan already had.

The object of her thoughts walked into the room at that moment.

Her breath caught. Freshly showered, his hair still damp, he wore a white polo shirt and jeans, looking fit, casual and entirely too sexy. Her heart picked up a rapid pace, a hunger coursing through her that had nothing to do with food.

His gaze shot to hers, nostrils flaring as if he were breathing in her scent.

She'd seen that look between pack mates before. In heat.

Oh damn.

"Dylan," Noah said, stepping over to him. "This is Lamont Burkhart, the San Francisco pack leader. Lamont, Dylan Maxwell."

Chantal hadn't even known his last name.

Dylan shook Lamont's hand.

"We are terribly sorry about the unfortunate event that has brought you here," Lamont said, casting a chastising look at Chantal. "We hope you accept our humble apologies for what has happened to you."

Dylan shrugged. "I'm not sure I know exactly what's happened. But I'm slowly grabbing a clue."

"It is Chantal's responsibility to guide you through this process," Lamont explained. "Come, you must be starving. The impending change will cause you to be ravenous. You need to eat."

They sat at the table and ate. Chantal sat next to Dylan, breathing him in. Soap and the underlying scent of pure male that she attributed uniquely to him. It was burned into her olfactory senses now. She could probably pick him out of a crowd of thousands by scent alone.

Dylan downed his food like a man starving, tearing through two thick, rare steaks until nothing was left but bone. They consumed a couple bottles of wine, which Lamont explained would help relax the agitation within him.

Chantal was pretty damned agitated herself. And at a loss for what to do for Dylan. Or for herself.

Dylan wiped his mouth and took a swallow of wine. He stared at the remains of the two steaks he'd damn near inhaled. Two huge steaks. Almost rare. Damn, he'd been hungry. He always liked his meat well-done. Scorched, in fact.

What the hell.

"You'll find your tastes changing," Maia said, smiling at him.

A petite woman with the body of a stripper, she had unusual violet eyes and short, spiky blonde hair. "A lot of your tastes will change. More meat, less of the side foods."

"Uh-huh." All the people at the table looked so . . . normal. They ate, they drank, had normal conversations, even laughed and cracked jokes. Just looking at them, one wouldn't notice anything unusual at all. Did they finish dinner, clear the dishes, then turn into wolves and run wild through the parks?

"All your appetites will be more enhanced. Especially at the beginning," Lamont said. "Food and sex."

His gaze shot to Chantal, who turned a bright crimson.

"Chantal will see to your sexual needs."

His brows lifted. "Is that right?"

"Yes. You will have a voracious sexual appetite before the change occurs. She will satisfy all your requirements. Anything you need, just ask her."

Interesting side benefit. "Tell me about this change."

"Even now your physiology is changing. All your senses are heightening. You are growing stronger. During the full moon you will complete the transition and shift for the first time. It will be painful. Extremely painful. Chantal will assist you through that too. Trust her, let her help you. Do not leave her side at all for the next few days. It is important you stay here at the compound."

Dylan's gaze shot to Lamont. "Wait. Can't do that. I have a job."

"It'll have to wait." Lamont crossed his arms.

Dylan shook his head. "It can't wait. I need to leave." How could he have forgotten his goddamn job? All this shit had messed with his mind. Werewolves and sex and fucked-up transformations didn't matter. A killer was on the loose and he had to find him before he struck again.

"You cannot leave the safety of the compound. You will have to contact your employer and ask for time off."

"It's not that simple." He looked to Noah.

"Lamont, we need a minute in private to discuss this," Noah said.

Lamont nodded and looked at the others. "Leave us."

The others rose and exited the room immediately, leaving Dylan, Chantal and Noah alone with Lamont.

"Dylan works for the NCA as an agent. He's investigating the wolflike murders," Noah said.

"Oh, I see. Well, that's rather ironic." He looked to Dylan. "We have nothing to do with those."

Dylan steepled his fingers. "Any idea who does?"

"We have thoroughly investigated these killings within our own justice system. It's no one in our pack. We think it's a rogue. Definitely a werewolf, though."

Dylan's gaze shot to Noah. "Would have been nice if you'd let me know about this before."

Noah shrugged. "It's not like we go about revealing our identities to the Feds, man. I couldn't tell you. Would you have believed me anyway?"

"Not before last night." Shit. "I still have to do my job. I was in the park last night because I was supposed to meet an informant. Some woman with dark hair who had a lead for me. I thought Chantal was the informant."

Lamont looked at Chantal.

"Don't give me that look," she said. "I didn't even know about these murders until Noah told me about them this morning."

Dylan stood. "I have calls to make, leads to follow up on. I'm on assignment here. I need to report in to the NCA or they'll be sending a shitload of field agents to look for me. You don't want that. Let me go do my job."

Lamont sighed. "Very well. But I want Noah and Chantal with you at all times. And they do have the inside track on the werewolf population here in the area as well as around the country. They can be of use to you."

Dylan shrugged. "If it's okay with them, it's fine by me."

Lamont looked to Chantal.

"I can take a few days off work. I just finished a case."

"I'm free for a few too," Noah said.

"Good," Lamont said. "We do, of course, require your discretion in this and would appreciate you not notifying the government of the existence of werewolves."

"Considering my current predicament, it would be a death warrant to my career. You have my word."

Lamont nodded. "And night of the full moon, Dylan, you come back here for the change. It's dangerous for you to be out there."

"Fine."

"Then it's settled." He stood. "Chantal will see to any of your other needs and questions. If you require anything else, please don't hesitate to ask."

After he left the room, Dylan turned to Noah. "Doesn't he remind you of Lurch?"

Noah snorted. "He's a little dry and humorless, yeah."

"More like those movie vampire types than a werewolf if you ask me."

"And just what are our 'types'?" Chantal asked.

"Not sure yet. Y'all seem pretty normal to me. Except for the snarling and biting."

"You haven't seen the half of it yet," she said with a half smile.

"Show me." He tilted back in his chair and laced his fingers over his stomach.

"Uh, yeah. That's my clue to leave before I get icked out." Noah stood. "You need me, Chantal, buzz my phone. I'm going out but I'll be nearby."

"I need to make some calls," Dylan said.

"Make your calls," Noah said. "You won't be going out for a few hours."

"Why's that?"

"Urges, my man," Noah replied with a snicker as he walked out. "Urges."

Dylan turned back to Chantal. "I feel like there's a private joke I'm not privy to."

"Sexual urges. Now that you've eaten, they'll be hitting you shortly. Better make your calls." She stood. "I'll be in my room."

"Naked? Legs spread? How nice of you to act like a whore for me during this transition."

She calmly pushed back from the table and leaned over him, her mouth inches from his, her gaze boring into his. "Guess I deserved that since I put you in this predicament. But get this straight. I'm no man's whore, Dylan. I'm doing this out of guilt and pack responsibility. Nothing more. When you're ready and the urge hits, I'll be ready to take care of it for you, because that's what I'm supposed to do. Don't assume I'll derive any pleasure from it."

She turned on her heel and walked out of the room.

Well, that was strangely unsatisfying. But goddammit, he didn't choose to be a werewolf. Sex kitten Chantal Devlin had decided she wanted a romp in the park, took a bite out of him and as a result his whole life had changed overnight.

Didn't he deserve to be a little pissed off about that?

As far as her not getting any pleasure out of fucking him? Huh. He'd see about that.

Chapter Four

Chantal paced. Stopped in the middle of the room and stared at the door. Nothing. She resumed her pacing until she reached the center of the room, then halted again, crossing her arms over her chest.

She looked at her watch. It had been an hour.

Where was he? Her panties were damp just thinking about how it would be with Dylan again. Hot, carnal and wild, just as it had been last night.

She might be irritated as hell with him, but she couldn't deny wanting his cock inside her again.

So why hadn't he shown up yet?

She finally grew tired of wearing a hole in the rug with her heels. Disgusted at her nervous anticipation, she kicked off her shoes and fell onto the bed. Exhausted, she figured she'd just close her eyes for a few minutes. She'd hear Dylan when he showed up.

When she opened her eyes the room was dark. Damn, she'd slept the rest of the day. Of course, she hadn't gotten any sleep at all last night, so it was no wonder. She yawned and grabbed her pillow, snuggling deeper into the soft down. Warmth. Oblivion.

Her eyes shot open when she caught a familiar scent and heard movement. She wasn't alone in the room.

She started to move.

"Don't."

Dylan's voice, tight and strained.

"Stay just like that. God, you look hot, sprawled out on

your belly with your legs spread and your skirt hiked up to your thighs."

He was panting. She scented his arousal in the air around her, her panties flooding with moisture as she breathed him in. She heard a zipper drawing down, the rustle of clothing as it dropped to the floor.

"Where've you been?" She hated asking the question, but couldn't help it.

"Fighting this. My cock's been hard for the better part of four hours. I paced, I worked out, I read, I made some calls. I did everything I could to keep from coming in here. I even thought about jacking off, but I knew it wouldn't even begin to take the edge off. It's you I crave. I need you, Chantal. I don't want to, but I do."

The bed creaked as he climbed on the end and came toward her. She gripped the sheets in her hands, anticipating, wanting, squirming as she rubbed her pussy against her wet panties. Her clit swelled and she moved it against the mattress, feeling the burst of sensation sparking inside her.

"I can't promise to be gentle," he muttered, his body surrounding her.

"I don't want you to be."

He touched her calves first and she jumped at the contact.

"Shhh," he whispered, smoothing his hands upward, over the backs of her knees.

Slow. Too slow. He crept to her thighs, raising her dress as he moved his hand underneath the fabric to her upper thighs. When he reached her panties, he growled, "These are in my way," and tore them with a harsh rip.

She gasped. "Those cost twenty dollars."

"Send me a bill."

The animalist nature of the act only served to heighten her excitement. She lifted her hips, begging silently for his cock. He patted her ass and ran his finger between her cheeks.

"I want to fuck you everywhere. Including here. I'll bet your ass is just as tight and sweet as your cunt."

She shuddered at the sensation of his fingers teasing back and forth along the puckered hole. When he bent and kissed the small of her back, she whimpered. When his mouth went lower, his tongue finding her drenched pussy lips, she cried out and dug her nails into the mattress.

She could shift, could take over. He wasn't lupine yet. She was stronger. But, oh, she felt so feminine under his assault. And she needed to let him have his way, let him do this to her. She owed him that much. God, she needed him inside her.

She gasped when he flipped her over onto her back, then held her firm with his hand on her belly. He tortured her with his tongue, lapping at her pussy with warm, wet strokes, sucking at her clit until she was afraid she was going to die from the sweet pleasure.

She couldn't take it anymore. "I thought you said you weren't going to be gentle."

He laughed. "Impatient for my dick?"

"I want it."

"Tough. I've been waiting. Now you wait. I want you to come. I want to taste that sweet honey again. It's like a goddamn drug, baby. Give it to me."

She didn't like the tone of his voice, ordering her to have an orgasm. Then again, it was damned hard to not have one the way he was licking her clit, sucking it, tugging, then swirling his tongue around it. She was going to come and she couldn't hold back if she wanted to.

Hell, she didn't want to. She lifted off the mattress, ground her sex against his face and let go.

"God, Dylan, I'm coming," she moaned, the hot rush of fluids pouring from her. He clamped his mouth over her pussy and drank from her as she crested the wave over and over again.

She panted, breathing deeply to gather some semblance of wits. Though he hardly gave her much time before he snaked his arm around her waist to lift her up. He flipped her over and shoved a pillow under her hips.

Now he wasn't gentle as he kneed her legs farther apart and positioned himself between them, his cock head finding her slit. Before she could even draw a quick breath, he shoved inside her, burying himself balls-deep.

"Oh yeah, that's perfect," he groaned, grinding against her ass as he fit against her, drawing out and thrusting hard.

He was thick, pulsing with heat and she'd never felt anything so good. She rose up and back against him, needing him deeper. He placed a hand on her back, pushing her down.

"No. Let me."

His growl of irritation only turned her on more, his hand large, hot and powerful splayed across her back, holding her steady. Visions of him holding her in place with his teeth while he mounted her in wolf form sent pools of desire pouring from her.

"You always get this wet when you fuck?" he asked, withdrawing almost completely, only to slam hard against her again.

She grunted, fisting the sheets and pushing back. The answer was no. No man had ever turned her on like this. But she wasn't about to tell him that since her emotions were conflicted enough where he was concerned.

In the darkness, every sound, every scent was magnified. Her senses caught and held the musky, totally male smell of his soap, heard every intake of breath he made, the slapping sounds of their moist bodies connecting. It was hot in the room despite the air-conditioning, and their bodies slid against each other as he lay fully on top of her, swept her hair to the side and sank his teeth into the back of her neck.

She screamed in pleasure, came in a flood of crashing sensation. He growled against her neck as he jettisoned inside her, keeping his teeth buried in her nape, possessing her, riding her.

It was phenomenal. She'd never climaxed so hard or so long. By the time he let go of her neck and raised off her, she felt like a limp dishrag, unable to move, let alone speak.

Instead of leaving the bed, he rolled to the side and took her with him, drawing her against him. Admittedly, she kind of liked that.

She shouldn't like it. She didn't even like him. Okay, she didn't even know him. She was never supposed to know him. That was the whole idea with men and sex. Last night Dylan was supposed to be a quick, anonymous fuck, and he had been. Only the quick fuck had turned into something more . . . binding. Now she had to keep him satisfied while he made the transition. Which meant she couldn't just up and leave or kick him out of her room. Her bed.

Dammit.

She had to let him stay.

"You smell good." He kissed the back of her neck.

She shivered and tried to elbow him. He laughed.

"Not much for after-sex snuggling, are you?"

Glad for the darkness, she shrugged. "You hardly seem the snuggling type yourself."

"You don't know me very well, then. I enjoy women. Everything about them. I'm not a fuck 'em and leave 'em kind of guy."

He was right. She didn't know him. Nothing about him other than he was an agent for the NCA and human. Well, formerly human. She scooted away and sat up, pulling her hand through her hair. "Why did my brother call you Legend when he first saw you?"

"It's my code name with the NCA."

"Oh. Why that code name?"

"Let's say I tend to get myself out of pretty sticky situations in rather legendary ways."

She wanted to hear about those ways, but that would require intimacy and conversation, and that she wouldn't do. "Didn't you have to go out?"

"Yeah, actually, I do. You in a hurry to get out of bed?" He inched toward her again, teasing her inner thigh.

She melted, her clit tingling at the thought of how easy it would be to lay back, spread her legs and let him rub those big, hard hands all over her pussy. Spend the entire night in bed with him. Exploring, learning his body, getting to know him.

Too dangerous. When he demanded it, she'd fuck him and leave it at that. "Want to prowl around in werewolfland?"

He paused in his mapping of her body. His fingers disappeared from her thigh and the warmth of his body left her side. She felt cold. The harsh light on her bedside table flipped on. She squinted, then glared at him.

"That's actually a great idea," he said. "Can you take me there?"

She was the one who suggested it. No point in being irritated with his boyish excitement. "Sure. Give me an hour to get showered. Nighttime is when everyone prowls. We might be able to find out something about the killer."

He bounded out of bed and grabbed his clothes, climbing back into them so fast she barely caught a glimpse of his body. Too bad.

"I'll shower and change too," he said, exiting her room in a hurry. With a resigned sigh, Chantal slid off the bed and headed into her bathroom and turned on the shower.

She turned and regarded her reflection in the mirror. Her face was flushed with the aftereffects of great sex, something she could still be having if she wasn't so damn skittish about getting close to a man.

"Dumbass," she said to her reflection, then stuck out her tongue.

Well, great. Instead of a night of hot sex, she was going to help Dylan hunt for a killer.

• • •

Excitement churned inside Dylan. Adrenaline pumped through his veins. He didn't know whether he was more sexually charged or if it was the chase for the killer. Either way, he was keyed up.

Chantal had recruited Noah to come along, so the three of them headed out into the city. Not the typical tourist traps, since they were closed by now. Noah drove them to a nondescript brick building with no windows. The building stood two stories tall in the middle of what looked to be a business district.

"What's this place?" Dylan asked as they parked in front and stepped out of the car.

"Party central for the werewolves around here," Chantal said, smoothing her skirt.

Correction. What skirt there was. The tiny scrap of fabric barely covering her ass could hardly be called a skirt. Typically he'd enjoy ogling a woman wearing a short skirt. But for some reason, knowing they were going into some club where other men could look at Chantal made the green monster rise up in a huge way inside him.

And he didn't like that. Why should he be jealous? He had no claim on this woman. He'd fucked her, and according to this whole werewolf thing going on inside him he'd get to continue to fuck her for a while longer, which was just fine with him. But that was all they had going. They had no relationship. Hell, he didn't even really know her.

So why did the thought of those long, shapely legs and firm thighs about to be displayed for every pair of male eyes to see really piss him off?

Music pumped through the heavy oak door. Noah rapped on it. A window slid open in the door and a mean set of dark eyes glared at them. Noah showed an ID.

"Okay. I know Chantal. Who's the new guy?" the man behind the window asked.

"Human. Newly turned. He's Chantal's."

The guy looked at Dylan for a second, then nodded, slammed the slider shut and opened the door.

The interior was pitch black inside with the exception of lights strobing down from the ceiling and hitting a dance floor. Dylan followed Noah and Chantal's lead to the bar. The place was packed, both on the dance floor and off, every table occupied.

"Are all these people werewolves?" Dylan asked, bending low to speak in Chantal's ear over the loud music.

She tilted her head back and nodded. "Yeah. No humans allowed."

Damn. He had no idea.

A group got up and left, so they took their table and sat, giving Dylan a chance to sip his beer and survey the crowd. A mix and match of all ages, all robust and healthy looking, smiling, laughing and partying their asses off. It could be any nightclub in any city, with the exception that these people were lupine.

"So why do they hide out? Why the exclusivity?"

"Kindred," Noah explained. "Plus, if anyone shifts or things get out of hand, no one will be shocked and our covers aren't blown. It happens. Fights break out, tempers flare, passions rise. Things are just warming up in here. It looks normal right now. Just wait."

"Werewolves are a very primal, passionate lot, Dylan," Chantal added. "Anything can happen."

He cast a heated gaze at Chantal. "So I've noticed."

Lifting her chin, she said, "You haven't seen anything yet."

Noah cleared his throat. Loudly. "You two gonna practice verbal foreplay all night, or are we here to do something else?"

Dylan dragged his gaze away from Chantal's challenging stare. "Ever see any bad element among your kind? Anything suspicious?"

Noah shrugged. "There's always a dumbass or two in the population who want to step outside the secrecy we try to so hard to maintain. Think the rules don't apply to them. But they're easily brought in line. Or eliminated."

"Our rules are very clear," Chantal added. "Break them and you die. The sanctity of the pack is everything and all of us work very hard at maintaining the cloak of normalcy. If one of us is found out, it threatens us all."

"So it would be unlikely that the pack would protect a killer of humans."

"Protect? No. We wouldn't turn him over to the authorities either," Noah explained. "We'd just deal with him ourselves. But he wouldn't be allowed to run amok. If werewolves were discovered to be living among humans, they'd hunt us all down. The potential for war would be great. We would never risk the possibility of elimination of our species."

"None of us want that," Chantal said. "We'll do anything we have to in order to stop this killer. What do you know about him?"

"He struck a couple years ago in southern California and Nevada, then nothing until a few months ago. Then he hit in Oregon and Washington about six months ago. Last three attacks were here in the San Francisco area."

"So he's a traveler," Chantal said.

"Or someone who likes fucking with us," Dylan said. "We get a lot of serial cases that move around for the sheer fun of watching us chase them. That's their thrill."

Noah drained his drink, then shook his head. "This guy's pissed off about something. Or at someone."

"I wish I knew who the woman was who had called saying she had information," Dylan said, casting his dark gaze on Chantal.

If he'd met that woman instead of Chantal, none of this would have happened.

And he wouldn't be a werewolf feeling this hunger churning inside him right now, wishing he could strip Chantal down at the club and fuck her.

His head was swirling. It was getting hard to concentrate on work. His stomach hurt. His cock throbbed. How long had it been since he'd eaten? Since he'd fucked Chantal? A few hours? Several?

Too long.

He was getting hungry again. For food.

And for Chantal.

Chapter Five

Chantal caught and held Dylan's gaze, reading the hunger in his eyes.

"Let's feed you," she said, shooting Noah a warning glance.

Noah took a look at the feral expression on Dylan's face and nodded. "Get him some food. And whatever else he needs. I'm gonna do a little recon around here, see if I can get to know some of the locals."

"Okay." She signaled for the waitress and ordered meat. Rare. And in a hurry. The waitress took a quick look at Dylan and seemed to catch Chantal's drift, scuttling off to the kitchen.

Chantal reached across the table for Dylan's hand. "Hey, hang on. We'll get you some food."

He seemed in a trance, his gaze fixated on her. He nodded. "It hurts. Everywhere."

"I know." Dammit, she didn't know, but she understood now that she'd have to be more careful over the next day or so until he made the transition. Keep him fed and keep him fucked, Lamont had told her. She hadn't been doing her job.

The music pulsed around them. Hard, heavy and driving with a sensual beat that entered her bloodstream, pumping the primal sensations within her. It had to be making Dylan crazy because he wasn't used to the experience yet. She could handle it, could control the wildness within her.

From the looks he was giving her, she wasn't sure he was going to be able to tame the impulses.

Fortunately the waitress came back with a huge piece of meat. Dylan dove into it with a vengeance, polishing it off quickly. He never once took his eyes off her as he ate. Her pulse began to thrum with a wild beat as he watched her, and with every bite he took, every time he swept his tongue over his full bottom lip, she began to feel as if she were his meal.

It was getting warm in the club. The music churned, the urge to move, to dance, becoming a need she couldn't ignore. She stood and reached for Dylan's hand.

"Let's go."

"Where?"

"Dance floor."

He frowned. "Don't feel like dancing."

"We'll be doing more than dancing, trust me."

After studying her with a surly frown for a few seconds, he slid his hand in hers and let her guide him into the middle of the throng of undulating dancers. She turned and wound her body around his.

"Feel the music, Dylan. Let it enter you."

He wrapped his arms around her and jerked her against him, none too gently. The thick heat of his cock brushed insistently against her hip. "I'd rather enter you."

Sensation took flame and caught, igniting her into heated arousal. The frenzied beat of the music pounded as hard as her clit. "I know what you want. You'll get it."

"Good. Let's go."

He pulled away and tugged on her wrist but she stood firm, then advanced on him once again, holding him there by lifting her leg and wrapping it around his hip. "Just dance. And keep watching."

She began to move against him with the rhythm of the music, undulating her hips against his, driving her clit against his pelvis. The ache intensified, pleasure bursting and making her clit swell. She let her head fall back and just went with the mood, letting go.

Dylan frowned and grasped her hips while she wound her arms around his neck. "You're playing a dangerous game, Chantal. I don't have much control."

She raised her head, opened her eyes, drinking in his chiseled features, the frown that signaled pained arousal. "Look around you, Dylan."

He tore his gaze from hers and surveyed the dance floor. She already knew what he'd see. The smells and sounds of sex surrounded them, permeating the entire room.

The party had begun.

Dylan didn't want to look at anything or anyone but Chantal, but the sounds of moaning crescendoed even over the ear-splitting music. Various stages of foreplay or downright sex were happening all around them. People were either dancing and ignoring what was happening, or they were getting down. Right next to him a woman had straddled her dance partner. His pants were unzipped and they were going at it as they danced. Across the room one guy had his woman spread-eagled on the table and was snacking on her pussy. Another woman was going down on a guy while he leaned against the bar.

Christ. Was this some kind of sex club?

Chantal leaned into him. "I told you we're a passionate lot. This happens at the parties. Since we don't kill for sport anymore, we fuck to let off tension."

He pulled her back and searched her face. "You do this often?"

She shook her head. "Never, actually. Been to the clubs before, but never . . . engaged."

"Why not?"

Her lips curled in a teasing smirk. "I'm picky."

He liked that. "Guess I should be flattered, then."

"Yes, you should be."

Dylan searched the room looking for Noah, but couldn't find him.

"Where's your brother?"

Chantal shrugged. "Probably took off after he looked around a bit. He knew what we were going to do here. I doubt he wanted to witness it."

"And what do you think we're going to do here, Chantal?"

Her eyes darkened, lips parted as she moved her hips against him. "We're going to fuck."

That wasn't why he'd come here. But it's what he needed. The mission be damned, he needed to be inside Chantal. His balls were twisted in a painful knot, throbbing tight and hard against his body. His lust for her was overpowering, driving every thought away except the need to mate with her. It burned within him to the point where if he didn't take her right now . . .

Oh, fuck it. Enough thinking. He shuffled her backward, off the dance floor and through the crowd, holding her close to his body and using his hands to push people out of the way. Not that anyone paid attention to them. They were too busy doing their own thing.

He slammed her up against the wall and latched onto her lips, driving his tongue inside her mouth. She tasted of raw passion, of the same hunger that burned within him. It fired his blood, making the lust churn inside him. Soon he forgot where he was, didn't care about the people around them, the fact they were in a public place.

With a low growl against her mouth he tugged her skimpy little skirt over her hips and slid his fingers underneath her panties, desperate to make contact with the heat of her flesh.

She was wet and pulsing. He rocked his palm against her sex, then inserted two fingers inside her. She moaned against his lips and thrust her tongue against his.

Rock-hard and ready, he couldn't stand this. Playing was one thing when he had patience. Now he didn't have any. He withdrew his fingers and unzipped his jeans, tugging them down enough to withdraw his cock. He didn't even ask if this was what she wanted. One look at the glazed expression in her eyes, the way her tongue swept over her bottom lip, and he knew.

He pushed against her and entered her with a quick thrust. She cried out, the sound absorbed by the loud music. Only he heard and her cries were the sweetest music in the place. He pushed her hard against the wall, pistoning his cock deep, feeling her pussy grip him as she welcomed him inside.

Chantal clawed his back with her nails, scraping along the tops of his shoulders, trailing them into his hair, tugging it fiercely.

"Fuck me," she demanded in a low, sexy voice. "Harder."

He slammed against her, pulling back so he could watch where their bodies met, could see her cunt grab on to his shaft every time he withdrew and reentered her. She fit him perfectly, accepting the thick heat of him fully. He was on fire from the inside out, his balls aching with painful pleasure, filling with the cum he would soon jettison inside her.

Music blasted louder, harder, the beat driving through his nerve endings. He pumped to the rhythm, grabbing Chantal's wrists and raising them above her head, pinning her to the wall. Possessing her was his driving force now. Her eyes were open windows, letting him see inside to the passion, the need, the wild creature that lived within her. Instinctively he knew she'd never let anyone this close. Chantal was guarded, but not with him. He wanted to crawl inside her, to mark her, to make her his in a way that had never been as compelling as it was right now.

"Dylan!" she cried, her pussy squeezing him with relentless pulses.

With measured, frantic strokes, he took her over the edge, burying his head in her neck and biting down on the soft tissue between her throat and shoulder. She shuddered against him and spilled hot cream over his balls as she came. He shuddered, climaxing against her, erupting with fierce contractions that sprang from his spine upward. He emptied into her with blinding pulses until he had nothing left to give.

Panting, he released her arms, wrapped his around her waist and pulled her skirt down, protecting her from those who might see.

Fuck. He'd lost it. Utterly lost it.

And the odd part was, he didn't give a shit that he'd just fucked Chantal in a very public place. Nor did he care who had watched. She didn't seem to either. Just lifted her lips in a very satisfied smile.

"Feel better?" she asked.

"Much."

"Good."

He took her hand. "Now let's find Noah."

"He's probably long gone by now. With the car. But it's not too far back to the house. We can walk."

They headed out the front door of the club. Night chill bit into them. "You sure you're not too cold?"

"I have . . . internal insulation to keep me warm," she said as they started walking. "I don't tend to feel the cold."

"Oh. Good to know." That was convenient. He supposed there'd be benefits to this werewolf thing.

"Are you cold?

The wind swirled around them, biting into his skin. He thought about it. "Actually, no."

"Good."

They cut through the park, Chantal leading the way. In about two hours it would be dawn. Typically this wouldn't be a wise decision since wandering around a dark, deserted area like this in the middle of the night wasn't the safest thing to do, but he had a weapon.

And a very sexy werewolf by his side.

He slanted a glance at her, finding it hard to believe the slight little wisp of a woman holding his hand could shift into a feral beast. He'd like to see that.

A sound to his left dragged his attention away from the beautiful woman at his side. He stopped, sniffed the air, looked around, his senses catching something on the wind.

Something foul.

"What's wrong?" Chantal asked.

"I smelled something."

She inhaled. "Wolf."

He couldn't describe the sensation, but it prickled down his spine like a sixth sense of foreboding. He grabbed his gun and released the safety. Chantal's eyes widened.

"Do you think it's the wolf you're looking for?"

"Maybe. Could be nothing, too. I don't have a handle on these new senses slamming around inside me. But I'm not going to take any chances."

He stalked the area, tuning into his senses. Chantal followed, staying behind him and a little to his side, remaining within his field of vision at all times. Good girl.

Was the wolf following them, or was it stalking other prey?

A rustle in the bushes ahead and a scream made him start.

He had the answer to his question. The wolf hadn't been after them. Ballsy sonofabitch, though. He'd known they were there and just hadn't cared.

"There." He shot straight ahead, Chantal hot on his heels.

A wolf had a dark-haired woman backed against a tree. Dylan pulled his gun and fired at the ground in front of the wolf, the shot spraying grass and dirt in front of the wolf. The wolf started, jumping back and turning to snarl at Dylan. Dammit, he couldn't shoot the thing, it was too close to the girl. If he missed, he'd hit her.

The wolf's eyes glowed like golden flame in the darkness, its sleek muscles undulating under its gray fur. For a second Dylan was sure it was going to lunge at him, but then it turned to the left and sprang through the dense bushes, disappearing from sight. The young woman sank to the ground in a heap, out cold.

"I'm going after him," Chantal said, pulling her clothes off in a hurry. Dylan watched, transfixed, as within seconds and at a dead run, a naked Chantal shifted from woman to wolf and disappeared into the brush.

He checked the woman for injuries. Other than a few scratches on her arms and legs, she seemed okay. Probably in shock. He took out his phone and called Noah, reporting what happened while he waited for Chantal. Goddammit, he wanted to be able to shift and go with her. Wasn't that just the oddest thing? He didn't want to be a werewolf, didn't want this upheaval and complete change in his life that had been thrust upon him. But it sure as hell would come in handy right now. Because he'd like to chase down that sonofabitch who'd tried to attack the girl.

He looked up at the moon. Almost full. He felt the draw to it, immersed himself in its power.

It was almost his time.

Chapter Six

Chantal hadn't been able to catch up to the wolf. Once she hit the end of the park, the trail ended at the fence leading onto the Golden Gate Bridge. The bastard. No telling where he'd gone from there and his scent had gone cold. If he was in human form she wouldn't be able to follow his scent. Only when he was in wolf form. He must have shifted and taken off over the fence where he had a car waiting or he'd walked across the pedestrian part of the bridge.

She'd hurried back to Dylan and found him and Noah with the girl. She was conscious, but her memory was a blank. She didn't even remember the wolf, only that someone attacked her and she fainted. Said the last thing she remembered was meeting some friends for drinks at a bar called The Joint on Market Street, a popular nightspot. The police arrived and everyone gave their statements, saying they'd come upon an unconscious woman while walking in the park. Dylan identified himself as NCA and indicated he'd fill his superiors in on what happened. Then they left the scene and headed back to the house.

Dylan ate a pound of bacon and some eggs while they sat around with Lamont and Maia and a few of the others from Lamont's higher echelon.

"The others who were killed also were young and hung out in very trendy bars like The Joint, where the woman was last night. Our wolf is obviously targeting his victims there," Dylan said.

"Maia and I hit that bar a lot. We know all the regulars. It's a popular place for the downtown crowd," Chantal said.

Lamont frowned. Chantal shrugged. "We go before dark, okay? And only one or two drinks."

"Lighten up, Lamont," Maia added. "We *are* allowed to mingle among the human population. It's not like we ate anyone. Well, not in the werewolf way, anyway," she finished with a cocky grin.

Noah snorted. Maia shot him a lascivious gleam. Chantal shook her head, having seen that look from her friend before. Her brother was in serious trouble. Then again, Noah might enjoy being "eaten" by Maia. And that was somewhere she didn't want to go, mentally.

"So how about a double date tonight at The Joint?" Dylan asked. "Since Chantal and Maia are regulars, they'll fit in and we won't look out of place."

Maia shrugged. "Sounds fine to me."

"And you, Dylan? How are you holding up under the impending change?" Lamont asked.

"I'm fine and handling it."

Lamont's brows lifted and he looked to Chantal, who nodded. "He's right. He's doing okay. And I'm taking care of him," she added before he asked.

"Tomorrow is the full moon. I don't think I need to remind you that Dylan will need to be kept here when the change occurs."

"Noah and I will take care of it." Geez, like she didn't know when the full moon was?

They'd slept during the day. She woke to dusk settling over the room, Dylan's even breathing behind her.

Interestingly enough, Dylan hadn't gone to his room to sleep. He slept in her room. Even more interesting was that she didn't mind when he followed her, undressed and slipped into bed, drawing her against his body and pulling the covers over them both. She'd passed right out, cocooned within his embrace.

She was getting used to having him around, which was a very bad thing. As soon as she got him past the transition, she'd go back to her job and he'd go back to doing his. Wherever that was. They had no relationship—okay, other than the bond they would always share because of what she'd done. But that didn't make them partners forever. It didn't mate them. Not unless it was by choice on both their parts.

Dylan didn't know the first thing about lupine society and its rules. And Chantal wasn't ready for that kind of commitment. She had . . . things to do with her life before she settled down in a pack with one mate.

Though at the moment none of those "things" came to mind. The only thing pressing on her mind was Dylan's long body stretched out behind her, his warmth surrounding her, his hand resting in the hollow between her breasts, one leg over hers.

Possessive. She'd never even let a guy spend the entire night with her before. She might fuck them, but she never slept with them. But Dylan had slept with her. And she was comfortable with him. What did it mean? Was it because she had no choice, or was there some special quality about him that other men she'd known didn't have?

The sex was phenomenal, that was for sure. She smiled in the darkness and inhaled a satisfied breath. Admittedly, she'd never been quite so . . . pleasured, before. And they'd only scratched the surface. She knew there was more. So much more.

In fact, that "more" was lengthening against her ass right now, the heat of his awakening cock sliding between her legs. Dylan cupped her breast.

"I feel you're awake," she teased.

"Uh-huh." He moved his hips against her. Her pussy responded with a flood of moisture. God, she was so easy where he was concerned. Her nipples puckered, begging for his attention. He rolled her over onto her back and took one hard peak between his lips and sucked.

She arched, thrusting the bud into his mouth, letting him graze on her nipple in lazy abandon. Waking up this way, letting him love her body in a slow, leisurely fashion, was another new experience for her. Her nerve endings tingled in anticipation as a desperate rush of passion surged to life. The yawning awakening had been replaced with hungry need. She lifted her hips to his, trying to edge closer to his cock.

He used his own hips to push her back down on the mattress. "Not yet, baby."

Damn him. "Quit teasing and just fuck me."

"You're too impatient." He licked her neck, causing chills to pop out along her skin.

"You're too damned irritating. We need to get going."

"Plenty of time," he murmured against her breast as he shifted lower, licking at her nipples, sucking them, gathering one between his teeth and lightly biting. She nearly came off the mattress at the exquisite sensation. Twice, because he did the same thing to the other tortured bud before moving his way south, sliding his tongue into her belly button and tormenting her.

"Dylan," she warned, trying to throw him off. It was useless, like trying to crawl out from underneath steel. He had her pinned. At least her bottom half, his hands grasping her hips as he kissed her inner thighs, then teased her sex with his rough bearded chin.

"Yeah, babe. I know what you need." He kissed her clit.

A feather touch, not at all what she needed. All it did was prime the pump, make her want more. She twined her fingers in his hair, trying to direct him to her pleasure spots. But the damned man wouldn't budge. He looked up at her and smiled.

"You in some kind of hurry today?"

"Yes. I want to come. All over your tongue."

His lips curled and he stuck out his tongue. "This tongue?"

She couldn't help it. She laughed. "No. Your other one, jackass."

"Oh, you must mean this tongue, then." He pressed it down on her clit. Warm, wet, he swirled it around her sex, licking her up as if she were the best ice-cream cone he'd ever tasted.

She melted, pouring over his tongue. He lapped her up and came back for more until she was writhing underneath him, mindless, her only driving thought to climax. She fisted the sheets and clenched her butt cheeks as she approached the edge of reason. When he slid two fingers into her pussy and began to pump them inside her, she lost it.

"Oh God, Dylan, I'm going to come," she cried, thrusting her hips against his mouth and his fingers as her orgasm tore through her. He latched onto her clit and sucked as she came, sliding one more finger into her pussy and fucking her cunt with a maddening rhythm that made the waves crest higher and higher until she sobbed out his name.

And still, he didn't stop, licking her from her clit all the way to her ass, lifting her up so he could tease the tiny hole. He invaded her there with his tongue and mouth, wetting her beyond her own juices pouring down there.

What was he doing to her? She was going out of her mind and loving every minute of it. But she guessed his intent and a fire grew deep in her belly at the thought of having him embedded there, where she'd never let a man in before. Oh, she'd fucked herself in the ass with her toys, but she'd never been filled with a thick, hot cock. Her pussy quivered at the thought, anticipation wrenching her arousal a notch higher.

Dylan stood and dragged her to the edge of the bed.

"Fuck your pussy with your fingers," he ordered, stroking his cock. "I want your ass."

He pulled her legs up and braced them against his chest, his gaze focused between her legs as she skimmed her flesh with her fingers, teasing her already swollen clit.

"Yes, like that," he whispered, draping her legs over his arms and spreading them apart. "You have lube?"

His voice was tight, barely restrained. She nodded and pointed to the bedside table. He leaned over and grabbed the bottle and poured the liquid onto his hand. He coated his cock, then her, positioning his shaft at her entrance. He inched forward, pushing past the tight barrier. The burning hurt.

"Rub that pussy for me, baby," he said, leaning over her. "Make it feel good."

She focused on the sensations around her clit, and on his eyes, the darkness within them, the pleasure she saw in his face as he forced past the muscles in her ass. With careful, measured movements he inched his way inside, stopping with every push so she could grow accustomed to his invasion. He'd pull back, watch her caress her clit, let her feel the pleasure instead of the pain.

Even though it hurt, it felt good too, the mix of agony and delight easing the pain of his entry until there was nothing but the sensation of being filled, of having him thick and hot and buried inside her. She dipped her fingers into her pussy, where the thin membrane that separated one part from the other allowed her to feel him moving inside her.

"So tight," he murmured as he gripped her legs and began to pump against her. "Fuck yourself, Chantal. Fuck your pussy for me."

The double penetration brought out the wildness within her. She felt the beast begin to surface, and she let Dylan see it, growling at him, scratching his arm with her free hand. His fingers bit into her legs as he began to power deeper, harder, and she cried out, demanding it, needing each punishing thrust he gave her. The animal within him, though not visible, was present. She could see it in the swirling darkness in his eyes and she reveled in its power, its match for her strength. The mating was savage as he pistoned his cock deep in her anus.

She thrust another finger in her pussy, using her other hand to tease her clit.

"You ready to come?" he asked, lifting her even higher off the bed as he fucked her, his voice low, deep, like a growl.

"Yes," she hissed. "Fuck me hard."

She dug her fingers deep into her pussy as he slammed his cock into her ass. When her climax hit, she howled as the pleasure splintered her, making her shake so hard she rocked the mattress. She screamed, unable to control the sensations as every nerve ending came alive with her orgasm.

Dylan yelled and shot hot cum into her ass, pressing deep, his body plastered against hers as he raised her legs over his shoulders and shuddered against her. She saw the light in his eyes, the yellowing glow as he soared through his orgasm. Though brief, it was still there and she knew then, his change was coming soon.

Panting, shaking and drenched in perspiration, they showered afterward. Dylan was achingly tender with her as he washed her all over, his lips pressed to her skin as he rinsed her body. He caressed her, then positioned her up against the wall of the shower and took her again, this time slowly, his cock moving inside her with sweet, oh-so-gentle strokes. She came again with an explosion that nearly sent her to her knees. He kissed her, soft kisses like a spring rain instead of their typical hard passion, until he came inside her with a torrent of shudders, gripping her so tight and so close to his body that it brought tears to her eyes.

He was an enigma. Hard and passionate one minute, soft and tender the next. Challenging her in every way, meeting her head-on and giving her everything she could ever ask for in a mate. A true partner.

Damn him. She was falling in love and she didn't like it one bit.

Chantal Devlin had never loved a man in her entire life. And she had no idea how to handle this.

Because she wasn't keeping Dylan Maxwell. He wasn't her mate.

He wasn't!

• • •

The Joint was jammed up with all the usual people. Chantal led them to the table she and Maia typically occupied near the front window. Their favorite waiter, Joe, came over.

"Hey, you two," he said, grabbing his pad from his pocket. "Been awhile."

"Where've you been?" Chantal asked. "We missed you."

Joe grinned a boyish smile. "Visiting family while on break from college." He rolled his eyes. "Obligations, you know. They drive you crazy if they don't get to do a visual inspection at least a couple times a year. But I'm back now. And I see you two lovely ladies brought dates this time, huh?"

"Yeah," Chantal said. They ordered drinks and she surveyed the room.

"No one looks out of place," Maia remarked. "Typical crew."

Chantal nodded. "But we'll give it a couple hours and see who wanders in and out."

While they sat and drank, Chantal watched Dylan. He seemed unsettled. Fidgety. Like something was bothering him. And he wasn't making eye contact with her. She was sitting next to him, but he kept looking out over the crowd and didn't once look at her. She tugged on his shirtsleeve and he turned to her.

"You okay?"

"Yeah. Why?"

"You seem . . . anxious."

He shrugged. "Just want to find the guy." He looked away.

It was more than that. She felt weird vibes emanating from him. His anxiety was rising. She took a glance outside at the moon. Almost full. By tomorrow she'd have him safely locked up at the mansion where she could keep watch during the transition.

Then her duty to Dylan would be finished.

And she could let him go, get him out of her life and off her mind. Return to some normalcy.

That's what she needed—her real life back. She'd chalk up these feelings to a little minivacation from her regular routine. She wasn't in love with Dylan. She never fell in love. Men were for fucking, not making a life with. Geez, what had she been thinking?

Too much about Dylan, that's what. She decided to look around The Joint and see if she could figure out who looked out of place. The staff were all the same people.

No, wait. Bartender was new. She hadn't seen him before. She motioned Joe over.

"Need refills already?" Joe asked.

Chantal smiled. "No. Just wondering about the bartender. New guy?"

Joe glanced over his shoulder and frowned. "Oh. That's Lance. He started about a month ago. Comes in and works the late shift but has to leave before closing. Weird schedule but he's a med student. He has to be on staff at the hospital so can't stay for cleanup. We have to do his dirty work." Joe shrugged. "Cushy schedule, huh?"

"Hmm. Sucks for the rest of you."

He laughed. "He's a nice enough guy and the ladies go crazy for him. Must be his pheromones or something but he draws them like flies to honey. I'll have to figure out his secret," he said with a wink.

After Joe left, Chantal slanted a look at the rest of them. "Okay, that's strange."

"Very," Maia said. "Especially the pheromones part. If he's lupine he might be deliberately drawing out the human females. They wouldn't be able to resist him."

"Which means he's got a captive population, especially in a bar, and if they've been drinking, they're easy marks. Asshole," Noah said, grimacing.

"So what do we do now?" Chantal asked, focusing her attention on Dylan.

"We stay here and keep our eye on him. When he leaves tonight, we leave. See where he goes."

"Our wolf from the park didn't make his kill last night," Noah added. "That means he's hungry. If that dude behind the bar is our guy, he'll want to finish what he started."

Chapter Seven

Didn't it just figure that tonight Lance would stay until almost closing? But he finally finished up and left. And one of the women he'd been chatting up at the bar the entire night shot out the door right after him.

Damn good thing too, because if Dylan had to sit there one minute longer he was going to explode. His skin felt like it was prickling with some kind of rash. Every part of his body itched and burned and he was dying to shed his clothes and sit in an ice-cold bathtub.

He was boiling from the inside out.

And irritated. And antsy as hell. He wanted this case over with, wanted to find the killer and tear him to pieces. Food hadn't calmed him down and this wasn't exactly the type of place where he could fuck Chantal up against the wall to help ease his tension, so he did his best to ignore her.

Not that he could, with her sitting next to him. Her scent permeated his senses. Primal, earthy, musky, like the sweetest honey, tantalizing him to take a taste of her.

Taste, hell. He wanted to devour her. The urges were growing stronger and he was finding it hard to control them.

"Let's go." He stood and pushed the chair back with his legs. It banged against the one behind him.

"Hey, dude, be careful," the guy behind him said.

Dylan turned and growled at him. One more word and the scrawny little shit was going to go flying through the window.

The guy took one look at Dylan, his eyes widened and he held up his hands.

"Sorry," the kid said. "No harm done." He sat back down and turned away from Dylan.

"Jesus, Dylan, get a grip," Noah said, grabbing his arm and leading him toward the exit.

The woman who'd left right after Lance caught up to him. They stopped for a few seconds, talked, then Lance threw his arm around her and they started walking together.

Chantal sidled up next to Dylan. "Is she his next victim?"

Dylan shrugged. "Could be."

"We need to stop him."

"We need to make sure he's our guy first," Dylan snapped. "Be patient."

Chantal shot him a glare and moved behind him to walk with Maia. Fine. He couldn't handle her standing so close anyway. He needed his mind on work and she distracted him in the worst way. His dick was throbbing and he couldn't chase down a killer werewolf while trying to harbor an erection the size of a giant redwood tree.

They followed Lance as he made his way down the street toward the parking garage. Noah went off to grab their car while the rest of them kept an eye on the parking garage exit. Noah pulled up first and they piled in, then Lance exited the garage and they followed.

Lance headed to the park. Dylan's gut tightened. "This might be our guy."

Noah purposely kept far enough back so Lance wouldn't become aware he was being followed. Noah cut the lights once they entered the park and pulled over when Lance did.

They waited.

Lance and the woman didn't get out of his car. Dylan frowned and looked over at Noah. "You think he'd do her in his car?"

Noah shook his head. "Doubtful. Bloody mess and hard to clean up. He's priming her with foreplay, then he'll convince her to get out and take a walk in the park. At least that's my guess."

"Makes sense."

After about fifteen minutes, Lance and the woman exited the vehicle. Her clothes were disheveled and her hair mussed up.

"Definitely foreplay," Dylan said. The thought of it made his balls ache. Primal hunger surged through his bloodstream. Good thing Chantal was in the backseat.

Damn good thing he wasn't back there with her. He needed her, badly. This whole transition thing was a pain in the ass. His concentration was shot and he was forcing what little clarity he had left. Right now he was operating on instinct and years of experience. He hoped to God they could get this case wrapped up tonight, grab Lance before he did any damage to this woman and end things so he could go back to the mansion and get through this fucking nightmare of becoming a werewolf.

He wanted his old life back. He didn't want this change, goddammit.

"Okay, they're out of sight," Noah said. "Let's go."

Dylan popped his door open, and turned around to look at Chantal and Maia. "You two stay here."

Chantal shot him a look of pure venom. "Like hell. You need—"

"Don't argue with me," he shot back, cutting her off. "The more people tramping around leaves and twigs and making noise, the more likely he'll hear us and run. Noah and I can handle this. Now stay put."

If looks could kill . . .

He left her in the car, no doubt fuming and calling him every dirty name in the book. But at least she stayed there. She could cuss him out later.

While she was fucking him.

They circled behind a copse of thick trees, trying to remain out of sight while they followed Lance and the woman into the depths of the park. Lance and the woman were holding hands, stopping every now and then to kiss.

Frustration ate away at the last of Dylan's patience. He wanted action, dammit. He wanted Lance to make a move, to see him shift into a wolf so he could shoot the sonofabitch and have it be over with.

Lance led the woman to almost the same spot as he had the girl last night. Asshole. Not very careful, was he? Either that or he was supremely confident he wouldn't get caught.

He pushed her up against the base of a tree and lifted her skirt, then squatted. From their vantage point, he and Noah had a clear view of him eating the woman's pussy. The girl dug her nails into the tree trunk and moaned, thrusting her cunt against Lance's face.

Watching Lance pleasuring this girl wasn't helping the ache in Dylan's balls. Too reminiscent of what he and Chantal had done that first night in the park. The pain throughout his body was intensifying. He was shaking all over like he had a fever with chills.

"You okay?" Noah whispered.

Dylan raised his hand and gave Noah the okay signal. No way in hell was he going to get pulled off this case or in any way alert Noah about something wrong with him. He could hold it together a little longer. He had to. They were almost at the point they could capture this guy.

All Lance had to do was even look like he was gonna shift, and they had him.

• • •

Chantal sat in the backseat of the car thinking of the thousand different ways Dylan was going to suffer for dumping her while he got to run off and play crime solver.

"Pissed, are ya?"

She shot a glare at Maia. "Like you wouldn't believe."

Maia grinned, the spiky ends of her short, silvery blonde hair glimmering in the moonlight shining in through the back window. "He's right, you know. All of us out there stomping around would make too much noise."

"I realize he's right. Doesn't mean I have to like it." Maybe she'd squeeze his balls in her fist while she was sucking his cock. A little pain with his pleasure. She and Noah and Maia could have shifted and followed Lance. As wolves, they could be deathly silent.

She stared out the side window at the darkness, wishing she could be out there now. She really wasn't good about following directions. If they shifted and snuck behind them . . .

Movement caught her eye. Through the trees to her left, she caught sight of something gray flashing by.

"Maia, did you see that?"

"See what?"

"Look there." She pointed.

Maia stared, then her eyes widened. "Holy shit."

"Yeah." She looked to Maia. "Are you thinking what I'm thinking?"

"Yes."

They began to undress, wrapping their clothes into cords to wear around their necks.

"Hurry," Chantal urged.

• • •

Dylan groaned. Lance was into foreplay. He'd licked the poor girl's pussy raw. Now he was finger-fucking her while he sucked on her clit. Hell, he could have gotten off with Chantal in the backseat of the car, smoked a couple cigarettes and been back watching them again during the time period this dude had been pleasuring the woman.

He began to have his doubts about Lance being the wolf they were looking for. Unless he was into well satisfying his victims before he tore them apart.

He shot a glance at Noah, who shrugged and rolled his eyes.

After another screaming orgasm from the dark-haired woman, Lance stood and unbuckled his pants, shucking them to the ground. He stood in front of her and stroked his cock. Smiling at him, she sank to her knees.

Turnabout.

Sighing in disgust, Dylan realized they were wasting their time here.

He'd wanted this finished tonight.

"Let's go," he whispered to Noah.

They headed back to the car. His pulse was racing, his body warming to the point of great discomfort. He needed Chantal. And she was pissed. Maybe a walk home, just the two of them. They could talk.

But when they reached the car, dread dropped his heart to his feet.

"Shit," he muttered. "Where are they?"

"Knowing my sister, they walked home," Noah said. "She's not one for cooling her heels, especially when she's pissed off."

Great. "I guess we should search the area for them before we drive away and leave them."

"I think we should leave. If she decided to take a walk instead of staying put like you told her, it's her own damn fault if she gets left. She can walk home."

Dylan crossed his arms. "There's a killer wolf out here somewhere, Noah."

"Who targets humans, not other werewolves," Noah reminded him. "Chantal can take care of herself, and I'm sure Maia can too."

So maybe he was overworrying. And maybe his plans to take

a long walk home with Chantal and fuck her on the way had just been screwed.

Still, a Southern gentleman didn't leave a lady out wandering. Some things were just ingrained. "I'm gonna look for her. You take the car and head on back to the house. I'll just walk back. I need the air anyway."

Noah rolled his eyes. "Fine. Call me if you need a ride."

Dylan nodded and headed north into the dense brush, figuring he was probably wasting his time. Noah was right—Chantal had been so irritated she'd decided they'd just walk back to the house. But he'd at least search a bit.

He pushed through the bushes, cursing when a thorn jabbed into the skin of his upper arm. By the time he threaded his way through the brambles he was pretty scratched up.

Damn woman. No way would she have gone through here.

He was about to turn back when a dark flash sprang across his field of vision. Shit! He tore off after it, but no sooner had he launched into a full run than he started to sweat, hard. Then he began to shake, violently. So badly that he had to stop and drop to his knees.

What the hell?

Racking pain shot up his spine, white-hot and unbearable. He screamed as it burned like someone had lit a torch inside him.

His vision blurred. He couldn't see anything but shadows now. Every sound around him was magnified, including his own blood rushing in his ears. His heart pounded and panic set in.

And he was hot. So goddamned hot he couldn't stand it. He tore at his clothes, stripping them from his body in a hurry, desperate for any cool air to wash away the heat incinerating him from the inside out.

Even his bones were on fire.

He dropped forward, slapping his hands to the ground as he

felt the first crack of his bones. His skull was splitting apart and he screamed in agony, tilting his head to the sky.

He was dying.

• • •

Chantal circled back toward their origination point, having long ago lost sight of the wolf.

And of Maia, who'd gone off in another direction. They were hoping they could cut off the wolf and meet him head-on, but no such luck. But they decided if they got separated and didn't find the wolf, they'd just meet back at the car, or at the house.

As she headed that way, she heard a half howl, half cry of pain, so mournful and piercing it made her pause and shudder.

God, it was awful. She hurried in that direction, praying the wolf hadn't attacked someone.

Her heart thudded when she came upon a naked Dylan, crouched over and clearly in agony. She shifted to human, tossed aside the rope of clothing and hurried over to him.

"Dylan, can you hear me?"

He was bent forward, his head touching the ground, his body curled up so tight she couldn't shake him loose.

"Dylan! It's Chantal. Answer me!

"It hurts. Goddammit, it hurts."

His voice was low, strained, a guttural whisper filled with agony.

Shit. It wasn't full moon yet. Why was he going through transition? She smoothed her fingers over his back, feeling the bones there. They were starting to move.

"Baby, listen to me. Try to roll over onto your back."

"Can't. Hurts."

"Yeah, you can. Just try. I can make this easier on you if you let me."

She moved him, slow and easy, onto his side. He grimaced with every movement.

"I'm sorry. I promise to make it better. Now onto your back."

"Christ, Chantal. I know you're pissed off, but are you trying to kill me?"

She smiled. At least he had a little sense of humor left. "The reward will be worth it, trust me. On your back, stud."

He finally rolled with a loud grunt of pain. Success! His cock was thick, erect, and she didn't waste any time. She knew what he needed to make the transition easier.

"Dylan, open your eyes and look at me."

He pulled his eyes open, squinting. They were golden, shimmering.

"Okay, you're going through transition a little early."

"No shit."

She smiled and threaded her fingers through his hair as she straddled him. "Fuck me, baby. It'll make this easier."

" 'Bout damn time you showed up. I need you."

She knew he needed her for this, not for any other reason, but just the words tumbling from his lips made her wet and ready for him. Oh, who was she kidding? She was always wet and ready for him.

He gripped her hips and thrust inside her, sheathing himself to the hilt. Sweet pleasure burst inside her at his invasion. Her pussy gripped him in welcome. She settled on him, moving against him in tandem rhythm, placing her palms on his chest while she leaned over and captured his lips with her mouth.

His mouth was blazing heat, his tongue liquid fire as he slid inside her mouth with desperation. She sucked his tongue while she lifted up and down on his cock, feeling it lengthen and thicken inside her, filling her walls, stretching her until her juices poured over his balls.

She pulled away and sat up, grinding against him, rubbing her clit against his skin. She was lost in sensation, in the need for him that superseded any sense of duty. She fucked him because she wanted to, not because of any requirement. Because being close to him had become a necessity, a joy in her life that made each day complete.

His skin glistened under the moonlight, the tight strain he was under visible in the lines furrowing his brow.

"Don't fight it," she said, reaching forward to smooth her hand across his face. "Accept it and it'll be easier to bear."

She rocked against him, absorbing the sensations, wishing she could take away his pain. But she felt him relax as she moved, his fingers lessening their tight grip on her hips.

"That's it, baby," she said. "Relax. It's your time. Breathe in and out deeply. Concentrate on fucking me, on how good my pussy feels gripping your cock, squeezing it, milking the cum right out of it."

His eyes widened and he lifted his head, reaching for her hands as he began to buck his hips against her, driving his cock upward. Strong contractions pulsed inside her as she reached the edge and flew over, crying out with her climax. She squeezed his hands and rode him hard. He groaned, then howled, coming in shuddering bursts.

The sounds he made were more wolfen than human.

Finally, he relaxed. She lifted off and kneeled beside him and he made the full physical transition to wolf. God, he was beautiful, his silvery coat sleek and shiny under the moon's light. She shifted alongside him so she could teach him how to communicate in their lupine language, with psychic thought, the human part of them remaining even though they were fully wolf.

Dylan explored the sensations of being a wolf. Every sight, sound and sensation magnified in incredible ways. And he could hear Chantal talking to him, though they weren't speaking. And the speed he could run—incredible. Not even winded, either. He felt . . . invincible.

He stopped, sniffed the air, scenting another wolf. He turned to Chantal, who nodded.

Maia and I saw a wolf flash by the car earlier. That's where we were, out trying to find him.

That's our guy. They followed the scent upwind, catching sight of the wolf where Lance and the girl were still entwined and going at it.

The wolf growled. Lance and the girl were fucking and panting so hot and heavy they didn't even hear it.

No way was he going to hurt anyone else. Dylan howled and Lance leapt off the girl. The girl screamed and stood, grabbing frantically for her clothes as she spotted the wolf approaching. Dylan and Chantal circled in front of the wolf, getting between it and the humans so he couldn't attack. Lance at least had the presence of mind to start backing away from all of them.

They ran like hell. Dylan heard the slamming of their car doors and the roar of the engine. They peeled away in a hurry.

Good. No witnesses.

They're mine, the wolf said, raising his lip and showing his sharp canines.

I don't think so, Dylan replied. *Your game is over.*

He wished he had his gun. Fighting a wolf was new to him. But he felt powerful. He could handle this.

The wolf lunged for him, teeth bared. Dylan braced for the attack and sidestepped him, then jumped, biting down on the back of his neck. Instinct roared to life and the battle was fierce. He drew blood, tasted it flowing into his mouth, feeling it increase the surging need for battle inside him. He wanted more. He wanted death, to tear this creature apart.

Chantal entered the fray, snapping at the wolf's hindquarters, pulling him off balance. The wolf turned on Chantal and bit her. She yelped.

Goddammit! Dylan lunged at him, and at the same time Noah showed up, jumping into the battle, leaping onto the back of the wolf.

Outnumbered, the wolf went down and Dylan grabbed him by the throat. Without hesitation, he bit down and ended the wolf's life.

Instinct. Part of him couldn't believe he'd made a kill, but the wolf side of him knew there was no other choice.

He returned to human form, as did Chantal and Noah.

So did the wolf.

Obviously, it wasn't Lance as they'd suspected.

It was Joe, the waiter from The Joint.

"Holy shit," Chantal said.

"We need to get out of here and fast, Noah said. "Lance has probably already called the police. I'll get the car. Get your clothes and get dressed."

Dylan nodded. As they hurried to get their clothes, Dylan grabbed Chantal's arm. There was a bite mark there and it was bleeding. He reached for her wrist.

She smiled. "I'm fine. It's already healing. Werewolves have amazing recuperative powers, remember?"

"You shouldn't have jumped in the middle of that. You could have been seriously hurt."

She frowned. "I can take care of myself, Dylan. And you're welcome."

She stalked ahead of him, obviously irritated.

Well, damn. He had a lot to learn about this werewolf thing. And about Chantal. She had no fear. She'd taken up position and had his back like a seasoned agent.

Or like his mate.

His mate. His woman.

God, he wanted her. Needed her. In a few days she'd become ingrained, a part of him.

She was saucy, annoying, opinionated and hardheaded. And beautiful, sexy, intelligent, warmhearted . . . the kind of woman he'd been looking for his entire life.

He was in love with her.

He couldn't let her go.

Chapter Eight

Joe took frequent breaks from his job at The Joint. Not long enough that anyone grew suspicious. He claimed to have family obligations and trips to take. But the NCA has placed him at the scene of every murder," Dylan said. "And his death has been pinned on another series of wolf attacks, which will now cease completely without explanation. It's the best we can do under the circumstances."

"At least he's been killed and the wolf murders will stop," Lamont said, nodding his head. "This is good for all the packs involved."

"Did you ever figure out who the woman informant was?" Noah asked.

"No. It could have been a false lead, but I doubt it. My guess is someone knew about Joe. Maybe a girlfriend or something. Either way, we never heard from her again so he either found out she was going to inform on him and took care of her or she was too scared and decided not to come forward."

"Well, it's over now," Maia said. "That's the important thing."

"And everyone can go back to their lives," Chantal added, though she was looking at Dylan when she said it.

"I'm out of here. I've got business to take care of somewhere else." Noah stood and wrapped his arms around his sister. "Walk me out?"

She nodded.

He said his good-byes to Lamont, Maia and Dylan then walked with Chantal to the front door.

"Don't be stupid," he said to her.

She cocked a brow. "What the hell does that mean?"

"It means don't be typical Chantal and blow him off."

"Still not understanding."

"You're in love with Dylan. Don't push him away just because you're scared of having a mate."

"Don't be ridiculous. First, I'm not afraid of having a mate, and second, I'm not in love with Dylan."

He kissed the top of her head, leaned back and grinned at her. "Yeah, little sis, you sure as hell are. Now I'm the last person in the world to claim settling down is a great thing and you know that. But when it's time, it's time. Give it up and accept it. You and Dylan belong together. Even someone as jaded as me can see that. Call me if you need me."

He turned and walked out. Chantal scrunched her nose, then stuck her tongue out at the closed door.

Like he knew what she needed. Hmph.

She turned on her heel and found Dylan leaning against the doorway.

Shit.

"You are too in love with me," he said, smirking.

She brushed by him and headed up the stairs to her room. "I am not."

He followed her and shut the door behind him. "Yeah, you are."

Ignoring him, she started packing her things in her suitcase. "You don't even know me. It was just great sex."

"It was, wasn't it?"

Oh, she hated when his voice went all low and dark like that. It made her pussy wet and trembly. Dammit.

"I don't want you to leave."

She paused. "Why not?"

"Because I think we have something together."

"Yeah. Fucking. You can't build a foundation on great sex, Dylan."

He approached and wrapped his arms around her. "You can't? We have chemistry, Chantal. That's what made me a werewolf in the first place. That blind fuck, you and I in the park that first night, remember?"

God, did she ever remember. It was burned into her memory banks forever.

"I need you to guide me through this being-a-werewolf thing. I can't do it without you."

"Sure you can. You're a big boy."

He exhaled, ruffling her hair. "Okay, so I can. But I don't *want* to do it without you. I've kind of gotten used to having you around."

"I don't even know where you live."

"I don't really live anywhere. I'm on the road all the time with the NCA, but I'm originally from Oklahoma."

"I've never been to Oklahoma." Her eyes filled with tears. Dammit, what was wrong with her?

"You tell me where you want to live and we'll work it out from there."

"Why are you being so accommodating?"

"Because I'm in love with you and I don't want to lose you."

Shit. Shit, shit, shit. He could have said anything but that and she might have been able to walk away. She turned in his arms and looked up at him. "You love me."

"Yes."

"I'm difficult."

"No kidding."

"I'll make your life a living hell."

"I'll love you in spite of it."

She sighed, already knowing she'd lost the battle. Noah was right. It was time. She'd known it since that night in the park. "I love you too. You'll be sorry."

He laughed. "I like a challenge."

"You'll get one."

He swooped her up in his arms and pressed his lips to hers, kissing her with a maddening passion she would never tire of. Her body flamed to life, her nipples puckering and pressing against the thin silk of her dress.

Dylan put her down and took her hand, leading her toward the door.

"Where are we going?" she asked.

"To the park, to that spot where we first met. I've got this thing now for fucking in the park."

She grinned, her pussy moistening. "You're a very bad boy, Dylan Maxwell."

"That's why you love me, Chantal Devlin."

Jaci Burton

After spending too many years to count in the high-stress business world, Jaci Burton is thrilled to be living her dream of writing passionate romance. Now she occasionally writes in her pajamas while surrounded by yipping little dogs that she adores but who drive her crazy. She'd like to say she lives a glamorous life, but it's all too normal. She still has to do laundry and dishes and feed her family, and wouldn't have it any other way. She lives in Oklahoma with her husband, who inspires her to create stories about sexy, stubborn alpha males who don't always do what the heroine wants them to.

Jaci is a multipublished author who writes in multiple genres, including paranormal, contemporary, futuristic, fantasy and BDSM. She was awarded Romantic Times Reviewer's

Choice Award for Best Erotic Paranormal. She is a member of Romance Writers of America, Futuristic, Fantasy and Paranormal's RWA Chapter, Passionate Ink, Romance Writer's Ink, and EPIC.

You can find Jaci on the web at http://www.jaciburton.com

Eternal Triangle

ANN JACOBS

Chapter One

His houseboat rocked gently at its moorings in the wake of a fast-moving motor launch. His soft, willing slave was on her knees before him, giving him head not for a club scene but because she loved him. As he loved her. Pretty much satisfied with his life, Chad Lalanne tunneled his fingers through Katie's long dark hair and encouraged her to deep-throat him.

There was just this one thing. If only she weren't a vampire. Two months ago he hadn't even known about vampires other than that they weren't to be messed with, but then Katie had been bitten by an out-of-control Dom who'd happened to be one. It stung Chad's soul that he hadn't been able to protect her.

"Yes, like that, my angel," he said when she took him deeper, sucked him harder.

In order to be able to accept his guilt, Chad had dedicated himself to understanding everything about vampire culture and needs. It still made him feel impotent when he considered the fact that his own considerable strength meant nothing when it came to protecting his woman from the overzealous attention of a vampire.

He knew, though, that she needed a vampire companion to mentor her as well as satisfy her need for nourishment lest she lose control and feed on Chad or worse, a member of the club. Much as he hated to admit it, she also needed the protection of a male vampire. So when Katie had gone to feed at the only vampire bar in New Orleans's French Quarter and run into Philippe, a member of the honorable and powerful d'Argent clan, and when she'd subsequently told Chad that Philippe was a sexual submissive, Chad knew what needed to be done.

Not that bringing a third party into their private lives didn't have potential for bringing trouble of a different kind, but as he saw it he had no choice. As a Master, he'd been struggling with his own feelings ever since checking out the tall, powerful-looking vampire and inviting him to join them tonight at the club for a ménage à trois. The idea of bringing a male into their relationship, one who might consider he was Chad's as much as Katie was, tempted him for dark reasons he'd barely let himself think about, much less share with her. He would take Philippe d'Argent as his second slave because Philippe could provide what he could not—a safe, portable supply of blood for Katie and protection from male vampires who might assault her.

But the vampire posed dangerous temptation to Chad. He'd felt it the moment Philippe had met his gaze, recognized him then deliberately broken the visual connection and lowered his eyes provocatively, much like Katie had done when she'd first knelt before him. Chad's reaction had been much the same, a tightening of his muscles with need, the absorption of his mind with every aspect of a new potential mate.

He wouldn't utilize his new slave's admittedly tempting holes. He wouldn't. After all, he was a Dominant. Master of his own sexual destiny. He hadn't used another male sexually in over ten years, and he wasn't about to do it now.

"Suck me, my darling," he said, his voice tight as he framed Katie's head between his hands and tried not to picture himself sucking d'Argent's cock, shoving his own up the buff vampire's ass or down his throat. "That's it." When Katie inclined her head and swallowed his full length, Chad let out a moan of satisfaction. "Oh, yeah," he croaked, drowning in the feelings . . . the love . . . the sense of receiving as well as giving sexual pleasure.

• • •

Katie swallowed the last drop of her Master's hot ejaculate and pulled away, looking up at him and reading the worry in his dark eyes. Even though he'd been the one to propose this ménage, she sensed a confusing reluctance in him. She knew men as well as women attracted him sexually, knew from the way he spoke of Philippe after meeting him that he was intrigued. Something he wouldn't discuss, something buried so deeply in his head that she couldn't put her finger on it, was holding him back. She wished Chad would confide in her, but the only reason he admitted for bringing another party into their relationship was to provide her with the one thing she needed to survive—a regular supply of fresh blood. That need had kept them tied in New Orleans since she'd been turned. She hated that because she knew how he missed the frequent trips they used to make into the bayou country where they'd both grown up.

She'd seen their new partner first. Something about Philippe d'Argent, with his brooding blue eyes and a look of loneliness, had caught her attention when she'd been in New Orleans's only vampire bar, trying to get used to the idea of regularly feeding her blood requirement. Working so long at *Club de la soumission* had given her a sixth sense about men and their intentions. She'd known from the outset who he was, sensed he wouldn't harm her even though something she couldn't put her finger on about his imposing appearance disturbed her. What had amazed her was to learn he was a submissive. She'd dared to speak to him, and he'd told her about his lost Master . . . his need for a strong Dom to help him over his grief. What she'd learned had been enough to take her back to tell Chad about him. Her Master had checked him out then issued the invitation.

Tonight would begin what she hoped would be a lasting arrangement, but she was in no way certain. Katie couldn't help wondering if Philippe would agree to handing over control of his sexual being to a mortal Master, and whether Chad might accept an active third party in their relationship. She wasn't at all sure he could set aside the prejudices she saw as products of a mortal upbringing much like her own, and welcome another male—submissive or not—as an equal participant in their sexual games. Their lives.

A muggy breeze blew across the waters of the Mississippi River, making the boat rock gently on the water. A sea bird squawked his mating call from a perch on an upended oak tree that lay on the other side of the river, half on and half off the swampy land where it once had grown, its roots rising toward the sky. Katie closed her eyes against the late afternoon sun, turned away from the shuttered window and traced her Master's taut golden skin with one perfectly manicured nail. "You know, his skin will be even smoother than yours."

"Yeah, I know. More like yours?" Chad lifted her hand, brought it to his lips then sucked her forefinger inside. "Are you looking forward to having both our cocks working inside your tight holes tonight?"

The question sounded casual, but Katie's sometimes off-putting vampire intuition allowed her to sense some of her Master's underlying qualms. "If that's your pleasure, my darling Master." His reaction puzzled her, for they frequently partici-pated in dungeon scenes where another man or men joined Chad in forcing her to the releases she sometimes found difficult to achieve.

"It is. Come. If we don't hurry, we won't make it to the club in time to meet your vampire pal." Chad stood and pulled her up. "Or for me to punish you for having looked at him while you were feeding at that bar."

•　•　•

Philippe couldn't quite shake the feeling someone had been watching him earlier. Probably the female vampire's Master, he thought, since it would have been only natural for a Master to go out of his way to protect his slave before coming to him and issuing an invitation for ménage. He checked his watch then glanced out his office window, wincing at the brightness of the late afternoon sun. The temporary job he'd taken on—reorganizing a fellow vampire's importing business—was going faster than he'd imagined. On Monday he'd go check on the warehouses being built on higher ground than those washed away by the killer hurricane almost two years earlier. Then he'd report back to Sam, and his time would once again be his own.

He had little to take his mind off what he'd agreed to do tonight. Though grief still ruled his heart, his body had suddenly come back to life. It was time. Time to assuage the ache in his balls, put Jacques out of his mind and move on to a new sexual relationship. Philippe sat back, fighting the compulsion to leave now and make his way to the BDSM club. Would the shy female vampire's Master take him, or would he order Philippe to service her instead? Would he remember how to fuck a woman? He sat back, closed his eyes and recalled the chance meeting he had a feeling might change his life—only he wasn't sure the change would be for the better.

This restlessness had begun last night as he'd sat alone in his room . . .

• • •

He was hungry, but he didn't want to go to the nearby vampire bar. It was too soon to face the place. Only one year had passed since Philippe had wakened from an evil vampire's poison to see Jacques laid out on the edge of the dance floor there, destroyed beyond redemption.

Now Philippe stared out the window at New Orleans. The French Quarter with its promise of dark and sensual pleasures had a way of bringing back memories long buried beneath his single-minded quest to avenge his lover's death. Memories of long nights' vigils and longer days' steamy hours spent in this third-floor room of a small hotel off Decatur Street. Bodies entwined, taking each other and loving it, oblivious to the heat and humidity as the blades of an old-fashioned ceiling fan cooled them. They'd drunk from each other, symbiotic nourishment that required none other.

Philippe laid alone on that bed staring out at the gold ball of a moon lighting an indigo sky. Since the evil vampire clan that had kept Philippe too busy to think about his lost love was no more, he now had time to grieve. To remember his Master's hands skimming over the planes of his vampire body, the sensuous stretching of his lips when he'd sucked his Master's cock . . . the pleasure-pain when Jacques had first claimed his virgin ass. The joy of fulfillment when Jacques had occasionally allowed Philippe to pump his own male essence into his Master's accepting mouth. Those days were gone, gone with Jacques to the sky to which dead vampires' ashes went to spend eternity.

A hundred years had passed since Jacques had changed him. A century since Philippe had enjoyed the softness of a woman's body, the thrill of feeling her hot, wet sheath surrounding him, drawing out his seed. Well, not quite a century. Jacques had sensed his occasional need for a female's softness and had found them one to share from time to time. Philippe wrapped his fingers around his own flesh, tried to remember . . .

It had been too long. He'd spent too many nights in his Master's strong arms to have more than a few vague memories of long-ago encounters with women. He'd loved Jacques as he had never loved another being, mortal or immortal. His cock hadn't stirred since his love had died, not even during the vampire orgy held a month ago in celebration of the d'Argents' final victory over their archenemy.

It stirred now, almost as if it had a mind of its own. Getting up and crossing the room, Philippe opened the rosewood box on top of the dresser and stared down at the elegantly curved silver sounds Jacques had given him for their love play. He missed the sex but more than that, Philippe grieved for the lost friendship, the knowledge that he was half of a whole, an extension of his lover and Jacques an extension of him. Still, he'd never forget his first night as a vampire or the feel of first one sound and then the next making their way down the flesh of his cock, through his bladder and scrotum and on to nudge his prostate gland. Or the lust that had overcome him when the largest of the sounds was secured by piercing his flesh and passing a thick gold ring horizontally through his penis, through the eye in the sound and out the other side. Jacques had closed the ring with a captive bead. Then he'd lapped away the lubrication that seeped out around the blunt, circular end of the sound that capped the tip of his cock head.

Philippe had become acclimated to life in the sophisticated world of the d'Argent vampires. But losing Jacques had laid his sexuality dormant. Picking up the box, Philippe took it to the bed and sat beside it, the wispy mesh of the mosquito netting blowing gently in the breeze, tickling his flesh as a lover might. Many times he'd been on his knees on this bed while Jacques had taken him from behind. Now Philippe saw nothing but a crowd of noisy mortals apparently in search of yet another bar . . . yet another drink. Their collective restlessness seemed to rub off on him. With one hand he stroked his cock. With the other he rubbed the polished rosewood box, tracing the elaborately carved pair of lovers forever captured in flagrante delicto.

He laughed. Strange, he could recall the Latin phrases pertinent to his mortal calling as a lawyer, but he couldn't conjure up even the faintest memory of the lovers he'd had before an angry client's bullet had sucked out his mortal life—and Jacques had rescued him with a vampire kiss.

Philippe felt his fangs elongate. His cock thickened and throbbed against his fingers. His nipples swelled and hardened as though longing for a lover's kiss. He opened the box once more, searched by feel for the slender foot-long sound Jacques used to insert deep within his body for love play, long after the ritual was finished. With the fingers of his other hand he twisted the threaded end of the thick barbell he wore in his Ampallang piercing until it loosened. Then he slid the bar through his cock and out the other side.

As the sound moved through his scrotum, Philippe felt drops of lubrication well up around it. A sense of sexual urgency surged through him when he found his prostate and began to stroke it with the blunt end of the sound. Gods, but he wanted to drink his partner's come, or feel the total ecstasy of a massive cock pounding against the sound, of hot, slick fluid spurting up his ass. Just imagining that had Philippe's cock jerking, stimulated by the sound and his imagination. Yet he did not come. His climax was for his Master, and his Master was gone. Giving his full attention to his newly awakened cock, Philippe carefully threaded the barbell back through the piercing just behind his cock head, fed it through the eyelet in the sound and secured it.

The thick ring he'd had at first had been much more convenient for securing a sound. But his Master had preferred the smoother feel of the barbell on the rare occasions when he'd allowed Philippe to penetrate his throat or his tight, inviting ass. *Perhaps I'll change it to suit myself. Perhaps I'll cut my hair.* But he knew he wouldn't. Not unless he found a new Master.

His need to feed, a dull pang of hunger before, now raged in Philippe's head. His fangs elongated when he spied an elderly tourist passing on the street below and pictured himself sinking his fangs into her throat. He had to feed quickly. A vampire could only suppress that bodily urge for so long. Not wanting to revisit the scene of his Master's death but unwilling to prey on an unsuspecting mortal, he made his way downstairs and the few yards down the street to the bar.

• • •

From his seat at the bar he studied the early evening crowd, a few dark-skinned Owenga in colorful native garb, some businessmen winding up the night's activities . . . and one very lonely-looking female vampire perched three stools down from him. From her dark hair and honey-colored eyes, he guessed she hailed from one of the southern European countries. She had a lost look about her . . . a look he imagined mirrored his own.

"Would you like an introduction?" Philippe looked up when the waiter spoke, saw an expectant look in his eyes.

"Just a draft of O negative, if you please." Unusual. Most vampires had a sixth sense about each other's sexual preferences, but then Philippe himself wasn't all that certain of his own when his cock twitched, making the sound inside it reverberate off his flesh when he ogled the female's rounded ass cheeks covered with jeans so tight they must have been painted on. They'd be soft, and so would her breasts, he knew, pulling from vague recollections from long ago. He itched to wrap his hands around her tiny waist, hold her . . . sink his cock into her and come. His balls ached, and his cock throbbed urgently beneath his loose linen slacks.

He wanted her like he hadn't wanted a woman in over a century. Yet he sensed submissiveness in her downcast eyes, her shy demeanor. And gave up the notion of having her ease his lust. He had to have a Master . . . or a Mistress. He could manage a complex business with ease, control the work lives of scores of employees. But it did no good to deny that in sexual matters he was purely submissive. "Au revoir, mademoiselle," he said softly, and from the look in her eyes he sensed she understood.

But he couldn't look away. Something about the slight angle

she held her head, the dainty way she sipped her wineglass full of rich, red blood . . . the occasional furtive looks she shot in his direction fascinated him, made him want to challenge her. Deliberately he moved back from the bar and turned so she couldn't fail to notice his erection. And they talked, exchanged names, danced around desire neither one of them had been able to deny.

• • •

Philippe turned back to his desk, tidied the stacks of papers and shut down the computer. Maybe if he focused on the mundane he'd be able to treat the coming evening as what it was—a BDSM scene, nothing more.

Then he picked up the card the Master had handed him, looked at the elaborately scripted scarlet lettering on a black background etched with a subtle rendition of handcuffs and a coiled whip. *Club de la soumission.* Philippe had heard the name before from some of the d'Argent males who had made use of its facilities. His cock felt as though it might explode, so loudly was the sound reverberating against its inner walls. Turning the card over, he looked once more at the note on the back, scanned the small, no-nonsense block print.

Tonight. Nine o'clock. Give the card to the manager and ask for Katie and Master Chad.

Philippe could hardly wait. He remembered the times Jacques had found a female they could share, recalled the joys of working with her to serve their Master's pleasure. The prospect of doing it again—sharing a Master with Katie—had him more eager than he'd been for decades. But it wasn't only joining her in serving her Master that had him reacting this way. It was the Master himself, the way Philippe had reacted to meeting him. He'd never thought another Master would stir his cock the way Jacques had. But that flesh had leaped to life, startling him, when the mortal Master had appraised him, his aggressive stance spurring an urge in Philippe to submit. Philippe had lowered his eyes, but it had disturbed him. The first time he'd felt this way since Jacques, so of course guilt and resistance had stirred. When he'd looked up in defiance against his long-held grief, Chad was already gone. But his hard-on was still with him.

Eager to take Katie's lush body at the Master's command. To bring their woman pleasure with his cock while Chad fucked him . . .

• • •

She saw him the moment he stepped inside the club. Her pussy swelled. Her nipples turned hard as stone. She swore the smell of sex began to fill the room as she stared shamelessly at the bold outline of his cock beneath those loose-fitting trousers. No one would mistake Philippe for anything but a d'Argent vampire— tall, muscular, with dark hair that lay in waves past his broad shoulders, over the fine material of an aqua dress shirt. He looked elegant, self-assured. Not the least bit submissive except for the downcast eyes, the slight tilt of his head that had his hair obscuring one side of his handsome face.

His hair. That was what had struck Katie as unusual about Philippe. The d'Argent males she'd encountered before wore their hair short—except for the submissive ones. They shaved their heads as a sign of their sexual enslavement, unlike her mortal Master, who kept his own head clean-shaven as a statement of his Dominance. Philippe's brilliant blue eyes marked him a made vampire, for as she'd heard it, all the born d'Argents had green eyes.

She lowered her gaze to his crotch, eyeing the impressive bulge of his sex. He'd be pierced, she hoped, because according to what she'd heard, all made d'Argents who were able to function sexually wore rings through their cocks. It would have been a shame if that monster hard-on he'd displayed so blatantly last night had been just for looks.

Katie loved her Master. She'd loved him since they'd both been mortals indulging their sexual preferences with members at *Club de la soumission*, before a vampire Dom had lost control and changed her. Still, she couldn't help imagining this gorgeous stranger forcing her to her knees, stuffing his cock into her mouth. Or mounting her from behind, filling her ass or cunt and ramming into her over and over until he screamed with the force of his climax. She'd like for him to tie her up and discipline her. Take her blood for his sustenance and give her his. Be as much her Master in the bedroom as Chad was.

But I am submissive, like you. I cannot be what you're looking for in a lover. He'd said that last night when they'd been two lonely vampires taking their nourishment in a vampire bar. She'd met his gaze, found his mind so open she'd been able to read not only his conscious thoughts but also his ambivalence. He wanted her yet he didn't. He wasn't sure he could take a dominant role, or even if he could make love to her. That hesitance was what made her certain he'd be ideal as a partner for her and her mortal Master. If Chad would accept a male vampire submissive as their partner *en ménage* tonight, perhaps he'd invite Philippe into their relationship and make it whole.

His gaze settled on the padlocked collar around her throat then moved to sear her breasts with vampire heat. *Come to me,* she projected, for her voice had deserted her. *Please.*

His desire came through strongly, a vampiric projection of thoughts too private to put in words. *I want you to reach down, caress my cock. Roll my testicles between your palms while I feed from that vein you've deliberately made so vulnerable.* Katie hesitated a moment then crossed the room, oblivious to all eyes but his.

She held his gaze, took his hand, tried not to notice the wetness of her pussy or the tightness of her nipples. Instead she concentrated on the weight of her Master's collar, the jingling of its padlock against the gold hasp. "If that is what our Master desires, it will be my pleasure. Welcome to *Club de la soumission*. You'd best hurry and disrobe. Our Master awaits us in the observation chamber."

Chapter Two

Philippe followed Katie, his feelings mixed. Dungeons had never been a major turn-on for him, and he found the constant thwacks of floggers hitting flesh a bit distracting as he crossed the main salon. Not that he hadn't enjoyed the occasional discipline sessions Jacques had meted out, or the humiliation of being shared by Jacques with their vampire friends. But being watched by strangers? Mortals?

It would be all right. After all, Katie and Master Chad were employees here, and she seemed quite at home. She'd made him comfortable at the bar last night, at a time when he'd thought nothing could have taken his mind off the chilling memory of Jacques lying on that very floor, destroyed. Philippe found himself focusing not only on her soft and willing body that might be his tonight, but also on the Master who might choose to claim them both.

After all, having dozens of mortals watching their scene couldn't be all that different from participating in one of the d'Argent clan's vampire orgies, Philippe told himself as he stripped down in one of two anterooms outside the torture chamber. If he'd been mortal, he imagined he'd have been slick with sweat. As it was, his skin was flushed and his pulse raced with anticipation as well as a good bit of dread. Sitting on the bench, he inserted the sound in his cock and secured it with the barbell. He brushed his hair and restrained it at his nape with a black leather thong.

He hadn't cut it since Jacques . . . No, Philippe wouldn't think of his dead Master, not now. He gathered his courage and walked through the swinging door into the torture chamber. Katie was already there, secured over a side horse while her Master cracked a cat-o'-nine-tails over her lush ass cheeks.

A golden god, the Dominant laid another stinging blow on that delectable flesh, his well-defined muscles bunching beneath his skin. Philippe couldn't take his eyes off the mortal's rippling muscles or his tanned, hairless skin. His perfectly sculpted oiled scalp gleamed in the glow of several muted spotlights. Obviously comfortable in his own sexual Dominance, the Master wore nothing but black leather chaps that drew Philippe's eye to his large, low-hanging balls. Philippe's mouth watered at the sight of the Master's cock, long and thick and already erect, its head purplish with a drop of lubrication glistening at its tip. As far as Philippe could tell, the Master wasn't pierced except for his left ear, where a large gold hoop dangled.

Philippe's own sex hardened when he imagined the buff mortal invading him, taking him, punishing him the way he was punishing Katie. He'd whip him first then ram that big, hard tool up Philippe's ass and make him come. Chad must have sensed his presence because he laid the whip down and turned to Philippe, who quickly lowered his head and focused his gaze on the chamber's polished marble floor.

Chad's mouth watered when the vampire approached, not on hands and knees as Chad expected of his subs but upright. Only his downcast eyes and respectfully lowered head hinted at the submissive role he intended to play, but Chad assumed this was the vampire's first club scene and refrained from chastising him. Besides, he made an arousing picture, his pale skin a stark contrast with shoulder-length dark hair, muscles rippling beneath skin so smooth no amount of waxing could have achieved it. Vampire skin. The pierced cock—an Ampellang studded with a hefty barbell—jutted straight out from thighs as thick as tree trunks. The gold cap covering the tip of the vampire's cock head confirmed the presence of a sound or wand inside the impressive length.

"Look at me, slave." Dark lashes fluttered, and the sub looked up at Chad with clear blue eyes, just long enough to give a hesitant greeting, and his full lips curved into a smile that revealed gleaming white fangs. And desire.

Chad could tell that look, he'd seen it often enough, working as a Dominant here at *Club de la soumission*. To Master this one Chad would have to touch him like a lover, fuck his vampire ass—kiss those delectable lips and feel them on his own cock, sucking out his come. He told himself he didn't want to do it, that he'd promised his father years ago never to sodomize a male or let himself be sodomized again.

But then again he'd vowed to Katie when he took her as his permanent sex slave that his greatest wish was to see to her care and sexual pleasure. Since she now was a vampire, caring for her properly included taking a vampire partner *en ménage*. A male vampire whose strength could protect her against the threat of another male vampire's attack. "Move closer," he spat out, angry with himself for having become so aroused at the idea of fucking another male.

The vampire obeyed, stopping within Chad's arm's length. The look he shot at Chad was a clear challenge. Chad took it, reached out and squeezed the jutting cock that practically touched his own belly. "Does it work without the jewelry?" he asked, turning so his own throbbing cock nudged the vampire's.

"If you wish it to."

"If you wish it, Master." For a sub, this vampire lacked the tone of groveling respect Chad was used to hearing from the ones who frequented the dungeon.

The vampire inclined his head, focused his gaze on Chad's cock and his own. "Master," he said, bowing his head the way a proper sub should.

"On your knees, vampire. Katie, tell this vampire what you want of him." Chad gave Katie a light slap on one reddened ass cheek.

"His cock, Master, if that is your desire."

Chad turned back to the vampire, tried to tamp down his own unholy compulsion to see if that pale skin felt as smooth as it looked. To feel the big pierced cock penetrating his ass. To cool his lust he reminded himself his considerable strength would be as nothing if his male vampire slave should decide to turn on him. "You heard Katie," he snapped, furious that the vampire fired forbidden desires he'd long kept under wraps. "Stand up. She wants to feel your cock in her ass. First, though, lick her pussy. Stick your tongue inside and taste her cream. You'll like her rear hole. Unlike mortals', it's tight, clean, made for nothing but fucking, but then you'd know that, wouldn't you?"

"Yes, Master." The vampire bent and began licking Katie's pussy, obviously paying special attention to soothing the welts that had almost healed in the few moments since Chad had whipped her. Though he certainly possessed a vampire's superhuman strength, this one would be a gentle sub . . . one who'd take Chad's sexual orders without question. Realizing that had Chad imagining . . .

His own cock spurting into the vampire's mouth, his ass. Him watching the vampire fuck his woman. Removing the sound from his slave's jutting penis and sucking out his seed.

Chad settled his gaze on the vampire's tight ass cheeks, imagined them beet red from a flogger. *Would his vampire ass be as inviting as Katie's? Of course it would be. That sound would vibrate against my cock like . . .* He wouldn't wait any longer. "Fuck her now," he ordered. The vampire stood and rubbed his cock head along Katie's exposed cunt, the tip of the embedded sound stroking soft, wet female sex. Chad's own cock swelled to bursting, its slit opening, preparing . . . "Put it in her. All the way."

When the vampire spread Katie's ass cheeks and worked his big cock into her tight little ass, Chad almost ordered him to take it out and fuck him instead. But he didn't. Instead he stroked the vampire's straining buttocks, gave his seed sac a twist then let go as he prepared to penetrate. "I'm going to fuck your ass, slave. Fill you with hot mortal juice. When I do, you will give Katie a vampire kiss. You will not come unless I say so." With almost brutal force, he breached his lover's tight anal sphincter. Almost immediately the vibrations of the vampire's sound had Chad's balls tightening, his cock ready to spurt out his seed.

He was determined to hold out, endure the delicious sensations, slide in and out of the vampire's tight ass while the vampire slammed his thick tool in and out of their woman's rear hole. His balls collided with the vampire's. Katie's little moans fed Chad's lust. His own balls tightened. His cock felt like iron. Fuck but he had to come.

It was still too soon. But he couldn't help it. The vibrations . . . the vampire's tight ass gripping the base of his cock . . . The inner muscles clutching his flesh were hard, not soft. Erotic sensations flowed through Chad when their balls collided with every stroke. Vibrations stimulated his prostate almost as much as if he were the one wearing the sound. "Now," he rasped, sinking his mortal teeth into the vampire's muscular neck as the vampire pierced Katie's jugular the way Chad wished he could.

He bit down, tasting a drop of vampire blood, imagining puncturing the vampire's vein the way the vampire had done to Katie, taking his sustenance from his lovers . . . giving sustenance to them. His cock jerked wildly as he spilled burst after burst of slick, hot seed into the vampire's ass.

Spent, he collapsed over the vampire's broad back and buried his fingers in the long fall of his hair. Oh God, he'd had sensations like never before, not even when as a young man of eighteen he'd given in to temptation back home and fucked the new parish priest's tempting ass. He could see why the Greeks had idealized man-love, but homosexual relationships were frowned on in the modern mortal world where he must abide.

Most of the time Chad viewed that brief experience as an aberration and Father Andre as one who'd richly deserved the tar-and-feathering he'd received when they'd been caught. Sometimes—now included—Chad saw the priest for what he'd been, less one with a religious calling than one desperately attempting to deny how strongly he was sexually attracted to other men. And he hadn't been submissive by nature, only to God. The two elements together had been impossible for Chad to resist. He feared they were impossible to resist now with the vampire, as well.

Only thing, the stigma attached to submission and same-sex sexual relationships would no longer be there to cripple him with guilt . . . if he should join his lovers' vampire world.

• • •

Once his Master withdrew, Philippe did the same, desperate to have the sound removed before his flesh exploded. He entered the Master's mind, read the self-denial, the shame . . . the under-lying desire to leave the strictures of mortal society and join the world of the undead. And the denial of that unholy wish. Chad was a sexual Dominant who loved Katie, his female slave, with a love that transcended sex, and who desperately wanted not to want the sensations presently flowing through his body—those seemed the only facts of which the mortal was certain.

Tall, muscular in the way of a mortal who passed his days at a gym, the Master was almost as hairless as a vampire. His golden skin glowed from a recent oiling, and his skull gleamed. Funny. In Philippe's world a shaved head was the sign of a male submis-sive, where in the mortal world the style apparently indicated Dominance.

Philippe fell to his knees. Reaching on the underside of the sound's cap, he retrieved a small tool and held it out in his open palm. "As you said, Master, you control my coming. This opens the barbell so you can remove it and the sound when it serves your pleasure. May you have mercy." He lowered his head once more, tried desperately to ignore the vibrations that rolled with vicious regularity through his male flesh . . . his entire body.

"I am Chad Lalanne, and I am your Master. I want you to tell me your name, although rest assured I may change it."

"If it pleases you, Master, my name is Philippe. Philippe d'Argent." Philippe waited, barely breathing. He could crush the man's bones with barely a thought. Males of any species were competitive, and Chad would be highly cognizant of their differences in strength. But would he realize that as a Master, with Philippe as a submissive, he had a power over him that transcended vampires and mortals?

"Philippe." The Dom hesitated then reached down and clutched a handful of Philippe's hair. "It pleases me to call you 'vampire.' Stand and I will relieve you of the sound. You've endured enough pain to have earned a moment's pleasure."

"Thank you, Master Chad." Philippe felt his tension ease, even as he instantly wanted to hear Chad say his name. He would have to earn it by working for his Master's pleasure. His love. As Jacques had made him work for it.

The mortal's touch was surprisingly gentle as he unscrewed the cap and worked the barbell out of Philippe's cock. Now free, the sound shot out of his cock head and into Chad's hands.

Chad rubbed the end of the sound against Philippe's nipples, his touch light yet threatening enough for Philippe's muscles to tense. "That's it, vampire. With or without this stuck up your cock, you will come only on my command." He lowered Katie from the side horse and ordered her to her knees. "Katie, suck the vampire's cock. Suck it hard."

When her lips closed over his cock head, Philippe fought to maintain control as he tangled his fingers through her silky hair, held her to his groin. His own flesh throbbed, wanting . . .

The golden release. The sense of total obedience to a Master's will, of complete concentration on his own flesh. The light rasp of Katie's fangs along the length of his cock. Strong male fingers stroked his back, his buttocks, his inner thighs. Heady smells of arousal filled his nostrils. His ass ached for the Master to fuck him again. When large, strong fingers curled around his balls and pulled, he moaned.

He was going to come . . . No, he couldn't. Remembered the Master's order. Philippe tried to ignore the urgency, hold back. "Please, Master . . ."

A sharp tug on his balls brought him back from the brink, practically doubled him over with pain. But not for long. Katie moved on him again, took his cock down her throat. Sucked. Swallowed. Constricted his flesh until he wanted to scream. His Master's grip on his balls loosened, and he shoved his cock back up Philippe's ass. "Come now, vampire. It may be months before I decide to allow you this pleasure again."

As if he had a choice. Philippe's balls tightened. His cock swelled against Katie's throat. His ass contracted around the Master's throbbing cock. Waves of pleasure radiated from both as he came, long, wet bursts Katie swallowed like a dutiful slave. Bursts that matched the Master's steaming spurts up his ass.

As his climax ebbed, Philippe felt a tug on his hair. "You will join Katie and me for a week's journey. If you accept me as your Master, prepare yourself as a proper vampire slave and meet us at dusk tomorrow." He went on to explain that his houseboat would be docked near the gambling boats not far from Philippe's French Quarter offices. "I will spend a week showing you the bayou country where Katie and I grew up."

It was a good while later when it hit Philippe. On very short acquaintance he'd taken this Dominant mortal as Master and agreed to spend a week alone with them. It felt damn good to be owned again after spending so long alone.

• • •

Katie blinked at the sunlight filtering around the blackout curtains her Master had installed to ensure her comfort. Wake from passing boats lapped at the sides of the houseboat. She liked the swaying motion, found it anchoring in a world that was becoming more confusing each day. It still amazed her that Chad had invited Philippe into their relationship on such brief acquaintance, so much so that she wondered if the other vampire had used vampiric compulsion. "Will he come?"

Her Master sat beside her on the wide built-in cushioned seat at the bow of the houseboat, his touch incredibly gentle as he stroked her cheek. She loved that about him, his ability to dominate her with his mere presence as well as with his physical strength and the whips he wielded so well at the club. "Yes. He'll join us here in a few hours."

Chad might have told her he'd invited Philippe to join them in order to provide her a source of nourishment. He might have said he was doing this to bring her pleasure. Katie couldn't deny these things were true. But they weren't the whole truth. When she looked deeply into Chad's thoughts, she knew her Master wanted Philippe as much as he wanted her. Maybe more. Such a pity the mortal world frowned on what came naturally to vampires . . . sex in all its many forms, without rules. Without the shame that had sent Chad from his home, mired him in the BDSM dungeons of New Orleans. "I thank you, Master."

"Bringing in a third party will serve my pleasure too." He smiled, his teeth startlingly white against his deeply tanned skin. When he drew her hand to his chest, she realized he'd spent the hours while she slept being groomed by one of the attendants at the club. His taut muscles flexed under her fingers, beneath freshly waxed and oiled skin. His beautifully shaped skull gleamed as though it too had been waxed rather than shaved. Without running her hands over every inch of her Master's magnificent body, she knew the only hint of hair she'd find would be the barely discernable stubble on his cheeks and chin. That single gold hoop dangled from his left ear, catching the late afternoon sunlight that invaded through the corners of the blackout curtains.

He'd make an awesome vampire. And she sensed part of him wanted to join her in her new, shadowy world. But Katie would never make him one. She didn't have the right. Or the ability to ensure he'd come through the change with his potency intact. But Philippe was a d'Argent. Perhaps he . . . No. Chad would remain mortal unless he commanded one of them to turn him.

She slipped a finger under the waistband of his olive green cargo shorts, looked up at him for permission to do more. "Not now, little one. Slide to the edge of the bench and spread your legs. I've brought you a present." He fished inside the bag he'd brought in and drew out a beautifully sculpted double-penetration dildo. "To fill you when I can't." He fitted the heads of the device into her pussy and ass and secured it with a simple pink leather harness she noticed had an empty pouch in front to accommodate the long, thick gel cock he handed her. "And this is for you to use to fill our vampire's ass when I decide he's deserving of such pleasure."

"And yours, Master?" Katie's juices began to flow when Chad set the vibrator in motion, holding the remote control against one of her nipples to enhance the tingling arousal that was spreading through her body. She recalled a scene at the club where a Mistress had fucked her male slave's taut ass with a similar strap-on, wondered if she'd worn a device similar to the one Chad had just secured to her for his pleasure.

"No." She'd known before asking what his answer would be. Masters fucked. Slaves were fucked. Apparently in this relationship slaves were to fuck each other too, whenever their Master willed it. She rubbed her finger over the dildo, tracing the ridge at the base of its head before setting it aside. "When will Philippe arrive?"

"You are to call him 'vampire.' Like you, he is my slave. Unlike you, my darling, he has not yet earned the right to be called by name." Chad lit the lamps secured to the walls of the houseboat's main room then turned to Katie. The flickering light caught wisps of smoke curling from brass incense holders set on a central table. A hint of musk and something heavily aromatic filled the air, heightening the sense of dark eroticism that was catching her in its sensual spell. "He will arrive at dusk, and we'll begin our journey then. Meanwhile, I command you to enjoy the anticipation while I check out the boat."

Katie lay back, enjoying the feeling of fullness within her body, the variation in vibrations as the boat swayed from side to side when Chad moved about on the deck. She closed her eyes, imagined her Master and the vampire fucking each other, their hairless bodies glistening, Chad's from the sweat that came with his mortal arousal, the vampire's slick with the oil the Master would have ordered her to rub onto his pale vampire skin. Her nostrils flared as incense filled the small room with its heady aroma. And her fangs itched to taste the blood of her fellow slave.

She slipped her hand beneath the curtain of her hair, felt the barely palpable marks above her collar where Philippe had sunk his fangs into her vein last night. It had been his nourishment, taken on their Master's order. Yet there was the potential for much more. For her and Philippe, but for Chad too, if he accepted what she knew he wanted, deep inside beneath the mortal machismo, the posturing of an alpha male not yet sure of the extent of his own Dominance. Her arousal growing almost to a fever pitch, she sat up and gathered her hair high up on her head and braided it into a silken whip she imagined her Master using to enhance their pleasure.

Chapter Three

A soft breeze caressed Philippe's freshly shaved scalp, its feathery touch curling around his ears, teasing the sensitive flesh so long left unexposed, covered by the now absent evidence of his grief. He'd stiffened and braided the severed hair into a short flogger and fashioned a handle from hard leather engraved in gold leaf with his Master's initials. A gift, one he hoped his new Master would appreciate. The new, thicker ring Chad had given him to thread through his piercing bounced against his thigh, a constant reminder that he now answered to a new Master. Eager, Philippe made his way through the darkening streets toward the dock—and Chad Lalanne's houseboat that would be his home for the coming week.

As instructed, Philippe had brought nothing but the gift, his box of sounds, the barbell, a large anal plug and a set of piercing needles and stretchers. Though his vampire intuition was strong, he hadn't been able to discern the purpose for the latter items. His only clothing was the loose gray sweats he had on. And a pair of leather deck shoes. He had the feeling—the hope—the garments would be permitted only for journeys to and from the boat. The air smelled of fish and seawater as he got closer to the docks. His heartbeat, normally so slow as to be indiscernible to most, thumped in his chest.

Dangers lurked in every alleyway, for New Orleans was in many ways a lawless city, but Philippe paid little heed to the occasional thug who darted back into the shelter of narrow alleys upon being shown his fully extended vampire fangs. Of the many shadow dwellers of the city, only an Owenga would dare challenge Philippe, for his vampire prowess was obvious, undiluted by his equally obvious sexual submissiveness.

There, in the distance, was the dock Master Chad had mentioned. The houseboat straining at her moorings was smaller than Philippe had imagined, an unassuming deck and cabin riding on pontoons. Its two idling motors churned the water at its stern to a brownish froth.

After stepping on the dock, Philippe hesitated. He sensed his potential new Master was standing in the shadow of the cabin, watching him. He knew what he wanted to do, but wasn't sure how he would be accepted. If he would. There was only one way to find out. He went to one knee, then the other. Then to his hands. Hopeful yet not certain of his reception, he began to move forward that way.

He got halfway to the cockpit before the boat rocked and he saw two bare feet planted in his path. Following his heart, he kissed the tops of those feet then lifted one foot at a time. Being careful to keep his fangs retracted, he drew each toe into his mouth and laved it with his tongue. After paying homage to all ten toes, Philippe lay facedown on the ground and lifted one of his Master's feet to rest on the back of his neck.

A sign of trust. Of perfect vulnerability to another's will. Of giving one's self, one's life into the hands of a Dominant alpha male, be he vampire or mortal. Philippe tried to squelch the rush of arousal that threatened his Master's total control over him.

Chad kept the pressure light, his deep voice more a whisper than a shout. "I know you lost a Master you loved. His training and his presence in your memories are honored by your proper act of submission now." He lifted his foot and placed it on the deck beside Philippe's cheek. "On your knees, vampire slave."

When Philippe complied, he felt Chad slip a heavy collar around his neck. The snap when he shut it had a ring of finality, even before he ordered Philippe to lift his chin and fed the hasp of a hefty padlock through the clasp. "Feel it. Tell me if it is positioned so my woman can feed on you."

The collar was smooth, heavy . . . and positioned low enough around his neck to give Katie plenty of room to puncture his jugular vein and drink her fill. "Yes. She can feed. I thank you, Master, and I will do my best to please you. Take this as a small symbol of my submission," Philippe said as he drew out the flogger and laid it in the Master's hand. The weight of the collar felt good, a tangible reminder he belonged to Chad. Just as his shaved head let other vampires know his status, the collar announced to the mortal world that he was a sex slave, bound to a mate who controlled his very existence.

"Never fear, vampire, you will please me. Your gift pleases me. Go inside. Undress and plug your ass while I get the boat underway. I am happy you chose to acknowledge me as Master." Chad rubbed his calloused palm over the crown of Philippe's closely shaved head, sending a shiver of hot arousal through his body. "You will find Katie there. Finding our way into the bayou country will require my full attention, so you have my leave to give her sustenance. You may feed on her, as well, for I want my vampires full of energy for the days to come."

"What about you, Master? Do you not need to feed?" Philippe sensed his Master's nagging desire to join the vampire world, wondered if Chad realized how close he was to asking to move to the dark side with his slaves.

Chad laughed. "I bought a po'boy and beer on the way back from the club. I'll leave the blood drinking to you. Oysters and French bread are more to my taste." He rearranged the collar so the padlock fit nicely in the hollow of Philippe's throat then extended his hand and pulled Philippe to his feet. "Can you tolerate mortals' food?"

"Some. Very little. A sip of wine . . . a small taste of forbidden fruit . . ." He imagined Chad knew that what vampires ate they must absorb since they had no means of elimination.

"I thought as much. Go now. Feed Katie and yourself. And sleep. You will waken in the morning, in the paradise that's Cajun country."

• • •

Philippe was beautiful, almost as breathtaking as their Master. Once he toed off leather deck shoes and shed his baggy sweats, Katie watched the moonlight reflect off the gold collar locked about his muscular neck and the large, heavy-looking ring that dangled from just behind the head of his fully aroused cock. Her mouth watered to taste him—not just the blood that pulsed invitingly in a vein above their Master's collar but the smooth, pale column of his vampire cock, the bursts of salty cream he'd give out when he came. When he bent and inserted an anal plug almost as long and thick as their Master's cock, she noticed the perfectly oval shape of his denuded skull and longed to sample its smoothness, find the erogenous zones that would make him go crazy with lust.

"We are ordered to feed while our Master takes us on this journey," he said, taking a careful seat beside her on the bench, as though afraid of incurring the Master's ire.

"I know." She couldn't resist. She had to touch him, feel the barely leashed power beneath that pale, smooth skin. Did his heart beat slowly like hers, or after so many years as a vampire did it remain still in his chest? She splayed her fingers over his chest, searching out and finding a strong, slow heartbeat below the surface of his skin. As though to stop her exploration, he laced his fingers through hers and brought her hand to his lips.

"You may feed first," he told her as though eager to get on with following the Master's order. "You should have easy access, for he fit my collar loosely to facilitate your feeding."

ETERNAL TRIANGLE ~ 141

"Yes." If she didn't know better, she'd say Philippe didn't want this—didn't want the intimate contact with her alone. Katie met his gaze, saw kindness there along with confusion. He wasn't sure he could do this, was silently asking her forgiveness and her help. "Lie back on the bench and let's play awhile. We needn't feed right away. It will take hours for us to reach our Master's beloved bayou."

When he did, she stroked his scalp, found each spot that always seemed to fuel Chad's lust. Philippe rewarded her with a growl and a thrust of his hips toward her belly. She laid soft kisses on his chest, laved his flat coppery nipples with her tongue. Her own arousal intensified when she wrapped her hand around his steely erection and rubbed it back and forth. "You changed your jewelry," she said, lifting the large, thick ring and rotating it through the flesh of his cock.

"On our Master's order. It's almost as effective a preventative as a locked Gates of Hell."

She shouldn't have needed the reminder. Chad was her Master. Philippe's too. He controlled their sexuality as surely as if he kept them locked up separately, unless he had immediate need of them to provide his own sexual satisfaction. She gave the ring one last tug and let it go, laughing at herself as she did. "Almost as effective as the plugs we're wearing. Mine has a vibrator . . . and he holds the controls."

Philippe seemed to relax when she made light of their situation, and he tilted his head back, giving her easy access. "Drink up. The sooner we feed, the sooner we can sleep and escape temptation."

When she put her mouth to his throat and pierced his jugular vein, he framed her face in his big hands and held her to him as she fed. Warmth swirled through her veins, along with the arousal her Master controlled, and as she released Philippe her lust dissolved, replaced by a sense of satisfaction—not quite orgasm, but almost. Her release came later, a slow roll of erotic sensation that began when Philippe pierced her throat and started to feed. Her last memory before slipping off to sleep was of him releasing her, sighing and snoring quietly against her naked breast.

• • •

As dawn began breaking, turning the eastern sky to shades of pink and blue and purple, Chad anchored the houseboat beneath the heavy canopy of a huge live oak tree and draped the deck with a net that let in the breeze but kept out the mosquitoes. It shaded the worst of the sun's rays, too, which would be good for his slaves' pale, sensitive skin.

Then he lay on a cushion at the stern and enjoyed listening to the murky water lap at the pontoons, the mating call of a bull gator in the distance. A fish broke the water, mouth open to take in a bright blue dragonfly flitting along the surface. He loved this primitive and treacherous land, the rivers that changed course from week to week, the wealth of creatures that made the bayou their home. Shifting his gaze to the starboard side of the houseboat, he watched a pair of water moccasins slither out of the water and sun themselves on an uprooted tree trunk nearby.

As much as Chad enjoyed New Orleans with its dark pleasures, he claimed the bayou country as his own. It would have been better if he'd been able to put it from his mind since he could never go back to Bayou Vert, the nearby fishing village where he'd spent the first eighteen years of his life.

Chad would never forget the shame. The humiliation of being discovered in the rectory with Father Andre on all fours, his bare ass in the air while Chad fucked him. Most of all he'd never forget the shock on his family's faces when they'd heard about it, the disbelief that their son and brother had let another man—never mind a man of God—desecrate his body.

Like the others in Bayou Vert, his parents were simple people, deeply religious, with strong ideas about right and wrong. But they'd stood by him while their neighbors had tarred and feathered the priest. They'd protested Chad's innocence to no avail then tried to paint him as an innocent victim, but no one had bought it. Not even Pop, who'd exacted a promise from Chad never to commit such sin again even as he'd launched Chad in his pirogue and ordered him to hightail it out of there. Mama and his brothers had stalled the townspeople—he'd never figured out exactly how. His escape had taken some doing. For hours he'd slithered like a snake through overgrown streams that sometimes got so narrow he had to carry his pirogue through. It had taken what seemed like forever, but he'd finally reached smoother sailing and made his way to New Orleans.

Nope. He could never go back, stir up all the shit that hit the fan back then and splattered his family with shame.

I'm not gay. I wasn't then, when curiosity made me get it on with the priest. Chad hadn't admitted otherwise then, even to himself, and he wouldn't do it now. After ten years working as a club Dom, he'd seen and participated in every manner of sexual kink except male on male. He'd promised Papa he wouldn't do that, and he'd kept his word until two nights ago when he'd taken a male vampire as his sex slave. *I did that for Katie. She needs the vampire's blood and his protection. I promised to take care of her when I collared her, and that's all I'm doing.*

But was it? Chad looked down at his bare feet and couldn't help remembering feeling the vampire's soft lips and tongue there. Or recalling the sense of responsibility he'd felt when Philippe had prostrated himself and placed Chad's foot on his neck. He'd submitted as completely as Katie had done years ago, when she'd still been mortal like him. Chad doubted he could trust anybody that much. He knew he couldn't lay his life in any other mortal's hands. Not for the first time he wondered what it would be like to turn his back on his mortality, join the vampire world where his slaves belonged.

If he became one of them he wouldn't have to worry about indulging his sexual fetishes. From Katie he'd learned vampires celebrated their sexuality with abandon. They enjoyed orgies where nothing among consenting adults was off-limits. BDSM wasn't limited to clubs or the privacy of one's own home, but instead was practiced freely by those with a bent toward Dominance and submission. If he became a vampire he wouldn't have to worry much about getting a dread disease, or dying young . . .

Yeah, there was a lot to recommend going over to the dark side. But there were downsides, not the least of which was the fact Chad enjoyed his beer and crawfish . . . and another fact that he was none too fond of the idea of risking his sexual potency to some restorative ritual his new slave's d'Argent clan supposedly had a monopoly on. Chad's cock began to swell and lengthen, as though reminding him how necessary his sexual prowess was to his calling as a sexual Dominant. Would Philippe d'Argent know the secret of restoring a new vampire's potency? Chad forced that question to the back of his mind. It wasn't time. Probably would never be.

When a lazy breeze caught and ballooned the netting, he reached for the remote control and activated the vibrator in Katie's cunt and ass. Soon afterward she showed up on deck, a plate of hot boudins and biscuits in hand. The vampire trailed behind her, carrying the battered tin coffeepot that had come with the houseboat . . . and a single mug. Chad sat at the helm, enjoying the breakfast his slaves had prepared. How would it feel to see food, smell the mouthwatering aromas but not be able to savor the spicy sausage or let a fluffy biscuit melt in his mouth? He wished he knew. He sipped the sweet chicory-laced coffee, looking over the steaming cup to meet the vampire's gaze.

"Did you drink your fill?" he asked Katie, who sat on her heels at his feet.

She smiled at him and at the vampire who stood by, ready to

refill Chad's coffee. "Yes, my darling Master. I fed on the vampire, and he drank his fill of me. We both thank you."

"You're welcome." His collars gleamed around his slaves' necks in the muted sunlight, reminding Chad the vampires probably weren't enjoying the damp heat of early morning on the bayou— or the sunlight filtering through the oak tree's broad canopy. "All this good food has made me sleepy. Let's go inside."

He might as well have been a creature of the night, he decided as he stepped off the open deck, leaving the sunshine to the swamp creatures. Since leaving home, Chad had worked all night and slept away most of the days, except for occasional treks like this one where he renewed himself in the quiet, sometimes treacherous backwaters of the Mississippi River, communing with fish and fowl instead of his fellow man. This trip, he'd savor the night . . . a golden moon and starlit sky, the vast darkness that cloaked a thousand forbidden fantasies. A hundred dark desires that never met the light of day.

• • •

A ceiling fan swirled lazily in the center of the boat's main cabin, its four leaf-shaped blades churning the humid air. Lingering smells of strong coffee and spicy Creole sausage hung in the air, not unpleasant yet a sensual reminder of the fact his Master was a mortal. Swamp creatures croaked at one another from the shore, their low, menacing tones punctuated occasionally by loud bellows.

Wild. A little threatening yet irresistibly seductive. Like Chad. Philippe turned toward the cabin door, trying to decipher the unfamiliar sounds.

"You curious? That bellowing's a bull gator's mating call," Chad said. "The bullfrogs are croaking too. Fishermen'll be out tonight, giggin' them by the hundreds. Frog legs. Almost as much a Cajun delicacy as crawfish."

"You want crawfish jambalaya for dinner, Master?" Katie asked from her perch at Chad's feet.

Chad reached down, laced his fingers through her hair and lifted her to her feet just as Philippe was about to kneel beside her. Then he looked back at Philippe. "*Mais* yeah. You ever taste it, vampire?"

"Afraid not. The smell reminds me of bouillabaisse, though. I often ate that before I was changed." Philippe's mouth watered at the memory of the spicy fish stew he'd enjoyed whenever his mortal business had taken him to coastal France.

"How long have you been . . ." Chad motioned for Katie to take off his T-shirt.

"A vampire?" Strange, Philippe thought, how a lot of humans hated to say the word.

"Yeah." Chad's muscles rippled when he bent and raised his arms so Katie could pull the shirt over his head. "I've often wondered . . . Never mind, finish undressing me."

"I was changed a little over a hundred years ago." Philippe knelt and slid Chad's cargo shorts off. Gods but the man was hung. Of course Philippe had realized that the moment that cock had reamed his ass during the club scene. He longed to take the thick, plum-shaped cock head in his mouth, suck out the cream that even now pearled in its eye. Instead, for he hadn't been given permission, he rubbed his sensitive scalp against Chad's muscular thigh, sighed.

"Later, vampire." Chad strode to the bench and stretched out along its length. "Get rid of the toys, both of you." Philippe complied first, sliding out the butt plug then taking the ring out of his piercing. With luck he'd soon have the Master's throbbing cock filling the void where the plug had been.

But it seemed that wasn't going to happen. He knew it before Chad adjusted the blackout curtain above the sleeping bench and told Katie to lie down. Chad stretched out on his side beside her, his cock pressed against the pale skin of her belly, his free arm draped over her shoulder. "Come lie down with us."

Chapter Four

Skin on skin. Silken skin over taut male muscles. Philippe stretched out behind his Master, his cock nestled between the cheeks of Chad's taut ass. To calm his lust he tried to focus on a lightning bug that sparkled against the blackout curtain, its movement a tiny beacon in the dark. Philippe laid one arm over Chad's narrow waist and let his fingers drift up to play with his Master's taut nipples. When Katie moaned softly he realized Chad must have been playing with her nipples too.

Arousal built slowly, not only in Philippe but also in his partners. Unlike the club scene they'd played night before last where physical sensation had been everything, this seemed real. Philippe sensed the love . . . the unconditional trust that flowed between Katie and Chad. Love that reached out and included him here in this primeval wilderness of raw nature, unfettered emotions. He felt Chad's need to give pleasure, his confusion as to the path he'd take.

When Philippe delved into his Master's thoughts he sensed again that one part of Chad wanted to join them, give up his mortal existence for one that promised no sexual boundaries, no mortal rules of right and wrong. But he also sensed Chad's fear, his reluctance to leave the familiar for something unknown and more than a little frightening. Philippe understood. He'd felt the same a century before when he'd been dying, but he'd grabbed at the chance Jacques offered to stay alive. Perhaps he'd been a latent submissive even then, undisturbed by the thought of acceding to the wishes of the vampire Dom who'd enthralled him.

It would be so much harder for a Dominant male to put his future into the hands of his vampire slaves, but that was what Chad would have to do if he wanted to make this relationship permanent.

Philippe stretched out behind Chad. Needing to touch his Master, he found the sensitive spot at the base of his skull and laved it with his tongue. Chad tasted good, like fresh herbs and spices—cinnamon and ginger, Philippe recalled from long ago—spread over smooth, slightly salty skin. When Chad moaned and thrust his ass toward Philippe, Philippe slid his hand down and encircled his Master's hard cock. The backs of Philippe's fingers brushed Katie's plump mound, eliciting a whimper and a fluttering motion of her hand as though she sought a stronger connection.

Her small, cool hand found Philippe's, closed over it. She dragged it upward and pressed it against their Master's chest. Philippe scissored his fingers over the rigid nub of Chad's nipple then freed his hand and rubbed Chad's cock along her damp slit, searching for and finding her cunt.

Chad shuddered. "Put me inside her. Now."

As though they'd done this countless times before, Katie slid closer, impaled herself when Philippe positioned their Master's cock within her honeyed slit.

The Master's silent order might as well have been shouted for all to hear. *Fuck me, vampire. Fuck me while I fuck Katie.* Philippe wanted to obey. His cock throbbed against his Master's ass cheeks. But while he read Chad's desire loud and clear, he also sensed his ambivalence. The fear that kept the Master from coming out and demanding what he wanted.

He nipped Chad's neck, careful to keep his fangs retracted. "Do you want this?" he asked, moving back slightly and shifting so his cock pressed tentatively against the Master's tight hole. "I know you do. But I need you to ask for it. Please, Master."

"No . . . Yes, damn it, fuck me."

Philippe took his time, entering Chad's tight ass inch by inch. "Like this, Master?" he asked, rocking slowly in and out of Chad while Chad fucked Katie.

"Yeah. Oh God. Don't stop." Chad's skin grew hot, damp as he approached his climax. His inner muscles milked Philippe's cock while Katie's milked Chad's. Slow motion. Two loving slaves fucking their loving Master, one Master pleasuring both of his beloved slaves.

As though they'd choreographed the move, Chad rolled Katie to her back and rose above her while Philippe followed, never losing the connection . . . the sense of oneness. Chad stiffened, growled, shot burst after burst of semen into Katie's womb as Philippe felt his own release teetering on the edge. "Come, slaves," Chad ordered just as Philippe knew he couldn't hold back much longer.

• • •

When the sun had practically disappeared on the western horizon, Chad called his lovers out onto the deck. "No. Sit here with me," he said when Katie was about to kneel at his feet. "You too, vampire."

Philippe rose gracefully for one so large. As though unaffected by the Master's offhand order he settled onto the bench at Chad's other side. Katie knew, though, that he longed for the dignity of a name.

She was a vampire too, but Chad called her by the name she'd had when she was mortal like him. Her mind attuned with her partners, she rested her head against the canvas boat cushions and watched a pelican fish for his supper. Like Chad, Katie was a child of the bayou—but one who'd left of her own accord when she turned eighteen, determined to escape a domineering father who'd wanted to keep her as unpaid labor servicing his customers in the back room of his dingy crab shack. Now, with Chad and Philippe at her side, the bayou represented peace it never had when she'd lived there. Then she'd viewed it as a prison without bars, a place from which she'd only wanted escape.

"Tell me, vampire, what is it like to make the change." Katie sensed that Chad's mind was churning, first urging him to join them in their world then holding up, enumerating his doubts and fears. To ease him, she laid a hand on his thigh, traced the pattern made by the setting sun shining through the leaves of the live oak tree. She noticed Philippe had reached out too, his large hand draped over their Master's knee.

Philippe spoke slowly, seductively. "The feeling is indescribable. Like I always imagined it would feel to die and be reborn. I came as I never did before or since . . . and then I slept. When I woke I was no longer Philippe Simon but rather Philippe d'Argent. A vampire. Submissive lover to a Dominant vampire and member of a vampire clan whose members embraced me, made me whole again."

"Tell me exactly how they did that." Excitement coursed through Chad's body into Katie's hand, but she still felt his doubt.

"My lover—Jacques was his name—turned me. Then he swept me into the air and took me to the seat of his d'Argent clan for the ritual that restored my potency." Philippe made a brief explanation of the preparation and the ceremony itself. A quick visit into Chad's mind let Katie know he was intrigued yet still afraid.

Chad cleared his throat. "Is this ritual foolproof?"

"I've never known it to fail, Master." Philippe grasped Chad's cock, stroking it to full erection. "By the time the ritual began, the pain from my piercing was long gone."

"Do you want to join us for eternity?" Katie had to ask. She had to believe Chad had conquered his doubts before she'd encourage him to come over to the vampire world she'd quickly learned to appreciate.

He took her hand, brought it to his mouth and nibbled at her knuckles. "I don't want to lose you. Or you," he said, turning to Philippe and kissing him full on the lips. "I want to love you both and not be riddled with guilt. To feel no pain, only love and lust. And I want the superhuman strength I need to offer you both my protection."

Philippe laughed. "That strength takes time and effort to develop, just as it requires a certain amount of practice for a vampire to move smoothly through space and time. As you once were an infant mortal, you will be a fledgling vampire for a good time after you've been made."

A fledgling vampire. Chad mulled over the words, imagined himself submitting to vampires older and more experienced than himself. No. Chad Lalanne submitted to no one. He hadn't since that awful day he'd let the elders of Bayou Vert send him running from the only home he'd known, like Papa's old hound dog when it had been caught one Christmas gobbling up Mama's roast turkey.

Or had he? For ten years now he'd lived in the shadows, feeding his kinks by performing for members of *Club de la soumission* not so much for his own pleasure as for money. He'd met Katie there, but instead of taking her home to meet his family and putting a ring on her finger, he'd made her his sex slave and allowed her to keep working at the club. If he hadn't, she wouldn't have encountered the vampire Dom. She'd still be mortal.

Perhaps the club had simply been the gateway, his preparation for a world even more on the shadowy outskirts of the mortal world than BDSM. Chad realized it now. He might call the bayous home, but he'd never truly belonged in Bayou Vert with its rigid notions of right and wrong, natural and unnatural. He belonged to Katie, perhaps also to Philippe. He belonged with them. He'd learned to live without his family and friends, but he couldn't survive without his lovers.

Doubt faded in his mind, replaced by eagerness. Eagerness to join the female vampire he'd always loved and the male vampire he knew he was falling in love with in an unbreakable bond. A bond as sacred as any marriage lines spoken before a mortal priest.

"Turn me."

• • •

For five days they'd explored the bayous. Chad had gorged himself on the sights and smells and tastes of his childhood, seeming to enjoy them more because he knew the tastes at least would soon be forbidden to him. As though preparing for a vow of marriage, or celibacy, he slept alone on the deck after taking his slaves one by one, leaving Katie and Philippe to feed on each another— and prepare for the transformation Chad had determined would take place at the end of their journey.

Tonight the full moon hung in the sky, lighting her Master's way to the dark side.

"We'll join in an eternal triangle." That's how Chad had taken to calling the event that only Philippe knew exactly how to orchestrate. The one Katie could only fret about as she scurried around tidying the houseboat. She couldn't help recalling times she'd enjoyed with Chad on the boat when she had still been mortal. They'd fished for their supper, celebrated the wealth of nourishment teeming in the water and on land.

Tonight there'd be no pungent smell of jambalaya, no shared bottle of wild muscadine wine from a winery they'd discovered in Gonzales on a rare car trip from New Orleans to Baton Rouge. A tear made its way down her cheek, for the many mortal pleasures Chad had savored that soon would exist only in his memories.

"Don't cry, little one." Philippe joined her, rested his hands on her shoulders. "It will be all right."

"He still will be our Master? You're sure?" She couldn't imagine Chad as a submissive, or her or Philippe as Dominants.

Philippe laughed, a deep rumble that echoed around the room. "I've never known a changing to turn a Dom into a sub, or vice versa. I imagine our Master will be the same as he is now, except that he'll be a vampire."

Katie wished she were as sure, but then she supposed Philippe had gotten plenty of experience in his hundred-plus years in the vampire world. "I hope so."

They'd lie down together tonight, and sometime after midnight Chad would order them to turn him. In spite of her misgivings, Katie felt her fangs elongating, anticipating . . .

• • •

He loved them. Both of them. But was it enough? Chad stood on the deck, naked as the day he was born, staring up at the full moon. Stars sparkled in a black sky, and an occasional fish jumped in the dark water, its scales catching the silvery moonlight.

When he walked back in that cabin he'd be walking away from life as he'd known it. Laying his life and future in the hands of his beloved slaves, trusting they'd guard him on the journey they'd both taken. Was he ready?

Yes. He didn't understand the mechanics of it, but he was ready. Chad said a silent adieu to the life he'd known and strode into the cabin to Katie, Philippe . . . to an incredibly seductive prospect of completing their eternal triangle.

They met him on their knees as proper slaves. Moonlight streamed through the open cabin door, illuminating their golden collars when they bent and kissed his feet. Touched, for he'd never stood on such ceremony outside the dungeons, Chad reached down, raised them to their feet. "Tonight we are equals."

Philippe smiled then laid his hand on Chad's chest. "Come. We will make love, and then . . ."

"Then you'll become one of us." Katie stroked his cheek and laid her head on his shoulder.

Chad took them both by the hands, led them to the bed where they'd made love each night since coming to the bayou. Where they'd bonded physically and included Philippe in the emotional bond that had cemented Chad with Katie for so long. Determined not to relinquish control before the very end, he drew them down on either side of him, kissed Katie first and then Philippe, plunging his tongue deep, welcoming the slight abrasion of their fangs on his flesh when he withdrew.

They stroked him, searching out and teasing the sensitive spot at the base of his skull . . . his nipples . . . the dimples at the base of his spine. With each touch Chad relaxed, a willing victim of the vampiric compulsion he'd invited. When Philippe slid down and sucked his cock, Chad squelched the twinges of mortal guilt he felt when his male slave's wet tongue excited him as much as Katie's. Her damp, swollen cunt beckoned his own mouth when she pushed him to his back and straddled his face.

He was eager. Eager to make Katie and Philippe come and come and come, until they couldn't come any more. Eager to come in them over and over, filling them with his essence. With himself. Chad drew Katie down on his mouth and sucked her sensitive clit between his teeth, reaching up and twisting the hard nubs of her nipples until she squealed with pleasure.

Philippe cradled Chad's scrotum while he deep-throated his cock. With strong fingers his slave massaged Chad's testicles. God but it felt good. So good Chad wanted to complain when his lovers changed places and Chad found himself taking Philippe's hard cock down his throat while Katie impaled herself on Chad's erection. He raised a hand, slipped one finger up Philippe's ass while Philippe reached down and finger-fucked Katie's tight rear entrance.

His first climax rippled through him, out of control. Chad

clamped down on Philippe's cock, sucked for all he was worth. Vampire semen shot down his throat as he let go and came in long, hard bursts in Katie's womb. From the feel of her steaming wet cunt and the way her inner muscles clamped down on him, Chad knew she'd come too.

"It's time, Master." Philippe untangled himself from the heap of arms and legs. The way they'd planned, Katie lay on her back. Chad knelt above her and fit his cock into her steaming pussy. He felt Philippe's steadying hands at his waist before Philippe slammed his full eight inches up Chad's ass. Their balls collided. Philippe's slow, cool breath tickled Chad's neck from the back while Katie's teased his Adam's apple. He fucked Katie, and Philippe fucked him. Slow. Deep. Incredibly arousing. His ass burned. His cock felt ready to burst.

"Give me your throat, Master." Philippe's deep voice rumbled against Chad's ear, its tone compelling. What had once seemed so fearful now felt right. Inevitable. Chad turned enough to expose his jugular to Philippe and felt sharp fangs pierce him there. On his other side Katie also was giving him a vampire kiss. Two lovers, one male, one female. Both vampires, both his lovers. Both his slaves.

As they drank from him, Chad's senses rushed. Arousal, lust, the need to come. All those feelings flashed through his mind, but the overwhelming sensation was love. Commitment as strong as any a religious man might feel for the church, as deep as what he'd felt for Katie from the moment they first met. For Philippe as well. As Chad lost consciousness he came again, each burst of semen longer, harder, more satisfying than any he'd ever known.

When he woke he found the ritual had begun.

Chapter Five

*K*atie, Philippe and Chad stood in the main salon at the d'Argent family's Paris town house. Her heart pounded in her chest, full of pride in her newly turned Master . . . and fear that something about this ritual Philippe seemed so confident of would go awry.

The journey had been quick, from the dock in New Orleans, where she'd brought the boat while Chad had slept and Philippe had prepared him, to this elegant home. She and Philippe had supported their Master on his first vampire flight. Now her pussy creamed as she watched her Master and her fellow slave standing side by side, identically pale. Identically naked but for the wide collar that proclaimed Philippe his Master's slave, the single earring that marked Chad a Dominant. Their cocks jutted forward, the flesh filled with sounds held in place by the gleaming rings dangling from their Ampallang piercings.

"Sorry I couldn't be downstairs to greet you when you arrived," said Claude d'Argent, the clan's new leader, whose prominent fangs were evident when he smiled. "My bride just presented me with a bouncing baby boy."

Philippe had filled them in on the flight over the Atlantic, so the birth came as no surprise. Rare among vampires, Claude's fatherhood at such a young age seemed practically a miracle. "Congratulations, sir," Katie said, hoping the brief delay in performing whatever the d'Argent ritual was wouldn't keep Chad's potency from being restored.

Claude shot her a cocky grin. "Never fear. Your mate's potency will be safe with us. We're about to begin. Chad, are you ready to join our clan?"

"I'm ready." Chad's eagerness to have his sexual potency back didn't require special vampire skills to discern.

"Then let's get started." Claude gave a signal and a door opened. A handful of d'Argent vampires surrounded them. "In the year of our Lord 935, Alain d'Argent was born a vampire . . ." Claude told the incredible story of the d'Argents' beginnings then instructed everyone to shed their clothes. "Tonight if the fates are with us, we will restore the potency of Chad Lalanne so he may be Master to Philippe and Katie."

One of the vampires—Katie thought Claude had introduced him as Marisa's brother Raul—knelt and sucked Chad's cock while Claude's cousin Stefan fucked his ass. Stefan's wife, a gorgeous blonde American who looked not far from her own delivery, stroked Chad's satiny skull. When he began to come, she steadied him and sank her fangs into his throat, a tender vampire kiss. Claude moved forward, kissing Chad full on the lips and welcoming him into the d'Argent clan.

"Remove the jewelry from their cocks, Katie." Claude stepped back, giving her space. Trying to control the trembling in her fingers, she removed the jewelry and the sounds. Then she knelt, took first one hard cock then the other in her mouth, felt the hard flesh grow warm. The first drops of semen seeped from Philippe, then from Chad. Their balls tightened against her fingers when she swirled her tongue along each pulsating shaft.

The d'Argent vampires backed away, sought their own partners as Chad took over, bringing Katie to her feet and enclosing her and Philippe within his strong arms. "Let's get the hell out of here." Taking to the air, he tossed a heartfelt "Thank you" over his shoulder as they floated into the night.

A few minutes later they landed back on the houseboat, on the wide sleeping bench from whence they'd left on their journey the night before. Chad lay on the bench, his lovers hovering over him as though they thought he might vanish before their eyes. "I'm here. And I'm hungry. Come here and let me feed."

• • •

Once again the Dominant Master, Chad sank his fangs into Katie's throat, sipping the pungent fluid that now sustained them all while he thrust into Philippe's inviting ass. Philippe positioned Katie's damp pussy and licked her, his cock throbbing. He wouldn't come yet, no matter how fantastic it felt to serve the Master's pleasure, no matter how the sweet smell of female sex aroused him.

No matter how the sting of the flogger he'd given his Master made him ache for Chad to fuck him harder, make him come and come and come.

Over the coming hours they changed positions, all of them sampling every hole, every inch of smooth vampire skin. Philippe wound Katie's silky hair around his hand, positioned her for a vampire kiss as Chad jerked his cock and sucked his balls. Katie raked her long nails over Philippe's nipples as he sank his fangs into her and drank his fill.

None would be denied. Katie fed on them both then laved their cocks, the way she'd done during the ritual that restored their Master to her . . . and Philippe.

The Master spoke, his voice tight with passion. "Fuck us, Katie. Both of us. You, my darling Philippe, lie back and let her ride you. Now, for dawn's breaking over the river and you soon will need to sleep."

Philippe doubted this was the time to remind the Master he too was now a creature of the night, so he obeyed, stretching out on his back and loving the feel of Katie's hot pussy surrounding his shaft, milking it. When Chad knelt behind her and filled her rear end, it felt almost as if he or his Master still wore the sound. Delicious sensations flowed among them, building to a fever pitch as they moved faster, harder. "Come, damn it, come now. Oh, yeah, I'm coming."

The Master's climax triggered Philippe's. Katie's too, if the way her pussy rippled around his spurting cock was any indication. Waves of sensation still coursed through his veins as they rolled to their sides, still joined as they now would be as long as they all lived. An eternal triangle bound by love.

Ann Jacobs

Ann Jacobs is a sucker for lusty Alpha heroes and happy endings, which makes Ellora's Cave an ideal publisher for her work. Romantica™, to her, is the perfect combination of sex, sensuality, deep emotional involvement and lifelong commitment—the elusive fantasy women often dream about but seldom achieve.

First published in 1996, Jacobs has published over forty books and novellas across practically every subgenre of erotic romance. Several of them have earned awards including *The Passionate Plume* (best novella, 2006), *The Desert Rose* (best hot and spicy romance, 2004) and *More Than Magic* (best erotic romance, 2004). She has been a double finalist in separate categories of the EPPIES and From the Heart RWA Chapter's contest. Three of her books have been translated and sold in several European countries.

A CPA and former hospital financial manager, Jacobs now writes full-time, with the help of Mr. Blue, the family cat who sometimes likes to perch on the back of her desk chair and lend his sage advice. He sometimes even contributes a few random letters when he decides he wants to try out the keyboard. (Most of the time Blue just curls up and sleeps!)

She loves to hear from readers, and to match faces with names at signings and conventions.

Lady Elizabeth's Choice

SAHARA KELLY

AUTHOR'S NOTE

This story is set in the London of 1816. A year after Wellington's victory at Waterloo spelled the end of Napoleon's reign of violence and war in Europe, all was still not calm and peaceful either in England or elsewhere on the continent.

Adding to the postwar difficulties was the weather, which is mentioned by the characters as being uncommonly cold. In fact, this year was known as the "year without a summer" or "eighteen-hundred-and-froze-to-death." London recorded its lowest ever daily temperatures during that summer and there are many reports of snow falling in America, specifically during August in New England, where crops were damaged and often ruined.

The year before had seen a massive volcanic eruption in Indonesia, when the island of Tambora blew up in an explosion that has never been equaled in violence. There was incredible, immediate devastation from this event, with many thousands losing their lives. Over the long term, expelled ash particles reduced the global temperature by several degrees, an effect that changed the weather for many months.

Given that this period was also the midpoint of one of the sun's extended periods of low magnetic activity, and concurrently it was experiencing one of its cyclical shifts in position relative to the rest of the solar system, conditions were ripe for an extremely abnormal weather pattern to cloak the northern hemisphere.

Famine was widespread, crops never germinated, let alone flourished, and for most of the year dismally cold conditions sent Europeans and Americans alike shivering indoors to light their fires.

Chapter One

G ood *God, nooooo* . . ."

The howl of outrage shook the small breakfast parlor and sent Little Ted skittering from his master's lap to cower beneath the sofa. He peered from beneath the sturdy frame, cat eyes wide and pupils mere slits in the morning sunshine.

"What the fucking *hell* . . ."

Sheets of newspaper flew across the table and sent the Sèvres cream jug teetering on the edge of disaster.

Little Ted eyed it hopefully.

"*Tedson*—get in here." Sir Spencer Marchwood shouted for his faithful butler who until recently had been his loyal batman. Coincidentally Tedson had also served as the inspiration for the name of the cat. Spence had commented that they both tended to look at things with the same expression of superior disdain.

Thus the kitten had become "Little Ted" although the butler remained Tedson, resolutely refusing to be summoned by the degrading term of "Big Ted."

The older man stepped quietly into the room. "You screamed?" He lifted one eyebrow.

But this morning Spence was not in the mood to be amused. He shook the pages of the *Gazette* he still held fast in his hands. "Did you see this? *Did* you?" He felt the blood thrumming in his veins but couldn't tamp down his anger.

"Not yet, sir. If you'd release your death grip on the paper and take a breath, perhaps I could read what has driven you to the brink of apoplexy." Tedson took the liberty of patting his master paternally on the shoulder. "Since fighting Napoleon quite failed to do it, I can only assume there's a woman involved."

"She-she—*aaaargh*. I will kill her. Kill her *dead*. I swear."

"Yes, sir. Of course you will."

Spence felt the pages eased from his fingers and leaned back in his chair. His brain still reeled from the shock he'd received along with his kippers and toast.

Tedson shook the creases from the sheet and focused intently on the section that had so upset Spence. He nodded. "I assume you are disturbed by this one particular announcement, sir. It contains a name I recognize." He quoted the paragraph. *"Lord and Lady Lionel Wentworth announce the engagement of their daughter, the Lady Elizabeth Wentworth, to the Right Honorable Gregory Sanderson."*

Spence clenched his teeth. "Gregory fucking Sanderson. I *ask* you. *Gregory fucking Sanderson.*"

"I do not believe that *fucking* is Mr. Sanderson's middle name, nor is it a seemly word to use over breakfast." Tedson glared down his nose at his master. "I'm assuming you had cherished some hopes yourself in Lady Elizabeth's direction?"

"Cherished hopes? Cherished *hopes*? You make me sound like some sort of fribblish Almack's debutante." Spence winced as his voice rose to a squeak.

"You're repeating yourself and I don't think *fribblish* is a word."

"Lady Elizabeth Wentworth and I . . ." Spence bit off the words angrily and gulped, fighting for composure. "Lady Elizabeth and I had an—an *understanding*." He paused and frowned. "Of sorts."

"And what sort would that be?"

Spence ran his hand through his shock of unruly blond hair. "Dammit, man. I *claimed* her. I made her a woman. I took her innocence. I—" He cut himself off.

"Ahh." Tedson nodded sagely and poured more tea for his master, retrieving the Sèvres jug and destroying Little Ted's hopes at the same time. "*Now* I see. Right makes might. Droit du seigneur and all that stuff. You took her virginity, thus she belongs to you. That sort of understanding?"

"Well yes. No. Something along those lines." Spence frowned at the inoffensive teacup. "Devil take it, Tedson. I simply can't have her marrying somebody else. It's not acceptable. She's *mine.*"

"It would appear that the lady herself is not cognizant of that fact." Tedson pointed out the obvious.

"Grrrrr." The angry growl forced its way between Spence's teeth as he realized the accuracy of his butler's statement. "I need to see her."

"Might be a tad late in the day for that."

Spence's heart thudded uncomfortably. "Not as far as I'm concerned." He rose, scraping the chair backward and towering over his butler. "Have my horse brought round."

Tedson sighed and reached for the plate of leftover kippers, which he lowered to the floor for an ecstatic Little Ted. "Sir Spencer. It is incumbent on me to point out that it's barely nine o'clock. Morning visits are never paid before eleven and even that is considered early in some homes."

Spence paused, the momentary silence broken only by the sound of kipper bones being enthusiastically crunched betwixt small but effective teeth. "Too early?"

"Yes. Definitely. When I said *late in the day*, I was speaking metaphorically." Tedson gently tugged his arm, pulling him back down into his chair. "Now, in addition to the hour, you must also consider that you've been gone from her for *how* long now? Let's see . . . it must be at least half a year."

Spence swallowed. The sun wasn't quite as bright as it had been first thing that morning.

"So haring over to the Wentworths' . . ." continued Tedson, "full of indignant passion, attempting to claim a woman you say belongs to you when she's just announced her engagement to somebody else smacks of folly to me. Especially since said engagement has been approved by her parents. You *know* what that means." Tedson bent a stern gaze on Spence. "If Lord and Lady Wentworth are in favor of this arrangement, you've got some serious obstacles to overcome. Think, lad. *Plan.* You led military campaigns in France for no less a commander than Wellington himself. Isn't this equal in importance?"

A tiny burp from the floor at his feet distracted Spence and he glanced down to see Little Ted contentedly washing his whiskers. He knew the answer to his butler's question. "Absolutely."

"Good." Tedson cleared away the rest of the unused breakfast dishes. "I'll leave you to it, then."

The offensive newspaper disappeared with Tedson, but Spence's dark thoughts remained. He'd been home in England for less than two weeks, after traveling the length of Europe at the command of his government.

And he'd left at the worst possible time too.

The vision of Elizabeth's face swam back clearly into his mind as he stared unseeing at his own breakfast table.

• • •

Long black hair like silk flowing over limbs of ivory. Eyes as blue as the sea in sunlight. A smile that had enchanted London when she made her debut and sent more hopeful bachelors into a tizzy than he could begin to imagine.

Looks like hers, coupled with her heritage and fortune, made her a most eligible prospect, but she'd refused to be shackled or hobbled by marriage. Elizabeth Wentworth possessed a spirit that yearned for freedom, adventure and passion. And Spence thought he'd given her all three.

They'd loved with abandon and desire, her body welcoming his intrusion with heat and hunger. He'd taken her gently, lovingly, cherishing each cry of pleasure and every drop of sweat that dewed her skin. They'd been slightly tipsy from her special "tea"—a brew she'd obtained from a friend of a friend . . .

They'd been relaxed and comfortable with each other, excited at their nakedness, stimulated by touch and sight and smell. Elizabeth was no shy miss. She'd run her hands over his body in exploration, learning every nook and cranny and following her path with her lips and her tongue.

When he'd finally begun to take her, to slide his cock past heated pussy lips and into her soft tight cunt, she'd watched him, eyes wide open, lips parted, breath coming in quick pants of delight as he penetrated farther and deeper where no one had ever gone before.

Her virginity was no barrier to his passage, a flimsy check in his forward momentum. Neither paid attention when he slid past the remains of her innocence and carried her into womanhood on the head of his cock. They were fixated on each other's gaze, lost in the wonder that each saw reflected there.

Tall yet feminine, Elizabeth's body melded with Spence's like two pieces of a puzzle. Pieces designed to fit together snugly as they coupled into a single whole. Never had he found such physical satisfaction with any other woman. Even though this was her first time, Elizabeth had given him a night unlike any he could ever remember. They'd exploded around each other, her cunt seizing his cock as she screamed out her climax, muscles taut and shivering, eyes glazed with astonishment and the savagely wonderful shock of her orgasm. Her breasts had trembled against him as he followed her into the madness, filling her with endless spurts of his come, dousing her fire with his essence until he felt her overflow around him.

It had been the most amazing and overwhelming experience and he'd never forgotten it.

Nor had he forgotten the sight of her, naked, holding a dueling pistol and staring at the body of the man she'd just shot dead.

Their paths had begun to diverge from that moment on. She'd saved them all, including her friend Charlie and Charlie's future husband, *his* friend Jordan Lyndhurst. The Lyndhursts had moved to the Colonies, the matter of the insane killer had been smoothed over and buried along with the body—all was as it should be.

Except for Elizabeth.

Spence had been a soldier for many years and fought in Wellington's train. He knew what it was like to kill, to come to terms with the fact that his hand had taken another human being's life. He guessed that it would not be an easy thing for Elizabeth to accept, although she'd come through it better than he'd expected. But he hadn't anticipated her withdrawal from him, or her refusal—eventually—to see him at all.

It had hurt. And hurt a lot. He determined to woo her, to seduce her once more and make her his for life. But then the damned government intervened; his orders took him abroad into a Europe recovering from Napoleon's devastation and kept him there for six long months.

Too long, apparently, for Elizabeth.

Well, he was home now. He'd reclaimed his title as heir to the Marchwood estate, turned in his epaulettes and was ready to assume his position in society. The plan was to do so with a wife at his side. He knew there could be no other candidate for that role but Elizabeth.

Now he just had to convince *her* of that fact.

With that very intention in mind, he found himself facing the Wentworth butler a few hours later.

"I'm sorry, Sir Spencer. Lady Elizabeth is not receiving this morning." The man inclined his head politely and stared down his nose at Spence, who was still standing outside the Wentworths' front door. "I will, of course, relay your good wishes for her future."

Spence felt his arm quiver with the restrained urge to grab this superior idiot by the throat and choke his way past him into the house. "Will Lady Elizabeth be available later today?"

"I could not venture to say, sir." The butler gently but firmly closed the door, leaving Spence staring at an ornate door-knocker.

He spun around with a curse and strode down the elegant steps to the street where his horse was tethered. For a moment he paused, hand on the reins, a furious anger sweeping through him. It was coupled with a sharp pain—the pain occasioned by the thought that he might have really lost her. Lost the one woman he knew could complete his life.

"*Pssst.*"

He blinked and stared at his horse. The horse stared back uninterestedly.

"*Pssst.* Sir Spencer. Over *here* . . ."

Casually Spence turned his head and glanced behind him to see a face peeking through the railings that led to the servants' entrance. "At the corner. Meet me there in five minutes. *Pleeeease* . . ."

The face disappeared, leaving the lingering plea rattling in Spence's ears. It had been a maid by the looks of her, but what could she possibly want with him? His horse sidled and stamped his hooves as Spence swung into the saddle. He had nothing better to do with his time now than to meet some maidservant at the end of the street.

Come to think of it, Spence didn't have anything better to do with his *life* now that Elizabeth apparently wouldn't be a part of it.

His shoulders slumped and he dispiritedly turned his horse into the street. Perhaps there was *something* he could do, some way he could get to see Elizabeth. To talk to her at least, to find out what was going through her mind. But at this moment, his spirits were lower than his boots.

It did *not* look good. Not good at all.

Reaching the corner, Spence paused, staring at the carriages and the strolling pedestrians, wondering why they weren't all staring and pointing at him. *Loser. You've lost Elizabeth. She's left you. She doesn't want you. You weren't enough for her.*

Stupid and senseless recriminations galloped through Spence's head screaming invectives at him until he wanted to open his mouth and scream back. But a tap on his boot distracted him from his misery and he looked down into the face of the maid beneath her tidy bonnet.

"Sir Spencer, *please*. I *must* speak with you. It's about my mistress . . ."

"Your mistress?"

"Yes . . . *Lady Elizabeth* . . ."

Chapter Two

The lady herself was sighing—something she found she was doing more and more these days.

Sitting demurely in the small salon, she was supposed to be listening to Gregory as he expounded on the joys of their upcoming life together. Her hands lay folded in her lap, the lace around the high neck of her blue silk gown brushed her chin as she moved, and her hair was smoothed back into an elegant chignon.

She knew she presented the ideal picture of a young woman about to set sail on the sea of matrimony. Demure, a little embarrassed by all the fuss and paying close attention to her betrothed.

She also knew that inside she was ready to mutiny—or at least throw herself overboard. Hence the big sigh, which her fiancé mistook as awe.

"I know." He tucked his thumbs into his waistcoat and assumed a man-of-the-world pose. "It is rather overwhelming, isn't it? But you'll get used to notion, Elizabeth dear." Not tall or blindingly handsome, Gregory was best described as "sweet." He could also fit the adjective "verbose," since he loved the sound of his own voice.

"I think a house near Mama's will suit us for the season. At least until I get established in Rutherford's office. Mama says there's a couple available we can choose from and they'll be close to Whitehall." He smiled. "And of course close to Bond Street— and your parents too, Elizabeth dear."

Of course. I shall spend the rest of my life shopping and visiting my parents. How . . . unspeakably delightful. And I shall forever be known as "Elizabethdear." Elizabeth managed a small smile. Gregory was doing his best. If she'd revealed any dissatisfaction whatsoever, he'd have bent heaven and earth to rectify it—to make her happy. His feet were firmly set on the political path and it was a safe bet that he'd end up in Parliament or running the whole dratted country someday in the not too distant future.

And Elizabeth knew she'd probably make an excellent political hostess and mother of future generations of wordy and dull politicians.

If she didn't die of boredom first.

A sound from the hallway indicated more visitors. Elizabeth wondered who it might be, then dismissed the thought. This morning's announcement in the *Gazette* had brought her more than her fair share of curious, pleased and just plain nosy people. Being closeted with Gregory was an excellent excuse to avoid the pleasantries she was supposed to utter upon such an auspicious occasion. It would be bad enough tonight when they made their first appearance together as an engaged couple.

The noise in the hall faded. Apparently her butler had obeyed her wishes and informed the caller she was not receiving visitors. She closed her eyes for a moment in thanks and absently ran a hand over her brow.

Gregory immediately noticed. "Oh poor dear. You have a migraine, don't you? I know the signs. Mama suffers too, you know. You must go to your room and have your maid prepare you a tisane." He tenderly assisted her from her chair and rang for a servant. "Tonight is important and you must look your best. Mama is so excited." His gentle brown eyes smiled kindly at her. "You will be as beautiful as always, I'm sure, Elizabeth dear. But do try to get some rest, won't you?"

Shepherded to her room, Elizabeth barely had the chance

to nod farewell. There was no suggestion of a kiss or anything, of course. Gregory was far too well brought up for that sort of behavior.

Which, realized Elizabeth as she shrugged out of her gown and prepared to nap for a while, was the root of the whole damn problem. Her engagement, her future—all of it. Shaped by a decision based on the appallingly *bad* behavior of the most incredible man she'd ever met—the shockingly badly brought up Spencer Marchwood.

He'd kissed her breast! She still shivered as she remembered the first time they'd met. It had been in the quietly tasteful salon of a house that catered to gentlemen and their needs, but had also managed to become the "in" place to visit for the curious and more adventurous ladies of society.

Somebody had tried to throw a bomb of sorts through the window and Elizabeth's gown had caught some glowing embers. He'd stepped on it roughly, grinding out the flickering ashes and also tugging it down much farther than the designer had intended. Her breasts had popped free without her even realizing it. Her lips curved into a smile as she remembered how he'd bent low, dropped a fast and hard kiss on one sensitive nipple and then laughed.

"Ma'am, I think your dress is extinguished, but the fire has spread to my breeches."

Spence's words still sounded loud in Elizabeth's brain. As did images of what else they'd done together when they'd met for the second time.

It had been fate, destiny—whatever it was called—it had brought Elizabeth into Spence's arms for a night of passion that surpassed her fantasies. And it had also ended with a savagely violent death.

Funnily enough, she regretted neither event. Killing had been hard, but done out of necessity and the desperate urge to protect.

Loving had been much easier, but the aftermath had been more shattering, more terrifying than she'd expected.

Spencer Marchwood had touched a place within her that she did not know existed. And *that* fact was what had scared Lady Elizabeth Wentworth down to her very elegantly shod feet and sent her running away from him. Because if Spence ever found out—he'd have her in his power for as long as they both had breath in their bodies.

And Elizabeth Wentworth had sworn never to be in *any* man's power. *Ever.*

• • •

"Tedson."

Spence was yelling and he knew it. But he was burning with a plan, ideas running amok in his brain and he stormed through his own front door as if he were leading a charge against Napoleon's troops.

"Sir?" The patient man appeared from a side door as Spence erupted into the hall.

"I have a plan, Tedson. I have intelligence, I have strategies, I have—I repeat—a *plan.*" Spence tossed his riding coat aside and rubbed his hands together. "Damned lousy weather too. Whatever happened to the sunshine?"

Tedson picked up the discarded coat and shook it out. "I have no idea. They're calling this year unusually cool."

"I'll agree with that. But it works in our favor." Spence walked to his study and opened the door. "Come on in, my friend. I need you. And only you. This will be a delicate operation . . ."

Sighing, Tedson followed his master into the cozy room and shut the door behind him. "Are we going to do anything illegal? If so, I should probably check to see that my final will and testament is up to date . . ."

Spence chuckled. "Don't be a wet blanket, Tedson. This plan

will—if all succeeds—get me a wife and the Marchwood estate a mistress."

"Ah. Behold me overcome with joy."

"Scoff if you wish. But"—Spence leaned on the desk—"the intelligence imparted to me this morning by one small but nosy maidservant has changed everything."

"Really, sir?" The eyebrow rose sarcastically. "*One* small maidservant?"

"Yes." Spence folded his arms. "I have it on the best authority that Elizabeth—*my* Elizabeth—is as miserable as sin about her upcoming marriage to Geoffrey whatshisname."

"Gregory whatshisname, sir. And you've verified this by talking to the lady herself, have you?"

"Er . . ." Spence paused. "Not exactly. But I will."

"Very well. You've made an appointment to visit?" Tedson pursued his line of questioning in a patiently logical manner that irritated Spence to no small degree. Of course, it was one of Tedson's unique skills. Spence appreciated it when it was directed at others. When it was directed at *him*, however—that was a different kettle of fish.

"Not exactly," said Spence once more. "We're going to invite Elizabeth for a visit."

"Ah." Tedson stared thoughtfully at Spence for the space of a few moments. "Let me guess. She will not be allowed the opportunity to refuse our invitation, will she?"

Spence knew his grin was spreading from ear to ear. "No. She won't."

Tedson sighed. "I think I put my will in your safe, Sir Spencer. Would you pull it out for me and make sure you witness it?"

"Oh, come on, man. Where's your sense of adventure?"

"Not up my arse, sir. Which—if you'll pardon the thought—is where you seem to be keeping your brains these days."

Laughing out loud, Spence clapped his servant on his shoulder. "It'll be *fun*, Tedson. I want this woman for my own, for the rest of my life. I've *never* been this sure about anything. All I have to do is convince her she feels the same way."

"And if she doesn't?"

Spence's gut tightened at the thought. "She will. I'll make sure of it."

"And where is all this convincing going to take place?" Tedson slumped. "Since it appears there's no talking you out of it, I suppose you'd better outline the plan. Knowing you, you've probably forgotten something—like those poor chicken farmers we nearly invaded just outside Brussels. I couldn't eat eggs for at least a month after that . . ."

The two men emerged from the study an hour or so later, both looking fairly relaxed. Spence's heart was tinged with excitement at the prospect of seeing Elizabeth again that very night.

Tedson—well, what his heart was tinged with was anybody's guess. But Spence did note that he'd stopped asking to see his will. That probably meant he was a little more enthusiastic about the proposed strategy.

Or that he'd given up even hoping they'd come out of it with a whole skin.

Whatever Tedson's feelings on the matter, Spence was all for it. If it would get him his desire, he was more than all for it . . . he was over the moon for it. Just the thought of Elizabeth set his blood burning through his veins.

And the thought of being with her again, naked, skin to skin, sent the blood rushing to one vein in particular. He cursed his tight breeches, adjusted the growing erection that bulged uncomfortably beneath them and hurried to his room to throw a few essentials in a bag.

They were off on a wild journey. Where it would end, heaven only knew.

But if Spence had anything to say about it, it would end in

bed. And the heaven that was Elizabeth's body. It could not
sibly end anywhere else—not for him.

This was more than a lighthearted gamble for a woman's
affections. This was a step Spence had not imagined himself ever
taking. It was a commitment—a pledge—to the only lover he'd
ever found who was his complete and total match in every way
that mattered—in every way there could possibly be.

No doubt about it, Elizabeth was destined to be his. And
from tonight on, there would be no question in anybody's mind
of that fact, least of all *hers*.

• • •

Elizabeth spared barely a glance at the sober brougham awaiting her at the foot of the steps. She'd received a message from
Gregory that he had been delayed and would meet her at the ball.
It was like him to thoughtfully send a carriage and very like him
to make it a dull and undistinguishable brougham.

It rather described the man himself—sober and dull. And
tonight, Elizabeth was planning on presenting herself as his
future wife, thus putting all the eccentricities of her past behind
her. Closing the door on the "wild" side of Lady Elizabeth Wentworth.

She would stand next to him, her arm resting on his and
accept the congratulations of the curious, the vicious, the relieved
and the just plain couldn't-care-less. In other words, the *ton*—the
cream of London society. Her mother would be there, having torn
herself away from her charities devoted to "poor unfortunates"—
women who had fallen by the wayside and into prostitution of
varying degrees.

Her father would not be present this evening. Most likely
he was somewhere enjoying the services of some "poor unfortunates," thus ensuring there was always somebody to keep his wife
occupied.

It was an unending cycle of unemotional detachment that Elizabeth had lived with all her life. Her parents seldom spoke. Her mother looked pale and bitter at times, her father appeared awkward around his family.

Elizabeth sighed as she pulled her fur-lined cloak more snugly around her. It was cold, much too cold for this time of year. She found herself thankful for the small oasis of warmth inside the closed carriage. A hot brick took much of the chill off the air and she sighed with relief as the coachman shut the door against the harsh wind.

Her gown was of the most delicate silk—shades of blue and lavender emphasized her pale skin and made her eyes even more brilliant. She'd eschewed jewelry this evening, knowing she was to receive Gregory's mother's engagement ring. Another public link in the chain of her forthcoming nuptials.

And all the while, Elizabeth fought an inner war against a foe who haunted her dreams, dogged her footsteps and would not be denied. She'd not spoken his name in months, nor would she. It was as if by giving voice to it, he would become real again—too real for her to ignore as she so wished to do.

Because along with the vision of the tall, blond Viking good looks came a fear of the passion his touch could arouse. A fear of the overwhelming ecstasy he could create within her body. And a fear that with him she would really and truly lose control of the one thing she could call her own—her soul.

In spite of the heated interior, Elizabeth shivered again. This time it was not, however, a result of the unusually cool spring. It was totally and completely a result of thinking about one man. The man who had taken her innocence in a heated rush of loving that would provide the benchmark for intimacy the rest of her life.

The carriage slowed and Elizabeth was recalled from her musings to a sense of her surroundings. It was icily dark, another unusual feature of this strange time when the world refused to acknowledge spring and clung to its winter mists and winds. Deducing that she must be close to the Havers' mansion, which was on the outskirts of Mayfair, Elizabeth straightened her shoulders and shifted her cloak more closely around her knees.

Tonight was to be the first step on a road to a quietly appropriate future.

It was also going to close the door on a somewhat reprehensible past. Elizabeth tried to ignore a little voice whispering in her mind that thoughts of that past would be all she would have to keep her warm in the future. Marriage to Gregory certainly wasn't going to suffice.

Tears blinded her for a moment as Elizabeth mentally said farewell to the man she'd refused to allow herself to love. And she broke her vow . . . promising herself it was just this once and would *never* happen again.

"Oh *Spencer* . . ."

The carriage lurched, a gust of cold air blasted into her face and Elizabeth shrank back against the squabs as a large shadowed figure filled the gloom.

"Hello Elizabeth."

Chapter Three

Oh my *God . . .*"

"Well, thank you. But I think that's overstating things a tad, don't you?" Spence chuckled warmly, happy to be in the same carriage with his woman even if he was taking his life in his hands. Of course, if she'd had a weapon at hand she'd have shot him already so he was probably safe. For the moment, anyway.

"What the *hell* are you *doing* here? Get out of my carriage this instant."

"As a matter of fact—and although I hate to contradict a lady—this isn't *your* carriage. It's *my* carriage."

"But—what—you—"

Spence slid onto the cushioned seat next to Elizabeth and fought with the many folds of her cloak, hampered by the fur, the wool and the darkness. "God *damn* this thing. I know you're under there *somewhere.*" He finally peeled it away from her gown and wrapped his arms around her slender waist as she wriggled in an attempt to evade him. "Now that's *much* better."

He pulled her close and found her mouth with his lips. Cool full flesh met his on an indrawn gasp, but he ignored it. This wasn't a time for subtle wooing or gentle kisses that presaged more to come.

This was a claiming—a laying on of hands that would brand her forever. And a laying on of mouths.

Spence devoured Elizabeth, starving for her sweet taste on his tongue. He forced her lips apart, tearing a hand from her waist to hold her head in position for his invasion. Heat exploded in his gut, a fire that burned every thought from his brain and focused searing hunger down to his cock as it swelled beneath his breeches.

For a few seconds, Elizabeth was limp in his arms, her heart thudding frantically beneath the delicate silk and the soft breasts. Spence pulled her even closer, a fierce movement, demanding she respond, refusing to let her deny the desire rising between them.

Then she moaned. A tiny little sound that barely escaped her throat but Spence caught it and swallowed it down with the air she exhaled. He thrust his tongue deeply into the hot darkness of her mouth, slipping sensually over the ridges of her teeth and sliding over the slick flesh. She began to move her head, turning a little to admit him more fully and lifting her own tongue to return his rough caresses.

Her arms wrenched free from his embrace only to lift to his shoulders and twine around his neck. Fingers tore at his hair and with a lightning-quick movement Elizabeth launched herself into his lap, straddling his thighs, all the while keeping her lips glued to his.

Heedless of her gown, her cloak or anything but their embrace, she returned his fire with an inferno of her own. As if he'd uncorked a volcano with his kiss, Elizabeth erupted into a wild and passionate mass of writhing womanhood, body pressing against his, hips grinding down onto his groin and pushing against his erection in a frantic dance of desire.

It would have taken less than a second to unfasten his breeches and a scant second more to rip her gown free of his thighs. He could be inside her cunt and making her come in the space of a heartbeat.

Spence's hand quivered against the urge to free his cock. This wasn't how he intended their joining to take place. Although he wanted her with an urgency that passed anything civilized and had journeyed into the primal realms of lust, Spence knew he had to act carefully. His future was on the line now—this was no simple fuck in a carriage, this was the foundation for the rest of their lives.

"Elizabeth . . ." He eased his mouth from hers, a last tug at her tongue making him shudder.

She returned his sensuality with her own, sliding her lips over his and licking him hungrily. "Spence . . . oh *Spence . . .*" Her hips pushed down as her knees clamped against his thighs. "Fuck me, Spence . . . dear God, *please* fuck me . . ."

He swallowed down the urge to *do* just that. He had a plan, somewhere in the sex-fogged recesses of his brain. If he could manage to dredge some sanity out of that maelstrom, tell his cock to go to hell for a while and still hold Elizabeth on his lap, then there was a chance his plan would work.

"No."

The word was harsh, rasped through a throat that was seriously clogged with desire and the taste of his woman. But Spence held on to that word with his mental fingernails, knowing it was time to start convincing Elizabeth of a fundamental truth.

She was *his*.

• • •

"What?"

Elizabeth knew she was clenching her fists in Spence's hair, but at this point she didn't care if she tore out clumps of the damn stuff. Her jaw dropped as she absorbed the implications of his answer.

She said the first thing that came into her head. "Why not?"

He huffed out a laugh, rough and uneven against her body. "Not for lack of wanting, my sweet." He let his hips roll suggestively beneath her, catching her pussy with his hugely distorted breeches and the erection beneath.

"So? Why hold back?" Elizabeth shook her head, trying to clear it of the passionate mists swirling around inside.

Firm hands grasped her waist and lifted her, settling her once more on the seat beside him. She blinked, struck anew by the strength that lurked within his tall body. Spence never presented the image of a heavily muscled strongman, but the power was there nonetheless.

"We won't hold back. Not ever. But the time is not right. I won't fuck you here in a carriage where I can't touch you the way I want."

"You won't?"

"No. I want . . ." He paused and Elizabeth felt rather than saw his hand as he ran his fingers through his hair in the darkness. It was a gesture she remembered so well. "I want all night with you. Hour after hour to explore you. I want you naked and I want to be able to see you. I want to watch as I sink my cock in you and I want to see your face as I tease your nipples with my mouth . . ."

She shook as the force of his words washed over her, a hot tide of emotion and need. "You do?"

"Yes. I do. I've wanted that since the first time I saw you. Since the time we spent in bed together. And every minute that I've been apart from you."

"You never told me."

"You never gave me the chance." Spence shifted as the carriage bounced over a rut in the road. "You withdrew, Elizabeth. After that night—and the terrible way it ended—I thought you needed some time to adjust. To deal with what had happened."

Elizabeth drew in a shaky breath. Visions of that night still plagued her occasionally. "Indeed I did need time. It was clever of you to know." And it was part of Spence's charm . . . he knew when to push and when to back away. But she'd pushed him further, much further away from her than necessary. And it had nothing to do with the violence or the shooting.

It had everything to do with their loving. Of course, she could never tell *him* that.

"Then I got sent back to Europe on a mission and upon my return, *what* do I find?"

There was accusation in his tone, something that stirred Elizabeth's hackles and brought a lick of temper to her voice. "*Do* tell. Perhaps you found that I had decided to continue with my life, rather than put it on hold while awaiting your return. *If* you returned at all."

"I found . . ." This time there was no mistaking the anger beneath his careful words. "I found that my woman had gone and gotten engaged to somebody else. Another man—if he can be called that—was going to marry what was *mine*. Was going to spend the rest of his life with what was *mine*." His fingers found her wrist and clamped around it—hard. "Was going to *fuck what was mine*."

"*Your* woman? You're taking a lot for granted, aren't you?" She snorted and pulled her arm from his side, trying to dislodge his grip. She failed.

"Am I? I don't think so. But then again, perhaps your precious Geoffrey's kisses turn you into a spitfire the way mine do. Perhaps he makes you scream when he fucks you, the way I can."

Elizabeth felt him turn toward her. "Well, Lady Elizabeth? *Does he?*"

Anger blossomed within her, an anger born of passion and unfulfilled desire. *This* was the sort of thing that frightened Elizabeth. Spence's ability to send her flying into a place where she had no points of reference. No map to guide her, no safe handholds—just an ache that only he could ease.

"His name is *Gregory*—"

Her words were interrupted as the carriage rocked and slowed.

Lights appeared beyond the dark interior and Spence's silhouette loomed large as he moved to stare out the small window. "We're here."

"At the Havers'?" There was a sudden silence. Elizabeth frowned, her brain whirling through suspicions like a child's toy windmill in a savage gale. "We're not at the Havers' ball, are we?"

Spence unfastened the door and the vehicle swayed as he jumped down and turned to her.

"Spence. What have you done?" She shrank back in a futile effort to stay within the darkness. *Where am I?*

"With me." The dim light showed Elizabeth his eyes gleaming as he held his hand out to her. "You're safe. You're with me."

She snorted. *Safe* and *Spencer Marchwood* were not words she tended to use in the same sentence. "You've kidnapped me, haven't you?"

"I suppose you can call it that if you want." He shrugged. "It's just a word. I prefer to think of this as a visit. A few hours together when we can catch up on old times."

"I need to leave, Spence. I *have* to be at the Havers' ball. I'm announcing my engagement tonight. Everyone will be there . . ." Her voice tapered off. "*That's* why you took me tonight, isn't it? So that I can't get engaged."

Spence sighed. "Elizabeth, I'm freezing my arse off here. We can discuss this much more comfortably inside." He nodded over his shoulder to where some dim lights were shining through drawn draperies. "You'll enjoy the fire, some hot food and a rather nice brandy. Couldn't we continue this conversation in there?"

Elizabeth swallowed. She was cold too, even wrapped in her cloak. But she knew that the man standing before her could warm her with a mere touch. He was danger personified to her peace of mind and a challenge to her spirit. He always had been. He knew how to fire her imagination and ignite her desire. He *saw* her— the *real* Elizabeth—and it was to her that he was speaking.

The real Elizabeth knew there was only one acceptable answer. "All right."

With a relieved sigh that sent white misty breath swirling around him, Spence pulled her from the carriage and swept her into his arms.

"Good God, Spence. I can walk." Elizabeth gasped as her feet never touched the ground.

"I know. But I like carrying you. So be quiet and allow me to enjoy myself. Besides I wouldn't be surprised if there were a few icy patches here. This damn cold wind—"

Shivering, Elizabeth nodded. "They say 'tis the coldest spring ever and the summer will likely be as bad. Did you know the Thames froze? It hasn't done that since . . . well, I understand it's been a long time."

They might have been two acquaintances discussing the weather. Two people who had met over tea in a drawing room, or in front of a painting at a gallery. The conversation was impersonal and correct.

But Elizabeth was uncomfortably aware of that all-too-familiar wetness between her thighs. The liquid evidence of a desire that only Spence could summon with a touch of his lips or even a look from his eyes. She wondered if he was similarly affected.

They reached the hallway and thankfully the front door slammed behind them, a signal for Spence to lower Elizabeth gently to her feet.

As she slithered down his body her cloak caught itself between them, snagged around a very solid erection bulging from his breeches. He winced as she glanced up at him.

Oh yes. He was indeed similarly affected.

In spite of the circumstances that faced her, Elizabeth permitted a small grin to cross her face. Perhaps he was telling the truth. Perhaps he *had* wanted her all those months they were apart. Only time would tell.

She allowed Spence to take her cloak and lead her into a small warm parlor where a fire blazed and heavy drapes were drawn against the night. A tray rested on the shining sideboard and Spence moved to serve himself from one of the chafing dishes.

"Eat, Elizabeth. I know you women and these parties. You don't eat a thing beforehand and end up starving hungry halfway through the night."

She joined him, nibbling at a lobster patty, her appetite for food negligible. Her appetite for Spence, however, was burgeoning. To distract herself she looked around. "Are you going to tell me where we are?"

"At a friend's house. He's away and I often come here when I need some quiet time to think. There are few servants and what needs I have Tedson attends to."

"Ah. The redoubtable Tedson." She smiled. "I will assume he was our driver this evening."

Spence grinned. "You are very astute." There was a warm and genuinely amused curve to his lips, which melted Elizabeth's small remaining knot of anger.

She put down the food. "Not really. I just know you."

"Yes, you do. And I know you." Spence also put down his plate. "For example, I know that right now you'd probably enjoy a brandy."

Elizabeth moved to the warmth of the fire and stared into it. "Yes, that sounds nice."

Glasses clattered and then he was at her side, offering a snifter with a splash of rich golden aromatic liquid. "Cheers, Elizabeth. To us." Spence held his own drink out and raised an eyebrow in challenge.

"And if there is no *us*?"

"There will be." He clinked his glass to hers. "Never doubt it, sweetheart. There will be. And do you know why?" He sipped and then put his glass on the mantelpiece as he moved to stand close—too close—before her.

"No, why?" She held her place, refusing to step away from him, from the challenge he presented.

The glass in her hand trembled as Spence slid warm palms up over her arms to her shoulders where his fingers toyed with the delicate fabric of her gown. "Because I know *you* too. Because you're a woman who won't spill her drink. A woman who knows that the finest brandy is to be savored, yes?"

She ignored the heat of his hands and sipped, relishing the fiery caress of the brandy as it trickled down her throat. "Absolutely." She lifted her chin.

"You'll keep holding that glass in spite of anything. Unruffled, undisturbed by anything or anybody."

"Of course."

"Good. Keep holding that drink."

With a swift and decisive move, Spence tore the gown away from Elizabeth's chest, revealing full breasts tipped with taut rosy nipples. The quick gasp she took lifted them shakily away from her body.

Spence wasted no time. He dipped his head and suckled one deep into his mouth.

The brandy glass shattered on the hearth.

Chapter Four

Lost in the wonder of Elizabeth's body, Spence barely heard the glass as it fell to the marble tiles. He only knew he was surrounded by her fragrance—the unique scent of woman that clouded his mind and filled his heart to overflowing.

He swept her up into his arms once more and carried her across the room to a sofa, all the while keeping his face glued to her breast, his tongue busy teasing and toying with one delectable nipple.

She was shifting in his embrace, panting a little, mewling tiny sounds as he suckled her harder, catching the nub against the roof of his mouth and tugging fiercely.

Elizabeth gasped. "*Christ Jesus*, Spence . . ."

He grinned inwardly. It was a rare and beautiful thing to have one's woman find religion beneath one's lips. Toppling down, they tumbled together, Spence finally releasing her breast only to slide his hands from her ankles to her thighs in one long rough swish of fabric and flesh.

She was bared to him, her breasts trembling, her legs parting even as his hands stroked the white skin glowing against the soft hues of her gown.

He pushed the silk higher, banding it across her waist, revealing all of her. All the secrets he'd discovered, the sights he'd lain in bed imagining whilst alone—he dined on the vision of her like a starving man at a ten-course banquet.

Her mound drew him as if it were a lodestone. Shining black

curls softly arrowed the way to bliss—gleaming pussy lips were dewing with her juices even as he looked at her. "*Elizabeth* . . . so perfect . . . so *beautiful* . . ." He stroked her mound with one finger, reverently slipping through the curls to reveal her desire.

She shook even more as he grazed the tiny knot of sensitive nerves lurking just beneath the skin and sighed as his finger traveled on to part the heated folds and slick her body's liquids over swollen petals of flesh.

Spence settled next to the sofa and continued his gentle petting, repeating his movements, attuned to every twitch and shiver of his woman. His fingers were encountering even more moisture now, her body weeping liberal tears of passion as he stimulated her.

Dragging his gaze from her pussy, he glanced upward, past the hard beads of her nipples to her face. Her eyes were almost closed, mere slits of gleaming blue, barely focusing. A hot blush suffused the white skin, turning it rosy from her chest to her forehead. Her lips were lush and parted, shining from his kisses and the movement of her tongue as it flicked at them, a quick and involuntary move echoing the passage of his finger across her most delicate flesh.

Lord how he wanted to fuck her. He wanted those lips on his cock almost as much as he wanted that cunt around his cock. She was everything he'd remembered and more—so much more.

His cock was strangling beneath his breeches, but for the moment he shoved that discomfort aside. This was all about Elizabeth, this moment was an integral part of his plan to make her his for the rest of their lives.

With that goal in mind, Spence leaned forward and thrust his face between her thighs.

Her scream echoed around the room.

• • •

Elizabeth felt the cry burst from her lungs and vaguely heard the high-pitched sound reverberate back into her ears. But it was a secondary impression when compared to the sensation of Spence's head between her legs.

He'd been the first to introduce her to this particular pleasure and the only one she could ever imagine doing it to her.

And oh my—did he know *how* to do it to her.

His tongue was gentle at first, lapping softly at her skin, loving the tiny spot that made her tremble. Little circles, little licks, hot breath from his nostrils fanning the heat that was spreading through her belly.

His fingers tightened on her legs and eased them farther apart, granting him better access to her secrets.

She didn't fight him. *Hah* . . . she *welcomed* him, eagerly moving so that he could touch her in all the right places in all the right ways. For as long as she could remember, Elizabeth had known she was a sensual and sexual woman. It was a dark, shadowy secret best kept hidden, even though this day and age prided itself on enlightenment.

It still wasn't enlightened enough to grant an unmarried woman license to explore her own sensuality. She'd had to bend some rules, dodge some restrictions and find like-minded friends. And after all *that*, she'd found Spence.

A man who'd taken her past the fleshly limits of her virginity without a blink, who'd held her hand and tugged her along with him into a world of passion, desire and incredible physical lovemaking.

Like now. Like this moment when his tongue probed deeper, moving faster over her clit, making her hips grind upward in need and her breath come faster as her arousal grew.

He'd push her, she knew. She wanted it—*demanded* it. There were heights Elizabeth had yet to climb. One night with Spence hadn't been enough. Would never be enough. All these thoughts ran rampant through her mind as she lost herself in the pleasure of Spence's mouth and the talents of his lips and tongue.

Then he sucked on her and plunged his tongue inside her. And she forgot to think at all. She could only feel.

Feel the subtle vibrations of his lips as he hummed against her while delving inside her body and moving his tongue curiously within the slick channel.

Feel the shivers of excitement build as her clit engorged and her pussy lips swelled in response to the touch of his skin to hers.

And then feel it all subside as he withdrew a little.

"*God*—" she cried out, scrabbling with her fingers for his head, reaching to pull him back against her.

"*Sssh. Wait*, Elizabeth mine. Wait—let it build—be patient..." His hoarse whisper percolated through the fog of need that swirled in her brain. *Patient?* He expected her to be *patient?* When she trembled on the edge of a massive climax that threatened to destroy her? Was he completely and totally out of his mind?

"Elizabeth. Look at me."

The command was harsh, surprising her, making her turn her head and focus on him with difficulty.

"See *me*, Elizabeth. Know *me*. Know who I am. Just as I know you." He met her gaze with his, eyes burning, color heightened, blond hair mussed and tumbling loose the way she would always associate with him—with sex. With how he looked when he fucked her.

"I know you, Spence." She rasped the words past an obstruction in her throat. It was lust, pure and simple lust, choking her with the force of its need.

"Do you?" He shrugged. "I'm not sure." His hand went back to her clit, lazily playing around it, keeping it awake, alive, still eager to erupt . . . "You know my body intimately. You know me in bed, you know the feeling of my cock inside you. Of my tongue against your pussy . . . my hands at your breasts . . ."

His words were blunt and erotic and Elizabeth knew they were all part and parcel of his lovemaking skills. She responded to them as much now as she had the first time they'd fucked—the first time he'd taken her beyond the stars into an orgasm that had shattered her girlish illusions of delicately polite sex forever.

"*Yesss . . .*" She moaned as he pressed on just the *right* spot . . . "*Oh please yessss . . .*"

"No. Not yet." Spence's voice was rough and unyielding. "I'm going to make you come, Elizabeth. You're going to shudder and scream and I'm going to watch you while you do it all. I might even suck on you as your pussy weeps and showers me with your honey. Yes, I believe I'd enjoy that . . ."

"I don't—I can't *think*, Spence—" His fingers were driving her insane and she spoke nothing but the truth. She couldn't think anymore. She couldn't do anything but squirm and thrust her hips into his touch, silently begging for more, for the ultimate touch that would relieve the tension making her shake like a leaf.

"More?" It was a single-word interrogative that offered so much.

How could he remain so detached? So impersonal? Elizabeth darted a quick glance at him through slitted eyelids. He was staring at her body as it drenched him. A muscle flickered low on his cheek and his lips were parted. He swallowed, a rough movement of neck and throat.

Her mind easing a little, Elizabeth closed her eyes. He was with her. Whatever he might say, he was with her. *He always was.*

"Are you ready?" His hand moved with purpose now, his caresses bolder and stronger. Fingers probed and flicked and as he knelt more closely even his hot breath became a stimulant.

"Are you *stupid*?" She ignored his quick chuckle as she choked on her response, rapidly approaching the edge of what had to be death. If he didn't make her come within moments, she was going to boot his body across the room and do it her-self, damn him.

But true to his word, Spence buried his face once more in her pussy, roughly this time, thrusting with his tongue and his nose and his mouth, urging her higher and higher until she found the sounds in the room were her own screams of pleasure.

His fingers dug cruelly into her flesh, her legs were stretched wide and still he devoured her, eating at her with every skilled muscle of his mouth, licking at the liquids she drowned him with and finally sucking—hard—directly on the seat of her arousal, her clit.

She cried out—a shriek of mingled pain and ecstasy—and then rocketed out of her body into someplace where there was only Spence and his hands and his face and his breath . . .

• • •

Watching Elizabeth's face as she flew into her orgasm sent Spence's heart winging with her. He licked his lips, tasting her tangy sweetness as he held her thighs and felt the shudders racking her body.

Making her come with his mouth and his tongue was an indescribable thrill for him, a sort of masculine moment of triumph— *look, I did that to her. I made her feel that explosion. And without even using my cock.*

Her flesh trembled with the rolling spasms that still ravaged her and those beautiful breasts rose and fell rapidly as she panted and gasped for air. He knew his fingers were probably leaving bruises on her thighs, but he couldn't help himself from holding her tight—as if by holding her that way he could keep her beside him forever.

He knew it was not so. There were decisions to be made and tonight he would risk his future and his happiness in a mighty gamble. Whether it would work or not, he had no idea.

As Elizabeth eased back into the reality of the salon, Spence sagged next to her and rested his head on the softness of her belly, dropping a light kiss on the damp skin. Fingers scrabbled at his hair, tugging him, moving his head so that she could look at him.

"Spence . . . that was . . ." She shook her head tiredly. "There are no words."

He grinned at her. "I know."

Her grasp tightened almost painfully as she managed to grin back. "And you're a self-satisfied, egotistically immodest man taking far too much pleasure in your male accomplishments." She paused. "And you haven't fucked me yet."

"Believe me, I know that too."

"Then shall we . . ." Elizabeth went to move, to stand perhaps, or part her thighs for him.

Spence swallowed. The dice were in his hand and it was time to throw them onto the metaphorical table. "Not yet, my heart."

She frowned. "Spence, you've said no to me twice tonight." With a quick gesture, Elizabeth tugged at her skirts, covering her mound and the slick shine of her desire. "Another woman might interpret your refusal as lack of interest. Another woman might think you're simply playing with her. Another woman might feel used . . ."

Spence watched her eyes, the play of golden flecks ebbing and flowing with her emotions. "But you're not another woman, Elizabeth. You know better."

"I thought I did." She gazed directly at him, not quite managing to hide the uncertainty lurking behind her stare.

Fighting for composure, Spence stood and shrugged out of his jacket. He knew his erection was obvious but cared not one whit. Casually he tossed the garment over a chair. "You do know me. You know me better than anyone, I believe."

His hands went to his shirt, pulling the cravat loose and sending it after his jacket. "You know how much I want you, how I desire you—how I could fuck you right this minute and keep on fucking you until we both passed out from exhaustion."

A smile crossed her face. "I think I have enough strength left . . ."

Spence turned away to hide his answering grin. "I can't do it, though. This isn't the same time and these aren't the same circumstances as before, Elizabeth. Things have changed. Our lives have changed. Six months ago we met and found incredible pleasure together. I fucked you, you fucked me. We explored each other in ways that I never imagined could be so amazing."

She swallowed, a ripple of skin along her neck. "Yes."

"I'd planned on wooing you, showing you how I felt and then asking your parents for your hand in marriage. All the usual stuff—what you'd expect from me—in spite of our history together." He shrugged. "The government got in the way and I found myself back in Europe."

"Yes. I know." She watched him.

"When I got back and read the announcement of your engagement, I realized that I might be too late. That I might have lost you to some traditional notion of marriage. Some ordinary chap who meets your requirements for the man you want to spend the rest of your life with."

He unfastened his shirt and pulled it loose, letting it hang freely over his breeches. "I couldn't believe that the woman I shared a night of ecstasy with could change like that. I won't believe it. I can't. So . . . tonight, Elizabeth, there's a choice to be made."

"I don't understand . . ."

Spence took a breath. *Here it comes.* "Tonight, you will *choose.* Here and now, you will choose the course of your life. If you choose to follow the conventional path and marry Geoffrey whatshisname, then simply ring that bell." He nodded to the bellpull by the fireplace. "Tedson will bring you warm garments and have the carriage ready to take you back to town and your future with another man."

Her face remained blank, expressionless. For once, Spence could read nothing of her thoughts. But he carried on regardless, knowing there was no other course of action at this point. "If you choose to follow what I believe is still in your *heart*, then go up the stairs you'll find behind that other door." He nodded to the almost-concealed exit in the shadows of one corner. "They lead to my bedroom." He strode away from her side to reach for the handle. "I'll be there, Elizabeth. Waiting for you. If you come to me, it will be because you are willing to spend the rest of your life at my side as my wife. Make no mistake, you'll be giving yourself completely and totally to me. As I have already given myself to you."

He opened the door. "It's your choice. I cannot make this decision for you. It's both our lives, but you are the one who must decide how they will proceed from this night on. I *know* what I want. Now you must ask yourself what *you* want. What you *truly* want." He glanced over his shoulder to see her sitting immobile on the sofa, eyes wide, a pulse thudding rapidly at the base of her neck.

"*Choose*, Elizabeth. I shall abide by your decision. *Forever.*"

Chapter Five

The door closed behind Spence with a gentle thud and a deafening silence fell over the room, broken only by the popping of a log in the fireplace and the loud thumping of Elizabeth's heart as it rang in her ears.

He wanted *her* to choose? To make a decision that would have unspeakably enormous consequences on so many lives?

Damn him to hell and back for leaving me in the first place.

Awkwardly she rose, limbs heavy and disconnected somehow, as if her body wasn't quite all back together yet. Her brain certainly wasn't where it was supposed to be, since all she could think of right at that moment was Spence, lying naked in his bed, waiting for her.

And planning wonderful things to do to her. All of which she knew she would enjoy enormously.

Her dress snagged on the arm of the sofa, distracting her and pulling her back into the present—into the dilemma facing her. She straightened the silk as best she could, covering her breasts once more with the remnants of the bodice. Her skirts were creased and limp, her thighs damp and sticky. She felt relaxed, content and almost sated. She also felt troubled, confused and indecisive.

Walking to the fireplace, Elizabeth stared into the flames as if they held the answer to her questions.

What do I want?

Spence. No doubt about it.

So why not just go upstairs and take him?

Because I'm afraid.

Of Spence?

No. Not of him—never of him. I'm afraid . . . of what loving him might *mean*.

And *that*, reflected Elizabeth, was the crux of the matter. For most of her life she'd awoken each morning to find her father irritable and distant at one end of the breakfast table. Her mother had been petulant and equally distant at the other.

It had been an example of "wedded bliss" that Elizabeth promised herself she would never emulate. Never would she love a man and give him the chance to disappoint her, to hurt her, to destroy her hopes—the way her father had destroyed her mother.

Always intelligent and quick to comprehend, the child Elizabeth hadn't taken long to discern the nature of her parents' marriage. Her mother had discovered charitable works, pouring her emotional discontent into the wounds of the poor women on the streets.

Her father had discovered the women on the streets. Well, in all fairness, his mistresses were probably of a much higher caliber than the lowly streetwalker, but the end result was the same. He debauched, she redeemed. An endless, lifelong cycle of discontent—at least that's how Elizabeth viewed it.

Loving Spence had shown her, in those weeks after their passion had played itself out at Jordan Lyndhurst's, that she too could fall deeply into a man's thrall. That Spence could easily wield sufficient power to destroy her in much the same way as her father had destroyed her mother.

In fact, when she learned of his departure for Europe, Elizabeth's heart had definitely cracked.

Gregory Sanderson had been the putty she'd used to heal the fissure. Nondemanding, quietly attentive, admiring—Gregory had done all the right things to calm her, had done all the right things to show her how precious she was to him. To demonstrate his lukewarm affections by dropping a light kiss on her hand, accompanied by a "speaking" look from his sweet spaniel eyes.

Lukewarm pretty much described their relationship and that was something Elizabeth felt she could live with. There was no fear of Gregory ever shredding her heart. Simply because she hadn't given it to him.

She had, unfortunately, given it to somebody else—somebody who was waiting for her right at this moment.

And it was at *this* very moment that Lady Elizabeth Wentworth stepped aside from the trappings of society. She pushed away the conventional wisdoms, ignored the prescribed behaviors demanded of her sex and her position.

She mentally stripped herself bare and took a long hard look at what was left, only to find she wasn't sure she liked what she saw.

A woman, possessed of intelligence and wit, of presentable physical attributes—some might say desirable—and a respectable income. She was blessed with good lineage, an education better than many and a curiosity about life greater than most.

She also possessed a fear that shadowed her accomplishments and threw her attributes into darkness, overwhelming her emotions. It was this fear that needed examining, because it was this fear that had sent her running to Gregory Sanderson and the safety he represented.

Elizabeth asked herself a difficult question. Was she going to let her life be dictated by fear—or by passion?

Could she live as the essentially proper and colorless wife of Gregory Sanderson? Or could she dare to seize the rainbows offered by Spencer Marchwood? Even though they might sear her hand—*and* her heart.

As she turned these matters over in her mind, Elizabeth felt the truth of her existence emerging within her. She was not a woman who could—or would—ever settle for less than the best. What had made her pick Gregory was an evasion, a lie—a refusal to be bluntly honest with the one person who really mattered—*herself*.

And the truth that now began to glow brightly in her brain set all these things in order and made her decision a foregone conclusion. Nobody but Spence would do for Elizabeth. Because although others had touched her hand and a few had even touched her body, he had touched what no one else had reached.

Her soul.

She blinked away the haze of her thoughts and looked around the room. There was something she had to do before going to Spence. But go to Spence she would. And once she had set foot on that road there was no going back—for either of them.

Ever.

• • •

Upstairs, Spence waited.

The silence of the house weighed heavily on his shoulders, since in spite of his resolution and his convictions, he wasn't exactly sure this gamble of his would have the desired outcome.

Elizabeth was a very intelligent woman. But she also seemed to be able to distance herself from that part of her where her emotions ruled her thoughts and her actions. Spence had known that from the beginning of their association—their night together had surpassed any he'd known. However, Elizabeth's emotional response had revealed a woman who had bottled up her desires, suppressed a portion of her personality to conform with some vague image she had created in her own mind.

He'd freed that part of her, relished it and loved it. That was the part of her that had responded so wildly to his kisses and his mouth and that was the part of her Spence hoped to see come through the small door in the paneling.

Which obstinately remained closed.

He stripped off the remainder of his clothing and slipped into a robe, needing the warmth of the wool around him more for comfort than for heat. The fire blazed and Spence doused most of the candles, leaving the room snug and lit by the orange-yellow flames licking around the logs.

She should have made her choice by now. She should be coming to him any minute now.

He threw himself down in a chair and hooked one leg over the arm in an effort to look casual. It failed, since the robe parted and his aroused cock thrust up into the air. Grimacing, he straightened, feeling like a hound who'd scented a bitch in heat. No point in looking like a . . . a . . . randy bastard. Never mind that he was. Randy, *not* a bastard.

A distant sound pulled Spence away from his absurd internal discourse.

It was the bell.

Oh God, no.

Spence's heart missed a beat as the implications of that little chiming from below him sank into his brain.

She'd rung for Tedson. She was leaving. Leaving him and their future—turning her back on whatever happiness they both could have seized from life. He'd failed to convince her, either with his words or his deeds.

Noooooo.

A red haze of fury descended on Spence, as he stood with his fists clenched staring into the fire. A chill poured over his skin in direct contrast to the fire of his emotions. His anger shook him, combined as it was with desolate hurt and a sense of loss that defied description. He'd been so sure . . .

A loud creak made him jump and he turned, expecting to see Tedson.

What he saw—was *Elizabeth*. Hesitantly she entered through the small door, shutting it behind her with somewhat exaggerated care.

"Hello, Spence. Here I am."

Speech had temporarily deserted him. He could only stare at her, devour her with his gaze, drink up the vision she presented in her tattered gown, blue eyes wide and staring back at him.

"I have made my choice." She swallowed, her throat moving as she glanced downward and away from him. "I choose you."

"So I see." His voice was harsh as he drove air past the obstruction in his throat. *She was here. She was in his room.* "And yet I could've sworn I heard the bell."

Her head jerked up. "Oh God, I never *thought* . . ." She winced. "I rang for Tedson. I needed him to take a note back to London for me. Or at least make sure it was delivered to Gregory. He deserved at least that courtesy." Elizabeth crossed the room, hurrying to his side. "I'm sorry, Spence. Honestly. It never crossed my mind that you'd misinterpret my actions."

She touched his sleeve, letting her fingers rest on the softness of the fabric and yet moving them so that she could dig down to the hardness of his arm beneath. "Spence, I'm sorry. God, I'm sorry. For everything."

Blue eyes begged his understanding, his comprehension. "There's never been anyone but you. Not really. Gregory was . . ."

Spence watched her. "Was what?"

She sighed. "*Safe.* In a word, he was safe."

"And I'm not?"

She choked out a laugh. "Christ, no. You're anything *but.*" It was her turn to stare into the fire. "Safe means uncomplicated. Safe means gentle, harmless, not likely to hurt me."

Spence moved, his immobility gone. He reached for her cheek, cradling it in his palm. "I'd die rather than hurt you, Elizabeth. Believe me."

She turned, her face a slick of softness against his skin. "I believe you. But the hurt I'm talking about is the sort of hurt you could inflict without realizing it. The sort of hurt that happens between two people who—who are as close as we are."

"You mean between a man and a woman who love each other?"

She stared at him once more, silent for a moment. "Do you love me, Spence?"

He paused, understanding the importance of those five simple words. How to answer? How to convince her that there would be no other—*ever*—in his life? That she was all things to him and that she'd driven thoughts of every other woman he'd had clean out of his mind?

That he could think of nothing and nobody else but her?

Finally, he sighed and pulled her into his arms where she belonged. "Yes." It was all he could say.

"Then that's enough. Because I love you too." Her arms slid around him and the heat of her breasts brushed a glancing caress against his chest. She dropped a kiss on his bare skin. "I am sorry I scared you." Her tongue flicked out to taste him. "I never thought, really, about the consequences of ringing that bell."

"No, you didn't, did you?" Spence moved a little, exposing more of his chest to her kisses.

"It was rather naughty of me, wasn't it?" Firm teeth nipped at his muscles, followed by another longer kiss.

Spence's hands slipped down past her waist and grasped her buttocks. They filled his palms, overflowing with softness. "It was very naughty of you. And you know what happens to naughty girls, don't you?"

Lost in her own private pleasures, Elizabeth barely heard him as she discovered a flat nipple and busily circled it with her tongue. "Hmmm?"

He squeezed her and then lifted her clean off her feet. "They get themselves a spanking."

Chapter Six

Once again Spence turned Elizabeth's world upside down.

Only this time, he did so in a literal sense, sweeping her feet out from beneath her and tumbling them both willy-nilly onto the bed. She found herself caught in a tangle of her gown, his robe and her hair, which had fallen loose under such rough treatment.

Hard thighs crushed her breasts and she realized that she was lying across his knees, head dangling toward the floor, her bottom right where he wanted it. And bare too.

"God, Elizabeth. You have what must be the world's most beautiful arse." A hand stroked her, caressing the flesh of her backside, smoothing from her spine to the tops of her thighs in a swoop of heat and sensuality.

"Spence . . . mwffummppp . . ." She spat past a mouthful of silk and hair. "What the hell . . ."

"Shhh." He pushed her head down and locked a strong arm across her shoulders, holding her right where she was. "You're about to get a demonstration of what a stern disciplinarian I can be."

A tickling finger dabbled between her legs and she fought down a giggle. "Stern, hmmm?"

There was a whoosh of air and suddenly a very hard palm collided with her buttocks, the resultant smack echoing loudly through the room. *"Owwwwww."* Elizabeth's legs squirmed and she writhed beneath his hold. "Spence, you *bastard*. That *hurt* . . ."

"Really?" She felt him lean over and drop a kiss where he'd spanked her. "Or does it feel . . . *arousing*?" His tongue licked at her skin. "Perhaps it's a little of both . . ."

Elizabeth explored the sensations she was experiencing. The brush of air over her naked backside was unusual and somewhat erotic. And the spot that Spence had punished now glowed with a sensitive heat. Each touch of his lips or his tongue was magnified a dozen times over.

"I . . . er . . ."

The words were driven out of her head by another sharp smack, this time low on her buttocks, near—very near—her pussy. Boiling hot nerves responded, sending a flood of moisture to her cunt and her thighs.

Spence, the ever-observant and annoyingly thorough man that he was, noticed immediately. She bit back a moan but he heard that too, chuckling softly as he pushed his hand between her thighs and played with swollen pussy lips. "So wet. I love making you wet, Elizabeth."

He let his fingers roam back toward her arse, daringly plunging between her cheeks and spreading her moisture on the exquisitely sensitive muscles he discovered there.

She moaned, this time making no effort to hide the sound of arousal. His touch was driving her mad, stimulating every sense she had.

"*Spence . . .*"

He didn't seem to hear her. "Such a beautiful bottom on such a naughty girl." He spanked her once more, this time catching the fullness of one cheek and making her gasp. "Look how pink your skin is when I smack you. All that hot flesh. And tingling too, I'll wager." Once more he delved between her legs and smeared her juices over her burning bottom. "And so sensitive here—"

"*God, Spence . . .*" It was nearly a shriek as his finger found the tight ring of muscles between her cheeks and pressed hard against it. Slick with her own moisture, Elizabeth's body responded to the intrusion with a shudder and a clenching spasm that echoed down through her pussy to her clit.

"I'm going to fuck you here one of these days, Elizabeth." He moved his finger against her, making her cry out with a mixture of pleasure and apprehension. "Not yet. Not for a while yet. But there isn't a part of you that won't belong to me. Do you understand?"

His hand moved, only to return with one more hard slap—the sharp sound of flesh on flesh ringing in Elizabeth's ears. "Yesss . . . oh *God . . . yes . . . Spence*, do it now . . . fuck me . . ."

She was lost. Lost in a realm of heat and fire stoked by the knowing hand of Spencer Marchwood. He'd seduced her, body and soul, into his world of erotic pleasures and she was his willing captive.

Gone were her inhibitions, her apprehensions about giving too much power to one man. It was too late to even worry about it—Spence had taken her heart the first time he'd touched her, smiled at her and kissed her breast.

Lying prone over his knees, her bottom naked and burning, Elizabeth realized that the thrum of her heartbeat was a rhythm of pleasure, of delight. That nothing Spence would ever do to her could destroy the trust and love that had grown so quickly between them.

She relaxed into the knowledge that they were two halves of one whole, that she'd been lucky enough to find the one man who could understand what she needed and give it to her without restraint. And she also knew that at some point she'd be able to share her fears with him, the reasons behind her withdrawal, her ridiculous engagement to totally the wrong person.

But for right now . . .

Daringly, Elizabeth freed one arm to dangle loosely, finding Spence's ankle and tracing up the muscles to his thigh and beyond. She knew he was aroused too, since his cock was digging into her side.

She wanted that cock. It was time to turn the tables on Sir Stern Disciplinarian and introduce him to Lady Wanton Woman.

With a final wriggle, Elizabeth slid off Spence's lap and onto her knees on the floor. Which, coincidentally, put her exactly in the right spot—eye to eye with his cock—to effect an introduction. She felt him freeze as she reached for his thighs and pushed them apart.

"Take this off." She tugged at his robe. "It'll only get in the way." She slithered closer, shedding what was left of her gown uncaringly to one side.

"In the way of what?" He obeyed, more than ready to share her nakedness.

"You'll see." Elizabeth licked her lips—and grinned.

• • •

That little smile went straight to Spence's balls, tightening the sac around its precious cargo. His cock hardened to an impossible rigidity under her gaze, weeping a tiny pearl of excitement as she moved near.

"Elizabeth . . ." He murmured her name just for the pleasure of saying it, more than anything else. She ignored him, her attention focused on the instrument of his pleasure between his legs.

With delicate precision, she curved her hand around his length, learning anew his contours and how best to hold him. With her thumb tracing the vein that ran from base to tip and her fingers resting around as much of him as she could grasp, Elizabeth dipped her head and lightly touched her tongue to the drop of liquid.

Could there be a more exciting moment than this? None that he could think of right this minute. He wanted to collapse back on the bed and let her mouth do its work. He wanted to sit bolt upright and watch her lips as they slid down his cock and back up again, leaving a trail of shining warmth behind.

He wanted to delve into the black silky hair and hold her head close to his body, thrusting himself down her throat, filling her, finally coming in great bursts of essence, marking her as his—forever.

Unable to decide, Spence simply leaned back and rested on his elbows, opening himself to her attentions and still retaining enough presence of mind to watch as she cherished him with her mouth.

Her tongue coiled and moved and slipped around, a living creature of pleasure within her head, devising its own torturous delights in concert with her lips. She shifted, one hand reaching for his calf and moving upward, fingernails dragging harshly through the hairs and over the skin. She was probably leaving marks, a brand of her possession of his cock.

He didn't care. The little sting of her scratches added to the sheer ecstasy of her mouth dragging across his arousal. She could carve her initials on his shinbone right this second and he probably wouldn't flinch.

Although he wasn't about to suggest it—Elizabeth was unpredictable, to say the least. She might find the notion charming and grab a letter opener.

Spence smiled as black hair tickled the inside of his thigh. The sounds of Elizabeth's mouth sucking at his cock, coupled with her little moans and grunts of joy as she pulled him deeply to the back of her throat, rattled more than his brains and the rafters.

They resounded deep in the very core of his being, crawling around the acoustic recesses of his soul and finally settling into the spots that seemed created just to hold them there.

A soft sigh of pleasure escaped his lips and she responded, drawing back from his cock, replacing her lips with her hand and continuing to stroke him. "Are you all right?"

It had to be a metaphorical question. He'd never been more *all right* than he was at this moment. "Yes. I'm very all right."

"Good." Her head dipped between his thighs once more, but instead of returning to lick and love his arousal, Elizabeth surprised him.

She moved his body a little and dropped a kiss on his balls.

"Good God, *Elizabeth* . . ." Spence jumped a little. They'd played together before with lips and mouths, but this . . . this was outside of anything he'd taught her.

"Sshhh." She continued her attentions. Soft kisses were replaced by warm and gentle licks, a massage that blew Spence's brains out of his left ear.

He wanted to squirm, to shudder, to erupt in a fountain of come all over her face, to bury his balls against her and coincidentally to shriek in fear. If she wasn't very careful she could be jeopardizing the future of a lineage that could trace its roots back to William the Conqueror.

When she delicately parted her lips wide and encased his balls within her mouth, Spence gave up the ghost.

"Holy fucking *Christ. Oh Jesus, God above.*"

He felt her lips curve as her tongue caressed him, then just as gently released him to fall free of her mouth. "Good?"

"I—uh—you—uh—" Speech was, apparently, beyond his capabilities, since she'd just damn near sucked his entire store of intellect down to his crotch. The head he was now thinking with wasn't up to conversation.

"I'm glad you are not displeased."

Spence dragged his eyelids apart and stared at her through a haze of erotic lust. Blue eyes blazed back at him from a face tinged with heat and excitement. Her hair was a tousled mass of black silk that spilled over his body and he realized he'd never seen anything so beautiful in his life.

"I wish I could paint. I'd paint you now." It was an abstract comment, but one that Spence realized said so much more than just a simple sentiment. He wanted to hold on to this moment with both hands. To preserve this instant in time when his world was truly perfect. When nothing but love surrounded him, and his woman was with him sharing a cocoon of passion. It was precious, unique and fleeting. It could not—sadly—be preserved for more than a heartbeat or two.

Elizabeth's lips curved and moisture sheened her eyes. "I understand."

Therein lay more beauty . . . she did indeed understand. He was never going to have to explain things to Elizabeth. They thought alike and comprehended each other's abstract concepts with no more clarification than a word or two. If only he'd realized all these things earlier . . .

"I'd like to paint you too. To capture the look on your face right now." Her words were soft, her hands just as soft as they caressed his cock and his balls. "To capture this . . ." She glanced down at his erection, dewed with her saliva and his own drops of excitement. "I'd like to capture the taste of you, the heat of you, the scent of you . . ." Her lips brushed the very tip of the swollen head and he groaned.

"And I'd love to capture the expression in your eyes as I do this . . ."

Spence knew his eyes were widening as her hand delved deeply between his legs and beyond his balls to a spot where her fingers paused. He choked then shuddered as she pushed upward into him. *"Elizabeth—what the fuck—"*

She lowered her head and sucked him deeply in tandem with slight movements of her finger against him. There was *something*— the place she was touching, massaging—it was sending jittering shivers of lightninglike shocks to his cock and his balls. He fell back on the bed, lost as she continued her erotic torture, alternately stimulating his cock and then that magic place she'd found between his legs.

A strange fog shrouded him, dulling all his senses except those wired to his groin. The world narrowed down to a tight focus—Elizabeth's lips, her mouth, her tongue and her fingers.

Heat bloomed at the base of Spence's spine—a sharp and intense burst of sensation presaging imminent release. "Elizabeth—*I can't*—you must stop—I'll *come* if you don't—"

He thought he heard her whisper two words. "Then come."

But he couldn't be sure. The roaring of his own lust through his veins drowned out all other sounds, deafening him, blinding him, sending him down the road to his release.

Her fingers thrust against his flesh and her mouth sucked him hard—deeply—back over her tongue until he swore he could feel her throat caress the tip of his cock. Her tongue flicked at the swollen ridge, an extra sensation that nearly stopped his heart in its tracks.

Spence was too far gone to exercise any kind of restraint. His hips were lifting of their own accord, following an ancient instinct, answering his body's call to arms. Muscles tightened and knotted, his toes curled and he felt the linens of the bed crumpling into balls as his fists scrabbled to anchor him against the oncoming rush of ecstasy.

Elizabeth never let him go. She sucked him all the way to the rim of madness and then stayed with him as he toppled into another universe, her mouth fastened to his cock like a limpet to a boulder during a storm at sea.

Shaking and trembling like the veriest maiden, Sir Spencer Marchwood erupted into a cataclysmic orgasm brought on by the skilled manipulations of Lady Elizabeth Wentworth.

And he heard her name echo through the heavens as he tumbled off the edge of the world.

He didn't realize that he had screamed it aloud.

Chapter Seven

A soft but distinctive sound woke Elizabeth. She'd fallen asleep tucked into the sweaty and sated body of the man she'd just loved to his peak, with the taste of him on her lips and the feel of him comforting against her skin.

She blinked, eyes bleary, body a little tired but content in the knowledge that it had wound up precisely where it was supposed to be—in the arms of Spencer Marchwood. A shiver ran through her at the mere thought of him and she smiled sleepily.

Something was digging into her backside and she reached beneath her only to find a couple of hairpins. The smile widened. They certainly had explored some interesting territory in this bed.

Then a clang followed by a muttered oath brought her fully awake and she glanced around, noting that the draperies hanging from the tester above her had been drawn closed to encase the bed in a little cocoon of warmth. It was somewhat medieval and quite dark, but snug nevertheless. Some ideas were still practical on cold nights.

She grabbed the coverlet, swung it around her shoulders in a makeshift cloak and peered out from her little nest. "Good Lord . . ."

"Sorry. I didn't mean to wake you . . . not yet anyway . . ." Spence was standing in unfastened breeches, manhandling a large bucket of steamy water that he dumped into a huge tub in front of the fire. "But seeing as you're up . . . come bathe with me, my lady. Allow me to tend to your ablutions . . ." He grinned at her.

Damn. Elizabeth realized when he grinned at her like that he could tend to anything he wanted. Anytime—anyplace. She gathered her hair into a knot, shoving a few hairpins into it to keep it in place. Then she slithered from the bed and crossed the room, hanging on to her blanket. "A bath? Spence, this is lovely—but how . . . ?"

"A lot of determination, a lot of buckets and a little help from Tedson." He stripped off his breeches. "Come quick, my love, before it cools off. I've stoked up the fire, but even so there's still a godawful draft from somewhere."

He gave a theatrical shiver, glanced at her from under waggling eyebrows and then stepped into the copper tub. "Ahhh." He sat, letting the water steam as it lapped against his chest. "That's better. Only needs one thing to make it perfect . . ." He held out his hand.

Elizabeth dropped the blanket and accepted the offer, heaving her own sigh of bliss as she sank into the water in front of him. He turned her, settling her comfortably against his chest. "Now *this* is what I call heaven."

"Mmm." A light scent—lavender perhaps—wafted around Elizabeth's nostrils, mixed with the distinctive fragrance of leather and man and musk that she always associated with Spence. He was right . . . this was heaven.

And when firm hands began rubbing lather up and down her arms and across her shoulders it got even better. "Spence, you're spoiling me." She leaned her head forward as he tucked a few loose strands of hair back up into the coil. "A girl could become rather used to this kind of decadent treatment, you know."

"I'm hoping so." Slick hands trailed down over her neck and gently whisked lather over her breasts. "I'm very *much* hoping so."

She leaned back against him, a sigh of pleasure drifting from her lips and mingling with the steam from the bathwater. "Why is it that when you touch me, I melt?"

"Because I know how to touch you." He lifted her breasts in his hands, cupping her, raising her nipples above the water for a few moments until they beaded in the cooler air. "Because I love touching you. And because I touch the *you* that nobody else has ever touched. Or will ever touch." His forefingers and thumbs separated to enclose her nipples and he rolled them, teasing her, arousing her, following with a quick dart of his tongue around the sensitive ring of her ear. "Because you're meant for me, Elizabeth. Because I'm meant for you." He nipped her earlobe, making her gasp. "Any doubts in that head?"

She swallowed down a moan of pleasure, content to drift on the beginnings of desire, the gentle stirring deep within her belly that presaged pleasures yet to come. Shaking her head in the negative, she answered his question. "Not anymore."

He shifted a little, keeping her breasts in his hands. "You *did* have doubts, though, didn't you?" He rubbed his chin against her skin. "It's all right, sweetheart. Tell me. Tell me why I had to kidnap you to persuade you we belonged together. Please? I want to understand. I need to understand how you could even *consider* marrying another man."

Elizabeth chuckled. "That stung, didn't it?"

He squeezed her breasts a little. "You'll never know how much, darling. Reading about your engagement to somebody else, imagining somebody else touching you—*here*—or maybe *here*—" Hands smoothed her nipples, slipped down over her abdomen to her pussy and then retraced their route back to her neck, ending at her chin. He turned her head and their gazes met. "It nearly drove me insane, Elizabeth. Totally and completely mad."

She lowered her eyelids, unable to maintain his stare. The emotions he was feeling were chasing themselves across his face and she couldn't cope with them—couldn't deal with seeing the pain she'd caused the man she loved. "I'm sorry." She turned her head and kissed his hand softly.

He breathed out. "You're here now. That's all that matters. But talk to me, love. Tell me. Was it the shooting?" He settled her back against him and leisurely ran a cloth over her thigh as he spoke.

She thought for a moment. "Possibly. Yes. No—I don't really know." Memories flooded back. "It was difficult for me afterwards, that's certain. Knowing I'd ended a human life—well . . ."

"I know."

She shrugged. "Yes, you would. I imagine killing in battle is not so different. The aftermath . . ." Her voice tapered off and they both remained silent for a few moments. There were no words to adequately express such thoughts, just two hearts synchronized to share a similar ache.

"He was a bad man, I know." Elizabeth straightened a little. "I have no regrets, Spence. He would have killed us all. You, me, Charlie, Jordan—he was insane and I did what was necessary. I will never believe otherwise."

"Agreed. But then you withdrew, love. You left me in more ways than one."

"And you left me." She sighed.

"I know." He cursed beneath his breath. "I had no choice. Damn government wouldn't let me go. I begged and pleaded with them. Told them I was no longer one of Wellington's staff— he'd given me permission to leave, for God's sake—but to no avail. They had *one last job*, Sir Spencer. *One last thing we need*, and *while you're in Brussels—*"

It was Spence's turn to sigh, a long breath that lifted Elizabeth as she lay in his arms. "You know what I mean. I was caught, good and proper, in Europe. I couldn't write, couldn't let you know where I was. There were diplomatic dealings to be taken care of, quiet negotiations, all that sort of silliness . . ."

Elizabeth lifted her hand and stroked his arm. "Not silly, Spence. Vital."

He snorted. "And we're supposed to be talking about you, not me. You haven't explained Geoffrey whatshisname yet. When did he come into the picture?"

She giggled. "I will not rise to your bait, you devil. *Gregory*— please note the name—was introduced to me soon after the shooting. By Mother, I believe."

"Ahh." Elizabeth felt Spence nod.

"What do you mean *ahh*?"

"Nothing. Go on." He slid one firm thigh beneath hers and parted her legs, moving the water with his hand and letting it lap gently against her pussy.

"Oooh."

"Go on. Your mother introduced you to . . . *him*."

Blinking and distracted, Elizabeth had to focus for a moment. "Yes. He seemed—*nice*, Spence. Quiet, attentive—you know."

"Undemanding."

"Very."

"Not like me in the least."

She bit her lip. "All right. Not like you in the least. As a matter of fact, I think Mother said something to that effect." She thought for a moment. "She said he was a sweet boy who would become a kind man and never hurt his wife."

"Ahhh."

"There you go again." She half turned, but he held her tightly, arms like bands of steel around her. "What do you mean by that rather cryptic comment?"

"I'll tell you in a minute. Right now"— he let his hands slide to where her thighs were spread wide—"I find myself somewhat occupied with other things . . . "

Fingers delved gently through the soapy water and found her pussy, caressing and stroking the soft flesh they discovered there.

"*Spence . . .* " His name was a caress, a whisper—almost a

prayer—and Elizabeth spoke it with a healthy dose of reverence mixed with growing desire.

"I think we're clean, don't you?"

Strong hands slipped to her armpits and hoisted her to her feet. "Time to dry off, my love." Spence stepped out of the tub and reached for a pile of neatly folded towels warming in front of the fire. "And I'm looking forward to making sure you're as dry as a bone."

The wicked grin on his face as he turned to her, holding the towel open in welcome, took her breath away.

He could dry her skin for all he was worth, but if he kept looking at her like that, there'd be *one* place he'd never be able to dry. In spite of her much-vaunted adventurous spirit, Elizabeth felt the heat of a blush creeping over her cheeks.

Yet again he read her thoughts. "Dry, of course, in *some* places. I intend to make sure you're wet in others, my sweet. *Very* wet." His gaze fell to her pussy.

The blush burned her skin as Elizabeth grabbed for the towel and smothered her choke of laughter.

• • •

Listening to his beloved's laughter sent a frisson of pleasure through Spence that had nothing to do with the sexual and everything to do with the emotional.

Just like that, all the bits and pieces of his life fell into step with one another and purred quietly in an enormously satisfying hum that settled into his heart. It was not unlike that magical moment when a new team finds its rhythm and draws the carriage musically down grassy paths to fresh adventures.

He reached for her, helped her from the tub and enveloped her in the towel, rubbing it against her skin, grinning at her yelps and generally fussing over her with great attention to detail.

Like her breasts, for example, which doubtless required careful drying and caressing. Or her ears and neck—certainly a few kisses could be employed to double-check that he'd missed no errant droplets of moisture.

Amid the fun, Spence realized that at last he'd reached a place where he was at peace with Elizabeth.

He *understood*.

All she'd had to do was mention that her mother had presented the unfortunate whatshisname and the puzzle was solved. No longer did Spence have to worry that the fault had been his— that something he'd done had driven a spoke between them and resulted in his dismissal from Elizabeth's life.

It had nothing to do with him and everything to do with her parents.

He decided to make sure she understood this as well. After a particularly thorough rubbing of her delectable backside, he caressed it, smoothing the rounded curves with great appreciation. "You know, besides having the loveliest arse in all of England—not to mention a good portion of Europe—you also have a somewhat annoying family."

"I do?" She blinked. "The family, I mean, not my arse . . ."

Being the incorrigible female she was, Spence knew that there had to be more to this statement. He was right.

She glanced over her shoulder. "You really think my arse is that good?"

Heedless of the towel, Spence pulled her tightly to him and cupped the subject under discussion with both hands. "Yes, your arse is that good." He squeezed and gently tugged her cheeks apart a little. "I can't wait to play with you there, Elizabeth. I'm thinking you'll enjoy it a lot."

Her hips tipped forward into his groin in a move that seemed almost involuntary. "I enjoy everything you do to me, Spence."

"Everything I do *with* you, sweetheart." He corrected her gently. "For you and me there is only *us*. We're a pair, a team, a couple joined by so much more than just plain desire. I love you, Elizabeth. I always will. I'm humbled that you love me in return." He kissed her swiftly. "Believe me when I give you my word on something here—you will never regret gifting me with your affections. I will never ever hurt you, I swear by all that's holy."

He felt a tiny change in the heat of her skin, coupled with a lessening of tension in the muscles of her spine as she leaned more fully against him and wiggled her hips in his grasp. "You understand, don't you?"

"I think so." He quickly slid his arms beneath her thighs and lifted her high, licking a nipple as it whisked past his mouth and then nipping delicately at her torso. Her hands dug into his shoulders as she gasped at the suddenness of her flight into the air, then she squealed as he tumbled them both through the half-drawn curtains and back onto the bed.

The towel was tossed aside and for a few moments, Spence let himself luxuriate in the wonderfully indescribable sensation of being naked and covered by a sprawling and equally naked Elizabeth.

He rolled them, bringing her into his body and letting her head rest on his arm. "Your parents are not a good example of married life, my sweet. Don't mistake what they have for what we will have. You are not your mother and I am not, nor could I ever be, like your father. We would never settle for that sort of existence."

She stared at him, blue eyes shadowed. "I am still afraid, Spence. Afraid of the power you have over me."

He reached for her hand and enfolded it in his, drawing it between them and holding it high. "See this? This is us. Intertwined. Embraced. Two halves of a whole. You have as much power over me in this . . ." He sucked her little finger into his mouth, laved it with his tongue then released it with a little pop,

" . . . this tiny finger of yours, as I ever do over you with all that I am."

"Ahh, *Spence* . . ." Elizabeth sighed and squirmed even closer. "There's only one thing I can say in response to that."

"Mmm?" Spence waited. She loved him, she was committed to him and he hoped she'd overcome her fears. At least her most immediate ones, anyway. He anxiously held her as words trembled on her lips.

"Fuck me."

He choked. Then nodded. "All right."

• • •

No sooner were the words out of Elizabeth's mouth than she found herself flat on her back with her arms pinned above her head. Once again, the strong body of Spencer Marchwood was pressed against her, holding her down—not that she was planning on going anywhere right this moment.

Hah. She was enormously content to be right where she was. Especially when he rubbed the firm muscles of his chest against her breasts—a roughly arousing movement that sent quivers of delight to her pussy and beyond. Truly, her toes curled at his attentions.

She sighed. "Oh—*so good.*" Closing her eyes, Elizabeth surrendered to the sensations involved in being loved by Spence. Her breasts were thrusting upward thanks to the position in which he held her on the bed and her body was his to do with as he pleased.

Of course, *she* was very pleased as well. The delicate touches of his tongue around her nipples made her moan and the flickering fingers burrowing through the soft flesh of her pussy brought a whimper of desire to her lips. "More, Spence . . . *more,* please . . ."

He obliged with a gentle yet intense loving, smoothly taking Elizabeth along a road to bliss, leading her easily from one threshold to the next without any interruptions to their progress. She reached for him in her turn, finding warm skin, solid and unyielding flesh and a cock that swelled magnificently between them, dewed with moisture at the tip. Elizabeth knew that the hunger within her could only be assuaged by this wonderful length of manhood.

It was long past time for her to be filled by Spence. To have his cock buried deep in her cunt, close to her womb, touching perhaps the portal to her soul. She wondered if she would ever tire of his touch, his scent—the passion he conveyed with just a single kiss.

All things considered, she thought probably not. How could one tire of something so precious? She slid beneath him, angling herself to his limbs, ready—oh so ready—to take him inside her.

"Elizabeth . . ." He whispered her name and she lifted her eyelids, trying to catch a glimpse of his face in the shadows of their bed. There—*there* he was—flushed cheeks, tousled hair and an expression curving his lips that could have been a smile or a grimace of lust.

She was happy with either—or both. And she kept watching those lips as she felt his cock press forward between her swollen folds of flesh. She watched them as Spence nestled into the vee of her thighs, pushing her legs farther apart with his hands against her knees.

He spread her wide, wider and wider still, until she wondered if she might split in two. But no, he held her steady, lowering his head to watch as his cock entered her pussy and found the place they'd known was waiting just for him.

He slid into her cunt, his passage made easy by the slick walls of desire surrounding him. She felt him stretch her, touch her in places unique to Spence and his loving. She heard the soft sounds of their flesh as they joined in the ancient moves of passion and erotic arousal.

She sniffed in the fragrance of their sex—his musky and tangy, hers a pungent sweetness that was familiar and yet new to her.

And she saw. She saw his lips part on a sigh of delight as their bodies finally meshed, merging into a whole joined by so much more than just a length of flesh. She echoed that sigh as they clung to each other, lost in the wonder of this closeness, this special and particular pleasure.

Then his expression changed, his body shifted and he began to move.

And Elizabeth lost the ability to see anything at all. She could only feel.

There were no words to describe the sensations and in truth she sought none. Who would have believed her paean of ecstasy? Would they understand the poetry that might have come close to depicting the flood of passion swamping her limbs and rendering her nigh to insane?

Spence claimed her. She'd given him that right when she'd climbed the stairs earlier in the evening. But now he truly took her as his mate, a savage rutting of bodies and an irrevocable blending of hearts.

He pounded against her, driving her with all the skill he possessed, bringing her arousal to fever pitch even as his own body neared its limits.

She cried out, breaths forced from her lungs by the power of his thrusts, whimpers of need, tiny mewling demands for completion, something he withheld—deliberately, she knew—until she was blind, mad and so desperate she screamed his name aloud.

"Spence—"

He froze then plunged one last time, deep—deeper—finding a place so deep within her core that she wondered if she'd survive the experience. The final brake had been released and her orgasm galloped upon her, trampling her with its violence and wonderfully devastating spasms.

She vaguely heard him choke out her name, but then all was gone—all was whirling lights and gale force winds and pleasure beyond imagination. There was only her blissful voyage into the eye of the storm—a storm named Spencer Marchwood.

She held on to him, fingers latched to his forearms, thighs clamped around his hips and cunt seizing and releasing his cock in a rhythm that matched her rapid heartbeat. In that instant he was hers—totally and completely hers—and in that instant she knew it would always be so.

There could never be another for either of them. Their fate was sealed.

As he collapsed limply beside her and sighed out his sated pleasure, Elizabeth smiled. Fate had truly accomplished a miracle. Spence was hers. She was his.

And for this one moment *everything* in the world was as it should be.

Epilogue

The London Gazette—1816
SOCIETY NOTES

Once again, the notorious Lady E_ W_ has shocked society! Instead of attending a recent soiree and formalizing her engagement to The Right Honorable G_ S_, the lady deserted her family, her apparent fiancé and the assembled guests in favor of an unseemly elopement with none other than a man recently cited in dispatches by our own Duke of Wellington as a hero to his staff.

While we can mention no names, we note that Sir S_ M_'s name arose some short while ago in connection with an unpleasant affair at the home of a fellow member of the Duke's staff, Colonel J_ L_. All these "coincidences" can lead us perhaps to conclude that the gentleman in question was no gentleman with the lady and that this elopement might be the result of indiscretions yet to be revealed?

While we cannot attest to this with certainty, we can report that a marriage license was filed on behalf of the eloping couple shortly before they embarked on a voyage to the Colonies. Ancillary to this interesting development is the information that Colonel J_ L_ and his wife currently reside in Boston.

Thus we bid a sad farewell to one of the more scandalous figures of the ton . . . the former Lady E_ will be sorely missed by many of us, but probably none more than her jilted fiancé. Perhaps he will find a more suitable bride amongst the cur-

rent debutantes, many of whom made their late-Season debut
last night under the aegis of their parents and the Patronesses
of Almack's . . .

• • •

"And still no decent summer warmth." Spence folded the paper
and tossed it onto the small desk beside him.

His wife stared out of the small porthole at the grey skies and
dark sea. "Even the sailors are talking of this strange weather. They
say the winds are much too harsh for August and that there has
been snow in the Colonies." She turned to Spence, an eager smile
on her face. "Snow, Spence. In *August*. Can you believe it?"

He chuckled. "Since you're bundled up in your pelisse, ready
for snow, yes . . . I can believe it." He stood and joined her at the
window. "I'm sorry this voyage has been so cold though. Your
first experience sailing anywhere and we've had to stay pretty
much belowdecks the whole time."

Elizabeth giggled. "I can't say I've minded, my love. You've
kept me busy. And warm."

"Just doing my husbandly duty."

"And very well too." Elizabeth leaned against Spence. "I hope
Jordan and Charlie will be happy to see us. I'm looking forward
to seeing *them*, that's for sure."

"And I know they'll enjoy a visit from us, no doubt about it.
However, it will be different, darling. The Colonies, I mean. It's
not London by any stretch of the imagination."

"It'll be an adventure, Spence. And you're here with me. I
can't ask for anything more than that." She turned in his arms.
"*Sir S— and Lady E— M— take the Colonies by storm.* Makes a
nice headline, don't you think?"

He nodded on a smile. "Yes indeed."

"Spence, d'you think we'll see one of those Indians everybody
talks about?"

"Maybe."

"D'you think we'll see mountains and wild animals?"

"We might."

"D'you think we'll have a real snowstorm?"

"Seems like a distinct possibility."

"D'you think—"

"Elizabeth." Spence turned her in his arms and kissed her—soundly. "I love you. That's really all I can think about right now."

She smiled up at him, all blue eyes and soft skin. "That's just fine by me." She stood on tiptoe and kissed him back. "I made the right choice, Spence. For both of us."

"Yes, you did."

"So . . . let's go to bed. I'm tired. Again."

With a completely male grin of contentment, Sir Spencer Marchwood swept his bride off her feet and into their small bedroom onboard the *Merry Maid of Margate*, where he proceeded to make her eyes roll back in her head and drive all thoughts of Indians and snowstorms from her mind.

She had indeed made the right choice.

She'd chosen *him*.

Sahara Kelly

Born and raised in England, Sahara Kelly spent her childhood not far from Jane Austen's home, reading the traditional classic literature of Shakespeare, Dickens and Hardy, while at the same time falling in love with Miss Austen's Regency novels. Although she'd love to describe herself as a jet-setting, best-selling author, currently having a hot fling with an internationally famous film star, the truth is sadly more mundane since she's settled in New England and only sees movie stars like everybody else . . . in the movies.

Married for more than twenty years to the same patiently loving man, Sahara became a stay-at-home mom, raised their son, sent him off to college armed with a sense of humor and a credit card (!), and then rediscovered her passion for writing with the arrival of the new millennium. Now that the nest is empty, Sahara is free to stretch her wings, spending long hours doing what she adores—writing spicy romances set wherever her imagination takes her. Fascinated by her characters, sex and the challenge of researching new times and new places, Sahara is the first to admit she is a truly blessed woman to be doing something she loves. Her argument is that if you're doing what you adore, you never really have to *work* at it. She simply indulges herself in fantasies—and that, she'll tell you, is very important. As her website clearly states—she thinks everyone should have fantasies. . . .

www.saharakelly.com

Selfless

SHERRI L. KING

Prologue

Cold and wet. Her hands pressing against the restraining glass, the fingertips shriveled like a crone's. Or a newborn's . . .

When she opened her eyes she couldn't see. Everything was blurry. She blinked and blinked again, harder this time, to clear the lenses of her eyes. Still blurry.

She swallowed . . . and gagged. Something was in her throat, her mouth. She looked down at herself and saw the thing—a tube, as wide and round and slippery as an eel—hanging from her lips. Past her lips and down into the blurry bottom of the tank, the white plastic rippled in places like an accordion straw. Again past her lips and down into her, into her throat, deep inside her chest it rested, rooted.

The tank, the tube feeding her air, the stubborn smear of her eyesight . . . she had no memory before them. She gasped, feeling her diaphragm expand as oxygen traveled down the tube and into the spongy tissues of her greedy lungs. Panic stung, like the serous liquid in which she found herself suspended. And it was cold.

Like any confused creature trapped as she was, she beat at the glass with her fists. Kicked it. Her muscles felt weak at first and then exponentially stronger. More powerful still until the feel of her blows against the imprisoning glass no longer hurt or bruised her tender hands and feet, or strained her trembling muscles, but began to feel almost sensuous. The glass seemed to expand, like cellophane over her knuckles . . . and then to shatter!

Until that moment she had been floating in the fluid, suspended, like a buoyant balloon, but when the glass gave way gravity won. She fell, outward and downward, as if from a great height. The floor rushed to greet her.

Blackness, like before, only now she was *aware* that the blackness existed. That *she* existed.

And then the light. She blinked several times in rapid succession and her eyes began at last to clear. Her body was cold, dripping wet, her skin smooth and unblemished, like that of a scaleless fish escaped from its aquarium.

Hands grabbed her. Rough. Textured. Disoriented, she rubbed her own fingertips together and, as the wrinkles faded away, understood that her skin had no such texture. No roughness at all. Her determined handler dragged her away from the wet puddle on the concrete floor, from the biting glass shards, his hands beneath her arms, digging into her armpits.

His hands. She sniffed the air, smelled the masculine odor of him—*thuja, vetiver*, honest sweat and suede. Yes, this was male.

Brighter pinpoints of light struck her eyes like nails. Murmured whispers, rushed and hurried words sounded through her compacted ears. She reached up, past other hands that swatted away her efforts, with a strength that must have surprised them as much as her because the hands fell away. She reached up unhindered now and dug in her ears, pulling out the plugs she found there.

Amplified sound—but only ambient sound, she understood—shocking and too loud to bear, made her cry out. A hand covered her mouth before she could make the noise. The textured fingers slammed over her lips, pressing hard.

These hushed voices, these shapes around her, wanted secrecy. There was a reason for that and until she knew what it was, she would keep silent too. It did not bode well that she'd awakened in a sort of prison . . . these people seemed intent on freeing her and that was good enough for now.

What concerned her most was *why* she'd been in the tank. And . . . why didn't she have a memory of before it?

The tube was crushed, her oxygen cut off by the pressure of the hand. She tried to breathe through her nose but choked on the glob of crud and liquid that slid down her sinuses into the back of her throat.

She coughed. Gagged around the tube.

"Goddamnit. Be quiet!" The hand lifted from her mouth. She swiftly grabbed the length of tube that lay on her chest and jerked it determinedly. It was seated in farther than she'd known. The pain of tearing it out made her lungs burn, her throat shred and her eyes water, but at least the liquid that blurred her vision now was her own, her tears, and not that strange antiseptic fluid she'd awakened in. The tube slid free, her lungs, her mouth were free, now she could breathe on her own. And the air was cold.

Was it all cold like this?

"Silence!"

She'd asked the question aloud? Odd . . . she didn't remember the sound of her voice in the strained silence.

"We're gonna get you out of here. But you have to be quiet." This voice, this was different from the first. This voice was softer . . . female. "That means stop thinking too."

Stop thinking? *How?*

The rough hands lifted her and they were up and running. She heard rather than felt her own feet slap against the hard floor. She faltered at first on unused muscles, then, after a dozen steps, she was running so fast the hands that supported her now held on to keep her from getting away.

She had to slow to allow the blurred shapes to show her the way through the dimly lit labyrinthine corridors.

Her eyes were growing clearer with each blink of her lids. She could now see some details of the company around her. Four in all, three male, one female. Dressed in black, two wearing night-vision goggles, all equipped with technological gizmos that creaked when they moved, they were otherwise careful not to make a sound. They flanked her, like some prized POW they'd liberated . . . and perhaps that wasn't far from the truth.

Still, none of that mattered, none of *them* mattered, none but the one touching her. He was their leader—she could feel it in the way the others regarded him. Feel it in his hand on hers as he turned her this way or that. Hear it in his breath, the way he paced himself and the others, the way he was assured of his every move through the concrete maze.

This one she would mind—the others meant nothing.

They were underground. She realized it instinctively—and just as instinctively accepted that she knew it without being told. Knew that they were climbing. Rising. She could feel their ascension deep in her bones. Making their way toward the light.

But the light of stars and moon . . . or sun?

"Shut up!" The rough hand squeezed her shoulder so hard it should have bruised but her muscles felt elastic, the bone and gristle beneath doubly so. His fingers sank into her. She found herself growing weary of the rough treatment.

She grabbed the hand and squeezed back, her own strength nearly crushing the bones. The man hissed but didn't pull away. Nor did he slow their pace. She let him go at once. She merely wanted to warn him that she would only tolerate so much.

Outside at last . . . liberation!

The stars greeted them, but no moon. It had passed beyond their horizon. The pungent scent of river water permeated the air. She felt sad and didn't know why.

She was pushed into the back of a dark vehicle. Van . . . the word seemed alien in her mind, but she put a fuzzy mental picture with the word and knew it was fitting.

The leader barked an order and the vehicle took off, throwing her off balance so that she fell onto her side.

The leader's textured fingers nearly scraped her tender skin raw when he caught her, righted her and held her stable. He draped a cloth around her and rubbed her arms.

Her eyes met those of the leader—he had ocher eyes, bright eyes, glowing gold and warm beneath the black war grease he wore.

Who were these people? What was happening to her? But most important . . .

"What is my name?" She startled everyone when she asked the question aloud. Her own voice sounded unfamiliar to her. Metallic. Unused.

The leader sighed and finally blinked his eyes. He looked sad for a moment, a fleeting ripple in a sea of time. But those eyes were steely once more when they refocused. "For now we'll call you Eva."

He turned away from her and the world grew colder.

Chapter One

S he's nothing at all like I imagined she'd be," Ryan Murdock observed from behind the two-way mirror. Watching as Eva flexed her fingers, cracking each joint over and over again, the sound like little fireworks exploding in the quiet of her room.

Her black eyes regarded the mirror, alert, unwavering, as if she could see them through the glass. Maybe she could, Ryan reasoned, how would they know? They'd been testing her for days and couldn't understand half the mystery of her.

So vexing that not even his best psychics could read her thoughts.

She was an enigma . . . and worse—for Sterling's scientists—Eva seemed to want to remain so.

"How did you imagine she would be?"

"More acquiescent." Ryan shook his head. "Curious, even. Certainly more sympathetic to our research and methods. She's literally a newborn. She shouldn't be so stubborn. So unyielding."

"That might be the reason she was cut off. Perhaps she wasn't quite what her creator wanted or expected her to be."

"And what would that be, Dante?" Ryan rounded on him but Dante didn't step back. Ryan's anger wasn't for him. Wasn't for Eva either, though she probably didn't know it. "What purpose could she serve? An organ donor?" Ryan spat. "A bodyguard—she's sure as hell strong enough for the work! Of what use could she be to the one who made her?"

Dante shrugged, watching Eva closely through the glass. She was still. Watching. Listening. Only the popping of her knuckles gave away any sign of life. "Who can say?" he responded carefully. "She's been a closed book since after that first night. She's learned quickly how to hide thoughts from us."

"Why? What does she want to hide? I want to help her—I do—but how can I? She makes it too hard."

"Perhaps she has as few answers as we do," Dante said softly, watching her watching them. "Perhaps she can't help us."

"Or *won't*," Ryan snapped. "Is she so corrupt? Already? Was she born with the hate of her creator already alive inside her? Is her purpose then to create chaos for the scientific community?" He snorted. "Because she's doing a damned fine job of it so far."

Dante almost missed the flicker of her eyes. Her lashes had grown so long, so fast . . . she'd been completely hairless when they'd first freed her. Now her hair was a canopy of straight blonde locks reaching to her shoulders. Her hair had grown so swiftly, in fact, that it had dreaded together at first, but her aides had been trying to keep her strands free of knots and tangles. Just as they'd been careful to help her exercise, to keep her quickly hardening bones from shattering or breaking. Eva didn't know it, but she was being treated very carefully by some of the best doctors in the world.

Still, she looked like a wild thing. Pale and dangerous . . . all of her the color of the autumn sun but for the blackness of her eyes.

Such strange eyes. They appeared to see everything, while giving away nothing of her inner thoughts.

Her pupils had not yet contracted. They'd been wide like the maw of a demon's gasp, gaping huge since day one. None of Sterling's finest could figure out why, or how to make them contract so she could at least have a light on in her room without getting halos in her vision.

"She's neither human nor monster." Dante said the words with flat, unyielding honesty. Eva turned her face away and regarded the shadows in the corner of her room. "We can't judge her as either." He watched as she swallowed, the movement of her throat compelling some hidden protective urge deep within him that he had to stomp on to immediately kill.

This wasn't the first time she'd made him feel so off-kilter.

"You're right," Ryan agreed. "But we need answers *now*. We don't have time to let her adjust, or to learn to adjust our own prejudices." He sighed. "I want another run of tests. I want you to call for them."

"I'm not a doctor, Ryan," Dante pointed out quietly. "Have someone else—"

Ryan's gaze was almost threatening, though the man was shorter than Dante by a few inches. "Call for them and join me in her room. I want you there. I'm going to speak to her myself. And then . . . I want you to speak with her." Ryan glanced back at the too-still subject of their conversation. "She understands authority. Power. Even the lowliest beasts do. If she won't respond to me, perhaps she'll respond to you—the others said she deferred to you on the trip here."

"It wasn't that long of a trip to make that assumption." But Dante had noticed too, that she'd listened only to his commands on the dark trip from Maine to Sterling's headquarters in Cleveland. He'd heard echoes of her thoughts—even as she'd built mental barriers to shield them—and known she dismissed the others in favor of his authority. It had, at first, made him more confident in the face of her alien stillness . . . but as the hours had passed, he'd felt something else. Something that had nothing to do with his duty or his purpose.

It had felt good, in that animal part of him, to feel his dominance over her. Her willing acceptance of it. She'd watched him the whole time, her black eyes never wavering, and he'd found himself returning her stare more often than was necessary or healthy.

It had taken every ounce of self-discipline not to look lower, at her naked flesh barely concealed by the covering he'd draped around her haphazardly.

Ryan was speaking again. "It's better than what we've gotten from her since her arrival. If she's going to suddenly cooperate with anyone, I've got a hundred bucks that says it'll be you."

Dante reached out before Ryan could brush past him. "This isn't my field of expertise. I did what I was supposed to do—I freed her and brought her here."

"You were the one who *found* her in the first place," Ryan pointed out mercilessly. "Don't you feel some responsibility to see this through? Are you no longer interested in finding out about her maker?"

"I don't have time for this," Dante growled, hearing the psychological prodding in Ryan's words.

"We don't have time to play any more games!" Ryan snapped back. "We need to know some things. *Now*. Before all this shit gets too real."

Grunting, Dante glanced one more time at Eva, at the gentle curve of her face and neck, and followed Ryan out of the observation room.

He missed the glittering tear that traced a path down her cheek.

• • •

I'm not a monster.

But according to them—to him—I'm not human either.

Eva shuddered, cold in her thin, sterile gown, and smeared the moisture of a hot tear across the soft skin of her cool cheek. The heat dissipated quickly, making her damp flesh even cooler after its absence.

What am I then?

Was she safe here at Sterling? Here where strangers poked and prodded her and asked question after question without mercy? Had they taken her from the darkness of the womb into the light? Or had they awakened her from quiet, peaceful dreams to the banshee wail of reality?

Were they her liberators? Or tormentors?

Her fingers furtively searched the planes of her belly, as if by scratching there, she could change something.

If she surrendered all her knowledge, answered every question, what then would they do to her? She who was neither human nor monster?

Her finger glided over soft, velvet tissue. A plane, unmarred.

She had no belly button.

What am I?

Not even the depths of her mind would reveal the answer to that secret. She knew everything, it seemed. Math, geography, history, biology—these were not unknown to her. But no matter how hard she tried to understand, no matter how clever she appeared to those who tested her, she could not understand the mysteries she most longed to unravel when she tested herself.

The mystery of what she was.

What was her purpose?

Who had decided that purpose for her—who had made her?

Both she and Sterling wanted to know—she knew her motives, but what were theirs?

Eva didn't know that either. With each day that passed, she felt the burn of that uncertainty, the heat amid the cold of this— her life—and she relentlessly stirred the warm embers, uncaring that those embers could at any time burst into a blaze of ravenous flame.

She liked the heat.

Chapter Two

hink hard. How do you know all these languages?
How do you know algebra? How did you learn these
things?"

The steel shackles binding her wrists to the bed were icy cold.
The back of the bed had been elevated so she could look her
questioner in the eye. Ryan Murdock's eyes were dark blue—the
color of the Caribbean on a summer day.

How could she know *that* and not know what she was?

She closed her own eyes, deep bruises in her skull thanks to
the stab of the bright fluorescent lights in the lab. "Ask what you
really came to ask. Do I know where my maker is—no, I do not.
Do I know why I was made? No. If I could tell you, would I?" She
opened her eyes again and stared hard into Ryan's gaze. "I don't
know." The words fell flat from her mouth.

His jaw flexed and his eyes glowed. "At least you're honest."

"For a monster, you mean." She watched his discomfort, relished it.

"You're not a monster." But everyone who heard knew he
wasn't entirely convinced. A nurse at her elbow flinched and Eva
sipped the woman's doubt and weakness into herself like a thirsty
vampire.

"No. I'm . . . let's see, how did you put it in your journals?"
Eva eyed everyone in the room defiantly. " 'A perfect physical
specimen. It has a working mind, independent of its creator, but
with no memories of its own. Knowledge is its memory. Its brain
operates like a hard drive, full of facts and data, languages and

literature instantly accessible. It's like a computer.' " Eva grinned slowly, ugly. "It."

The shocked silence that reigned almost made her smile.

Someone came closer—a woman Eva knew was called Diane. She was an oracle . . . a precognitive for Sterling. "How do you know that? Do you have extrasensory perception? Can you read minds?"

Eva closed her eyes again. How to explain that she didn't see the way Diane did, but listened instead to the scratching of pens and pencils as notes were jotted. In that scratching she could hear and track the point of the instrument, follow its path and pattern, and know what words it wrote upon the paper.

Just as she could watch a person move and know what motion they would make simply by eyeing the play of muscles beneath their clothes. Just as she could listen to the breathing of those around her and know which ones feared her and which ones dismissed her as an . . . it.

She wasn't psychic like many of these people were. She was just *aware*. Of everything.

Eva heard Diane step back. "Dante."

Against her will, Eva then opened her eyes.

Everyone in the room retreated, including Ryan. It was almost as if they were giving her some privacy at last . . . but she knew the respectful distance wasn't meant for her.

Dante looked far different without the black grease on his face. He'd seemed so dark to her that night, like the inky depths of space between the stars. But now she could see that he was light. His hair was a shiny sea of bronze waves reaching just past his shoulders. His eyes, still gold as the sun and twice as hot, looked over her as if he hadn't been watching her through the two-way mirror from day one. His tanned face was smooth, almost boyishly handsome, but his body was big and hard and supremely male beneath his sterile lab uniform. He had trained that body, pushed it and twisted it, shaped it into a mold that suited his use. He was a warrior. A fighter.

Eva believed that she too was a fighter.

The warmth of his skin emanated from him when he crouched at her side and met her gaze. "We can't help you if you don't let us," he said quietly, though Eva knew everyone in the room heard the words. As did the recording devices beyond the walls of her prison.

"I can't let you *use* me, if you don't even pretend to show me some human courtesy," she returned through gritted teeth, jangling the shackles around her wrists pointedly.

He sighed but met her gaze squarely. "You attacked one of the scientists—you broke three of his ribs. One blow and down he went. We can't afford to trust you. We don't know you." The hard line of his mouth softened. "Let us know you. Let us know you're deserving of human courtesy."

His voice was deep and rough, full of mysterious pits and hollows, like an unpolished basalt stone. She couldn't tell what he was thinking—by his breathing, the look in his eyes or the movement of his body—and that deeply troubled her. She felt some strange menace in him . . . and shivered despite herself.

"The man was rude," she found herself explaining. "He took my blood without even asking. Stuck the needle in and dug when he lost the vein. You may not know exactly what I am—but I *do* have feelings. I know what pain is. I know he liked making me hurt. I could see it in his eyes when he looked at me. He was afraid of me and wanted me to be afraid of him." She smiled to herself, knowing it unsettled their audience. "Well I too can be petty."

His eyes blinked slowly—his black lashes thick and dense. She noticed a tracery of onyx around his shiny irises—it made the ocher stand out in stark contrast. He was lovely to look upon.

When he came closer he brought his delicious warmth, but watching his face she felt a chill inside. "You don't know what you are. We don't know what you're for. But only you can decide what you will be."

Against her will, her gaze shifted away first. It made her angry, her own cowardice, and her hands were free of their restraints and reaching for him before she had time to think twice about it. The clank of the broken steel hitting the tiled floor echoed in her ears and the feel of his skin was almost hot against hers—his throat in her hands.

But he didn't fight.

Didn't block her move, though she was almost certain he could have.

He merely looked at her. Into her. Eye to eye.

He let her demonstrate her strength. She squeezed once, then immediately released him. The room exploded with sound and movement as guards entered the room with new restraints and the doctors that abounded remarked on her effortless power in breaking her bonds.

When someone foolishly tried to grab her wrist to apply the new shackle, Dante struck them away for her, already recovered from her swift attack. "Let her alone. She won't hurt me." His gaze never left hers, daring her to prove him wrong. "Everyone, leave us." There was an implosion of silence. "Go." He barked the command and the words were like stones falling upon stone. "She and I will speak alone."

"Dante." Diane stepped forward to intervene, eyeing Eva warily.

Dante turned his head, keeping one eye on her still. "Ryan, turn off the recorders. All of them. No surveillance. Leave us alone. Five minutes."

Ryan was silent a tick. "Five minutes." He nodded. Turning, he ushered everyone out of the room. A moment later, Eva heard the various recording devices being turned off. Heard the silence in the observation room behind the two-way mirror.

"You're not afraid of much, are you, Eva?" Dante asked softly, carefully, as if concerned his words might put her on the defensive.

No. Wait.

This was his *true* voice, she realized. His speaking voice. It was soft. Gentle. She liked it just as much as the commanding tone he'd used before.

"You don't feel fear like the rest of us. Yet you're wary of me." He let out a short, staccato sigh. "Why is that?"

"I don't know you," she answered truthfully.

"Is that why you're so wary of helping the doctors, then? Because you don't know them? You don't know us? Is it really that simple?"

"Y-yes." Was that a tremor in the lie? Truth was, she did all she could to help the doctors and scientists—she too wanted answers. But her caretakers were asking all the wrong questions, because they were afraid to tell her the whole truth of what they really wanted to know.

How can we use you to find our foe?

Dante shook his head. "We want to help you. We want to help all that we can. If there's someone out there with the technology and the power to create trans-humans like you, in total secrecy and isolation, we need to know who they are and why they've done this. It could save many lives. It could save yours."

Eva bowed her head, not looking at him. Looking only at the painfully bright white of her thin hospital gown. "Trans-humans?"

"For lack of a better term, yes. You aren't a clone—you're too sophisticated. Your DNA is not only identical to your creator's, you also look and sound exactly like her. You couldn't have spent more than a few months in that tank but are already fully grown. Your factual knowledge surpasses most of our staff's. Clones are subject to birth and life like any human. They grow from infant to adolescent to adult. They become individuals through life experiences.

But you're different. You . . . became. In that tank, you grew fast and perfect in every way. But with no past, no personal development to create your independent sense of self. How? Better yet, why?"

But he hadn't answered her question, not fully. He'd said trans-humans—plural. So there could be more like her . . . ?

How much were the people of Sterling hiding from her?

"Who made me?" she asked, whisper soft in her week-old voice. When he didn't answer she felt the heat of anger bloom in her chest. Felt it and liked it. Her voice was louder, harder when she continued. "You say I look like her, so you must know her."

Dante sighed as if in defeat, but when Eva glanced at him from beneath her forest of lashes he looked determined. "We know *of* her."

He folded his arms across his broad chest. His fingers, she noted while watching his hands, were long and lovely. But she knew from experience their gentle beauty was deceptive. Those fingers could bruise. She'd seen their marks on her own skin after that first night.

She was stronger now. But it was more than clear that he was her match—he hadn't even flinched when she'd broken her bonds and wrapped her fingers around his throat. This knowledge thrilled her in some elemental way she couldn't quantify.

"She was once a biochemist. A brilliant scientist," Dante elaborated. "Then, when the cloning phenomenon was young, she advocated experimental research. She was hard to dissuade and broke many laws. Eventually she was reprimanded. Fined. More than once. Then stripped of all credentials, all licensing. She seemed to fall off the face of the earth, disappeared completely. Now we find you. The product of her years spent in exile, you're a Pandora's box of unanswered questions."

Eva let that last go. "If she was in hiding, how did you know where to find me? Me and not her?"

He didn't meet her gaze. More secrets.

"Where did she get the money?" Eva tried not to let her frustration show. "Surely it must have been costly to make one such as me." Or more than one . . .

Dante shook his head, his bronze hair picking up glittering highlights from the fluorescents. "She was immensely wealthy."

"What's her name?" Eva asked the question with a hoarse voice.

He eyed her, then seemed to decide there was no harm in telling her. "Her name is Dr. Abigail Faria." He moved in closer. "But what good is a name? Does it have meaning for you?"

She met his gaze and had to keep from flinching at the seeking intensity in his regard. "I've never heard her name, if that's what you're asking. Or if I have, I don't remember it."

He was still for a beat, then nodded as if satisfied with her answer.

"Will you let us perform a few more tests? Ask a few more questions? After that, I promise, we will help you to build a life. A real life that is yours alone, no one else's. Will you work with us?"

Eva blinked owlishly, purposefully using her black eyes to unsettle him—if such a thing were possible. "I will work with *you*. The others, they don't empathize with me in any way." She let her words sink in, waiting for some emotion to cross his face but none did. "But you do. You're not like the others. I can tell by the tone of your voice when you address me. You don't see me the way they do." She pierced him with her stare, feeling almost reptilian as her blood ran cool through her veins. "And now I must ask . . . why is that? Why do I matter to your cause? What does the name Abigail Faria mean to *you*?"

He caught his breath. They both heard it in the stillness of the cold room.

She drank in this tiny slip, this small reaction from him, let it fill her up . . . but hated the way it made her feel. He was not like the others. He was not a toy. She wouldn't play this game of cat and mouse with him. "Never mind." She retreated hurriedly, lying back on the hard pallet that was her mattress. "Forget I asked. It's none of my business."

He turned to leave, but as his hand hovered above the doorknob he hesitated. Jaw clenched, Dante glanced at her over his shoulder, his gaze unreadable. "Her name means nothing. It's her methods I'm concerned with."

He was lying. Eva saw it in the line of his spine. Heard it in the resonance of his voice.

"You're right about me, Eva. I do empathize with you. I'm not a clone and I'm not like . . . what you are. But I am what I am because of rogue scientists like Faria. I was once caged as you were. I was once unsure of my true nature—human or beast."

"And now you're not?" she asked, voice hushed, needing to hear his answer.

"Sterling helped me find out who I am. They can help you too, if you let them."

Eva swallowed past a pain in her throat. "You freed me. Who freed you, Dante?" She said his name at last and reveled in the feel of it on her tongue.

He turned away. "We free ourselves, Eva." The door closed softly behind him.

Chapter Three

She freed herself exactly seven days later.

With Dante always in attendance, Eva let Sterling have their way, let them run test after test, interrogation after interrogation. She endured hours of psychotherapy that went nowhere and made her head spin. Without reservation she gave of herself all that she could, but no matter how deep the doctors dug, no matter how openly and honestly she answered their millions of questions, Eva learned nothing useful about herself.

She found herself chafing to experience the world beyond the walls of Sterling. Every day took her further away from caring so much about where she came from as where she was going.

On the seventh day, they told Eva that the next step was to probe her mind. Many psychics would be invited to participate.

Dante would participate.

But Eva didn't want anyone inside her mind. It was the only thing that was truly hers. From the beginning she'd hidden from their prying, safeguarding her thoughts as precious and sacred and wholly hers.

It had been easy. Eva knew it would stun Dante to know just *how* easy. Dante, who, Eva had learned, was perhaps the most adept at delving into the minds of others no matter how great and powerful the shields against him.

But Eva had no shields.

Eva had a cave.

There was an abyss in the center of her mind. A blank space that was neither cold nor warm. It was, however, comforting in an odd way. There, Eva could hide her self. There, in the darkness, she could bury her thoughts like seeds in the fold of a womb. She wanted no one to trespass there. This was her secret place.

She didn't know why the cave was there. The empty space seemed tailor-made for something beyond what she used it for. But it didn't vex her enough to wonder, so long as this secret space provided her solace from the hungry world of her waking and the jackals that would feed on her thoughts like it was carrion.

It was so hard to see Dante as a jackal . . . it was painful to think he would so easily betray her and crawl into her mind without a qualm. But by his own admission he intended to do just that.

Damn him.

Eva knew she wasn't an "it." She was a person. And each day that passed solidified this knowledge within her. Each moment was an experience. A memory that was real, that shaped her. She was unique, just like any other human being. Her thoughts were her own—no one had any right to them save her.

No one would take away her individuality, not with their prejudice or their probes. No one, not even Dante, would ever reduce her to a science project again.

Still, there were things that troubled her. The most alarming— if clues could be taken from the occasional slip from Dante or the others—the knowledge that she might not be alone. There might be others like her. More than one Eva.

Eva. A Hebrew form of Eve—the first woman. How droll. Dante had chosen the name on a whim—he'd told her as much. That it was he who had named her was the only reason Eva chose to keep the title. It was as good as any.

He'd chosen his name too. Unlike her, he'd been born with a name, but had forgotten it and chosen a new one. Eva didn't need to be told the details to know that Dante had forgotten it under extreme duress. Or perhaps had merely wanted nothing more to do with it and had simply erased it. Either way, he'd found his own name. His own way.

Dante. He'd been to hell and back, but had he ever reached heaven? Eva wondered.

Maybe we can reach it together.

When Eva heard that thought, like a hungry creature stirring in the deepest trenches of her mind, she'd immediately decided to leave Sterling. And when she learned that Dante himself meant to invade her mind, whether she liked it or not, she knew that time was now.

Every time she saw him her heart burned. Every time his skin brushed hers she felt her loins quiver and melt, like wax before the flame. His scent intoxicated her—she imagined she could still smell him half an hour after he'd left her side. The sound of his voice soothed her rough edges, her impatience with her keepers, and Eva found herself striving to please him, by pleasing the doctors and researchers of Sterling. Soon everything she did, she did for him, in one capacity or another.

Every night she dreamed. And she dreamed always of him. Them. Together.

She was becoming attached to Dante and that would never do. It was clear by his intentions to invade her that he could never accept her as she was. He could never love her if he couldn't even see how abhorrent it was to rape her mind.

And . . . what was she, after all, to be loved? No one had answered that question to Eva's satisfaction.

Only one person could.

It was clear that, despite her desire to let her past fade, she could never move forward in this world without knowing exactly where she came from.

And so it was that on the fifteenth night of her concious life, heartsick but determined, she easily broke the locks on the door to her cell and walked freely through the brightly lit hallways of Sterling.

It was quite simple and she was surprised that the few people she encountered paid her little, if any, notice. It must be commonplace to see someone in a hospital gown walking about.

Sterling, Eva knew, was more than just a prison for her. It was a hospital, a lab and home to many gifted individuals. The main goal of its people was to catalogue and study all things unique in the fields of science, biology and weaponry. Special attention was paid to paranormal cases. The majority of the scientists, doctors and soldiers here were gifted with paranormal talents of varying sorts.

Still, even knowing it was rare that anyone was *confined* here, Eva was surprised that no one sensed the forbidden nature of her intent, that not one person she passed glanced her way twice.

Perhaps, in the dark cave of her mind, she had hidden her thoughts better than even she had known.

She turned a corner, wiping her eyes.

"Where are you going?"

Eva gasped, opening her eyes wide despite the pain of the bright lights spiking into her gaping pupils. She halted in her tracks, the paper slippers covering her feet causing her to slide a few inches on the tiled floor. "Dante."

Her heart pounded. Her blood heated.

"Why aren't you in your room?" he asked, tone pleasant. Light.

Eva knew he really wanted to ask how she'd gotten out. No one, not even he, knew how strong she could be—she'd deliberately kept that information to herself. When she'd broken the locks on her door, the steel had been as pliant as butter.

She took a deep breath through her nose.

Something wasn't right.

Eva eyed him, tilting her head, puzzled. Her eyes hurt and halos danced from the lights, but she could see him. He was only a few feet in front of her. She could see him clearly enough to glimpse right through him. She sniffed the air again . . . nothing but the neutral scent of the well-filtered, air-conditioned halls.

Dante wasn't really standing there. Not physically anyway.

Still, Eva was cautious. "I was looking for you," she lied, the words smooth past her curving lips.

He hesitated. Eva wondered if he could sense the lie somehow.

"Follow my lead," he said, the image heading back the way she'd come.

Should she follow? Could he do anything to her in this state of nonphysicality? Could he stop her if she continued her escape?

He'd no doubt raise an alarm and that would certainly complicate the ease of her self-liberation. Eva decided to play it safe. For now.

"How are you . . . ?" She trailed off, for once at a loss for words.

"I'm an astral projection," he explained, ever patient.

"Oh." She understood this, without knowing how. Didn't matter.

"Follow me."

Would he take her back to her room? Eva couldn't let him see the ruin of her door—couldn't give him the chance to better improve the security of her cell. She wanted out of this place, tonight. *Think fast.*

"I want to see you, alone," she said in what she hoped was an intimate tone, feeling a strange thrill run through her at her own boldness.

His image shimmered in the lights. The outline of him was bronze, like his hair. For a moment it was as if his eyes blazed with heat . . . but she didn't feel it. He wasn't really there, after all.

"I'm this way," he said, image moving away from her.

Eva began to formulate a plan.

Heady, the anticipation of seeing him. Warm, the expectation. Hot, the desire.

As the image of Dante led her deeper into Sterling's labyrinth, Eva added to her mental construction of the compound. It was indeed vast—larger than she had suspected. Still, it would be easy for her to find her way out. She wouldn't lose her way, no matter that, she suspected, Dante was purposefully taking her through unnecessary routes to try to confuse her. He was very clever.

Her weakness—the need she had for him boiling in her blood—and his intuitiveness could have devastating results for her escape attempt.

She resolved to be more careful from here on out.

Resolved or not . . . she felt a fluttering in her stomach. Like a forest of leaves tickling her insides. If she listened, she imagined she might actually hear their whispering deep inside her. Echoes of her heart and all it wanted despite her best judgment.

• • •

The first thing he noticed was her hair. Though he'd seen her that very morning, not twelve hours prior, her hair was already noticeably longer. Almost reaching midway down her back. It was threaded, formed into thick locks or dreads—her cells regenerated so quickly it was a wonder the locks didn't reach her feet by now. While he knew she kept her white nails trimmed close, she left her aurulent hair alone, despite the difficulty of keeping it free of knots as it grew and grew. Carelessly, she usually ripped at her hair with her comb—he'd seen her do it. He'd also read in her daily evaluations that she'd taken to waxing off the rest of her body hair, morning and night, without fail.

It was almost as if she welcomed pain.

This had fascinated him. He understood pain. Understood its power to cleanse, to purify. Its ability to cement one's sense of self. It had also unsettled him. There was the suspicion she might *need* the pain. To feel more human. When he'd asked her, she'd told him in her frank way that pain was hot and she liked being warm . . . this made no real sense to him, but he could see that it made perfect sense to her. Eva was, as always, a puzzle.

But tomorrow he would change that. Dante was determined that it would be he who would at last delve into her, learn all her secrets. Her innermost self would be laid bare before him—he would know her completely. Perhaps then he could sleep dreamlessly again.

It was absurd that, in his dreams, she was always there.

Even more so that he should wake, hot and sweaty, almost mad with carnal need.

From the beginning he'd been attracted to her. But for Dante, his attraction had nothing to do with her shell so much as her reactions, to her world and to him. She was at times fragile, inspiring in him the need to protect her. Shield her. And at other times, she was so strong he felt overwhelmed by the glory of her.

It became increasingly difficult to be near her each day, after long nights spent dreaming of her in his bed. Beneath him. Above him. Sheathing his needy flesh in her tight, wet body. Every time she looked at him with her black eyes, he thought he saw within their depths an echo of his fantasies and he had to fist his hands at his sides to keep from grabbing her and making their dreams come true.

Being so close to her without seeing her thoughts was torture.

He had no time for dalliance. His purpose was to serve Sterling . . . and to find Abigail Faria. To find her and . . . then what? Punish her for her role, small though it was, in his imprisonment all those years ago? Punish how? As he'd punished the others—with death? He'd never killed a woman. Wasn't even sure he could.

Though he'd never met the doctor, he'd learned enough about her from the files he pilfered from the ones who'd made him what he was. As the lab that had been his prison for over a year crumpled to the ground around him, he'd crushed Faria's picture in his fist, vowing revenge on this one last guilty party, this woman whose knowledge had aided and abetted his captors. He'd long ago destroyed the picture, but he remembered every line of the woman's face.

When Ryan Murdock found him, saved him from a life spent in shadow and secrets, Dante had found new purpose. But he'd never forgotten his original one. Faria had to be stopped before she did to others what she had done to him. Sterling agreed, helping him without reservation.

Over the years Faria had somehow eluded even his great sight. He couldn't find her, despite his endless gifts—gifts he'd received against his will. He was a broad-spectrum psychic with the ability to astrally project himself anywhere he wished—but he'd been born a normal human. After his "rebirth" in the lab, he'd been able to find anyone he wanted, anywhere in the world—except Faria. He'd searched tirelessly, endlessly, projecting himself to all corners of the globe. It was how he'd found Eva . . . and known he'd been too late to stop Faria's penchant for toying with humanity.

Alone in her silent glass womb, he'd felt Eva's plight echoing his own. He'd felt it was his duty, as a member of Sterling, as a human being and as someone who'd been in a position similar to hers, to set Eva free. He'd felt that, perhaps by learning who and what Eva was, he could find Faria at last.

But these weren't the only things he felt. Not now. Not anymore.

Looking at Eva was like looking at a very young, very innocent Faria. When he was near Eva, hard with lust and longing after a night of fantasizing about them together, he nearly hated her for that. If only she had another face, he could want her without the guilt. Eva was smart, lovely, fragile and stubborn—appealing to every masculine sense he possessed—but she was a copy of *her*. His enemy.

It alarmed him that he had to remind himself of this again and again. And that no matter how often he reminded himself of this monstrous truth, every time he closed his eyes he dreamed of her. When they fucked in his dreams their violent passion had nothing to do with his vendetta. And Eva's face, soft with passion and ecstasy, looked nothing at all like that of her progenitor. She looked only like herself and Dante wanted her that way always in his thoughts.

And now Eva was coming to see him. Alone. Unguarded. He was certain he'd detected in her body language her desire for him. He'd sensed it before tonight, flashes of it, but now . . . she wasn't bothering to hide her motives from him at all. If the curve of her smile could be believed, she was more than willing to explore their attraction.

He wasn't sure how he should feel about that. What he did feel was eager. Hard. Wanting.

Cautious too. Always cautious around her. Not because of what she was, but because of who she was becoming. She was far too clever for her own good. Or his.

Her obsidian eyes were always unreadable. As were her thoughts. But tonight, that didn't seem so important. As he focused on letting his doppelganger lead her to his lair, his physical self set about making a bower of his apartment. A cozy, candlelit love nest. Eva wanted to see him alone? He too had wished for that. Many times over.

They would both get their wish tonight for good or ill.

His heart felt wicked.

His cock was hard as marble.

Perhaps his penetration into Eva could begin now, he thought, a sinuous curve playing at his own mouth. For the first time in his long memory, tomorrow seemed so far away. As if it didn't matter at all.

He dimmed the lights, mindful of her sensitive eyes, and thought of all the ways he could make her feel warm.

Chapter Four

Eva followed until Dante's transparent image walked through the door. And then it opened for her.

Even though she'd been following his image for several minutes, past the labs and into the private apartments of Sterling's residents, Eva wasn't quite prepared to see Dante in the flesh. To suddenly smell his delicious scent in the air. To feel the warmth radiating from his skin and breath. He was, for lack of a better word, potent.

His hand on her arm was hot as he pulled her inside his lair.

He let her go too fast. She stumbled a little as the door shut behind her.

The smell of fragrant, melting wax was thick in the air. The living room of the apartment a warm, golden glow that didn't cast hurtful halos in Eva's eyes and she was grateful for that . . . until she got a better look at Dante.

Her breath caught.

She found herself unable to blink.

He was naked.

Well, mostly.

She had to remind herself to breathe. No good. Her lungs were useless dry leaves in her ribs.

Dante wore only a skintight pair of midnight black boxer-briefs. They hugged his every curve, leaving nothing to her imagination. Eva had to tear her eyes away from the massive column of rigid flesh there . . . his cock. She'd never seen one in person, but she knew what it was. What it was for. What it meant for her now.

Eva shifted her legs, feeling strangely soft and flushed from her breasts to her loins and farther down to her knees.

His chest was so broad. Intimidating without the more civilized drapery of his clothing. His skin was golden and smooth. Every muscle was well defined and tweaked to peak performance. His pectoral muscles looked as though they'd been chiseled by a master artisan. Each of his lean abdominal muscles bulged, giving him a washboard stomach that caught and held shadows from the dim flicker of light. His waist was lean, dipping in to his hips before his thighs—each as massive as tree trunks—flared out artfully.

He stood, letting her catalogue his image, one hand on his right hip, that hip cocked to the side craftily.

Everything about him was in peak condition. Eva understood this in a clinical way, knew that millions of years of evolution dictated that he was a prime specimen, a perfect mate. What she was feeling, however, had nothing to do with her brain . . .

The warmth spilling from him was delicious.

Finally, she managed a breath. His scent overrode that of the candles—spicy, musky male. With so much of his skin exposed she could easily smell him, not his soap or shampoo, but his sweat and flesh and blood and . . . desire.

"What are you thinking?" he asked softly, watching her closely.

It took all her willpower to meet his gaze. Not five minutes ago she'd been plotting a way to escape him, escape Sterling, but now . . . she'd thought she understood the power of sexual need, understood how to manipulate it, but *this* was something beyond her scope of comprehension.

"I . . . I was thinking about licking your skin. To taste you and feel your texture on my tongue." She decided to be honest—he would see too easily through any lie she attempted in her present state.

Eva heard his sharp intake of breath.

Her senses were heightened, dancing on the edge of a knife.

Everything seared itself into her memory—the flickering of the candles, the scent and sight of him. The sound of their breathing, ragged, at times fast, others too slow.

Beneath those rich layers she could hear his heart. And hers. Hear the blood traveling like rivers in their veins. They shared the rhythm of one pulse . . . a steady seventy-five. Never wavering.

She blinked, breaking the hypnotic spell she'd fallen under. "That night, when you found me . . ." She couldn't bear to use "rescued." It wasn't the right word. "Your pulse never climbed over eighty. Not even when we were running. I remember listening to it."

He knew what she was getting at. Still, he made her work for it. "Yes."

"You're not entirely human either, are you?"

He shook his head slowly, his bronze hair picking up highlights from the candlelight, twinkling. Eva yearned to see him in the sun . . . but the sun was not for her wide eyes. Might not ever be.

"How are you different?" she asked simply.

He pursed his lips, eyes heavy-lidded. "I was born with a little psychic ability—nothing fancy. I could sometimes read minds. Move small objects a few inches without touching them. I was stupid and careless. The wrong people found out what I could do. They captured me and augmented everything I had, everything I was, until I am as you see me now."

"Then you do know what it's like for me. A little." She tucked that consoling knowledge deep inside her cave, so that it might warm her later . . . after.

"I know."

"I'm sorry for your pain," she said truthfully, seeing it there in his gaze—though he hid it very well. After a beat, she took a gamble and asked her most pressing question. "Was Faria involved?"

He nodded. "She was consulted. She had vast knowledge of the human body and what it can . . . withstand."

Eva hated that, for whatever reason, she too possessed vast knowledge of the human body. There wasn't a question regarding it she couldn't answer—as her cadre of doctors could attest.

What was I made for?

Eva winced and hoped he didn't see it. There were no answers here, so Eva let the question slide off her, as if she were a snake shedding its old skin. Her face felt smooth again and she was relieved that she could shuck her worries so thoroughly in his presence.

The room invited her deeper. Dante's eyes invited her. She saw a well-worn couch and moved to sit on it, tucking her chilled feet beneath her. "I like your body. It's strong," she said, seeing how her words threw him off. Enjoying her effect on him.

But a dark, feral sheen clothed his eyes and with a thrill of primal fear she wondered if she had gone too far. She was inexperienced in the mating rituals with which Dante was obviously so familiar.

He sat next to her on the couch and reached for her. Eva only barely kept herself from jumping to her feet and fleeing—not because she was afraid of him, but because she was so unfamiliar with how powerfully she *felt* around him. But he wasn't reaching to embrace her. His hand darted beneath her and captured one of her feet.

"Don't be afraid," he murmured softly, pulling off the slipper she wore, rubbing the sole of her foot with his warm, textured fingers. His eyes shone like polished I Ching coins.

His natural heat burned into her skin like a brand.

"I'm not afraid," she whispered hoarsely. "I'm curious."

He chuckled. "That's a good start."

She shivered . . . and for once it wasn't from being cold.

Her belly felt full of simmering honey. Her foot in his hand tingled with heat that spread upward, straight to the apex of her thighs, seeping into her sex even as her warm liquid seeped out.

Eva could smell her own arousal. When she realized that, she breathed deeper and smelled his as well—a similar but spicier, more *domineering* bouquet. It affected her deeply.

Dante motioned for her other foot and she eagerly gave it to his expert touch. He squeezed it as a small smile played about his smooth lips. Eva wanted his hands on her breasts, desperately. He seemed to sense the change in her from curious to yearning. He slid closer to her, gently pulling her legs over his thighs, almost cradling her like a child.

There was nothing in his gaze that made her feel like a child—quite the opposite.

His mouth hovered over hers.

She could taste the sweet flavor of his breath.

"This is dangerous," he murmured, so softly she shouldn't have heard it. Wouldn't have but for her near-preternatural senses.

"Afraid?" she whispered, deliberately goading.

His muscles rippled as his pride took the blow, refracted it. "Never."

She smiled secretly to herself.

"What are you thinking?" he asked again, the words a caress across her mouth, like a phantom kiss.

Eva felt herself frown, felt a pang like anger or frustration. Then let it go as she saw in his gaze that he didn't just want to know her thoughts . . . he *needed* to know them. In this moment, her thoughts mattered to him on a very personal level.

"I'm thinking you're taking this too slowly," she whispered.

It was all the permission he needed. His mouth crashed onto hers like a comet upon the face of a planet. The explosion of feeling was apocalyptic to her well-ordered mind. Her heart soared, even as it lay trapped inside her. She had never felt so free, or more captivated.

His arms were around her. A cage she welcomed.

His lips were soft, softer than she would have imagined even after their last week spent together. She'd seen his mouth pursed, relaxed, even smiling. But this was a kiss, a new experience for her, and no amount of knowledge could have prepared her for the reality of his lips on hers. Smooth, plump, hot and moist, his lips devoured her whole.

Mouth to mouth, breath to breath, she felt as if they were already one being. Each a part of the other, two made whole.

His palm discovered her breast. Eva discovered the stars.

Her back bowed of its own volition, pressing her aching nipple harder into the center of his hand. Her mouth opened on a gasp. Bringing her exhalation into himself, he silkily stroked his tongue stroked along hers, inviting her to do the same. She laved his tongue with hers, licked his lips and felt the ridges of his teeth and tasted the well of his mouth, an invasion he welcomed wholeheartedly.

She was beneath him on the couch. His weight was solid, the muscles of his shoulders and biceps smooth and rigid under her questing fingers as he held himself aloft so as not to crush her into the abyss of the cushions.

Eva tested his flesh with her nails and swallowed his growl.

Then his hands were everywhere. All at once. Everywhere he touched she felt the imprint of his heat and his texture. She felt like molded clay, sculpted for his pleasure.

She was naked, her flimsy coverings gone. There was no shame, no shyness, not on her part or his. She gloried in the feel of skin on skin. His golden glow warmed her, seeping into her paleness, lighting her sun-starved dark.

When his mouth kissed her nipple, she moaned low and long, startling herself with the uninhibited sound. The liquid lightning of his tongue flicking her sensitive tissues inspired her to cling to him, to kiss him wherever her mouth could find flesh, to murmur lovers' words in every language she knew between desperate gasps for air.

His hair felt smooth and cool, but for once she didn't revile the absence of warmth. She was burning up, fast and violent, like a supernova. For the first time in her life she perspired.

He sucked her. Licked her. Kissed her. From breast to breast, using his hands as well as his mouth. Nuzzling her, smelling her, reveling in her.

Eva was frantic for more. She rolled them, a wave of motion, and they fell. Dante was careful to take the brunt of their impact and then he rolled them again, so that he lay atop her once more.

Pressure built inside her. There was no way to release it but through her mouth, her cries, her moans and fragmented pleas. But Dante took his time, his patience for once nearly enraging her. She felt her fists beat at his shoulders, felt them captured in his, felt his kisses upon her knuckles. Felt him sucking on the tips of her fingers. Biting gently with his predator teeth.

"Please," she panted. In nine languages.

He wriggled out of his underwear. "Hold on to me," he said, enveloping her in his arms.

Their hearts beat together. Their sweat mingled. Their scents mated and formulated a new, unique perfume. She held him tight, pressing her mouth to the hollow of his throat. The burn of his hard cock in the cradle of her sex was a welcome shock.

And then he was sliding down.

There was a moment when she worried about her belly, about how it might repulse him, but he kissed the unmarked flesh and slid lower. She keened with delight, her worry gone.

Then a new worry as he opened her legs with firm insistence. As he dipped his head between them and . . . oh!

She cried out brokenly.

His tongue laved her, stroked her, burned her. Her cunt was wet already with the intensity of her desire, but now she practically wept with need. He tasted her, as he might sample an exquisite liqueur. Pressed his mouth to her sex as he had her lips. Sucked her clit as he had her nipple.

When his fingers penetrated her as his tongue lapped her cream, she orgasmed violently. Her thighs would have clamped around his head had he not the foresight to wedge his shoulders between them. Feeling her pussy muscles working, pulses that milked his fingers like a suckling mouth, Eva shrieked and rode the violent wave until it crested and crashed, leaving her beached and limp, but strangely innervated.

And then his blunt instrument, pressing into her, bringing her senses sharply back to focus solely on their union. She found his mouth with hers, tasted herself, tasted his mounting passion. Her fingers were in his hair, on his shoulders and back. As he penetrated her, filling her up and stretching her, she transferred the burn of her need into the clutching of her nails in his firm flesh.

The pain of her nails tore through him and he bowed his back, sending his cock to her depths. Sealing him in her wet heat.

They cried out together, ecstasy and pain combined, a maelstrom of sensations neither questioned nor fought.

"You feel . . . *perfect.*" The words were strained, an effort for him to achieve.

Eva was beyond the ability to speak. Kisses were the only language she knew and she used them to communicate her awe.

His hips undulated, his body moving over hers, his shadow a looming darkness that swallowed her whole . . .

Dante was lost. His feelings were an overwhelming force of nature, centered solely on the woman beneath him. His dreams had been aged watercolors compared to the vibrant oils on the canvas of reality. Her flavor was as wild as her origins. Her passion as honest as her words and just as raw, just as disarming.

If Eva felt a fraction of what he felt now, she would be his forever, body and soul.

How had this happened? How had his defenses crumbled so thoroughly? This wasn't sex—it was far too ethereal, too perfect for the physical world. This wasn't a way for him to purge her from his dreams—this would cement her in them. Forever. Beyond that.

Eva had destroyed him. But in doing so, she had remade him.

Gone was his intention to dominate her. Gone was the need to quantify her. She was beyond his mortal understanding. All that mattered, all that he cared for, was her happiness.

She moved like honey beneath him. Sweet and slow in her grace.

Wounding him with her deadly sweet kisses, her unselfish hands pulled him toward a dangerous edge, the precipice of glory.

As he felt his sac tighten he pounded harder into her. Feeling himself slip almost free of her innocent trap before plunging back down into her folds. She was wet and slick, tight—so tight—and small. But she welcomed him like an old lover, withholding nothing.

Nothing . . .

OhgodIloveitIlovehimdon'tlethimstop!

Dante gasped, his eyes flaring to look into hers. But her eyes were clamped shut tightly. Her mind, however, was wide open.

His orgasm crashed into him. With his ears he heard himself crying out, growling and snarling like a wolf. With his mind he heard her thoughts . . .

Gritting his teeth he found her clit with his thumb and rubbed it, needing her to find another release. Needing to feel the honesty of her body's response to him, needing it like a comfort or a balm.

Now that her mind was open, he wanted it shut.

When her orgasm hit, it struck him too, and for the first time since his teens he came a second time within moments of the first, the hot splash of his seed striking the heart of her. The echo of her thoughts following him into the dim cloud of absolute release . . .

The perfect heat. Let it last. Let it last past tonight, this warmth. Oh Dante, I'm sorry.

"Me too," he whispered, kissing the shell of her ear gently. Then silently, *Oh baby, I'm sorry too . . . but I can't let you go.*

Chapter Five

His breathing proclaimed his slumber but Eva was cautious, knowing how keen his senses were.

Dante lay behind her, chest rising and falling with each breath. He held her, arms wrapped around her like gentle ribbons of muscle and sinew. She gently, slowly repositioned them, opening a path of escape.

It was early morning but still dark outside. It was past time to flee. She should already be out of the compound by now.

But she'd lingered. She'd needed to. This was the first time she'd ever felt close to complete contentment. But her thoughts raced out of control, and she damned them for rushing her perfect moments with Dante.

Stolen moments. Get going.

Fine then. Eva crawled away from her lover, the cold absence of him already seeping into her marrow. A strange pain crippled her heart, made her eyes water even though it was almost full dark in the room, the candles long burned too low to offer any illumination.

Don't look back. Just go.

But she couldn't go naked. And though she didn't want to put on the horrible uniform of her time here, she had no choice. The cloth was cool, adding to her chill.

Dante stirred and she froze. His breathing didn't change, and Eva felt an almost overwhelming desire to lie back down and sleep next to him. To dream next to him, close enough that their minds might touch so that they could dream together.

Isn't that why I'm leaving now? To keep him out of my head?

She winced at her own savage reminder of what he meant to do in the coming hours and days. To force open her mind, to rifle through it like a filing cabinet.

The revulsion she felt at the prospect spurred her into motion. She left the haven of Dante's apartment and squinted against the frigid white glare of the light beyond. She ran through Sterling's labyrinth, blindly finding her way despite the even flow of her tears.

Tears that had nothing to do with the lights and everything to do with the dark emptiness welling in her heart.

When she opened the door that led outside, the last barrier to her freedom, the shock was enough to send her stumbling. The air here was fresh and natural, scented with all the impurities of the wide, open world. For a terrifying moment Eva felt how small she was, how vast the planet around her. The beauty and the savagery of her freedom were almost too harsh to bear.

A breeze, scented with the tang of Erie and the sting of burning fossil fuel, caressed her face, drying her tears to a stiff, salty stain on her pale skin. The moon was absent from the sky, the stars dimmed with the approach of dawn, but Eva felt them there, a constancy in the uncertain realm of her existence.

With the door to Sterling shut behind her and the world laid out before her, she balanced for a moment on the knife edge between her past and her future. Then with one step, she met the latter head-on.

No matter what dangers or disappointments the future held, she could hold on to the memory of her moments in Dante's arms. For those perfect hours the world had been small, only the two of them alive in it and Eva had felt safe.

Barefoot on the pavement she walked forward . . . and kept walking until she found a proper vehicle to steal. Safety be damned, she had questions—and only one person in the world could give her answers.

• • •

She actually managed to hot-wire the old jeep. Dante was astonished. Not because she knew how—the woman seemed to know everything—but knowing and doing were two different things. It took a certain skill, a *practiced* skill, to hot-wire any vehicle. It had taken Eva a few moments.

He'd been amused at first, watching her, knowing what she wanted to do, knowing it would be close to impossible without his help.

When the engine roared to life and she deftly put the vehicle into gear, he felt his jaw drop in stunned amazement. As she eased off the clutch and pressed gently on the gas, Dante jerked himself out of his shock and found himself running.

Nothing ever went according to plan with Eva. He'd imagined sneaking up on her in the dark and fighting to subdue her, to explain that he wouldn't rape her mind—her choice of words sickened and shamed him, but were apt, he had to admit—that he would keep her safe and warm forever. He'd imagined her relief and her willingness to be with him and the days spent after in erotic bliss.

But *noooo*. Now Dante had to run, sprint full-out, to catch up to Eva—she who had never driven any car before—as, like a pro, she worked the manual transmission of the jeep she had stolen. If he weren't so thrilled with her achievement, strangely proud to see her in action finally, he would have been a little pissed off.

His hand caught the tailgate of the jeep, slipped, caught it again. He gripped it, feet sliding on the pavement as she picked up speed, and heaved himself into the car.

From the time spent knowing her, learning her, Dante was well aware of the keenness of her senses. Still, her shriek of surprise and sudden stalling of the car jolted him.

"Dante!"

His name sounded so fucking sweet on her lips. Damn, he was already hard. Again. He was always hard when she was near.

"*Get out,*" she snarled, sparking the wires to ignite the engine once again—the neat trick took her only a second this time. She threw it into first gear, tires smoking, and drove with deliberately rough sways that threw him from side to side. He righted himself, gripping the headrest of the front passenger's seat and growled at her.

"Stop the car, Eva."

"Get out!" She screamed it now, her metallic voice in stereo as he simultaneously heard the shout loud and clear in her thoughts.

"Eva. What are you doing?" It took all his strength not to yell at her. She was still driving like a maniac, climbing toward fourth gear. He tried for patience and a reasonable tone. "I'm sorry I was so insensitive. I won't force you to let me read your mind. It was wrong to think I could. I'm sorry. You don't have to run away."

The speedometer kept climbing. She didn't even glance his way as he settled into the seat beside her. They were free of the vast parking lot flanking the Sterling compound now. Headed for the freeway.

How did she remember the way? She hadn't seen—there'd been no windows in the back of the van that had transported her. Then he remembered one scientist's theory that Eva's immense memory relied not just on sight, but sound and scent and other senses most people took for granted, all rolled into one efficient data-collecting process unequaled in the human scope. No doubt Eva had felt every bump and turn in the road and remembered the route as effortlessly as someone might remember the lyrics to a favorite song.

She never failed to awe him.

"You don't have to run," he repeated. "Eva, I've got you. The tests are done—I'll see to it. We'll start again, build a life. You and me." He hoped the offer was tempting enough. *She* certainly was, golden hair bedraggled, skin pale in the approach of dawn, her gown rumpled, her breasts bobbing beneath the thin cotton with each bounce of the vehicle.

She still wasn't saying anything.

"Don't you want that?" He remembered her impassioned response to his touch, her thoughts betraying her wonder and excitement at the height of their union. Had she forgotten so quickly how perfect they were together?

But Eva never forgot anything. She wouldn't—*couldn't*—forget that . . . could she?

"Eva?" His uncertainty beat at him with each second of silence from her kiss-bruised mouth. He was never uncertain, or had never been before meeting her, and found he hated the feeling. "Eva, say something." His words were much harder than he'd intended.

He probed her mind but found it closed . . . well, not exactly closed. Just . . . black. Abysmal.

"I have to know what I am before I can go forward." Her voice startled him when she finally spoke. It was dead—empty. Her words surprised him even more, though he knew he shouldn't have been surprised at all.

"Then we'll figure it out." He felt a seething pain emanating from her in waves and strove to calm the raging waters. "Eva, it doesn't matter what you are anymore. You're *you* and that's what matters. We'll learn the rest together eventually."

"No. You can't do that. You or Sterling. You've been trying for years to find Faria and the closest you've come is me. I can go further, Dante. I *know* where the bitch has been hiding." Triumph tore her voice to ragged edges.

"How?" The word conveyed clearly how stunned he was by her revelation.

She smiled mirthlessly. "I smelled something—a familiar scent, *familial* even. I smelled it the night you rescued me, only it didn't register right away." At last she glanced his way, and her eyes were black as the Stygian dark of a moonless night.

"She wasn't there at the time," Eva continued. "But she'd been there recently. She'll have been back. Maybe still there."

"No. Even if that was her base of operations, after you were taken she would have abandoned it."

Eva eyed him. "What about the others?"

He blinked, stumped by the unexpected question.

"It would take her time to move them, yes? She would want to move them."

The situation had spiraled out of his control. "Pull over."

"Did you think I wouldn't know about the others? Do you know how many times you and your cronies slipped up and said 'trans-humans' or 'experiments' or 'subjects'? As in *plural*? As in more than one scary, fucked-up Eva floating out there in a tube?" She laughed, the sound a little wild, like everything else about her, and Dante felt his heart breaking for the worry she must have suffered, the disquiet, knowing she might not be the only one of her kind.

He was ashamed to have hidden it from her. Eva deserved to know the truth. She was strong enough to deal with it, smart enough to understand, and she was human enough to need to hear it.

"We didn't know how to tell you," he started then paused, searching for the words that might erase fourteen days of doubt. "There are seven others."

"Did they . . . look like me?" she whispered, words breaking, jaw working around them stiffly.

"Yes." It hurt to see the look that shadowed her face then, neither fear nor revulsion, but a strange acceptance. "But you were different, Eva. I saw you while I was looking for Faria—just a vision and a feeling of you in that tank. Alone. When my team and I arrived, we were blown away that you *weren't* alone. But you—the tank you were in—had been pulled aside, separated from the others. There was a filtration system connecting the others—you had been cut off."

"Why?"

"We don't know. It's one of the things we've been working on." He exhaled, feeling relieved to have it out in the open. "Pull over, Eva."

"Why should I?" she asked calmly.

He watched her. Saw beyond her façade to the exhaustion, the hurt, but most of all the determination. "Because you can't drive in the sunlight."

She swore and he heard the tears in her voice.

"I can," he said and waited for understanding to dawn.

It didn't take long. "You'll drive?" she asked, voice softer, vulnerable.

He nodded. "I don't want to. I don't want you to ever go back there. But if it's something you have to do, I'll take you back to where we found you."

Eva pulled over, carefully checking the traffic around her before she eased the car into the emergency lane.

They switched seats without exchanging words. Dante was wearing a black jacket over a cream-colored knit shirt. He pulled the jacket off and offered it to her. "For your eyes."

He eased the jeep back into traffic.

"You don't think we'll find anything, do you?" she asked much later, voice muffled beneath the black cloth.

"No."

"What if she's there?"

"I'll let you ask your questions."

Eva reached out and placed her cool hand on his thigh. He felt her touch reverberate through his entire form. "And after?"

He was glad she couldn't see his face. After . . . if they were lucky—or unlucky—enough to find Faria, he would exact his revenge. For himself. And for her.

It occurred to him that he might have to kill his woman's mother.

It occurred to him that his woman might not like that.

In the wake of his prolonged silence Eva pulled her hand away and Dante felt its absence like the cruel kiss of a jagged knife in his gut.

But he held to the knowledge that for both their sakes, Faria had to be judged. Punished. Erased from their lives. Even if it meant losing Eva in the aftermath, Dante knew he had to take care of Faria, if only to set Eva free.

He stomped his boot on the gas pedal, needing the speed of the chase to ease the pain in his too-steadily beating heart.

It was roughly a nine-hour drive to the remote lake hidden within the Adirondack wilds. After stopping for gas and clothes for Eva, Dante made it in eight.

Chapter Six

The trail looked used but wasn't well maintained. The jeep drove over the pits in the pathway easier than the van had, but Eva felt each one deep in her bones.

This was the place. She remembered the way out well, especially this bumpy, rustic, makeshift road.

"We'll stop here. Just in case." Dante quieted the engine. "We don't want to set off any alarms."

"How did you keep from setting them off last time?"

"I'm telekinetic." His eyes glinted, feral and feline, darkened wood.

It was safe enough for her sensitive eyes here beneath the dense canopy of trees, but seeing the gathering violence in Dante's eyes, Eva almost wished she'd kept her own covered.

"You disabled the security system with your mind?" She knew she shouldn't sound so incredulous—she'd seen much in her time spent within Sterling's walls. But she'd never witnessed anything so . . . otherworldly as telekinesis. At least not from Dante, though she'd heard evidence of his power in the respect and awe of the voices of those around him.

"It's all about visualization. See the object move, and it moves. In this case, I visualized the wiring of the electronic sensors and saw them . . . malfunction." There was a bright flash of his teeth.

It was the only warning she had. And then her newly bought jeans unbuttoned, unzipped and were pushed by invisible hands down her hips. But she remained sitting and the denim could not go lower . . . so Dante had limits. It was reassuring, but only just.

He laughed, the sound thick and warm as molasses. She heard the echo of her own laugh before she felt it escape her lips.

Wind moved the trees. The shadows stretched and reshaped. She sobered. "Thank you, Dante."

"For what?"

"For bringing me here." She sighed. "For being with me."

He took her hand in his and kissed her knuckles. His skin was, as always, a welcome wash of heat against hers.

His breath played over her hand. "You don't have to do this. We can go. We don't have to go back to Sterling if you don't want to. We can find our own way."

She thought about it. Was tempted by it. "Could you do it? Could you let it go so that in years to come you won't dream of finding Faria? Let it go and not find yourself searching whenever you leave your body and streak through the ether?"

He sighed. "I don't know."

She could smell the truth of those words. "Me either," she admitted.

"It's what makes us human," he mused. "Our curiosity. Our need to know. Our need to right the wrongs."

Eva was enchanted that he'd said "us," including her in the human chain. She was further moved to realize he'd done so naturally and without hesitation.

The scent of the lake permeated her thoughts. It was a reminder of their wild flight on the night of her liberation. A reminder of the uncertain hours to come.

It smelled of rotted vegetation and dead fish.

And then came Dante's scent, washing away the distasteful lake with the cleansing tang of his maleness. His soap and after-shave also helped dispel the stench of the dark water. He smelled like . . . Dante. She knew if she put her nose inside her new T-shirt, she'd smell a little like him too.

"What are you doing?" he asked.

Eva realized she'd put her nose in the neckline of her shirt. She laughed and told him the truth. "I was smelling you on me."

His ocher eyes caught fire. Their golden glow burned through her and he didn't need to read her mind to know how deeply it affected her, the desire in his gaze.

He reached for her and dragged her across the seat. He opened his door and climbed out, still dragging her with him.

"Dante!" she hissed, mindful of the danger, but also incredibly aroused by it.

"You'll be surprised to know there aren't many cameras on Faria's compound." His hands pushed down her unzipped jeans. "And none that can see us here."

Eva didn't care, not one whit. He palmed her ass cheeks and squeezed, lifting her against him. There could be no doubt as to the effect she had on him. He was hard, hot and heavy against her.

Urgency riding her, Eva pushed at his clothes, putting her hands beneath his shirt to feel his rigid stomach and bulging pecs. The heat of his skin was like fire and she relished the burn.

His nipples were hard beneath her fingertips. She pushed his shirt up and set her mouth to one, biting him gently just to hear him gasp and growl. She brandished her claws on his skin, scoring him, leaving behind pink streaks on his golden flesh.

Her roughness inspired his own, and he turned her fast enough to whip her head around on her neck. She laughed, a deep and throaty sound, the sound of a woman in thrall to her man.

His tongue traced the line of her spine. He pushed her hard against the jeep, his fingers bruising the flare of her hips. With his warm, rough fingers he squeezed her ass again, separating the cheeks, letting the cool air kiss her.

Eva stepped out of her jeans, kicking them away in her eagerness, and threw her hair back out of her eyes, watching him over her shoulder.

Something about her tossing her hair must have enflamed him. He fisted her hair, pulling roughly but not cruelly, twisting her neck about for his kiss. He tasted wild, spicy and decadent, his lips crushing hers against her teeth.

He filled her mouth with his tongue. Filled her head with his scent and imprinted his touch on her skin. Then he freed her. Eva gasped, leaning limply against the vehicle. Dante bent behind her and used his teeth on her buttocks, kneading her with his hands, nibbling her with his lips.

Eva would have fallen if he hadn't been so strong, supporting her weight so effortlessly.

His fingers found a path between her legs. Found her wetness. Delved deeper, penetrating her, and she bit back her cries. It was delicious, sweet, nearly *painful*, the desire that racked her. But pain was warm, sometimes hot, and she welcomed the heat.

He rose and pressed tightly against her back. She felt him work the fastenings of his own jeans, felt his fingers seeking, felt the prod of his thick cock at her slickly wet pussy. He slid in, stretching her until she burned but she couldn't cry out her triumph, her ecstasy—silence was all that kept them secret and safe now.

She wanted to scream.

Instead she pushed her bottom back against him insistently, rising up on her toes, taking his cock deeper inside her. It was all the encouragement Dante seemed to need. He immediately began to pound his body into hers, riding her hard, hands heavy and strong on her hips.

She felt the bite of his teeth on her shoulder and nearly lost it. But she wanted it to last . . . she fought off her orgasm, but it left her knees trembling. Her mouth dry.

When he sucked the lobe of her ear into his mouth, when he used his teeth there, she couldn't hold back. Her climax slammed into her with all the force of a mountain crumbling onto her head. The pressure made it impossible to breathe, impossible to move. She rose up, taut like a dancer, muscles hard and shuddering with the strain of her enforced silence and violent coming.

The rhythm of his thrusts increased. The power doubled. His fingers dug deep into her hips, leaving perfect imprints of his possession in bruises that would later darken into a lovely violet.

The hot flood of his release inside her was enough to send her over the edge again. And again. She bit her lips ragged to keep from screaming. Gravity pulled his essence down, smearing creamily down the insides of her thighs.

He collapsed against her, breath bellowing.

A bird called from high up in the canopy. Another echoed the cry. *Perhaps they are mates,* Eva thought, a bleary smile curving her lips.

Dante recovered first. Eva's knees stayed weak, her thigh muscles shaking, her breath still coming in pants. He made sure she was steady against the jeep before retrieving her jeans. Dazed as she was, she was grateful when he tenderly helped her dress.

From passion to violence to tenderness, Dante made her feel . . . kept. *Taken care of. Safe.*

"But we're not safe," he reminded her. "Come on. We've got some loose ends that need tying."

It wasn't until they saw the camouflaged entrance to Faria's underground compound that Eva realized he'd read her mind. She was pleased to note that she felt no anger. Instead she felt less . . . alone.

His hand was warm around hers as he took her into the portal from which she'd been birthed.

• • •

Eva had prepared herself for this moment as much as she could.

She'd been naïve to think it would do her any good.

The long walk into the earth, deep into the bunker beneath

the lake, hadn't taken as much time as she'd secretly hoped. She'd wanted the moments to steel herself. To steady her nerves.

No, the walk had not taken long enough by half.

Seeing the tanks filled with cloudy liquid that did nothing to disguise the naked, hairless forms floating within made Eva gag. This was worse than she'd imagined.

Each form was a copy of her. Or close enough. They didn't have the lines of character she'd earned in her two weeks of life. They didn't have the wide eyes or wild hair or musculature that improved upon itself every day. But they were her twins, floating there in their glass wombs, tubes in their mouths, eyes closed as if in slumber.

Eva gagged again, sagging against the solid strength of Dante. She was a thousand times glad that he'd come with her now, a million times thankful that she hadn't come alone to witness this horror, as she'd originally planned.

God, had it only been last night that she'd broken free of her room at Sterling? It felt like a lifetime had passed from that moment to this. Eva felt old, the weight of her age not measured in years but in eons.

"So you've come back to your family? And you've brought a friend."

Eva and Dante both froze at the sound of that too-familiar voice. A voice so like hers but richer somehow, inflections in the utterance of vowels belying the neutrality of Eva's accent.

"Come forward, child."

The voice touched her like a clawed finger, digging into her cruelly with its benevolent but insincere veneer.

Eva stepped forward, compelled to see her, but Dante held her fast, his hand anchoring her by its grip on her upper arm. "Don't."

She frowned. Here, in the shadows of the crypt, where only the faintest light illuminated the concrete décor, she could see him more clearly than perhaps ever she had. He was frowning, his eyes glittering with a feverish intensity.

"Let me see you." The voice of her mother calling.

"Don't, Eva."

Why? she asked him, mind to mind, thought to thought.

You've seen enough. We can leave here, now, together, and never look back.

No. She shook her head to emphasize her quiet rejection. *I have to speak with her.*

Eva. Please.

I can't. She jerked her arm away.

I love you. Doesn't that mean anything?

She paused. *It means everything, Dante. But . . .*

Their gazes met in the shadowy cold and no more words were needed. He could see the determination in her eyes. Feel it in her mind, that great enigma he'd so longed to plumb, which now lay open and bared to him.

He nodded his understanding, his eyes hard and watchful, looking ahead to where her maker waited beyond the reach of any dim illumination.

Eva turned and walked deeper into the crypt. Her siblings lined her on each side, all quietly sleeping. Her footfalls sounded loud in her sensitive ears and she wondered if Faria's ears were as sensitive, or if that was simply part of her design, like everything else.

"Yes, that's it. Let me have a look at you." Faria's words sounded so proud, so *maternal.*

When Eva saw her at last, it was not at all like looking into a mirror as she'd imagined it might be.

At first glance the woman was beautiful. She had a golden halo of curls, long and shining hair that mocked Eva's tangled mess of locks. Faria was tall and straight, dressed in red velvet, like a partygoer in her designer dress. Her skin appeared creamy pale and unblemished, unmarred by time. Too young . . .

She stood by a massive wooden chair, behind an enormous antique desk, papers laid out upon it like pieces of eight on a pirate captain's table. Her research, her most prized and valuable asset, displayed like a trophy.

But when Faria stepped away from it, advancing, Eva scented the cloyingly sweet perfume of sickness. Saw clearly that Faria's body, constructed as artfully as her own, was nevertheless not regenerating cells fast enough to fight off the illness.

"My daughter is beautiful. Come and hug me, daughter."

Eva saw the taint of madness in the woman's eyes. But she hadn't come this far to turn back and flee without answers. She approached, not daring to breathe, and saw Faria open her arms.

Something broke inside her. The sight of those arms beckoning to her beneath that too-familiar face made her heart throb and ache. Tears choked her and Eva fell to her knees, enveloped at last in the embrace of her maker.

Beneath the smell of disease, Eva imagined she could smell the familiar scent of family.

"Mother."

Chapter Seven

*D*ante felt his jaw clench. His night vision wasn't a fraction as good as Eva's. But he could still *see* with his preternatural skills. When Eva hugged the thing that was Faria and yet not Faria, he almost ran to pry her away.

Now he knew why he hadn't been able to find Faria all this time.

He understood why Eva had been set aside. And why there were others like her in this horrible place.

It was a miracle he'd found her before it was too late. And now he'd brought her back, placed her right in the path of the monster that held her so close, deceptively gentle behind the mask of a mother.

Eva, don't!

But her mind was closed to him. Her thoughts dark and hidden as ever. As hidden as Faria's had always been.

He ran forward, praying he'd make it in time.

• • •

Eva felt the truth without Faria breathing a word of it.

Felt it . . . when Faria tried to inhabit her cave. When Faria tried to push out Eva—her memories, her independent thoughts, her personality—and inhabit her space.

Eva shoved the woman away, amazed at how frail this copy of her seemed. And then she understood. All of it. This was not Faria, the human. This was Faria the copy. Just as Eva was a copy. This was a shell containing the memory and personality of a long-dead woman. The shell Eva had been designed to be, a replacement for this defective one.

Abigail Faria had discovered immortality. But with a price.

Faria saw the knowledge on Eva's face and smiled. It was not a pretty or friendly smile, but it was an honest one in all its evil glory. "You were never meant to be."

The words were like a blow and Eva felt a wound inside her open and bleed. "Neither were you," she said hoarsely.

Dante rushed to her side and grabbed her arm. "Let's go."

She stilled his urgency with a touch. There was much to do yet before they could leave this place. He didn't let go of her, however, and she was glad of his strength. She would need it, of that Eva had no doubt.

"You were an accident. You were the next ripe vessel. I prepared you as I've prepared two others before you. I weaned you from my mother's milk." Faria grinned, her gums dark with her illness. "I imprinted your mind with a hundred years' worth of scholarly knowledge. A perfect instrument for me to use when I transferred from this stinking, dying sack into your strong and youthful form. And then *he* came," Faria spat, pointing at Dante with a clawed hand, bones crooked and misshapen.

Faria's monstrous intent given form in her monstrous body.

"And now you're a . . . *thing*. I don't even know what you are." Faria snorted disdainfully. "I don't know how you developed a personality. But then, I have performed miracles before this."

Eva's flesh crawled. "I am what I have made of myself."

"You are what I made you!" Faria snarled. "You're a freak. A failed experiment."

"Don't listen to her, Eva." Dante tugged at her arm again. "Let's go."

But Eva wasn't finished. So her questions were now answered— she was an accident. But an accident of nature, thank heaven. Her form was unnatural, a construct erected by a mad genius, but her mind was hers and hers alone. She was unique. Somehow, through whatever magic created the minds and individuality of other humans, Eva had a soul. She had a life. She had a future.

But what of the others? Her siblings in this farce of a family? She couldn't leave them as they were, empty shells with no hopes or dreams or thoughts of their own.

"Look at you," Faria sneered. "You haven't even aged properly yet. You've still got baby fat. You should be svelte and thin by now. Your hair shouldn't be so thick." Faria looked puzzled now, insane and confused. "You should be prettier, your face narrower. Your eyes are all wrong . . . you don't look right at all."

And Eva saw that the disease of Faria's current shell might not be her fate. Perhaps Faria's unnatural occupation of her creations deteriorated the flesh, like a cancerous cell that did not belong, growing and spreading until the vessel decayed, forcing Faria into a new body again and again. Or perhaps, like any other living organism, each new copy of the original Faria had a flaw.

Regardless, Sterling's had doctors assured her a thousand times over that Eva was beyond healthy. But for the weakness of her eyes, she was physically perfect.

This cycle of madness had to end. Here. Now. Faria should, for whatever reason, be long dead by now. Her time was over and done. Eva had to set herself and her sisters free.

She felt tears spill past her eyes, hot and stinging. For once she did not like the heat. Turning to Dante, hoping he would understand and forgive her, she shoved him away with all the great strength she possessed.

Despite her preternatural power, it was still hard to move a man as solid and strong as Dante. But something in her face must have warned him and he didn't fight, didn't stand against her when she struck him. He flew backward, crashing inelegantly to the floor twenty feet away.

Then Eva turned back to face her doppelganger. She reached

out, a smile softening her mouth. Faria eyed Eva warily. But the health and strength that radiated from her hoped-for vessel must have been too great a temptation to resist. Now it was Faria who fell to her knees before Eva, Faria who nuzzled into her embrace like an orphaned child.

"You will let me in, then? Become my new body?" Faria whimpered the plea, shivering.

Eva took the woman's head in her hands, cradling the golden curls. "I am what you made me." One last tear slipped down her cool cheek. "Mother."

Faria's neck snapped like a twig.

Eva sobbed and lowered the limp form onto the concrete floor with as much care as she could.

Turning her back on her past, Eva went to Dante's side. Where she belonged . . . if he'd have her after what she'd done.

"Are you all right, baby?" Dante asked softly, his eyes empty of judgment, empty of condemnation. Full of empathy. And love.

A hiss erupted from one of the tanks. Then another. The life support systems that had kept her sisters alive were failing, one by one.

"No!" Eva rushed to the nearest tank, uncertain what to do, knowing only that she must do something.

"Babe." Dante's voice was full of sorrow for her plight. "There's nothing you can do. It was Faria's 'mother's milk' keeping them alive."

Eva frowned, gasping as tiny alarms began to sound all around her. The sound of the machines dying. Of her sisters dying.

"She was a psychic," Dante explained, reaching for her. "It's part of why it was so hard to find her. That and her ability to hide in the dark corners of her mind—same as you. She spread herself thin—using her strengths to help power the life support systems. To keep their hearts beating."

And Eva had killed her. Killed Faria's psychic mind, breaking the chain of power that kept her siblings alive.

"Don't think like that," Dante said, reading her easily, pulling her away from the dying wombs. "These others weren't prepared. They weren't anything close to what you were when Faria was ready to inhabit you."

Eva accepted that, accepted too her guilt. She'd broken the circle at great cost . . .

"Wait. Her research." She tugged at Dante.

He was immovable. He kept his arms around her, nearly dragging her from the chamber.

"We can't leave it there for anyone to pick up where she left off!"

"We won't. Let the river have it," Dante said, steel in his voice.

And then she felt it. The power rolling off him in waves. She heard it behind them, the cracking of the bunker's ceiling as Dante's telekinetic power bombarded it, destroying it. She smelled the powerful scent of the oncoming lake.

It no longer stank of death and decay. The scent of the lake as it flooded the chamber of horrors, the laboratory of the late Dr. Abigail Faria, smelled of cleansing rain.

It swallowed the lair back into itself, where it belonged, in the depths of the deep, dark waters where the dead could sleep forever.

• • •

"Where will we go?" Eva looked up at the night sky. At her long-lost moon. It was large and shining, a silver face looking benevolently down upon their naked forms. Her first moon . . . and it was lovely to behold.

"Wherever you want," Dante replied, stroking her hair away from her face.

She listened to the beating of his heart. Listened to the pounding rhythm of her own. "You've given your life to Sterling. So many years . . ."

He chuckled. "I'm not old, babe. But yeah, Sterling has been home for a long time. We've been valuable to each other. They don't always treat newcomers like a lab project, you know."

"Hmm." She wasn't convinced, but was perhaps willing to be coaxed.

"They didn't know how to treat you. You were . . . unique."

She smiled against his warm, muscled chest. "If we go back, will they know how to treat me?"

"They'll treat you like a queen." He kissed her head. "Or they'll answer to me," he growled menacingly.

Eva grinned. *I love you.* She gave him the words in her thoughts, which meant so much to him, and moved to straddle him. He slipped into her, hand in glove, key in lock, man in woman.

She was wet and tight.

He was thick and hard.

Everything natural. Everything right.

The moon smiled down, watching the lovers dance from its cradle in the deep, dark blanket of outer space.

Sherri L. King

Sherri L. King lives in the American Deep South with her husband, artist and illustrator Darrell King. Critically acclaimed author of The Horde Wars and Moon Lust series, her primary interests lie in the world of action packed paranormals, though she's been known to dabble in several other genres as time permits.

Wild Ride

CHEYENNE McCRAY

Chapter One

Tess Marshall shifted on her stool in Red's, the most popular bar outside the town limits of Douglas, Arizona. Smells of stale beer, perspiration, perfumes and cigarettes made her wrinkle her nose. The sounds of people talking and laughing were almost as loud as the beat of the band on the other side of the room.

She sat next to Catie Savage at one of the high tables across the room from the bar. Tess tugged down on her miniskirt, pressed her legs tight together and bit her lower lip as she wondered why in the world she'd let her friend Catie talk her into dressing in such a skimpy outfit—a jean skirt that showed off her long legs all the way to her upper thighs and a white blouse that tapered down to her waist and exposed her belly button. The blouse was also so low cut it practically bared her breasts, showcasing her generous cleavage. Her dark red hair hung in waves to her shoulders and she'd never had on so much makeup in her life.

The corner of Tess's mouth quirked into a smile. The men who'd asked her to dance so far had been guys she'd known for years who hadn't even recognized her. She'd never been seen without her hair pulled back in a braid or ponytail, and wearing jeans and T-shirts.

So far she'd turned down every single guy, half afraid her skirt would slide up to her hips, showing off her little red thong, and half because she was waiting for someone who would really set her blood to boiling.

Catie leaned over and practically yelled into Tess's ear so that she could be heard over the beat of the band and the noise of the crowd. "You need to get your ass out there and dance. Stop turning all those poor guys down."

Tess shook her head and raised her voice to respond. "I'm waiting for the right guy."

Catie rolled her eyes before saying, "Good lord, Tess. We're talking *Douglas* here. You can't do a whole lot of picking and choosing." She nodded toward one end of the bar. "But some of those Border Patrol agents and those cowboys over there aren't too bad-looking. And, honey, if you aren't turning them on, I'll buy drinks for the whole damn bar."

Tess's gaze scanned the crowd and warmth crept up her neck to her cheeks as she saw that Catie was right. Men *were* staring at her, and looked like they wanted to eat her up. She quickly looked away and back to Catie. "I don't know about this."

Catie's eyes focused on the doorway and a smile curved her lips. "Goddamn, but Santiago's hot. If I hadn't married the best-looking lawman in the state, I'd jump his bones."

Tess's skin prickled all over at the mention of Santiago's name. She'd seen the man quite a few times here and there, and knew he was Jess Lawless's partner but she'd never had the opportunity to actually meet Santiago. From what she knew of him, he was a real badass.

Her gaze followed Catie's, and Tess couldn't help sighing as her eyes perused Santiago from head to toe. He wore a long black duster that made him look sexy as hell and a black Stetson that shadowed his eyes. He was well over six feet, had a strong jaw, high cheekbones and an intense look about him. From his Hispanic heritage, his skin was bronzed and she knew his hair was dark and his eyes gunmetal black. Beneath his open duster he wore a snug T-shirt and she already knew he was *built*. The guy had to work out with weights or something. From his broad chest, trim hips and powerful thighs it was obvious he was fit. Her gaze rested between his thighs at what looked like a *really* nice package.

Tess glanced up to see a sensual look on Santiago's face—and he was looking right at her. A flush rushed from her face down to her toes at being caught checking him out. His gaze swept her body slowly, from the three-inch heels Catie had talked her into wearing on up her long legs to her hips, to her midriff and then gradually to her cleavage. Tess's nipples tingled and hardened beneath his perusal and she felt her thong grow wet. She thought she was going to die from embarrassment when his eyes met hers again and he gave her a sexy grin that about made her melt and slide off her bar stool.

He touched the brim of his Stetson, turned and shouldered his way through the crowd toward the bar.

Disappointment lined her belly like lead, but immediately her resolve hardened. She could do this, she *could*. By God, she *would*.

She turned to Catie and leaned closer to talk in her ear. "Santiago's the man I want." At Catie's chuckle of encouragement, Tess inhaled deeply and added, "And I want to have him *tonight*."

Catie grinned and patted her hand. "You go, girl. That man wants you as much as you want him."

Tess managed a grin, even though she was nervous at the thought of being so bold. "You get on home to that sheriff of yours, and I'm going to take care of business."

Pulling the brim of his black Stetson low over his eyes, DEA Special Agent Diego Santiago pushed his way to the long bar in Red's. After tonight's bust, adrenaline surged through his veins like wildfire, and he had to find a way to put it out.

A cold beer and redheaded Tess Marshall might just do the trick.

But first he had an informant to meet with.

He'd never seen Tess look so hot. He'd seen her around town and knew her father, Mike Marshall, who owned the Double M ranch. Santiago had always thought she was good-looking, but *damn*. His cock was so hard after getting a good look at her that it strained against his jeans and caused him to grit his teeth.

Thank God for his duster. He'd adjusted it to cover his no-doubt obvious erection. It felt a little warm in the heat of the bar, but it had been damn cool outside.

When he reached the bar he ordered a cold one. It wasn't long before Raul slipped up beside him and ordered his own beer, without looking at Santiago. The informant tapped his fingers on the bar like a nervous tic. Raul was about five-four, almost emaciated, with scars on his arms from doing big-time drugs over the years.

"Well?" Santiago said without looking at Raul.

"Torrez," Raul said in a shaking voice.

Keeping his eyes straight ahead, Santiago said, "The head honcho is a Torrez?"

"*Sí*. He has a big shipment Friday at—"

Raul's voice cut off so sudden that Santiago nearly jerked his head to look at the man, but he kept his calm, even though his gut told him the informant was gone. Out of the corner of his eye he glanced down and saw he was right.

Shit.

A sudden sensation—and not a pleasant one like he'd enjoyed when he'd caught Tess staring at him—came over him that he was being watched. No, this time his instincts told him something was off.

Keeping his Stetson low, he let his gaze slowly peruse the bar and sweep the room. He saw Tess leaning close to Catie, the two obviously talking. He continued on, cataloguing all that he could in those few moments.

His gaze caught two men staring at him, but Santiago turned

back to the bar after a quick once-over. In the instant he'd looked at them, he had taken in their stats. Blond man, approximately five-eleven, medium build, tanned skin like he'd seen plenty of sun, tattoo on left wrist. The other man was Hispanic, about five-eight, slender, wavy brown hair, thin nose and thin lips.

Santiago didn't recognize either of the men, but his instincts told him the pair was what set off his radar.

He glanced where the men had been standing. Both were making their way out the door, and Santiago gritted his teeth. It flickered through his mind that the men might have something to do with the drug dealer they'd taken down tonight, a dealer who was part of an extensive organization. It was possible the men worked for the drug lord himself. And no doubt they were who had caused Raul to scurry away.

Shit.

When the hairs at the nape of his neck settled, and he no longer felt as if he was being watched, he looked in the direction Tess had been sitting. He frowned when he saw that Tess was gone and even Catie Savage no longer perched on her bar stool at the high table.

Damn. Maybe he'd misread the look in Tess's gaze. At the thought of the redhead, his cock refused to back down as he turned back to the bar to grab his beer. He dropped cash on the bar, took a sip of his beer and started to face the crowd.

He nearly choked on the sip he'd taken when he found Tess Marshall beside him, looking up with her grass green eyes.

She gave an uncertain smile that did *not* go with that bold blouse and tiny skirt. He had the sudden instinct to wrap her inside his duster and lead her outside the bar so that no other man could get such a good look at her body.

"Hi, Santiago," she said, the innocence in her gaze and the breathlessness of her voice not helping the hardness of his cock one damn bit.

He gripped his beer in one hand and touched the brim of his hat with his other. "Tess."

She glanced to the throng of dancers and back to him. Her tongue darted out to touch her lower lip. In his occupation he'd had a lot of experience reading expressions, but he didn't have to use his experience to tell that Tess was nervous.

"How about a drink?" Santiago asked, his eyes focused intently on the beautiful woman. His animal instincts kicked into gear and what he wanted to do was drag her out of the bar and kiss her senseless before fucking her out of her mind.

She shook her head. "No thanks. I—I, um . . ."

"Why don't we grab a table?" he said to make it easier on her. Hell, easier on him.

She nodded and gave him another shy smile before letting him guide her through the crowd to an empty table. He held his hand at the small of her back and the warmth of her bare skin singed his palm and fingertips.

A feeling of possessiveness rose up within him and he wanted to growl at the men in the bar who watched Tess as they made their way across the room. He took her to a table away from the band so that at least they could talk without yelling at each other. When they claimed a table, Tess was careful to tug down on her skirt and to keep her knees tightly together.

Good girl. He sure as hell didn't want anyone else getting a look at what he intended to have tonight. One incredibly sexy woman who was lighting his body on fire.

Tess shivered despite the heat emanating off Santiago as he sat close to her. He set his beer on the table and turned to completely focus on her. She swallowed and warmth flushed through her at the way he was looking at her. She'd never been so close—within kissing distance of the man—before. She wanted to touch the hard, angular lines of his face, slide her palms over his stubbled cheeks and move her hands on down his muscled body.

He gave her that sexy grin again that seemed to say he knew what she was thinking. "Why don't we dance?" he asked as the band struck up the chords of a slow song.

"Sure," she said, trying not to stutter. The man made her so tongue-tied she could hardly think. Where was all that bravado she'd had when she'd told Catie she was going after him?

His eyes seemed impossibly darker as he took her hand and helped her to her feet. Her ankles wobbled in the high heels Catie had made her wear as he led her onto the dance floor. The heels added three inches to her five-foot-six height, but he still was a good eight inches above her.

When they slipped into the crowd of dancers slowly moving to the tune, Santiago wrapped her in his embrace as if they knew each other *really* well. She slipped her arms around his neck as he brought her body flush against his. Her eyes widened and she couldn't help the surprised look she gave Santiago when she felt the hard press of his erection against her belly. The expression on his face was absolutely wicked, as if he enjoyed letting her know that he wanted her.

And lord, did she want him. Her thong was so wet she was afraid he would catch the scent of how aroused she was. No doubt he could feel her hard nipples rasping against his chest through the T-shirt he wore beneath his duster.

"Damn, Tess." He squeezed her tighter to him, moving closer to speak to her. "You've always been a knockout, but *damn*."

Tess swallowed. "Um, thanks." *And thank you, Catie.*

Then she realized what he'd said. He'd always thought of her as a knockout? *Yeah, right.*

Slowly they moved on the dance floor, their bodies swaying to the music. Tess couldn't help staring up at him as he guided her by holding her waist with his big hands. Her lips parted at the intensity of his gaze. His mouth was just inches from hers, then a mere fraction.

Kiss me, kiss me, kiss me.

Santiago's hands gripped her tighter, his jaw tightened and she felt as if he was holding himself back. The warmth of his breath teased her lips. His body enveloped her, making her feel on fire everywhere they touched. And God, the way he smelled— a spicy masculine scent and a hint of the outdoors.

The tune changed to another slow song and they continued to move in a slow circle. She was mesmerized by his lips. Firm lips that she wanted to kiss so badly she ached with it.

I want him, I want him, I want him.

Before the impulse went away, Tess reached up and kissed Santiago.

She felt his start of surprise, but immediately he returned the kiss and his arms tightened around her. The brim of his cowboy hat bumped the top of her head as she slipped her tongue into his mouth and tasted the beer he'd had along with his own male flavor. She was barely aware of making soft mewling sounds as he took her mouth with force, dominating her as if he was branding her.

He moved his hands from her waist, up the soft bared skin of her midriff until he reached the material beside her breasts. He slid his hands back down, over her waist to her ass, then back to her waist.

Santiago's caress made her squirm against him. His belt buckle and his cock ground into her belly and when he bit her lower lip she gasped into his mouth.

With her fingers, Tess toyed with the ends of his hair that curled slightly at his nape, just below the brim of his Stetson. She moved her hands down to his chest inside his duster. Every time she'd ever seen him, she'd wanted to touch him. Her shyness vanished as she placed her palms on his chest and felt the heat of his body along with the flex of his muscles.

The kiss was so exquisite she didn't care if they ever came up for air. She ran her hands all over him, feeling the tautness of his abs, but stopped when she reached his belt buckle. She wanted to cup his erection, but she didn't dare in a roomful of people.

He broke the kiss and she opened her eyes to see him studying her with heavy-lidded eyes. "Go ahead," he said in an incredibly husky voice. "Touch me. With this coat on, no one will see you."

Tess didn't know if she'd ever stop flushing with heat around this man. But she couldn't begin to stop herself as their eyes remained locked. She slid her hand down over his belt buckle and instantly felt the thickness and hardness of his erection against his jeans. He closed his eyes for a moment as she cupped his balls, and despite the loudness of the music, she swore she heard a groan coming from his lips.

When their eyes met again, Santiago said in a gravelly voice, "Why don't we get out of here, baby?"

She raised her hands to grip his T-shirt in her fists and reached up to kiss him again. This time his kiss was hungrier than ever and she knew she wanted him more than anything. Her heart beat so fast she could barely catch her breath.

Tess moved her lips over his stubbled jaw to his ear. "Okay."

Chapter Two

*W*hat the hell am I doing? Tess asked herself as they walked out of the bar, Santiago's arm around her shoulders. The answer came just as fast as her question had. *Exactly what I wanted to.* It had been too long since she'd been in the arms of a man, and no one excited her like this man did right now.

Even though it was early spring, colorful Christmas lights were strung along the eaves of the bar and flashed blues, greens, reds, oranges and yellows that reflected on the paint of a range of vehicles from expensive automobiles to old beaters. Fresh air greeted her. The scent was pleasurable after being in the bar filled with the smells of so much cigarette smoke, stale beer and sweat.

From the corner of her eye she saw Santiago searching the parking lot with his gaze, as if looking for something. When they got to his truck she noticed he even checked the bed and glanced into the window of his truck cab before using his remote to unlock the door.

Her legs were shaking when he helped her into the passenger side of his big black truck. It was so black it all but absorbed the night sky. The pounding of her heart grew even harder when he closed the door behind her, went around to the driver's side and climbed into the cab.

After he shut the driver's-side door, Santiago glanced at her. "Hold on, baby." He pulled a cell phone out of his pocket and keyed in a number.

"Lawless," came the voice on the other end, loud enough for

Tess to hear. Must be her friend Trace's husband, she thought. Trace and Jess Lawless had been married for a good four months now. Tess sighed. All her friends were married—she was the last of the bunch.

"Raul gave me a name. Torrez," Santiago was saying. "There's a shipment due in Friday but he was scared off before he gave me all the info."

"Got it," Lawless said, and Santiago snapped the cell shut.

When he got off the phone, he stuck his keys in the ignition, but didn't start it. He turned to study her. His expression had changed from sensual to serious. "Are you sure you want to go home with me, Tess? Once we're there, I'm not going to want to let you go."

Without hesitation, even with her heart beating so rapidly, she said, "Yes."

The look he gave her was so damn sensual that her thong was absolutely soaked. She leaned over and kissed him, letting him know she wanted this.

When they broke away from the kiss, she still tasted him on her tongue and her lips were moist. He gave her another smile, started the engine, backed up and drove out of the parking lot and onto a stretch of highway. She noticed he kept looking into his rearview mirror as if watching for something.

While he drove, Tess kept darting glances at Santiago. He was such a big, powerful man, and even though she wasn't exactly thin or small, she felt that way around him. She felt strangely comfortable with him, yet nervous at the same time.

They finally pulled up to a ranch house out in the desert, only about ten miles from where she lived on the Double M ranch.

After he parked, she climbed out of the truck and met Santiago at the front of the truck. There was a porch light glowing from the front of his house, and when she looked up at Santiago she could make out the hard planes of his face.

For a moment their eyes locked and she couldn't look away from him. Her body responded to the heat of his closeness, his musky male scent and the way he was looking at her. It was as if neither of them could move. Her nipples drew into taut nubs and, God, her pussy ached. How she could respond like this to a man she didn't know *that* well, she didn't have a clue.

His voice was incredibly husky as he reached up and brushed her hair over her shoulder. "It's chilly out here. Let's get you inside."

With that he took her by the hand and strode toward the house. Tess shivered as she realized he was right, it *was* chilly.

When they were both inside and the door closed, she scanned the masculine home. The leather furniture was deep brown and the coffee and end tables were made of rough, chunky unvarnished wood. A newspaper was scattered across the coffee table, shirts were draped over a recliner and an empty plate and cup were on an end table along with an empty pizza box.

Santiago removed his Stetson, took off his long black duster and put them on a chair by the door. She couldn't help watching his every movement. She'd been right. *Damn*, he had a nice ass. She never could resist a man in Wranglers, and he was no exception. More than no exception. He withdrew an object from inside the duster and as he came back to face her he slipped something into his back pocket. All she got a glimpse of was a bit of shiny metal.

When he had turned away from her, she'd immediately noticed the gun at his back in the waistband of his jeans. When he faced her again, he hadn't removed the weapon. His eyes met hers and she couldn't read his expression.

Tess cleared her throat. "Your home is nice."

He glanced around the front room and shook his head. "It's a mess, but it's my place."

Tess found her hands itching to touch Santiago again and

instinct led her to move toward him. He held completely still, studying her as she came up so close she felt his body heat again. She reached up, moving her hands slowly, and placed her palms against his chest. He sucked in his breath but didn't move as she eased her hands up his chest to his shoulders, then slipped her fingers into his dark brown hair. He had the most beautiful black eyes she'd ever seen. His lashes were dark, his nose was a little crooked, he had high cheekbones and a mouth she was just dying to kiss again.

Santiago still hadn't moved but she saw the desire in his eyes. She had no doubt he wanted her like she wanted him. There was some kind of connection she felt with him.

Tess didn't hesitate. She rose up on her toes at the same time she pulled his head closer to her and kissed him.

Santiago didn't know what the hell to do while he stared into Tess's gorgeous green eyes. Damn, he wanted her. But he had his doubts. Tess Marshall wasn't known for sleeping around and he didn't want to take advantage of her if this wasn't what she wanted.

In the next moment Tess was kissing him, her mouth soft and pliant beneath his. When she nipped his lower lip, he groaned and she immediately thrust her tongue into his mouth. All thought fled his mind as his cock responded to her, hardening to the point where his jeans were killing him. He grabbed her hips and drew her close enough to grind his erection into her belly.

She never stopped. If anything, her kiss became more intense, hungrier. She moved her hands from his hair, exploring his shoulders, his biceps, down to his hands that held her hips. Then she brought her palms to his chest again, her investigation leading down his abs to his belt buckle and the waistband of his jeans.

He sucked in his breath when her bold hands cupped his balls and squeezed his erection through his jeans, just like she had on the dance floor.

Santiago took her by her arms and pinned them to her sides so that she couldn't stroke him anymore. Her eyes were such a dark green. Her dark red hair was tousled and her mouth moist and swollen from their kiss.

He sucked in a deep breath. "Are you sure this is what you want? If you push me much farther, I don't know if I'll be able to stop."

Tess tried to shake off his hold. "One thing I've always known is what I want. And I want *you*. Now."

Santiago didn't release her arms even though the force of his need for her was causing him to tremble. "I plan to fuck you all night and well into the morning. Is that what you want, baby?"

She gave him a smile that held a hint of her former shyness, yet was one of a seductress too. "I'll make sure you do." She shook out of his hold and pressed her body tight to his, her arms around his waist. He knew she had to feel his rigid cock against her belly. And his damn erection was getting harder by the moment—so hard his jeans were definitely too damn tight. All the blood and his good intentions were rushing straight to his groin and he was almost beyond thought.

Tess reached up to kiss him again and this time he met her halfway. Goddamn, he'd never felt a kiss straight to his boots before. The way she kissed was so damn intense.

She took his hands in hers and brought them up so that his palms rested on her partially covered breasts. The moment he cupped her, she moaned and went wild in his arms. Her hands were everywhere, her body rubbing against his. "My nipples," she said against his mouth. "Pinch then. Play with them."

In his lustful haze, that was one order he had no problem obeying. He unbuttoned her blouse, then pulled her bra down so that her breasts were bared. She sucked in a breath and whimpered her excitement as he rolled her nipples between his thumbs and forefingers. Tess felt so silky, so soft to his calloused hands.

She reached down and grasped his cock, rubbing his jean-clad erection hard. He groaned and took her mouth with all the savagery he felt surging through his body.

Tess had never wanted anyone so badly in her life as she did this tall lawman. Having sex with a stranger had always been a fantasy of hers, and even though he wasn't a total stranger, he was the right man. A man who turned her on like no other. Maybe it was the air of danger about him, how tightly he guarded his emotions, his expression whenever she'd seen him around town or at the ranch when he'd visited with her father. She wanted to break down his barriers, to have him opening up to her. She'd never been with a man she hadn't dated a few times, but with Santiago she felt entirely different.

She was so into the incredible kiss that she didn't want to break it just yet. But when he started moving his lips over her jaw, down her throat and toward her breasts, she was all for that. The only problem was that he was taking too long. He licked a warm path along her skin, nipping at her then licking the spot he'd just bitten. He rubbed his stubble over her sensitive skin, causing her to gasp with pleasure.

Tess squirmed in his hold, beneath his touch, his mouth. She explored him with her hands, her palms running over his powerful muscles. As he kissed a path down between her breasts she squirmed and clenched her hands in his T-shirt. Even though her breasts were bared from when he had pulled her bra down, he wasn't licking her nipples like she wanted him to.

"Suck my nipples." She was begging, but she didn't care. "Please, please, *please*."

"Slow down," he murmured when his mouth reached the sensitive skin between her breasts.

"I can't, Santiago." She released his shirt and raked her nails over his nipples hidden by his T-shirt. "God, how I want you inside me."

That got a deep-throated growl out of him. He latched his hot mouth onto one of her nipples and sucked. Tess whimpered, slipped her fingers into his thick hair and clenched it in her fists. He gave a soft groan as he moved his lips to her other nipple and drew her into his warmth.

"That feels so good." She arched her back so that her nipple slipped deeper into his mouth. "I want to be naked. I want you naked."

Santiago rose up so that his eyes met Tess's and the fire in their depths was so hot. "You're sure, baby? You're absolutely sure?"

In response she released his hair and took a step back. She shrugged out of her blouse and let it flutter down. Cool air brushed her skin, causing her to become even more excited. Before her blouse even made it to the floor she'd unfastened the back clasp of her bra. She let it slide down her arms and it ended up at her feet. She kicked off her heels and the only things she was still wearing were her skirt and her thong.

He groaned and it looked like he couldn't take his eyes off her. "God, woman. You're killing me."

She smiled and snuggled up to him, rubbing her nipples against his T-shirt. She drank in his spicy, musky male scent and felt his muscles ripple beneath her as he reached down and grabbed her ass. He slid the jean material of her skirt so that it bunched at her hips and his hands were on her bare ass and he groaned again.

When she pulled away from his hold, he watched her with those dark eyes. His hands clenched and unclenched at his sides and she could see the barely contained lust in his gaze.

Tess smiled as she unfastened her skirt while he watched. She shimmied out of her jean skirt and damp thong at the same time, then stepped out of her clothing. She started to move closer to him. He stopped her by taking her by the shoulders, holding her away from him with his strong arms and firm grip.

A muscle twitched on his jaw as his gaze lingered on the patch of trimmed red hair on her mound and she grew wetter between her thighs. "God, you're beautiful, baby."

"Let me touch you." She tried to reach for him, but he kept her an arm's length away. She whimpered when she couldn't reach him.

In a movement that caught her off guard, Santiago jerked her to him and captured her mouth with an intense kiss. Tess melted against him, her whole body feeling like liquid silver in his embrace. There was something so erotic about being completely naked while he was dressed. His T-shirt scraped her nipples, his belt buckle scraped her belly and his jeans rubbed against her mound. The well-worn denim was rough against her thighs.

She couldn't get over the way he kissed. He bit her lower lip hard and as she gasped he rubbed his tongue over the spot, causing her to moan. She wrapped her arms around him as he worked his mouth over hers.

"Damn, woman." He drew back and she saw that his eyes were so dark they were as black as his hair. "You're not the Tess Marshall I've always seen. Where the hell did you come from?"

Tess gave him what she hoped was a sensual smile. "I want you, Santiago."

His jaw tightened. He grabbed her ass and lifted her up. She wrapped her thighs around his hips and held on to him as he carried her through his house. She nuzzled his neck, drinking in his male scent and the hint of aftershave. Butterflies swirled in her belly when she realized they were in his bedroom, and then he was laying her on his bed, her head on his pillow.

His sheets were rumpled and his blanket thrown aside. His scent instantly surrounded her from the bedclothes.

Santiago raked his fingers through his hair as he studied her, making her feel a little shy. Here she was, completely naked and he hadn't taken off any of his own clothing yet. But then he got on the bed, straddling her with his jean-clad thighs, fire in his eyes. He took both her wrists in one hand and pinned them above her head.

She shivered then gave him a naughty smile. "Going to hand-cuff me?"

"Don't tempt me." His voice came out in a growl that sent thrills curling through her belly.

With her hands still pinned over her head, he kissed her hard before moving his lips to her ear and tracing the skin around her sapphire earring with his tongue, causing her to shiver. She struggled against his firm hold, wanting to touch him, to help him out of his clothes. She wanted them off and now.

Santiago nuzzled her neck and she heard his deep inhalation. "You smell so good, baby. I can't wait to taste you."

Tess squirmed and then gasped as he licked a trail down the curve of her neck to her throat. "You're really driving me crazy here."

He gave a husky laugh. "I'm trying to figure you out," he said before adding, "I need more evidence."

Before she could get out any kind of retort, he latched onto one of her nipples, taking it into his mouth and sucking hard. Tess gave a shout and arched her back so that her breast pressed against his face. She could swear he chuckled, as if enjoying teasing her, when he moved his mouth to her other breast. He sucked on the hard nub with the same intensity and the sound she made was between a sigh and a cry. He moved away from her nipple and kissed the soft skin between her breasts, trailing his tongue in small circles, then bigger and bigger.

Her skin felt flushed and she sizzled all over. "You know how to make a woman squirm."

"Mmmmm . . ." he murmured as his lips reached her mound and he released her wrists.

Without thinking, she slipped her now-free hands into his hair and pressed her pussy closer to his face. This time he gave a groan. He kissed the soft hair of her mound before delving into her folds, his face pressed tight between her thighs, his mouth and tongue on her. Licking, sucking. He trailed his tongue around her clit in circles and she clenched her hands tighter in his hair.

It felt so incredible and she felt so out of control that she turned her head from side to side and wriggled beneath him. She couldn't have stopped the moans rising up in her throat if she wanted to.

He raised his head and looked at her with his intense dark eyes. "Goddamn, you taste good, baby."

"Don't stop." She thought if he did she'd die. "Please don't stop."

He gave her a slow and sexy grin. "And if I did?"

Tears threatened at the corners of her eyes at the intensity of her need to come. "Don't mess with me, Santiago."

"Or?" The teasing in his gaze only made her hotter.

"I'd have to get even." She tried to force his head back down to her pussy, but he wasn't budging.

"Play with your nipples." His voice was husky. "Pinch them hard."

Tess immediately obeyed, letting go of her grip on his hair to roll her nipples between her thumbs and forefingers. The moment she did, he delved back into her folds with his tongue and she shouted out. He kept his eyes on her as he licked and sucked.

God, having him watch her only made her come even closer to climax. When he thrust two fingers into her pussy at the same time he watched her, he licked her clit. She squeezed her nipples and almost came. She was so close. So damn close. If he stopped again, she'd have to kill him.

But then she was beyond thought. She pinched her nipples harder as she rose higher and higher. Her legs began to quiver around his face. His stubble scraped the insides of her thighs and her pussy lips.

He thrust his fingers harder, sucked harder, and she went wild. Her entire world seemed to literally explode around her. She'd never seen stars during a climax, but this time little points of light sparkled in the darkness of her mind. Santiago continued to drive into her with his fingers, to lick and suck her and she rode out every throbbing pulse.

Just as she was coming down from her orgasm, he started again, driving her toward another climax. The second one hit her harder and faster and she couldn't take any more. She tried to squirm away from him, barely able to think, barely able to feel anything but the orgasm. She was sure her cries could be heard across the county.

Finally he stopped, and all she could do was lay there, her entire body boneless. "Oh. My. God." She let her hands drop to her sides. "I'll never be able to move again." Santiago chuckled and moved from between her thighs so that he was lying beside her. She was barely able to turn her head to look at him. "What the hell did you do to me?"

His sexy grin made her pussy contract again. He placed one of his palms against the soft skin of her belly and leaned over to kiss her. This time it was slow and sweet, and she sighed. She caught her own scent mingling with his at the same time she tasted herself on his tongue. She still felt the power of her orgasm swirling through her, but it was gradually subsiding.

When Santiago broke the kiss he smiled. "Let me see your wrists."

A little confusion flickered through her sated mind, but she moved her arms together in front of her.

He grasped both her wrists in one of his hands and raised them over her head. Still completely relaxed and content, she had no clue what he was doing. She saw him reach into his back pocket and in two seconds he had her handcuffed to a rail of the wooden headboard.

Chapter Three

A shot of alarm jolted Tess's body as she jerked against the cuffs and strained her muscles. They were real metal cuffs and she was really bound to one of the rails of the wooden headboard. That must have been what he pulled out of his duster and pocketed as he'd turned back to her.

She tried to slow down her breathing as she looked up at Santiago. "What are you doing to me?"

"Exactly what I wanted to do from the moment I saw you tonight." Still lying beside her, Santiago trailed one finger down her side and she shivered. "Admit it, baby. You like being bound and controlled by me."

At first Tess was going to deny it but then she realized it *was* turning her on. She was naked and at his mercy and it was sending thrill after thrill through her belly. Still her voice shook a little when she said, "What are you going to do with me?"

"Anything I want." He rose up to his knees, pulled his black shirt from his jeans, tugged it over his head and tossed it aside.

Her mouth watered. Seeing him in a T-shirt was nothing like seeing him in the flesh. His skin was naturally bronzed. He had a smooth, hairless chest and finely crafted muscles that flexed with every movement. Fascinated, she studied him from broad shoulders to chest and taut abs and trim waist. Her gaze settled on his erection pressing against his jeans. By the look of it, he had to be at least seven inches.

"Lord, you look good enough to eat," Tess said before she

realized she'd said it out loud. She would have clapped her hand over her mouth if one of her hands had been free.

"Is that what you'd like?" Santiago unfastened his buckle and drew the belt out of the loops. He brought the ends together and snapped the belt so loud she startled. "Or would you like a spanking first?"

"A spanking?" Her eyes widened and her heart raced a little faster. "You're not serious, are you?"

He grinned. "Not unless you're a bad girl."

Somehow the thought of being erotically spanked sent another thrill through her belly. "Um, what would qualify as being a bad girl?"

"I'll let you know." He tossed aside the belt and she watched it land on the blankets that were pushed to the side. With ease he moved off the bed, kicked off his boots and stripped off his socks.

He removed the gun that had been at his back and even though she knew he wasn't going to do anything with it, her heart still jumped. He placed the gun under his pillow, the barrel facing the headboard.

When he straightened, his hand went to the button fly of his Wranglers. Her jaw dropped when he removed his jeans. Her mouth watered again as she saw the length and girth of him. He *was* big, and he *did* look good enough to eat.

He stepped out of his clothing as he approached her side. If he didn't have her cuffed to the bed, she'd reach out and run her hands down his thighs right before taking his cock in her mouth. She'd dig her nails into his ass as it flexed against her hands. She'd never felt so wanton, so filled with desire in all her life.

Santiago never took his eyes off hers as he got onto the bed, which dipped beneath his weight. He straddled her waist and she licked her lips at the feel of his cock and balls against her belly.

He lowered himself by bracing his hands on either side of her breasts, palms flat against the sheet. His warm breath fluttered over her ear as he leaned close to murmur, "What do you want now, Tess Marshall?"

She shivered and her eyes met his as he rose back up to look down on her. "I want to taste you."

An intrigued expression crossed his features. "You want me inside your mouth, baby?"

She licked her lips and nodded. "Yes."

Santiago wasn't sure how long he'd last—and that was before she even touched him. Tess's dark red hair was in disarray against his white pillows, her lips still swollen from his kisses, and she looked so delicious with her arms stretched over her head. It caused her breasts to rise enticingly and she looked even sweeter and more vulnerable than ever. But he'd unlock the cuffs in a heartbeat if he thought she was scared or if she demanded that he did. He hadn't heard one word of argument from her though, and by the expression on her pretty face, he was certain she was enjoying this as much as he was.

He eased up so that his cock was directly over Tess's mouth. A bead of his come was poised at the tiny slit and she licked it away with a flick of her tongue. He hissed, then braced one hand against the wall above the headboard, and guided his cock between her lips with his other.

"Good God." He groaned as she swirled her tongue around the head of his cock, then brought him deeper into her mouth. The feeling of being in her mouth was incredible. Her eyes remained wide and focused on him as he started to slowly pump in and out, her lips smooth against his length while she applied deep suction. "Where did you learn to give head like that?"

She couldn't answer of course, but she gave a sound like "Mmmmmm" that reverberated through his cock and pushed him closer to the edge.

Santiago fought to hold himself back as he continued to slip in and out of her mouth and enjoy the sweet sensations. What was it going to feel like sliding into her pussy? He was careful not to slide too deeply into her mouth, just deep enough that she could take what he offered her. The thought of being able to bury himself completely within her just about made his head spin.

When he was almost at the point of release, he slipped his cock out of her mouth and tried to catch his breath. *Shit*. This woman was going to do him in. He could barely breathe as he looked at Tess. Her eyes were big and dark as he moved down so that he was straddling her hips again. She licked her lips as if savoring his taste.

"I've got to grab a condom," he said as he started to lean toward his nightstand.

She shook her head. "I'm on the Pill, and I can show you my blood donor card."

He grinned. "And I can show you mine."

"Come onnnnn then, Santiago," she begged as she squirmed some more.

Pleased that he'd be able to feel her slick core against his cock with no barrier, he proceeded to tease her a little more. "What do you want now, baby?" He blew his breath over one of her nipples and was rewarded with the sight of it growing tighter and the pink circle around it drawing up. He performed the same with her other nipple and both times she moaned.

"I want you inside me," she whispered and he saw her throat work.

He slipped two fingers into her pussy and pumped them in and out a few times. "Like that? I'm inside you."

Her face grew a little pink and she squirmed. "You know what I mean."

He slipped his fingers out of her slick core and slid them up her folds. "Tell me, then." He rubbed her clit and she gasped and raised her hips. "I want to hear you say it." The color in her face was so pretty he almost grinned. But he kept his face solemn and she writhed beneath his touch. "What do you want me to do?"

Tess was going to kill Santiago the moment he released her. He was torturing her with his hands and his teasing, and there wasn't a damn thing she could do about it.

Taking a deep breath, she forced it out. "I want you to fuck me, Santiago."

He slipped his fingers inside her pussy again and pounded his knuckles against her folds so hard she gasped. "With my hand?"

"With your cock!" Tess couldn't take it any longer. "With your cock, dammit!"

He gave her that sexy grin as he moved so that he was no longer straddling her, and he was now kneeling between her thighs. "Why didn't you say so?"

She jerked her hands against the cuffs. "Ooooh . . ." she started, then what she was going to say turned into a gasp as he spread her thighs wide and moved his hips between them. He pressed his cock against her folds, so close to the opening of her pussy that she wriggled to get closer to him.

Oh God, the look in his eyes was making her melt all over again. He wanted her with such passion that she hadn't even realized existed. She could see it in his gaze, in the tightening of his jaw. He'd been holding himself back, doing his best to draw her into a frenzy.

Well, he was doing a fine job of it.

"Uncuff me." She could hardly speak. "I want to touch you."

"Baby, I think you like being cuffed, don't you," he said as a statement, and heat rose in her cheeks. "Tell me you don't or I'm going to fuck you just like this."

Her face heated as she didn't answer and he gave her a slow, sensual smile.

He palmed both her breasts and kneaded them. The sight of his bronzed skin against her pale flesh and the feeling were so erotic that her body vibrated even more for him. She liked the way he looked between her thighs, loved the feel of his solidness.

"Seeing you spread out, your breasts raised high, your body just waiting for me," he said in a rough voice, "makes me want to take you hard and fast."

"Please." Tess whimpered, she wanted him so badly. "And do it just like you said. Hard and fast."

Santiago placed the head of his cock at the opening to her core. He was barely inside her and she raised her hips, trying to take him deeper, but couldn't.

He hooked his arms under her knees, raising her up high so that her thighs were almost to her chest. "You're going to feel me so deep, like you've never felt before."

"Yes." She clenched her fists, wishing her hands were free. She'd dig her nails so deep in his ass that she'd leave her mark on him. Oh God, she was truly going out of her mind. "I want you. Now. Please."

Santiago slammed into her in one hard thrust. Tess yelped in both surprise at the depth he'd taken her, the way he filled her, and the pleasure of it all.

He held himself still for a moment. A droplet of sweat trickled down the side of his face and he clenched his jaw, and she realized how hard it was on him taking her slow like this. "Did I hurt you, baby?"

"No. You feel so damn good." She shook her head and raised her hips. "Now ride me. Show me what you've got, cowboy."

With her words, it seemed that Santiago's control snapped. He drew out of her pussy then started pounding in and out of her. God, it felt so incredible to have his big cock in her, to have him driving into her so hard. Her eyes were nearly rolling back in her head.

"Look at me." His voice was a rough growl. "I want to see your beautiful eyes, baby."

Heat flushed over Tess's body from his demands and from the feeling of him inside her. She obeyed him and looked into his eyes. It made the feelings more intense to have him watching her as he took her.

His breath was coming out in harsher gasps. "Look at my cock as I take you."

Tess glanced down. The way he had hooked his powerful arms beneath her knees and had her spread wide, she could easily see him moving in and out of her. The sight heightened the sensations in her body, swirling from her pussy to her belly to her breasts.

"Look into my eyes, Tess." It sounded like he could barely get the words out.

She looked up at him and he kissed her hard, never stopping his thrusts. He plunged his tongue in and out of her mouth at the same time he plunged his cock in and out of her pussy.

The kiss, the feel of him so deep inside her, the strain of her arms against the cuffs made her wild, wild, wild for him. She bucked up, meeting his every thrust. He was reaching that place deep inside her that had never been reached before. A sweet spot, the G-spot, that was making her start to tremble with the early tingling of an orgasm.

When he broke the kiss, their eyes met again and she saw another bead of sweat roll down the side of his face. Her own body was slick with perspiration.

Uncontrollable feelings rose up within Tess. She tried to hold back, to make the moment last, but she was swirling, swirling, higher and higher. Just a few more strokes and she was going to lose it.

"Ready to come, baby?" His voice was so rough she heard the strain of his own control.

"Yes." Tess raised her hips higher, matching each thrust. "I'm so close. God, I'm so close."

In response, Santiago slammed into her so hard, so deep that he hit that sweet spot and she lost it. She cried out, her voice punctuated by every one of his continued thrusts. Her orgasm started at her toes and rippled throughout her body all the way to the roots of her hair. The stars in her mind were even brighter this time. Sparks that lit her mind so bright she felt blinded from them. Her body convulsed with every stroke as he continued to move in and out of her. She felt her muscles clamping down on him as her core contracted with every spasm of her orgasm.

Santiago shouted something that sounded like "*Dios mio!*" and she felt the heat of his semen as it was released deep inside her. Her pussy continued to clamp down on him with the remnants of her orgasm, and he slowed his strokes until he stopped and just pressed his hips hard against her, still deep inside.

She watched him through her own orgasmic haze, seeing the tightness of his jaw, his head thrown back, his eyes closed.

"Look at me," she demanded as her voice came out in small pants. "I want to see your eyes."

He lowered his head and his eyes met hers. Holding still inside her, he lowered her legs so that her feet were flat on the bed and her thighs no longer pressed up against her chest. He swooped down and caught her mouth with his in a kiss as deep as their passion had run.

The scents of their sweat and their sex surrounded them and her body ached from her bound wrists to her thighs. He had pounded into her so hard she was sure he'd left bruises on her thighs. And she'd loved every moment of it.

When he raised his head he looked at her with those incredible black eyes. "Goddamn, Tess. What the hell did you just do to me?"

"I think I just fucked you." She smiled up at him. "And damned if that wasn't the best sex on earth."

"No shit." Santiago kept the majority of his weight off her

by bracing his hands on either side of her breasts so she wasn't smothered by his bulk.

His breathing still hard, he finally slipped out of her. His cock was pressed up against her folds and to her surprise she felt him hardening.

"Believe it or not, I could take you again." Santiago kissed her hard. "You make me so hot, baby, I just want to stay inside you."

She was so relaxed from her incredible orgasm, but could still feel her body stir at the thought of him being inside her again. "Well, this time why don't you uncuff me and let me ride you?"

Santiago's expression went cold the same second Tess saw the flash of metal.

Her heart stopped in her throat as a blond man towered over them, the barrel of his gun pressed tight to Santiago's head.

Chapter Four

Santiago froze at the feel of the gun barrel pressed against the side of his skull.

Tess's eyes were wide, a terrified expression on her face. "Danny?" she said.

"The cuffs? I like you exactly the way you are, Tess," the man said to her as he kept the gun to Santiago's head. "We'll just leave them on." He gave a low chuckle as he added, "For now."

Fury boiled up within Santiago but he didn't move. He didn't recognize the voice, but Tess obviously knew him. "Who the hell are you?" Santiago said, his voice even and controlled, as if he wasn't lying naked on top of a bound and equally naked woman. "And what the hell are you doing in my home?"

The man pressed the barrel of the handgun harder against Santiago's head, but he was too pissed to feel any pain. "If I didn't have instructions otherwise, I'd shoot you now. The bullet would travel straight through you and right into Tess. Like killing two birds with one stone."

"How goddamn clichéd can you get?" Santiago growled.

The butt of the gun slammed into the back of his skull. Pain burst through his head and his vision wavered, Tess's face blurring beneath him. His arms almost buckled, but he managed to keep himself from letting his full weight drop on her.

He shook his head, trying to clear his mind, but then the barrel was pressed against his skull again.

"Get up, cowboy," the man said in a steel-cold voice. "I don't suppose you've got a gun up her crotch, so just get to your feet."

No, but he had one under the pillow, close to Tess, within inches of his fingers. If he could risk going for it and making sure Tess didn't get in the line of fire . . .

Thank God she didn't glance in the direction of the gun and give it away with her expression. She kept her gaze firmly fixed on the man bending over Santiago's head.

"Get the hell up," Danny demanded as the barrel of the gun eased away from Santiago's head. For one second he thought of going for his weapon, but the bastard added, "Got my sights set on Tess now, so just watch yourself."

Santiago ground his teeth and pushed himself from the bed, off Tess, and got to his feet. Her features were scarlet—he didn't know if it was from embarrassment at being fully naked and cuffed, or anger, or both.

"Turn around."

When Santiago obeyed, he moved slowly and found himself looking at the two men he'd seen at the bar—the blond called Danny and the Hispanic, the two men who'd been watching him and had scared off Raul. *Shit*. He'd been so goddamn sure that he hadn't been followed. But if they had been tailing him, he doubted they would have waited a good hour for him to fuck Tess. They'd probably had to figure their way out to his ranch one way or another.

Despite the fact that he was naked, Santiago felt no embarrassment, only rage. He clenched and unclenched his fists at his sides and narrowed his gaze at the man Tess had called Danny, who now had his weapon aimed at Tess's head. The other male had a gun pointed casually at Santiago, no expression on his face. Fact was, by the glazed look in his red eyes, the man looked stoned out of his mind. Danny seemed to be hyped on something too.

The man didn't waver as he pointed his gun at Tess while he glared at Santiago. "I don't particularly want to see your dick, so get your fucking pants on."

Santiago started to reach for them, but Danny shook his head. "First, Mike will check the pockets." Danny kicked the jeans in the direction the man he called Mike was standing.

Mike obeyed, his eyes just as glassy as they had been. He stuck his weapon in his waistband, crouched down and searched every pocket of the jeans. His search turned up the handcuff key, a pocketknife and a slim cell phone. He tossed the pants to Santiago who caught them in one fist, then Mike took out his gun again. Only now he was standing closer.

Santiago's mind raced, going through option after option. If Danny hadn't been pointing his gun at Tess, Santiago was close enough to take both of them out in five seconds flat.

He jerked on his jeans, his blood boiling and his head aching from the blow to his skull. He started to grab his T-shirt when Danny said, "Hold up, Santiago. I didn't say anything about the rest of your clothing."

Danny glanced at Tess and gave her a friendly grin. He reached over and tweaked her nipple, obviously squeezing it hard judging by her gasp and the look of pain on her expression. Santiago's jaw tightened and he cut Danny a murderous look.

"I'm not into rape, no matter how cute you look, Tess." He kept his gun pointed at her. "I'd leave you here, all nice and cuffed, but I don't intend to have any witnesses, especially an old school friend."

Tess's skin grew cold and goose bumps prickled over her body. Danny wasn't going to kill her now, but the threat was implied in his words. Once they were finished with Santiago, Danny and Mike planned to get rid of them both.

"Unlock her cuffs," Danny said to Santiago.

Santiago gestured toward Mike who had taken the belongings from Santiago's pocket. "Your friend has the key."

Mike dug in his own pocket and flipped the key to Santiago who caught it neatly. With a single glance at Danny, he leaned over Tess, blocking Danny's view of her face. He fumbled with the cuffs as he mouthed at her "gun" and glanced to where he'd hidden it, which was bare inches from her, beneath the pillow. Then his eyes darted up, over the pillow then back to her.

Heart beating faster, she gave an almost imperceptible nod. She knew better than to glance in the direction of the weapon and give it away. If she was lucky she could get to it and toss it to Santiago. She searched her mind for a way to do it and not get shot in the process. Danny didn't really need her, except as a way to get Santiago to do what he wanted him to do. She was a bargaining piece.

After he unlocked the first cuff, she slowly slid her hand across the sheet and under the pillow. Her fingers gripped the cold metal of his weapon at the same time he released the second cuff. The moment she was free, she passed the gun to Santiago. At the same time she threw herself over a mound of blankets, rolling to the other side of the bed, and landed on the floor with a loud thump, hitting her head so hard she saw stars.

Santiago snatched the gun from Tess's hand. Automatically his training kicked into gear as he shot Danny from under his arm and got the bastard in the shoulder of his gun hand.

Danny shouted and his gun fired, but his shot was wild as he tumbled to the floor.

Before Danny hit the floor, Santiago was in a crouch and whipped around to face Mike and discharged his weapon, shooting a hole through the man's shoulder too. Mike screamed as the weapon flew from his grip and skittered across the floor toward the bed.

Santiago whirled back to Danny—and found himself face-to-face with the barrel of the man's gun. Santiago's weapon was already trained on Danny, which put them at an impasse.

But from the corner of his eye, he saw Mike crawling across the floor, holding his hand to his chest as he tried to reach for his gun with his other hand. A long string of Spanish curses rolled out of his mouth. The air smelled of blood, gunfire and sweat.

Just as Mike's fingers reached for the firearm, Tess dove out from under the bed and snatched the gun. She didn't bother pointing it at Mike. Instead she got to her knees and fixed the weapon on Danny. "I grew up knowing a thing or two about guns, Danny," she said without a tremble in her voice, "and my sights are trained right on your head. You shoot either one of us and you're dead."

"Shit." Danny lowered the barrel of his weapon and Santiago eased forward and pressed his own gun to the bastard's temple.

He took Danny's weapon and stuck it in the back of his jeans before settling back into his crouch. It was then that Santiago saw Danny was trembling and gritting his teeth. The man slowly brought up his left hand to his right shoulder where blood was pouring down and soaking his white T-shirt.

Mike was holding the wound in his shoulder. Blood rapidly seeped into his shirt.

Santiago had done exactly what he'd intended—he had shot to wound, not to kill. He needed to know what the hell was going on. But he'd almost screwed things up royally. Danny had gotten to his gun a lot faster than Santiago had thought he would.

He glanced at the still-naked Tess, who hadn't wavered, still on her knees, her sights still set on Danny, a grim expression on her face.

God, you had to love a woman like Tess.

Santiago ordered Mike to give him his belongings, which included the cell phone. With a flip of the phone, and still covering both men, he punched in a number that dialed automatically.

"Lawless," came Jess's voice.

"My place." Santiago kept a wary eye on both men. "Backup and ambulance."

"Done."

Santiago snapped the cell shut, then ordered Danny to stand

as Tess scrambled to her feet. While he still covered the men, Santiago told Tess to put on the T-shirt he'd discarded. It would be a while before backup arrived because his ranch was so far out in the desert.

He searched Danny's pockets, where he found another handgun and a cell phone. He forced Danny to kick off his boots, where a dagger was hidden. After patting the man down, he turned his attention to Mike.

Santiago gave a quick glance at Tess.

"I've got Danny covered." Her stance was wide, her arms straight out, one hand supporting her gun hand. "My daddy didn't teach me to shoot to kill for nothing."

Santiago raised his eyebrows at that, but got to work patting Mike down and ridding him of an extra weapon and a baggy full of what looked like crystal meth and another loaded with marijuana.

When he was finished making sure the men were weapon-free, he cuffed them together and forced them to sit back-to-back. Both men had paled from their wounds and blood was dripping on the tiled floor.

Danny clenched his teeth from either pain or the fact that he didn't want to give Santiago any information.

"Who sent you?" Santiago leveled his gaze on Danny. "And why?"

The man grimaced. "I'm not giving you any names."

"Forget the names for now," Santiago growled. "I want to know why."

Danny's teeth started chattering, his face was growing paler, his eyelids were drooping. It was obvious he was going into shock.

"First-aid kit," Santiago said to Tess. "In the bathroom, under the sink."

"Gotcha." She whirled, her bare feet pattering on the floor as she hurried to get the kit.

"Smelling salts," Santiago said when she returned, and Tess flipped open the lid of the kit and handed them to him at once. The sharp smell of ammonia filled the air when he snapped the packet open and held it a few inches away from Danny's nose.

The man jerked his head up. For a moment he looked out of it, but then he started talking. "You made your goddamn bust of one of the head honcho's men, but that shit Raul tipped you off with more. We tortured that much out of him. Now the big guy wants to find out exactly what Raul told you."

"As if Santiago would tell him," Tess grumbled.

At Tess's remark, Danny gave a ghostly smile. "He's got all kinds of ways to get what he wants."

"Torture, you mean." Tess's features were grim. "Like with that other man you're talking about."

Danny's faint smile vanished, and was replaced by an expression of fear and pain. "The big guy's good at it."

No matter what Santiago asked Danny, the bastard wouldn't give him any names.

Santiago turned his attention on Mike. The man's agony had obviously jerked him out of his pleasantly stoned state and now his eyes were glazed from pain instead of drugs.

Boot steps sounded from the living room, and Santiago's gun was instantly pointed at the doorway to the bedroom.

"Santiago," came Lawless's voice from the front room. "Lawless here."

"Bedroom." Santiago lowered his gun and turned back to Mike just as Jess Lawless walked into the room. Lawless was also a DEA Special Agent and Santiago's partner. Jess had been on the earlier bust with Santiago and the DEA team.

Jess crouched down beside the two handcuffed and injured men. He glanced at Tess, and by the way he gave her the once-over he knew exactly what Tess had been doing with Santiago. By her blush, she obviously knew what he must be thinking too.

"Evenin', Tess." Lawless touched the brim of his hat before his features turned grim and he turned back to Santiago. "What have you got here?"

By the time additional backup arrived, Santiago was even more pissed. Neither Mike nor Danny would give names or locations no matter how much Santiago and Lawless tried to get them to talk. The backup arrived minutes after Lawless, followed by an ambulance and the sheriff, Jarrod Savage, Catie's husband.

After an endless night of following proper procedures, being grilled on what happened, and after being treated by the EMTs, Santiago's gut clenched when he glanced at Tess. She looked like she was about to drop. He'd wrapped her in his duster to keep her warm. Underneath she wore an old pair of his sweatpants that barely stayed up on her slender frame, and he'd had her put on a pair of his socks. Both he and Tess refused to go to the hospital to be checked out any further, although he'd tried his best to get her to in case she went into shock.

When everyone finally left, Tess sagged against Santiago. He ran his hand down her hair. "Are you all right, baby?"

She gave a long, shuddering sigh. "I think so."

"Goddamn it, Tess, I shouldn't have put you in danger."

She looked up at him with a puzzled expression. "How could you have anticipated this?"

He gave a deep sigh too. "I saw those men checking me out at the bar. I figured they hadn't followed me though."

Tess's eyes remained fixed on him. "That's why you checked the parking lot and your truck so thoroughly, and why you were looking in your mirrors so much."

Santiago raised an eyebrow. "Observant."

She smiled and rested her head against his chest, snuggling up to him. "I just want a shower and some sleep."

He tightened his arm around her. "You've got it, baby."

Chapter Five

Tess woke feeling exhausted yet comforted too. Santiago's big body was pressed up against her back, his arm draped over her waist, and they were cocooned in a sheet and blankets in one of his spare bedrooms. This time his alarm system was set and she wasn't worried about another break-in.

She snuggled deeper into his embrace and was rewarded with the feel of his morning erection hard against her backside. He reached up and stroked her hair, not saying a word, just lightly touching her. She was surrounded by his scent—it was like an aphrodisiac.

"Mmmm," she murmured with a sigh. She shook off the horrors of the night before, and concentrated on how wonderful it had been to be with Santiago. Every moment had been special—until Danny and Mike showed up, of course.

Santiago kissed her hair and she heard his deep inhalation, as if drinking in her scent. "I'm sorry, baby," he said softly.

Tess turned in his arms so that she was facing him. She was wearing one of his clean black T-shirts, and he wore only a pair of white briefs. She placed her palm against his warm chest and looked into his dark eyes. "If you apologize one more time, I'm going to have to kick your ass, Santiago." He'd already apologized a few times last night when they'd taken a shower together and then climbed into bed.

He grinned, his teeth flashing white against his bronzed skin. "After last night, I'd bet you could, too."

"Damn straight, cowboy." She reached up to kiss him lightly on the lips before drawing away. "I've probably got morning breath." She'd used his toothbrush last night, but that wouldn't keep her mouth minty fresh overnight.

He rubbed his nose against hers. "Then we'll just have morning breath together."

Tess laughed and Santiago nuzzled her neck.

"Up for a shower?" He reached around and caressed Tess's ass.

She reached down and cupped his incredibly hard erection. "Looks like you're up for about anything."

He closed his eyes for a moment as she stroked him, then opened his eyes so that they met hers. "Watch it, baby, or we'll never make that shower."

Tess gave a naughty grin, but Santiago rolled away, off the opposite side of the bed. "Come on, honey. Shower."

With a sigh she climbed out of bed on her own side. The guestroom they were in was sparsely furnished, like he didn't do much entertaining. Although she'd been a bit too, er, occupied, to really take notice of how the master bedroom was furnished. Like the rest of the house that she'd seen, the floor was tiled, and it felt cool beneath her bare feet as she padded across it to Santiago's side.

He took her by the hand and led her into the guest bathroom that was equipped with a couple of brown washcloths and towels, soap and shampoo. He turned on the faucet in a glass-walled shower and within moments the cool room filled with steam. She stripped off the T-shirt and Santiago pushed down his briefs revealing his thick erection. She sighed as she stared at his cock, but he pointed to the shower.

With a grin she stepped onto the ceramic-tiled floor of the shower. Warm water hit her full in the face and she felt Santiago's presence behind her as he walked in and slid the glass shut behind him. She grabbed one of the washcloths hanging on the bar inside the shower and scrubbed her face with it. When they'd taken a shower last night, she'd been too exhausted to make sure the heavy makeup she'd been wearing was off.

After hanging the washcloth back on the rail she turned so that she could see Santiago. God, he was just to die for. While their eyes met, she wet her hair and slicked it back.

The motion caused her breasts to rise too, and Santiago watched them with hunger in his eyes. "Baby, you are so beautiful."

"You're not so bad yourself." Warm water still pounding on her back, she snuggled up to him, rubbing her wet nipples against his chest and letting his cock press into her belly. She felt his chest move beneath her cheek as he sucked in his breath.

He slowly turned them around so that the water was at his back. He was so tall, so broad that he almost completely blocked her from the shower. With steamy eyes, he bent down and kissed her, his firm lips traveling over hers in a sensual movement that took her breath away. She sighed and whimpered into his mouth as she closed her eyes. Lord, how the man made her just want to melt into him, to become a part of him.

Santiago raised his head and she opened her eyes. "I just can't think around you, baby."

"That's what you do to me too." She raked her nails over his nipples and her fingers started traveling down to his firm abs. She glanced down at his erection before looking back to him. "Or rather, I become a little single-minded."

He gave a wicked grin that turned into a more feral expression as she gripped his thighs with her hands and got down on her knees before slipping one hand around his thick cock.

Santiago watched Tess as she slipped his erection through her lips. Her eyes remained fixed on his as she worked his cock with one hand while her head slowly moved up and down. She applied suction while swirling her tongue around the head.

Damn. He reached down and grasped her wet head with his hands and began pumping in rhythm with her strokes. "You give such good head," he growled and watched her smile around his cock as she lightly squeezed his balls.

He groaned and tipped his head back, all focus on his groin and the beautiful woman going down on him. Water from the shower ran down his face and his chest and worked its way down to where Tess was sucking his cock. He looked down again so that he could watch her suck him, watch as his erection slipped in and out of her mouth.

Wild sensations coursed through his body, to settle entirely in his groin. Santiago gritted his teeth. "I'm about to come, baby," he managed to get out even though he could barely speak at that moment. He wanted to give her a chance to pull away, but instead she sucked him harder. He gave a loud groan and braced his hand against the wall behind Tess as his climax exploded and he filled her mouth with semen. She kept sucking him, drawing out every drop until he thought his knees were going to give out on him. *Shit.* He'd never experienced that kind of orgasm before. So damn intense.

He drew his cock out of her mouth and shuddered when she licked the head again, teasing him. He caught her under the arms and brought her up so that he could kiss her again, hard. "Thank you, baby," he murmured against her lips. "Just wait until I fuck you."

She gave him a sultry smile. "Could it possibly be any better than the last time?"

He caught her nipples between his thumbs and forefingers and squeezed. "I think with you it can only get better and better each time."

Tess gave a soft sigh as Santiago rubbed her scalp with unscented shampoo as he washed her hair. "What's your first name?" she asked.

He moved his fingers down to rub the base of her scalp. "Diego."

"I like that name," she said as he soaped the ends of her shoulder-length hair. "Why does everyone call you Santiago instead?"

"Tip your head back so I can rinse." He guided her beneath the spray, obviously taking care to keep soap out of her eyes. She heard the shrug in his voice when he said, "My junior high football coach called me by my last name. It stuck."

"That's right, you were some kind of football star, all the way from junior high through high school." She caught a clean, musky scent as he applied conditioner. "I was at least four years behind you, but I remember hearing your name—lots of girls had crushes on you."

Santiago began rinsing the conditioner out of her hair and gave a soft laugh. "You're exaggerating, baby." He finished rinsing her hair and she started to turn around but he held her in place by gripping her shoulders. "I'm going to wash your back."

"You're so good at this." Tess sighed again with pleasure as he used the washcloth to scrub her back. Surprisingly a little jealousy stirred within her. "Do you do this often? Treat women to your shower skills?"

"That good, huh?" He gave a soft laugh and rubbed the cloth over her ass in slow, sensual strokes causing her pussy to grow wetter. "Nope, guess I'm just clean out the gate."

At that Tess smiled. "Good."

He chuckled again and crouched behind her to wash her legs. The water he'd been blocking began pounding on her back.

"Do you still have family in Douglas?" she asked. "You have a pretty big family, don't you?"

He touched the insides of her thighs. "Widen your stance." When she obeyed, he started washing her legs from her ankles to her calves. "Four sisters and three brothers. They've pretty much all moved here and there, but they're all still in Arizona." He moved the washcloth higher, to the insides of her thighs, and she didn't think she could talk if she had to. "My mother and father live in Douglas."

Tess groaned as he reached her pussy and began brushing the rag over the swollen lips. Lord, she wanted him. After she'd given him head, she wondered if he'd be up to the challenge of another wild round of sex.

As he rose back up and grabbed her shoulders, she felt his erection against her backside and she grinned.

Santiago moved around her so that the water still beat down on her back. With single-minded focus he started washing her front side. To her pleasure, he soaped her breasts first. Damn, that felt good. "So, how did you end up being a DEA agent?"

He shrugged one big shoulder. "I saw too many kids doing drugs while I was growing up. They'd get strung out on some serious shit and you could tell they were going to end up nowhere fast. One guy I knew overdosed. Really shook me up when he died." He moved from her breasts and rubbed the cloth against her belly. "Too much gets across the Mexican border, and I do the best I can to take them out."

Tess shivered as he worked his way down her thighs. "It's dangerous work."

With a grim expression, he said, "Last night was the first time my home was invaded, and I don't like it one damn bit."

"I'd be pretty pissed too." She trembled as he eased the washrag up the inside of one of her thighs toward her folds. "Well, I have to admit I *am* pissed about it."

He gave a low groan and kneeled again. "You have the nicest pussy." The change in topic startled her, not to mention the fact that he'd just slipped a finger into her folds and stroked the soft flesh. "So soft, so pink," he murmured just before burying his face against her mound and licking her from her core to her clit.

"Oh, jeez, Santiago." Her knees weakened and she braced her hands on his broad shoulders. The feel of the water pounding on

her back and ass added to the sensations of his mouth and tongue
on her.

He paused long enough to say, "Turnabout is . . ."

Tess popped him on the head with her fingertips. "Don't
stop."

Santiago chuckled against her pussy lips and then began sucking and licking at her in earnest. He thrust three fingers into
her core, and her legs started trembling. She looked down and
watched him and his eyes met hers. Somehow it was even more
erotic to be able to watch him like this, to see him pumping his
fingers in and out of her pussy and to see his tongue flicking
against her clit. His stubble scraped the insides of the already
sensitized skin of her thighs.

Her climax came out of nowhere. Fast and sudden. It was
like the heat of the shower was causing her to burn up, blending
with the heat of her orgasm. Her hips jerked against his face.
"Okay, you can stop now," she forced out. "Please. Before I pass
out."

Santiago kept hold of her as he rose up to stand. It was a
damn good thing, or she was sure she would have dropped to the
shower floor.

She clung to him for a moment before she said, "My turn."

Santiago smiled down at Tess, who still looked flushed from
her orgasm. "And my turn to grill you."

"Grilling, huh?" She raised an eyebrow. "You're going to have
to help me out here by bending over so that I can shampoo that
big head of yours."

He couldn't help smiling around Tess. There was just something about her that made him feel good deep in his gut.

"What about your family?" he asked as he bent over and she
started soaping his hair.

"This'll be a short conversation." She scrubbed his scalp like
he'd done with her. "My mom died right after she delivered me.

My dad never remarried, so I don't have any brothers or sisters." She guided his head up. "Rinse."

He closed his eyes as soap started running down his forehead, and Tess brushed the soap away from his eyelids and forehead with a washcloth. "Any other relatives?" he asked when he opened his eyes again.

"Sorry about the soap." She cocked her head. "Need conditioner?"

"Nah." He tweaked her nipples and she gasped. "Just soap me down, baby."

"With pleasure." She lathered the washcloth with soap. "Are we going to run out of hot water soon?"

"Could," he said. Tess moved behind him and started washing his neck and back. "I have two water heaters, but as long as we're taking, I wouldn't be surprised if we ran out."

"Then we'd better not take too long." She was soaping his ass with the washcloth and his cock was more than standing at attention.

"Back to my question." He widened his legs so that Tess could wash the insides of his thighs. "Any other family?"

"Not any that I really know of." Tess moved down to finish washing his ankles, calves. She moved back to his thighs, then teased his balls with the cloth. "My mom was an only child and my dad's brother died in a car crash when he was pretty young." She moved around him and soaped his legs from the front. "So, no aunts, uncles or cousins. My grandparents are dead too."

Santiago had a hard time imagining not being surrounded by a huge family. Their family gatherings could number as many as a hundred since on both sides of the family his grandparents had large numbers of children, who had large numbers of children and so on.

His thoughts stalled for a moment as Tess washed around his cock.

When she finally moved up to his chest, he said, "So that's why you've stayed with your father?"

Tess gave a shrug. "I figure until I move out he can use the company. He's got enough ranch hands to handle the chores, but I like to help out. While I'm at work at the courthouse in Bisbee, he's out in the middle of everything no matter that he's pushing seventy. I generally cook the meals. He could hire a housekeeper, but for now I think he likes having me around."

She finished washing him, and Santiago leaned forward and pressed his lips to her wet forehead. "I like having you around."

Tess felt heat flush up from her toes to the roots of her hair. She didn't know Santiago that well, but she kinda liked being around him too. More than kinda. A serious, deep-down-in-her-gut kinda.

"I've got to be inside you, baby." He gripped her hips and brought her closer to him.

God, his erection was hard, and his words and the look in his eyes were enough to make her fall to pieces. She'd do anything he wanted at this point. "Right here?"

"Not yet." He reached behind him and turned off the water then opened the shower stall so that he could grab a towel from the rack. He started rubbing her down from head to toe and she sighed in pure bliss. After that shower, the way he handled her body made her feel like she was in heaven.

When she finished drying him in return, he took her by the hand and led her to the bed in the guest bedroom. "I'd like to see you on your hands and knees," he murmured. She glanced at him with a curious look. Her heart pounded as she crawled onto the bed on all fours. "And why is that?"

He followed her, a seductive expression crossing his face. "I'm going to take you from behind."

Tess's pulse rate seemed to double as she eased onto the bed. Her wet hair fell over her shoulders.

"Spread your thighs, baby." He grasped her hips when her knees were just past the edge of the bed. "Hold up right there." He held on to her and then pressed his cock against her ass.

He leaned over her so that his chest was against her back and a tremor ran up her spine. "Do you want me inside you, Tess?"

All she could manage was a nod.

"Say it." He started brushing his lips across her skin at the base of her neck and moved his way down her spine.

Tess didn't think she was capable of speech at that point. But she wanted him so badly she managed to get the words out, even though her words were dry and raspy. "Fuck me, Santiago!"

"Mmmmm." The sound was a deep rumble in his throat. She felt the head of his cock at the entrance to her pussy at the same time the heat of his tongue left her spine. "You taste good—everywhere."

The ache between her thighs was so great she wanted to press her thighs together, but Santiago had her spread wide. She gave a little whimper when just the head of his cock penetrated her.

He held her tighter by the hips and drove deep into her.

The gasp that came from Tess's mouth was so loud that Santiago stopped for a moment, still buried within her. "Are you all right, baby?"

"Don't stop." She moved her hips back and forth, drawing him in and out of her.

He gave a low growl and gripped her hips so tight she knew he'd leave bruises. He slammed in and out of her as she rocked back to meet every thrust. The air in the room was cool on her damp skin, but Santiago was hot as he pounded in and out of her. Her breasts swung with the movement, her nipples rasping against the bedclothes, causing her to moan even louder.

Tess was thrown forward by one of his thrusts and her arms

gave out, causing her to lie with her cheek against the bed. She continued to move so that every time he pounded into her she met him.

She increased her movements, her need to reach climax was so great. But her orgasm was elusive. Just out of reach. She was so close. Damn, just a little more. "I need to come, Santiago."

"Hold on, baby." He thrust harder and deeper than she could have imagined.

Tess moaned and cried and clenched her vaginal muscles down on Santiago's cock. He slipped one finger around her and rubbed her clit.

"Thank you!" she shouted as she came. God, God, God, her orgasm was incredible.

A total head rush.

As she was starting to come down from the peak of her climax, Santiago gave a loud groan and slammed into her a few more times as she felt his hot semen filling her. He stilled, holding himself inside her, before collapsing on his side on the bed and drawing her into the cradle of his arm.

He smiled, and she managed a sated smile of her own. "Good thing today's Saturday," he said.

Tess raised a brow. "Why's that?"

"So I can fuck you all weekend long."

Chapter Six

Santiago hadn't been kidding. By the time he took her back to Red's Bar Sunday night, where she'd left her car, Tess was so damn sore from sex with him that she could barely walk straight. She swore they'd done it in just about every position possible. The man was insatiable, and she found she was just as insatiable with him.

When they arrived at the bar, Santiago parked and they just looked at each other. Then he roughly grabbed her by the back of her head and kissed her so hard he bruised her lips anew. *Damn,* could the man kiss.

He drew away, and his chest rose and fell as fast as hers, their breathing becoming harsh and ragged. "You know I could take you again, right here and now, Tess."

She smiled at him in the near darkness. "And I'd say yes."

Santiago kissed her hard again. This time he eased away only a fraction so that she still felt his breath on her moist lips. "I've got to see you again. Tomorrow night. Hell, every night."

Tess pressed her palm against his chest and felt the pounding of his heart. "I could live with that."

His expression was serious as he ran his thumb along her jawline to her lips. "I don't know if I'll ever be able to get enough of you, Tess Marshall."

"For some reason I feel connected with you." She swallowed hard, surprised she was even saying this aloud. "I don't think I could ever say no to you."

This time he kissed her softly on the lips. "Good," he murmured as they parted. "We'll just see where this goes."

Santiago was a man who knew what he wanted. And what he wanted was Tess. Heart, soul, body. He had always watched her from afar, but now that he'd had a taste of her, there was no letting go.

He didn't want to let her head back to her own home, but they both had work the following morning. Reality was that life didn't slow down for good sex, or a good relationship.

He'd had a conversation with Jess Lawless earlier that day, and Lawless thought he had a lead that they intended to follow up on tomorrow.

For now he just wanted to think about Tess.

With one last look at her, they both opened the doors to the truck—

Santiago heard a gasp from Tess at the same moment he found himself with the barrel of a gun right at his chest.

Shit.

He was certainly doing double-time on the fuck-up end of things.

Santiago sized up the man in front of him. He didn't recognize the sonofabitch. Dirty blond hair, about five-six, white T-shirt, jeans, expensive jogging shoes.

"Hands where I can see them," the man said in a low voice.

Without appearing to, Santiago's gaze swept the parking lot, but apparently everyone was inside Red's. Country music pounded from inside the building, coupled with the sound of loud voices. He and Tess could be shot right now, and no one would hear a goddamn thing.

Slowly, he raised his hands, his gaze focused on the man's blue eyes. "What the hell is it now?"

The asshole waved his gun, indicating that Santiago should

start walking. "Around to the other side of the truck where your girlfriend is waiting."

Santiago barely held back a growl. His heart pounded with rage, and adrenaline pumped through his body.

When they reached the other side, he saw a silver Beemer and Tess already in the back, hands bound in front of her, mouth gagged.

Double shit.

Another man now had his weapon trained on Santiago.

After the men frisked him, once again relieving him of his service revolver, cuffs, pocketknife and cell phone, he found himself with his hands bound behind him. The men shoved Santiago into the waiting car, not bothering to gag him.

Once they were on the road, Santiago looked at Tess, who was looking up at him with her big eyes. He read both fear and anger in her expression.

It didn't take long until they were out in the desert and the Beemer pulled up in front of a trashed-out trailer. The men hadn't bothered to blindfold them, and Santiago knew their exact location.

They were ushered up a set of rickety steps and into a trailer filled with debris and garbage. The stench of feces, urine and rotting food polluted the stuffy air of the confined space. Cigarette smoke clouded the room, adding to the foul odors, and his eyes watered.

Santiago immediately took in their surroundings and saw that there was one other person in the place, but he was in the shadows, away from what little light made its way into the trailer. All that Santiago could tell was that the man was fat and had a round face with layered chins.

From where he stood in the doorway of the tiny trailer, he saw no other means of escape other than the doorway they'd just come through. Tess was pushed into a chair that had stuffing coming out of the padding and a spring that was probably sticking her in the ass. Her gag was removed, but her hands remained bound in front of her. If Tess's eyes were lasers, her glare would have burned holes through their captors.

Santiago was herded to the right and shoved into another chair just as crappy as the one Tess was in. He was now face-to-face with the fat man and could better make him out. He had a pinched mouth, and eyes that looked small due to the layers of fat on his upper cheeks. He wore a wife-beater shirt that was torn and had grease stains across the front. He hadn't even bothered to button his pants.

Out of the corner of his eye, Santiago caught sight of something he hadn't been able to see when he'd walked into the room. Raul's mutilated body. His eyes were wide open, his body convulsing, and blood was pouring from a slit in his throat. By the sounds he was making it was obvious his tongue had been cut out. It was also obvious that he'd been tortured—his chest branded with cigarette burns, not to mention the cuts all over his body. In moments, the man went still, eyes wide and sightless.

Gritting his teeth, Santiago kept his expression as passive as possible as he gazed at Fat Man. On a table beside him were instruments he'd no doubt used to torture Raul. A hammer, nails, a knife, an ashtray with still-burning cigarettes.

Santiago was keenly aware of the two men with guns trained on him and Tess. This was getting fucking old, and fast.

His gut clenched at the thought of anything happening to Tess.

Fat Man pushed his bulk from his seat, struggling to get to his feet at first before managing to stand. He was a short man and could have passed for a sumo wrestler if he'd had one of those diapers on.

When Fat Man spoke, his voice was pleasant, conversational. He had a hint of a Spanish accent and his English was perfect. "What do you know?"

From where he sat, Santiago didn't have to look up too far since the man was so short. "About what?"

Fat Man picked up a lit cigarette and sighed. "Before we finished off Raul, he claimed to have told you nothing. But my men saw him speaking with you at length. We need to know the details of that conversation."

Santiago studied Fat Man as he silently praised Raul for remaining silent, no matter what he'd been put through.

When Santiago didn't answer, Fat Man sighed again, brought the cigarette to his lips. As he removed the cigarette from his mouth, a cloud of smoke spiraled from his mouth. He pointed the lit end of the cigarette at Santiago. It glowed bright orange in the dim light of the trailer. Fat Man pressed the cigarette against Santiago's chest and he heard Tess gasp. The smell of burning cloth soon joined the odor of burning flesh as the cigarette burned a hole into Santiago's T-shirt and his chest.

He focused on his anger, focused on what he planned to do to the fat bastard. The pain of the burn was shoved to the back of his mind.

Fat Man drew back and puffed on the cigarette again before removing it to blow out a steady stream of smoke. "Did he tell you about the drop?"

Santiago's mind raced as he figured out how to get Tess and him out of there alive. If he could just catch them off guard.

Again Santiago didn't respond, and again Fat Man pressed the lit end of his cigarette against Santiago's chest. This time his eyes watered from the pain and he clenched his jaw tighter.

Fat Man asked the same question. This time when Santiago didn't answer, Fat Man turned his attention and nodded to one of the men with his gun pointed at Santiago. When the man took his gun by the barrel, obviously intending to slam the butt of the weapon upside Santiago's face, it was the break he'd been waiting for.

At the same time the man swung at him, Santiago dodged and swept one booted foot against Fat Man's legs. The huge man went down in a crash that rocked the trailer.

Before the man beside him with the gun could react, Santiago dived for him. Santiago's hands were still bound behind his back, but he was able to come down hard with his elbow in the man's gut. The man gave a shout of pain and his weapon went flying across the trailer, toward Tess.

Santiago looked up to see the third man swinging around from Tess to aim for Santiago.

Big mistake. "Sonofabitch!" Tess shot out her feet and nailed the man at the backs of his knees. He went down hard on his back. His gun discharged at the ceiling.

Her hands still bound in front of her, Tess dove for the gun dropped by the man Santiago had taken down. She grabbed it, rolled onto her back and put a bullet into the third man's chest.

With the finesse of a trained law enforcement official, Tess got to her feet and had a bullet in Fat Man's neck before he could heave himself to his feet.

At the same time, the man Santiago had taken down slammed his fist into Santiago's eye. Pain burst in his head. With his hands bound behind his back he couldn't stop himself from being knocked up against a wall.

Man number two started to push himself to his feet, but he was close enough that Santiago was able to ram his boot against the man's face. He heard bone crunch and blood flowed from the man's nose immediately.

Before Santiago could go after the bastard, Tess had the barrel of her gun pressed against the man's temple.

"Move and die," she growled.

Santiago couldn't help smiling. You had to love a woman like Tess.

Chapter Seven

One month later, Tess was curled up in bed with Santiago. They'd just had wild monkey sex again, and she felt wonderful.

They'd each taken a leave of absence from work and had been inseparable the entire time. Yeah, it had only been a month, but Tess knew she'd fallen for Santiago, and she'd fallen hard.

She did her best to push out of her mind the insane events that had happened those weeks ago. The paperwork, the bodies. She'd killed two men, but she couldn't bring herself to regret it, considering the men likely would have killed her and Santiago. Thanks to the information from the informant, a huge drug bust had been made the following week. The location had been changed, but aware the drop was going to be made, the DEA agents managed to track it and the head honcho down.

Tess snuggled up to Santiago, breathing in his spicy male scent and the smell of their sex. She just couldn't get enough of the man.

Santiago raised himself up on one elbow and looked down at her with that incredibly sexy grin of his. He trailed one finger down her breast and circled her sensitive nipple.

"Mmmmm . . ." Tess closed her eyes for a moment as she relished the feel of his touch. When she looked into those gunmetal black eyes she melted all over again. She was *so* his. She would do anything for him.

"Beautiful." Santiago pressed his warm lips to her forehead and she heard his deep inhalation.

When he drew back, his expression had turned serious.

"What?" She traced her fingers over the healing scars on his chest from the cigarette burns, but she didn't take her eyes off his.

Santiago slipped his fingers into her hair and some of the dark red strands swung forward against her neck. "You do know, now that I have you, I'm not letting you go," he stated, the look on his face still serious.

For one long moment she studied him, her heart beating like crazy. "I think you've got it the other way around," she said with a smile. "Now that I've had you, *I'm* not letting *you* go."

He grinned and pushed her over on her back, sliding his hips between her thighs with the movement. Tess wrapped her arms around his neck and he pressed his forehead to hers. "I think it works both ways, sweetheart."

When he finally drew away, her lips trembled as she smiled. "All I know is that I can't imagine going a day without you."

"You won't." Santiago slid inside her in a slow thrust causing her to gasp in pleasure. "I don't intend to let you go."

Tess wrapped her thighs around his hips as he moved in and out of her at an easy pace, making love to her in a way he hadn't before. Their lovemaking was slow and sensuous, and she almost cried at the exquisite feelings that rose up within her.

When she finally climaxed, it was on a gasp and a moan. A different orgasm burned through her. One of fulfillment and completion.

Santiago's eyes never left hers as he slid in and out of her pussy. And when he reached orgasm, she felt his shudder of pleasure, felt the pulse of his cock in her core. He held himself inside her for a long moment, arms braced on either side of her chest, his gaze still locked with hers. His mouth took hers in a kiss that was sensual, but also possessive, telling her that she belonged to him.

He drew back and again their eyes met. "I can't believe I'm

going to say this so soon." He lowered his head so that his lips were close to hers. "I love you, Tess Marshall."

"Good thing." She raised her head slightly so that their lips brushed when she spoke. "Because I'm in love with you, Diego Santiago."

Cheyenne McCray

USA Today bestselling author Cheyenne McCray has a passion for sensual romance and a happily-ever-after, but always with a twist. Among other accolades, Chey has been presented with the prestigious Romantic Times BOOKreviews Reviewers' Choice Award for Best Erotic Romance of the Year. Chey is the award-winning novelist of almost thirty novels and novellas.

Chey has been writing ever since she can remember, back to her kindergarten days when she penned her first poem. She always knew one day she would write novels, hoping her readers would get lost in the worlds she created, as she did when she was lost in a good book. Cheyenne enjoys spending time with her husband and three sons, traveling, and of course writing, writing, writing

Wicked

LORIE O'CLARE

Chapter One

Mist soaked through his shirt, hung on his eyelashes, mixed with the sweat clinging to his spine. A perfect night for a good chase. He picked up the pace. Damned asshole ran faster than most mixed breeds.

That's it, fucking mutt, feel the triumph pump through your veins. You've met your match tonight. The punk's excitement that he'd gotten away with his crime drifted through the air. A blind man could have tracked him.

Perry Roth gritted his teeth, energy from his pure bloodline pumping through him as he raced around the corner. The street was quiet. Humans all tucked away in their beds.

His night vision sharpened, instinct demanding control. The dark figure ran hard and fast, gaining distance. There were several blocks between them now.

Sirens wailed blocks away. The gap between them lessened. Hesitation. Fear attacking rational thought. Let the mutt wonder if he'd pulled the law into this. Like Perry needed the help of humans.

The smell of damp pavement mixed with that of garbage from Dumpsters and the ever-present human scent that clung to the brick buildings created a nauseating mixture of odors. The smell of the creep was actually stronger than all the human scents clinging to the moist air, making the jerk an easy target.

Within minutes they'd be at the edge of town, the highway not too far. Open ground, free of humans, would make the change possible.

We can play in our skin, or in our fur. Your call, motherfucker.

The smells in the air changed quickly. He spotted the second figure immediately. Johann Rousseau wouldn't have sent backup. He wouldn't humiliate Perry like that. His pack leader had called him, and knew Perry would do the job. So who the hell was darting down the opposite side of the street?

"Steve. No! You idiot!"

The female's screams echoed off the buildings, violating the night. Attention would be drawn soon. The police called. Not good.

Time to end this game. Damn it. He would have enjoyed tearing at the creep's neck. There would have been a hell of a lot more pleasure in taking down the lawbreaking werewolf in his more pure form.

Perry's heart pounded through his head, his shoes hitting the pavement just as hard. As fast as he ran, faster than any human, the female across the street managed to match his pace. A *lunewulf.* And chasing down a mutt. Made no sense but not his problem.

He gained on the werewolf who'd attacked the unmated female at Howley's, outrage replaced guilt in the air around him.

"You are such a jerk," the female yelled, crossing the street and obviously trying to beat him to his target.

Long blonde hair fanned around her thin, petite body. She wore jeans and a pullover shirt, the simple clothes hugging the body of a goddess. Perfect curves, tight and fit, with the agility her breed was known for. Fuck. She chased after a rapist. A werewolf who probably would view her as icing on the cake.

Steve, the jerk, turned to look at her, and then glanced back toward Perry. He had him now.

"Show's over," he growled, leaping through the air.

Hard pavement tore at both of them as Perry took the asshole down. The scumbag wanted to fight, but obviously had no clue what he was doing.

He swung at air, twisting underneath Perry. "Get off me, motherfucker."

"Not a problem," Perry hissed in his ear as the stench of sweat and anger rolled off the guy's flesh.

Yanking him by the shoulder, Perry lifted him off the ground, reaching for his wrist and hiking it up his back.

"What are you doing? His den wants retribution!" The woman leapt on Perry, her body firm, yet light enough to toss across the street.

Except throwing a female wasn't acceptable—unless he planned on getting his dick wet.

Not many could control their actions quickly when attacked from behind. Every muscle inside him spasmed when he fought the urge to throw her. No way would he send a female flying.

"Stay out of this," he growled. He took a minute to glare at her, letting her know he meant business.

Her features were mind-blowing. Where the hell had this little *lunewulf* bitch come from?

Dark blue eyes glowed in the darkness. "Like hell I will. Turn Steve over to me. His mate and her den will see to his punishment."

Defiance glowed in blue eyes so pure they were like rare sapphires. He'd never witnessed such an intense shade.

"Not how it works." He shoved Steve forward, deciding a bit of distance from where he'd taken him down would be best. Just in case any nosy humans were up at this hour.

Then he'd call Johann.

• • •

There was no way Jaynie Rousseau could just walk away. If it weren't for her cousin, Wendy Amyx, she'd let this *Cariboo lunewulf* tear the life out of Steve. Wendy might end up a widow. But with Steve as her mate she would sooner or later anyway.

Steve did his best to look at her. "You go tell Wendy I've been set up. Have her sire—"

"Shut up." The *Cariboo* tightened his grip around Steve's neck, making his eyes bulge. He almost had his feet off the ground.

Steve looked like a cub in the *Cariboo's* grasp. Dear God. She'd never laid eyes on a werewolf so large. Sure, the *Cariboo lunewulf* were one of the largest breeds of werewolf on earth. But still . . . this one was a giant. At least six and a half feet tall, with arms as thick as tree trunks. And damn, the roped muscle that rippled underneath his jeans. He was so fucking huge. If he was going to break Steve's neck, Jaynie would enjoy watching. For all the grief he gave his mate, her youngest cousin, he deserved the worst of deaths.

They hurried down the street, on the edge of the industrial side of Prince George. She had no idea where they were headed. There hadn't been time since she got here to learn pack territory. The *Cariboo* didn't tell her to leave, and this was more excitement than she'd had all evening—hell, all month. The quick agility of the giant *Cariboo* stole her breath.

At the end of the block they paused. Rolling hills covered with evergreens sprawled out ahead of them. The mist held their scent in the air, and Jaynie filled her lungs with it. Damn, she'd wanted to get a good run in tonight.

Single bitches don't run by themselves.

Until she managed to establish a relationship with the queen bitch, she couldn't just prance around doing as she wished. Werewolves were annoyingly antiquated at times. And there was no changing it.

"You make one attempt to run and I'll break your fucking neck. Understood?" the *Cariboo* growled.

Steve muttered something incoherent under his breath and stuffed his hands in his pockets. He was just about the most stupid mutt she'd ever met, but even he had enough sense to know he didn't stand a prayer against this brute of a *Cariboo*.

"Are you here for a reason?" Perry asked.

Jaynie looked up at the *Cariboo*. And she had to look up. Standing a foot or so away from him, the top of her head barely reached his broad, packed shoulders. Blond curls hung almost to his shoulders. Blue eyes laced with silver—like lightning shooting across a clear sky. Dangerous. Deadly. And . . . oh my God . . . breathtaking. Her mouth went so dry staring at him that her tongue almost stuck to the top of her mouth.

She cleared her throat. "His mate is my cousin."

"You're standing as his defense?" His lip curled, his disgust apparent.

God. He looked dangerous as hell. All those stacked muscles, barely contained by the T-shirt that struggled to stretch over them, clinging to every bulge, damp from the mist and sweat.

Appreciating how well he was built at the moment wouldn't put her in this brute's good graces. She managed her best no-nonsense expression.

"He stands as his own defense. I'm part of his den, which wants its name cleared from his disgrace. We would love the right to see to his punishment." And no matter what this *Cariboo* thought of her, she knew she could kick Steve's tail until he begged for mercy.

The *Cariboo* grunted and didn't give her another moment of his time. Flipping open a cell phone, he muttered a few words and then grabbed Steve by the back of his neck, pushing him toward the edge of town.

Her gaze got stuck on buns of steel. Thick, corded muscles rippled as he moved. And if those weren't the longest, most powerful-looking legs she'd ever seen. Having a reputation for being a bit more on the wild side, more reclusive, a mountain breed, *Cariboo lunewulf* weren't a breed she'd spent a lot of time associating with. But damn, a dangerous excitement rushed through her at the thought of getting to know this one a bit better.

If she weren't careful, the damp air would soon be full of the smell of her lust.

Keeping a step behind, not so she could enjoy the scenery, but to keep from being growled at further, every breath she inhaled was full of his scent. Inhaling him gave her the chills.

Determination stronger than anything she'd ever sensed radiated from him. Anger, focused and powerful, mixed in with other scents. A strong male, never doubting his next move, a creature at the top of the food chain, this *Cariboo* feared nothing. It wouldn't surprise her if he'd never experienced the emotion. That made him a werewolf to be damn wary of.

Her gut twisted with excitement. Brutal and demanding, he'd be more aggressive than most. And rough. God. She almost tripped. Her thoughts already had his hands on her, ripping clothes while telling her what she'd do for him.

She exhaled, fighting her rapidly beating heart. This was ridiculous. Absolutely insane. *Cariboo lunewulf* were trouble. The brute probably had this job because he loved to kill—to mutilate and maim. Steve was a wuss and Jaynie saw the grief he put Wendy through. Like she needed some werewolf in her life who would be as intimidating and brutal. She'd seen the hell her cousin endured. No way Jaynie would allow any werewolf to chain her down like that. She'd be miserable.

All those muscles flexing in front of her looked like they would do anything but make her miserable.

At the curb a truck pulled up, tires grinding against gravel on the road while exhaust clouded the scent that had been driving her crazy. The driver was another *Cariboo*. Figures. Spending most of her time with her cousin in the six months she'd been here, she didn't know much of the pack. Loneliness didn't eat at her. She wouldn't let it. But she had no idea that so many of the larger, more reclusive breed of *lunewulf* roamed the streets at night. She definitely needed to find a reason to get out more.

And she wasn't drooling simply because she hadn't been around a virile werewolf in a while. Most of them were just trouble anyway. Something unique beat through this werewolf. He was a tracker, a werewolf who brought in the derelicts of their breeds. He sought out trouble, embraced it and forced it to belly up.

There was a small backseat and again her gaze was trapped when his arm muscles bulged as he pulled the front seat forward.

"Climb in," he told Steve. Then turned to look at her as if he'd just remembered she was with them. He studied her for a moment. "Get up front," he finally said, stepping aside so she could scoot in.

Jaynie found herself scrunched between two very large *Cariboo*. Damn.

When they parked and opened the truck doors, evergreens sweetened the air, almost drowning all emotions in the cab.

The *Cariboo lunewulf* got out on either side of her. For a moment Jaynie hesitated on which side to get out on.

"Go greet the queen bitch," the large *Cariboo* who'd brought her here growled at her.

She'd just been excused from witnessing any action that would take place with Steve. Had he doubted her reason for wanting to accompany them all along?

Her feet hit the ground and she straightened then dodged around him when he almost trapped her with virile arms as he moved to grab Steve out of the back.

"Perry. This is the instigator?" a *lunewulf* bellowed from behind her.

Johann Rousseau, pack leader and distant cousin of some sort, walked with a determined gait to the truck. Jaynie doubted he recognized her. She was from what had to be one of the largest dens in all of North America, and there was some vague memory of seeing him a few times as a cub. Keeping up with her den was an impossible task.

Walking away from this intense showdown of testosterone and muscle proved even more of a challenge.

"Yup. Caught him heading out of town." Perry grabbed Steve by his collar and threw him at Johann.

He stumbled but caught his footing quickly. Johann didn't move, but squared his shoulders when Steve almost slid into him. He made a show of straightening his clothes and glanced over his shoulder at the *Cariboo* before focusing on their pack leader.

Things didn't look good for Steve.

It was about time someone took him down. And she had a right to witness this after holding Wendy night after night while her cousin cried. The werewolf deserved the worst of deaths. Hovering against the front hood of the truck, the shadows hid her somewhat. Hopefully the warm engine would drown any smell of excitement or anticipation coming off her.

"Her den is on their way," Johann said, his emotions under check. She didn't smell a thing off him.

Steve's nervousness plummeted through the air though, quickly turning to fright. He straightened, a defiant sneer working over his expression. Like he could hide his fear from any of them.

"That bitch begged for everything I gave her," he lied, the smell of it turning Jaynie's stomach.

"You raped a virgin, an unmated bitch," Johann accused, his tone too calm. "The law on this matter is cut-and-dry. Her den will have their revenge on you."

And Steve wouldn't live through the night.

"Anything else you need from me?" Perry asked, muscles bulging in his arms when he flexed them. He looked like he ached to rip Steve's throat out himself.

"Nope. Appreciate your help." Johann walked past Steve, obviously satisfied that the *lunewulf* wouldn't try to run.

"Call me anytime you need me," the *Cariboo* offered.

Johann nodded, pulling his wallet from his back pocket. He laid a few bills in Perry's hand. The *Cariboo* nodded, shoving the money in his jeans pocket, and then he turned toward her.

But he walked past her, past the truck, and Johann returned to Steve, mumbling something profane under his breath and shoving him in the back to make him move toward the other side of the house.

She was left behind. Forgotten. The pack leader hadn't given her a thought, too pissed off at what Steve had done to a member of his pack. And Perry, the *Cariboo* who'd hauled her out here, obviously didn't see any reason to look after her either.

Perry's shadow faded quickly among the trees, dense foliage and darkness making it too hard to pinpoint him with her human eyes. Something about him compelled her. His scent called out to her. Running with him would be the only way to learn why he distracted her so strongly.

Chapter Two

ood little bitches don't run by themselves at night.

Shut up, Grandmother Rousseau.

Jaynie scowled as the old woman, who'd hovered over her whenever she'd had a chance as a cub, spoke in her thoughts. Shoving the unpleasant memory of her long-dead relative out of her head, she noted the pack leader's den was barely visible now through the trees.

And Perry, the *Cariboo* with way too many muscles for his own good, was gaining distance on her quickly. Well, he might be almost twice her size, but he didn't have twice her speed. The cold October air hit her like a brick wall when she stripped out of her clothes, almost tripping over her jeans and stumbling on the lace of her shoes.

God. Freezing and nervous made a bad combination. She shook worse than bare branches during a hard storm while twisting her clothes and then securing them around her waist.

Nervous energy leapt through her like a wildfire. Cold on the outside and burning alive inside. Is that why she wanted to chase after this *Cariboo*? Did going after some strange tail sound so appealing that she'd risk the wrath of the pack if they found her running alone?

Damn pack tradition to hell and back anyway. It wasn't like she didn't know how to take care of herself.

Sparks popped in her head, white tracers dancing before her eyes. The change from human to werewolf grabbed her hard enough to steal her breath.

She embraced the pain of the change, her teeth chattering and pricking her lip as they grew into deadly fangs. Coarse white hair punctured through her skin, covering the goose bumps from the cold.

Her lip burned, the quick prick of pain something to focus on while her bones stretched, lengthened and changed shape. Her skin hardened, a natural shield against the biting cold night. Warmth and strength coursed through her.

One with the night, she dropped to all fours. The peace that rushed through her was the high after the quick, sharp pain. Nothing compared to the clarity of emotions, of her senses.

Looking around her, sniffing the air, everything became clearer, easier to see, to smell, to hear. Her tongue thickened, darting over her quickly disappearing lips, tasting fur mixed with a tiny amount of blood.

Howls filled the air and her heart exploded, throwing the change into hypermode. She almost fell over her paws when stumbling forward, her tail lengthening to support her.

The den had arrived, ready to release their fury on Steve. Stupid son of a bitch. He deserved what he was about to get. She'd hold and comfort Wendy later, give her the support she needed after the pack contacted her. There were no doubts Wendy would be given honorary widow privileges. Although her cousin would mourn, it would be a relief to be unshackled from such a terrible werewolf.

The scent of the *Cariboo* faded beneath the scent of growing amount of werewolves at the pack leader's house.

Instinct kicked in and she dug at the earth with her claws as she ran. Time to get the hell away from her pack leader's den.

No longer did the cold air make her shiver. Instead she embraced it, enjoying the crispness of the night. Too much time had passed since she'd torn freely through the countryside, letting go and racing at full speed.

Time in the States had spoiled her. Having run from her pack ten years ago when pack law concerning mating grew outrageous, she never thought she'd tear through this beautiful land again. Nothing compared to the open wilderness outside Prince George.

A freak phone call in the middle of the night, her closest cousin crying over the phone from the abuse and neglect of her mate, had Jaynie returning to the pack. And she'd hated every minute that she'd been here—until now.

The moon appeared between parting clouds, giving light to the overgrown countryside. Birds squawked in protest as Jaynie violated their space.

I rule the night tonight, my dears.

And with that freedom came the reality that she wasn't too sure what to expect. This *Cariboo* could be mated. Although there was only one way to find out. She had no idea if he was even heading to his den. Not to mention how unsafe it would be to sniff her way around his den. But the mystery had its appeal. An adventure, taking on the unknown.

Inhaling his scent—he wasn't too far ahead—made her insides swell. Craving something a bit more wild, untamable and deadly powerful, she tracked him. Racing at a speed some cars couldn't match, she gained on him. Now to find out what he would do once he learned he'd been followed.

• • •

Perry almost took down his door when he reached the small cabin. His was the last on the row, a total of six cabins that housed the hired help on the Toubec ranch. A quick sniff of the air told him most of the cabins were empty, the help probably enjoying a communal run. That might make matters even worse.

Stupid bitch. What the hell did she follow him for?

Crashing into his tiny den, anger encouraged the change, the room spinning when he straightened. Yanking free the clothes that he'd tied around his neck free, he untangled them with a growl then dressed quickly, not taking time to mess with shoes. He grabbed his coat off the nail by his door. His human flesh was soaked with sweat and he'd freeze quickly in the autumn night air after such a hard run.

Not that he was a damn bit cold. Too outraged over seeing that little *lunewulf* chasing after him, he moved quickly, ready to knock some sense into her.

Keeping close to the wall of the cabin, he moved through shadows, his night vision grossly impaired in his human form. But he wouldn't take on the bitch in his fur. There might be a lot of bad things said about him but Perry didn't rape unmated bitches. And the damned fool of a thing was asking for just that, racing toward a line of cabins housing werewolves who didn't often get to spend a lot of time with a female.

And she raced toward them as if craving a formal announcement. Tiny paws crashing through underbrush. A full-blood *lunewulf*, blessed with speed no other creature on earth could match. If any of the ranch hands were in their cabins they'd pounce on her with one thing on their minds.

She slowed at the edge of the trees, and the moonlight caught her white coat, making it glow in the darkness. Limber and slim and so petite, she stole his breath with her intense beauty. Perry had been with this pack well over a year. He'd have remembered this little *lunewulf* bitch if he'd seen her before.

She sniffed the ground, her silver eyes glowing in the light streaming from his cabin. Perry stood very still in the shadows. Her scent drifted toward him. She moved warily, continually looking around her. If she searched for his animal scent, it would lead her to his cabin.

Mere feet from the entrance to his den, light shone over her smooth white coat. A beautiful creature, sultry in her movements. Almond-shaped eyes, glowing silver, stood out against the soft contour of her head. Even in his human form, his insides hardened in appreciation of the sexy female *lunewulf* who moved with either incredible bravery or as a complete idiot toward the dens of unmated werewolves.

He waited. Not breathing, not moving an inch. This bitch was no expert tracker or she'd have picked up his human scent. Her thoughts were preoccupied, with what, he would soon find out. But he patiently held his position until she was right where he wanted her.

"Inside. Now." Perry moved behind her, pointing toward the cabin door.

The little *lunewulf* turned on him, baring her long fangs and growling. Her hackles went up, not fazing him in the least.

"You can get inside and change," he hissed, staring into those intent silver eyes. "Or I can change and we can stay out here in our fur."

His meaning wasn't missed. In their fur, he'd fuck her first and ask questions later. Instinct and primal desire ran strong in his more pure state. Human hesitation and good manners fogged the natural instinctive reaction to fuck silly a sexy woman.

She backed up, pushing the door to his cabin the rest of the way open with her rear end.

Perry smiled, his cock hardening while the adorable little bitch backed into his den. No matter what form he took, a sexy female was just that. And one this full of energy and cockiness turned him on even more. Living on the wild side and more than likely completely untamable. Add that to beauty and defiance and you had the perfect female.

The door slammed in his face.

"What the fuck?"

Darkness enveloped him as quickly as his anger did. Like hell she would lock him out of his own fucking den.

He hit the door hard, pounding his shoulder into the wood. The vibration racked his body as wood split, jarring his muscles. The door swung open.

The female inside shrieked. And the sight of her made him forget how cold he was a second ago. Heat rushed through him as fast as his blood did. His cock danced back to life.

Her body glistened with sweat. She was slender with large breasts and curvy hips and holy shit—a beautiful shaved pussy. Unable to breathe, unable to move—hell, he wouldn't have been able to form a word if he tried. It was as if his tongue had made the change leaving the rest of him standing there in human form like a complete idiot.

"You made me change. Now turn the fuck around and let me get dressed." Bright blue eyes glared furiously at him while she fought to untangle the clothes she'd tied around her waist.

Perry shut the door behind him slowly. Thankfully it still shut, although he'd have to fix the broken doorframe and lock first thing in the morning. A cold breeze blew against his backside. This time it had no effect on him.

"You followed me here. Looks like you're going to have to face the consequences." No way would she start demanding anything of him. "Put your clothes on if you like. But then you're going to explain yourself."

Her nipples puckered and her full breasts bounced slightly as she fought with her clothes. He almost felt sorry for her, watching her shake like a leaf while trying to get her jeans straightened so she could slide them on. Long blonde hair fell down her front, parting around her breasts. Damn, she was fucking hot as hell.

"There's nothing to explain," she said quickly. "My cousin's mate is finally getting what he deserved. Forgive me for deciding not to watch."

"Yet you didn't run to her den to tell her?"

"Tell her that her mate raped an unmated female? That he

committed the most heinous of crimes and that she's now a widow?"

He wouldn't be anxious to share that news either. "You must know the queen bitch will contact her immediately."

She nodded, not looking up but focusing on her jeans, which she now had pulled up to her thighs. He would miss that awesome view of her pussy.

"Yet this cousin of yours sent you out to report back to her? What kind of den approves of an unmated bitch running on her own at night, especially into such dangerous territory?"

"I can take care of myself," she snapped, shoving her hair over her shoulder and glaring at him.

She didn't deny being unmated. Knowledge that she had no mate, was an available bitch, put an exciting edge to this little scene.

Her anger filled the air with its spicy smell. It didn't hide the slight tinge of fear he smelled too. She knew she wasn't out of the woods with him yet.

"I can see that." Maybe a fire would be a good idea.

Sweat had started to dry on his flesh, leaving the chill there. Moving to the wooden box next to his small fireplace, he pulled a fresh log and some kindling and dumped it into the hearth.

He smelled her defiance at the same time she made a bolt for the door—but not fast enough.

Perry dove on her, crashing to the floor with her soft body smashed underneath him.

"Shit," she hissed.

His cock nudged against her ass. Her jeans were pulled up although she hadn't zipped them, and she'd yet to bother with her shirt. Getting dressed had been a ploy. She wanted to escape, return to her fur and be gone. That didn't explain why she had come though.

"Leaving so soon?" he whispered into her hair.

She stilled.

Lifting the two of them up, he kept a firm grip around her naked waist, her large breasts almost touching his arm while he kicked the door shut.

"I don't think so," he told her.

She dared look over her shoulder, twisting her body against his. Firm and soft in all the right places. Damn it. It was a fight to keep all the blood in his body from draining straight into his cock.

"And are you a rapist as well?" Her blue eyes danced with defiance.

He almost shook his head with disbelief at her lack of fear and her outward cockiness.

"It's pretty hard to rape the willing."

She raised an eyebrow, twisting a bit harder in his arms. He really didn't want to let her go. Not that he would let her know how long it had been since he'd been with a female, or how hard she made him by twisting in his arms like that. Especially without her shirt on.

"Do you use the money you make tracking werewolves to buy your sex?"

Now she had intentionally insulted him. He smiled, knowing it probably looked more like a sneer. "If you didn't come here to sell yourself then maybe you should start behaving."

She moved quickly, doing her best to elbow him in the gut and kick his leg at the same time.

"Behave?" she hissed. "But I thought *Cariboo* liked it rough."

"You couldn't handle what I like," he growled.

Grabbing her arms, he pinned them behind her back, while shoving his leg between her legs. She couldn't move. Her hair fanned over her large breasts. Her body stretched out before him. But she stilled quickly. Either realizing how grossly outmatched she was, or contemplating what kind of sex he did like.

"Why did you follow me?" he asked.

"Because I want to track werewolves too."

Another lie.

He didn't rely on her physical reactions to his questions as much as he did her scent. The saltiness of her lie didn't hide the pungent smell of her sexuality. Him holding her like this, or maybe it was just the excitement of an unknown *Cariboo*, turned her on.

Either way, he was intrigued. She'd dared to follow him, take him on. For all practical purposes, she broke every rule held over a single bitch by the pack.

"I think," he said slowly, pulling slightly on her wrists so that she arched her back further. He cupped her chin with his free hand, turning her face to his. "You'll stay here with me until I hear the truth."

"The truth?" she whispered, the slightest hints of silver streaking through her large blue eyes as she stared up at him.

"Why are you here?"

Her breasts swelled with each breath she took, her brown nipples so hard they puckered into beautiful peaks. The shirt she'd gripped in her hands fell to the floor between them. He ignored the small action, her ripening smell of desire proving too much of a distraction.

"To learn more about you," she whispered. "But if you don't think I could handle you then you doubt my ability to handle any werewolf."

"I'm not any werewolf," he growled.

"You could be handled."

"By you?"

She bit her lip, looked up at him quickly, and the fire burning inside her made her expression glow. "I can handle anything."

Chapter Three

*J*aynie's phone vibrated against her leg. She tensed, watching the *Cariboo*, Perry, while hard muscle hit every overstimulated nerve ending in her body. Whoever called her right now wouldn't be bearing good news. Not at this hour.

"Not every day someone calls your bluff?" she chided him.

A nerve twitched next to his mouth. Silver suddenly shot through his deep blue eyes. His blond hair curled around his neck, ending at his shirt collar. Deadly looking and fucking hot as hell.

Then his cell phone rang, a loud chirping sound, and she almost had a heart attack.

"Yes," he said in a deep baritone into the cell.

The male voice on the other end of the line tickled her ear. Perry held her close, but making out what was said was impossible. Her phone vibrated again.

"Her name is Jaynie Rousseau?" His grip on her tightened and she froze.

Why the hell would he be getting a call about her?

"Yup. I agree." He grew before her eyes, anger filling the air around them. "I'll find her."

A deadly silence filled the room when he dropped his phone on the table. Her phone began vibrating a third time. Anything was better than smelling the fury that emanated around him.

"My phone is ringing." She struggled and he released her easily.

No way would he intimidate her, but getting a phone call

about her didn't sit well with her. She trembled as she dug her phone out of her jeans pocket.

"Hello."

"Jaynie. Oh God. I've been trying to call you," Wendy wailed into the phone.

Jaynie forced a small laugh. Her cousin didn't need her to cause any more stress. "I'm okay. I had to allow the change before I could answer," she lied, closing her eyes. Her cousin didn't need to know where she was right now. "How are you?"

"Samantha Rousseau is here."

Well, it hadn't taken long for their queen bitch to make it over to Wendy's den. She exhaled, doing her best to clear her head for her cousin's sake.

"Good. I'll be there soon."

"I was so worried about you. I mean . . . Steve . . . they caught him doing something terrible."

"I know, Wendy. I know."

"You do?"

"Yes. I told you I'd go find him."

Someone spoke in the background, another female, and Wendy whispered that she had Jaynie on the phone now.

"Jaynie. I can't stay here. I called my sire. I'm going home to my den," Wendy told her in a rush. "This den is dead to me. I don't care if you stay here. Samantha will talk to you about it. She has to talk to her mate."

It was like all the walls in that small cabin suddenly closed in around her. Her cousin was no longer mated and chose to return to her den, which was her right. That left her alone. Already the leash reached for her. Johann had called out his tracker. He'd called Perry. And she would be brought in for her pack leader to determine what to do with her. Single bitches had less freedom than a fucking slave.

"I understand," she managed to choke out.

"I love you, Jaynie," Wendy whispered.

"I love you too."

She almost crushed her phone in her hand, fighting the urge to hurl it across the room. The death of a scumbag werewolf had stolen her freedom. And the werewolf holding the leash stood right behind her.

"Jaynie Rousseau," he said from behind her.

What the hell was she supposed to do, deny who she was?

"You asked why I came here," she said, turning around until she found her shirt on the ground. She grabbed it and stuck her arms in the sleeves and then slipped it over her head. "I came here because I could. To be able to run, explore, take on the unknown—that can't ever be taken from you. You turn me in to Johann and it will be taken from me."

"And that's what you think I'll do?"

"Isn't it?"

He didn't answer. And when she looked up, questioningly, the intensity of his stare stole her breath. *Cariboo* were known for their height, their powerful muscle tone, but this werewolf was bigger than any she'd ever laid eyes on. More than likely he had a perfect track record, turning over any renegade werewolf whose name appeared on his list.

"You shouldn't have come here." He took a step toward her, filling the small space in the cabin with his overbearing presence.

Already her freedom crept away from her.

"Then you should let me go," she suggested.

Pulling her gaze from his might help her clear her head long enough to figure out how to get the hell out of there.

"Would you rather one of the other unmated *Cariboo* living out here had found you?" he growled.

"That wouldn't have happened."

"You were out running by yourself."

"Don't lecture me." She turned toward the door, the sight of the broken doorframe and useless lock twisting her insides with trepidation, a reminder of his raw, unbridled strength. Nothing would stop this *Cariboo*.

"Walk out that door and I'll catch you. And if we're in our fur . . ."

The small hairs on her neck spiked to attention. A tickle rushed down her spine.

"Don't threaten me either."

His tone deepened, his words sending chills rushing through her. "You know what will happen."

She reached for the doorknob. He bluffed. "You wouldn't turn me over to our pack leader after fucking me."

"It would have nothing to do with turning you over to Johann."

Her heart pounded so hard she couldn't move. Every breath she took smelled of him. His lust filled the space between them. Or was it hers?

"Why?" Her voice cracked. Heat rushed through her with enough intensity to make her stagger. "Why would you chase me down?"

"Because I want to."

Jaynie didn't move. She sucked in a breath, a deep one, her shoulders lifted and fell slightly. Long blonde hair streamed down her back, ending right above her ass. A perfect fucking ass. Goddamn. His cock swelled at the thought of burying himself deep in that tight hole.

He would deal with Johann later. That didn't bother him. He didn't answer to the *lunewulf*. Jaynie might be frightened about what the pack leader would do to her but for now, here with him, he would give her what he knew she wanted.

The smell of her lust dripped off her.

"Turn around, Jaynie," he ordered.

She moved slowly, hesitation warring within her. That in itself told him she wasn't a slut. Running alone would give her that reputation. But she'd told him, and he believed it—she craved freedom.

She craved him too, and that much he would give her.

Her tongue darted over her lips when she moved slightly, not completely facing him. But enough movement to ensure him that what he smelled on her was accurate.

He'd explode if he waited any longer.

Grabbing her arm, he pulled her to him, his hand tangling in her hair, pulling her head back. She opened her mouth, making eye contact with him just before he impaled her mouth with his tongue.

God, she was fucking hotter than he'd imagined. Muscles hardened throughout his body painfully. His brain boiled with a lust that had remained bridled way too long. Wrapping his arms around her, he crushed her against him, inhaling her scent.

And she didn't resist. Not that he thought she would. But instead her hands pushed against his chest, working their way up to his shoulders. Holding on to him, her small fingers dug into his flesh, clinging to him while she opened for him.

Fire rushed through his veins, the change bordering on the edge of his reality while he tugged at her shirt, almost ripping it from her body.

"Shit," she whispered, her breathing hard.

She looked up at him with almost silver eyes, her teeth extended slightly. Her blonde hair fell wildly around her, swaying over her shoulders and past her breasts as she panted.

"Okay, wolf man." She reached for him, grabbing his shirt and pulling it just as hard from his body as he'd done to her.

Blood pumped more furiously through his veins.

"Little bitch," he growled.

She would put him over the edge, beyond the ability to control his actions.

Running her fingers over his chest hair, she exhaled. His mind fogged, his vision altering from blurred to grossly acute while the animal in him begged to surface. He trembled when she reached for his jeans, her fingers fire against his skin.

"Holy fucking shit," she breathed when she released his cock.

Her singing his praises almost made him explode. But when she wrapped her fingers around his shaft, his world spun around him perilously.

"Come here," he growled, barely able to speak.

Taking her by the back of the neck, he led her to his bed, shoved in the corner of his cabin. He pushed her down, although she hardly fought him, her eagerness fueling his desire for her.

She was *lunewulf*, a fading whisper in the back of his brain reminded him. Smaller, petite, possibly not physically capable of taking all he wanted to give her. It was a whisper easy to ignore, and his brain boiled with so much need of pounding into her that he barely gave the words of warning any thought.

"Get out of those jeans," he ordered, grabbing his cock and squeezing his shaft, fighting for some semblance of control.

What a hot fucking body, so limber and petite. But she had a muscle tone that appealed to him, her strength noteworthy for her size. Slender hips and full breasts, a flat, hard tummy and that smooth, sweet, shaved pussy. God, she was more than fucking perfect.

Shoving his jeans down his legs, he climbed out of them quickly while watching her ass appear before him when she struggled to undress on his bed.

And then he was on top of her, feeling the softness of her body, the gentle curves and sweet scent that exploded from her body as she spread her legs. As she wrapped her legs around his thighs, her muscles shivered against him. Small fingers traced wicked patterns over his chest, up around his shoulders.

"Think you can handle me?" she purred, her voice thick with lust.

He chuckled and watched her tremble noticeably. She played coy with him, the all-knowing female. He saw through her though, saw the female who wanted all that he could give her, but wasn't sure what she asked for. Her craving for what she didn't know appealed to him more than he let her know.

"I'm going to handle everything you have," he said, cupping her breast.

So full and round, firm yet soft, her nipple puckered against his palm while she arched into him. He pulled and tugged then twisted the puckered flesh between his fingers, loving how her eyes fluttered closed.

He pinched her nipple and she grabbed the covers on either side of them. Then reaching up, her nails dug into his flesh, the sweet pain sending him over the edge.

"I love how your lust smells," he breathed, lowering his head to her chest.

Her breasts swelled on either side of his face as he took in her scent, let it fill him. She was putting her mark on him, and again that little voice in the back of his head sent out a warning cry.

They didn't know each other. And she ran too far on the wild side. His life had always been on the edge. And he liked it that way. But taking on a female that would fight to be trained wasn't on his agenda.

Fuck her. Enjoy her. Turn her over to the pack leader.

That rationale would do for the moment, allow him to enjoy her hot little body.

He sucked in a nipple, toying with it between his teeth. She convulsed underneath him, her nails dragging over his flesh.

"God. Please. Perry!" she screamed.

And the fire in his brain consumed all the little voices that argued with him.

"Come, little bitch. Give me what you've got."

He moved to her other breast, sucking and nibbling while she twisted underneath him. Her legs squeezed hard against him while she lifted up to him. That sweet pussy was soaked when it brushed against his cock.

Catching his breath suddenly became more work than he could handle. All blood drained through him. He was light-headed. Need coursed through his veins.

Fuck her. Fuck her hard. Make her scream.

He found her mouth again, devouring her taste. She wrapped her arms around him, holding on with everything she had while her tongue warred with his.

"Please," she cried into his mouth.

His cock throbbed so hard, burning like a fiery sword between his legs.

Letting go of her mouth, still tasting her on his lips, he rose over her. He grabbed her arms, pinning her to the bed. He adjusted his cock between her legs, and then thrust.

Her eyes rolled back in her head, her face contorting while she opened her mouth and screamed. The intoxicating heat that enveloped him burned him alive.

So fucking tight. Hotter than anything he'd ever experienced. And wet. So damned wet. He plunged deep into her pussy, feeling her muscles convulse and tighten around his cock.

Her arms struggled under his hands, but her strength didn't near his. He kept her pinned, loving the view while resting for a minute as her heat saturated him.

"Breathe, little Jaynie," he instructed quietly.

He fought not to move. Clarity ran through him while his senses altered, his vision growing more acute while the change burned through his veins. Changing while fucking her could do her serious damage. He needed a moment to gather his senses, keep himself in control.

"Fuck me," she growled, completely indifferent to his plight.

She did her best to thrust her hips upward and encourage his movement.

"Be still and I will," he told her, knowing her mind didn't consider anything other than her own satisfaction.

Well, he would see to it that she was satisfied.

She pursed her lips, scowling at him, and did her best to relax underneath him. The heat from her body burned him alive.

Slowly he pulled from her, his cock gliding over her inner muscles. They contracted, vibrated against him. He gritted his teeth, fighting for that control he'd had a moment before when he stilled his body.

But she was too much of an enticement. He had to hit that spot he'd felt seconds before. Diving deep inside her again, he could no longer stop the momentum.

"Yes. God. Yes." Again she twisted underneath him. "That's it. Fuck me, wolf man."

Fuck yeah. He let her have it, pounding her fiery cunt with everything he had. Muscles clamped down so hard he could hardly breathe. Her cunt wrapped around him, moisture exploding against him while she convulsed underneath him.

"Oh my God," she screamed, doing her best to wrap her legs around him.

Every inch of her hardened, her arms fighting under his hold, her body twisting. Her sexual scent filled the air, thick and heavy, making him drunk.

He thickened, his cock swelling and throbbing beyond his control. A pressure broke. He arched into it, pushing her hard down on the bed while gripping her small arms with all the strength he had as he plowed into her.

She grew too tight for him to move. His cock had grown and he released everything he had deep inside her. Locking down, his body shook, filling her, melting into her heat.

She was a blur underneath him. Her long hair streaming down her, clinging to her soaked body. So fucking beautiful.

Being a tracker had never been a job he'd despised. It was who he was, what he did, in his nature. But turning her over to the pack leader didn't appeal to him at all.

Chapter Four

Perry's cabin was more antiquated than anything she'd seen in a long time. One large room, a kitchenette on one end, fireplace on the other and a bed pushed into the corner. He hadn't done much to make it into a cozy den.

Although cozy wouldn't suit Perry's nature.

"Where do you shower?" she asked, muscles screaming throughout her body when she reached for her jeans and shirt.

Perry lay sprawled out over his bed. Although a good-sized bed, the large frame taking up a third of the space in the cabin, his feet hung off the end, and his massive arms, relaxed lazily behind his head, pushed against the headboard.

"You aren't showering there."

She struggled to comb her hair with her fingers and frowned at him. Even after sex he looked anything but relaxed. Tangles of curls lay around his head. Muscles rippled under tanned skin. A tiny scar, puckered flesh, ran in a thin line along his right nipple, surrounded by downy dark blond curly hair. Another longer scar formed a zigzag line on his outer thigh. Werewolves mended quickly, a scar remaining only if the wound had been fairly severe. Perry led a rough life, fighting, the continual aggressor.

"Why can't I use your shower?" She fought to bring her gaze back to his face.

"There's a communal shower at the end of the row of cabins. Toubec's unmated ranch hands live in the other cabins. You're damn lucky they were out on a run when you came prancing out here."

She sucked in a frustrated breath. Admitting her action to follow him had been foolish wasn't going to happen.

"I'm heading home, then."

"I'll take you."

As simple as Perry's home was, the Expedition he drove was new, black and sleek, classy yet tough enough to handle the narrow gravel road that led off the property to the highway. They drove in silence, but her thoughts were anything but quiet.

Where was he from? Did he have a home pack? Werewolves who called him family? She wondered if he'd always been a tracker. Not any werewolf could take on such an isolated lifestyle—such a dangerous way of life. Tracking criminals and scumbags would create enemies, cause you to always watch your back.

Perry said nothing, asked no questions, gave no indication that his thoughts strayed toward her at all. His expression was unreadable. Other than the still-apparent smell of sex that filled the space of the car between them, she detected no other emotions. His strong jawline and broad cheekbones set as if determined and satisfied with whatever action he would take next.

And that action was to turn her over to their pack leader.

Her stomach twisted at what might be decided during that meeting.

"My den is down the next street."

"I know," he said quietly.

"Oh really." She crossed her arms, watching him, but then scowled when she figured out that he probably knew where Steve's den was. If that were the case, had he spotted her before last night? Watched her as well?

He'd become a fucking closed book, not one emotion seeping from him. Well, that was just fine. She had a few years' practice at keeping her own feelings under lock and key as well.

Without instruction Perry pulled in front of her den and parked.

He growled when she reached for her door handle. "I'll get your door for you."

Getting out on his side before she could tell him she had no intention of being some kept bitch, he moved around the front of the Expedition with long strides.

He kept her close to him as if he were an overprotective guard dog. When she reached for her door, he took her hand, his large hand holding her firmly.

"Stay put," he told her when they entered her living room.

"Why?"

"Because I said so."

Okay. This little act could stop right now. She didn't hide her irritation as he inspected every room before returning to her.

"It's safe."

"Do you want to watch me shower too?" she asked sarcastically, although the thought sounded damn appealing.

He pushed her up against the front door. It clicked quietly as she was backed into it. He trapped her with his large body, his hands tangled in her hair as he yanked her head back.

"You aren't ready for me again yet, little bitch." The low rumble in his voice vibrated through her.

A pressure swelled through her, filling her with a quick, hard need. Damn if she cared how raw and worn out he'd leave her. She wanted him again—now.

He nipped at her lip, a quick, sharp pain that he immediately licked away. "Go bathe," he ordered.

"Quit telling me what to do." Her voice was a rough whisper.

Every inch of her tingled when she shoved past hard, solid muscle and somehow managed to get down the hallway on very shaky legs. No way would she look over her shoulder to see the disapproving gaze that she knew probably tore across his face.

The hot shower felt good but left her sated and sleepy.

"How does coffee sound?" she asked, leaving the steamy bathroom and walking barefoot down her short hallway to the living room. "Perry?" she called when she didn't see him.

His scent filled her small den.

She pushed open her bedroom door and paused. Her room was empty. Dressing quickly, she parted her curtains, blinking at the rising sun. The Expedition was still parked in front of her den. Perry leaned against the hood, speaking into his phone. He looked toward her, as if he'd heard the quiet movement of curtains being opened.

Letting them fall, she plopped down on her single bed. No way the two of them could ever do a thing on it. Shaking her head, she slid into her shoes. Already she plotted out when she could fuck him again. This was bad. In a matter of hours she'd created a list of damn good reasons why he'd make a terrible mate. A damn good fuck buddy, yes. But that was dangerous territory. Especially with a *Cariboo* who showed every indication of being way too dominating, too protective. And let's not even discuss how possessive he'd probably be. Hell, he didn't even want her opening her own doors.

Not that she minded a gallant werewolf.

It was being bossed around that would drive her nuts real fast.

"Shit," she breathed, amazed that she even pondered the possibility of a relationship. "That is not what you want," she reminded herself and then stared at her cell phone when it vibrated on the floor inside her jeans pocket.

"Hello?"

"Jaynie, where are you?" Wendy asked.

"At our den. How are you doing?"

"You shouldn't stay there alone. I know it's early but Johann and Samantha are expecting you." There was worry in Wendy's tone. But that was probably the least of the emotions her cousin was enduring at the moment.

"Please, Wendy. You know how I hate pack laws and tradi-
tions. I'll go see them, I promise. You need to take care of you."

"I'm fine. It's you I'm worried about. Steve's den is seeking
vengeance. They were just here. You might not be safe there
alone." Wendy let out a staggered breath. "I know you have a
habit of running from packs when you feel laws are closing in
around you. You've done this all your life."

"That's not always the reason I run. New places, new adventures . . ."

"And you don't want to be shackled down."

"Do you blame me?"

"No," Wendy said quickly enough for Jaynie to know her
cousin wished she'd run a time or two as well. The hard, quiet
tone she then took on was serious. "Look, Jaynie. Steve's pack will
move fast. They smell blood. And they feel revenge is their right.
I heard them. They were here talking to my sire."

Jaynie thought about the oversized *Cariboo* standing guard
outside her den. She was safer than any other *lunewulf* on the
planet right now.

"That whole den is a pack of lowlifes." Jaynie bit her tongue.
"I'm sorry, Wendy. I shouldn't have said that."

"You're right. I'm not arguing with you. My sire is worried
neither of us is safe right now. We're the only bitches in our den
here in town, and they're going to cause trouble."

She glanced up when a floorboard squeaked in the hallway.
Perry filled her doorway with his massive frame. A faint spicy
smell filled her room. He was angry. Amazing how his negative
emotions ran clearly through him. Somehow she had the feeling
he already knew what Wendy was telling her on the phone.

"I'll be fine. Don't worry about me, please."

"Gather your things. You aren't staying here," he told her
as soon as she hung up and shoved her phone into her pants
pocket.

She closed her eyes, fighting the sensation to strike out. No one told her what to do, where she would stay or not stay. She'd be smart to shake this *Cariboo* off her scent. At the same time, she wanted to know so much more about him. This was fucking nuts.

"I'll be fine," she said, repeating the mantra she'd used so many times in the past when told how she should live her life.

For a werewolf so large, he moved silently, touching her before she realized he'd reached her side.

"Jaynie," he growled.

She jumped at his touch, moving quickly, her leg muscles protesting loudly when she hopped off the bed. Having sex with this werewolf made her feel she'd run halfway across British Columbia.

"Look. I'm sure you have your orders."

"I don't take orders from anyone."

"Well, neither do I."

Surprisingly he smiled. Moved toward her slowly. His touch was gentle when a finger brushed over her cheek. She didn't want gentle. Gentle made her nervous. Compassion meant he cared. And caring would make her want to stay with him.

"Running toward danger isn't always the smartest move."

"That's what you do."

"I'm twice your size."

The damned brute. "Don't you dare imply I'm some feeble, helpless bitch," she sneered.

Being pissed at him worked a lot better than feeling compassion. If she fought him she didn't risk as much chance of falling hard for him.

He moved quickly. And she anticipated the act. He was right. Strength was on his side. But speed was her asset.

Leaping away from him, she jumped onto her bed and then flew off it, tearing out of her room and down the hall toward the front door. Her hand was on the front door when she paused.

With her heart pounding in her chest and her own emotions flying out of control, she'd almost missed it.

But not quite.

Another werewolf was on the other side of that door. His scent seeped through the door, outraged and obnoxious-smelling.

Shit.

She backed into hard, well-packed muscle.

Perry pulled Jaynie into his arms. As he backed away from the door, emotions soared through him harder than he'd experienced in years. The little *lunewulf* pressed against him possessed more fire in her than any female he'd ever known. Her energy, her passion for independence, not to be controlled, turned him on more than he'd thought traits like that would.

There wasn't room in his life for a mate.

At least not until a few hours ago.

Jaynie defied him. Told him off. Made it clear she didn't want to be told what to do. And it made his blood boil with a craving to possess her.

Fighting every emotion that soared through him, he backed them away from the door.

"Do you recognize that scent?" he whispered into her ear, lifting her off the ground, as he took a step backward.

She shook her head, showing enough sense not to speak. Soap and perfume, her damp hair, her warm body, traveled through his senses. A protector's instinct surged through him harder than he'd ever felt it before. No one would lay a paw on her and live.

The doorknob turned, and there was a slight creaking sound as the door opened toward them. A scowling *lunewulf* looked quickly at Jaynie and then glared at him.

He moved her behind him. A creaking sound made her stiffen.

"They're at the back door too," she warned him.

"This should save us a run." An older *lunewulf* chuckled with the confidence of an idiot.

"Yeah, both of them are right here." Another werewolf came through the back door.

"I get the bitch," the ugly fucker at the front door said, almost drooling as he stared at Jaynie.

"Lay a paw on her and it will be the last move you make." Perry's warning silenced the room for a moment.

"*Cariboo.* You messed with the wrong den today."

These were some stupid fucking *lunewulf.*

"Yeah. And you're in an Amyx den. We got a right to be here, and you don't," another werewolf spoke from behind him. "Get your overgrown paws off our bitch."

There were four of them. The fools had announced their presence. Each of them had spoken, their emotions running so hard with anger and plain idiocy, that he easily marked where each of them stood. This wouldn't take more than a few minutes.

Perry struck at the werewolf in front of him. The closest, and he had drooled over Jaynie. That won him the right to go down first.

"You need to learn to knock," he growled through clenched teeth while punching the werewolf in the face.

Bone hit bone and a cracking sound followed by a pathetic howl told him he'd hit his mark. Grabbing the werewolf before he slumped to the ground, he twisted his neck. Several pops vibrated against his hand. There was one less scumbag to annoy the pack.

Fire burned through him. Muscles stretched through his body. But changing wasn't necessary. A roar tore through him when someone jumped on his back.

"Take him down," the older werewolf yelled. "And get the bitch."

He threw the *lunewulf* from his back. Blonde hair flew before his face. Jaynie's scent, outraged yet so damned sensual, filled the room. He wouldn't be the only one to smell it. The little bitch had jumped into the fight.

"You want a piece of this tail?" she screamed, jumping into the air and kicking one of the *lunewulf* in the throat.

A mixture of pride and frustration distracted Perry. Jaynie pulled off an impressive kick. She could take care of herself. Her fighting style added to her sexiness, her appeal. A dangerous, erotic bitch.

Adrenaline surged through his veins too fast to sit back and watch her attack the Amyx den. "Get out of the way," he ordered her.

Her blue eyes were laced with silver when she turned to him, stunned. One of the werewolves, the youngest of the three remaining, lunged at her, and Perry grabbed the punk by the arm, throwing him into the other two.

Cars pulled up out front. He ignored the sounds of car doors opening and closing and moved faster to secure the area. He reached for the oldest in the den. No effort was needed in lifting the asshole off the ground by his neck.

The front door flew open.

"Put him down, Perry," Johann Rousseau yelled from behind him.

The command seemed to come from miles away. Defying a pack leader's orders would have him kicked out of the pack. He wouldn't accept the idea that Rousseau would side with this derelict den. More than likely he would play diplomat. Perry didn't feel like talking.

Rage surged through him. One of the *lunewulf*, the youngest in the den, bolted for the back door. Jaynie raced after him.

"Put him down now," Johann yelled a bit louder.

Perry threw the older werewolf toward the kitchen and leapt around the other two. Jaynie's scent faded quickly. What a fool little bitch! Running after a no-good *lunewulf* who more than likely had some of his buddies lying in wait. And if any of them got their hands on her . . .

"Perry!" Johann barked.

The remaining *lunewulf* already began mumbling their complaints about their treatment when entering their dead littermate's den.

Perry glared at his pack leader. "Do what you want with this trash," he hissed, glaring at the remaining Amyx den. "I'm going after her."

If there were any further comments, he didn't take time to hear them. Bounding out the back door, he searched the small backyard quickly then scanned the neighborhood. Her scent had faded and he'd have to track her from scratch.

Chapter Five

Three blocks later, Jaynie lost the *lunewulf*'s scent. The bastard. Prince George was up and moving with a new day, humans bustling off to work, getting their children to school. Racing at full speed down the somewhat busy street would draw attention. There were a few *lunewulf* on the police force who would be a bit more understanding if some human were to call in complaining of a rabid werewolf but she wasn't in the mood to deal with cops.

Or any human for that matter. They wouldn't understand her craving to eliminate a den because one of their kind had so terribly abused her cousin.

She huffed in cold morning air, filling her lungs with it, and dragged her fingers through her still-damp hair.

Exhaust from passing cars made it impossible to smell out any werewolves.

She jogged across the street, a small strip mall and a doughnut shop looking like a good place to regroup. One problem—she didn't have her purse or any money on her.

"Hell," she said with a sigh.

Hopefully the doughnut shop would be busy enough not to notice her slip into the bathroom. Her phone buzzed as she entered the warm shop. Hot grease, heavy fresh dough, strong coffee, aftershave, perfume—too many smells hit her at once. The place was doing some decent business. Good thing too. No one gave her a second glance.

She pulled out her cell phone and saw Wendy's number displayed on the small screen. It bugged her that she'd wondered if Perry would call. But he wouldn't call her. He didn't know her number. Shaking her head, she pushed through humans toward the bathroom. If he wanted her cell phone number he'd get it. A funny feeling twisted through her gut. Being stalked by such a giant of a *Cariboo*, stronger and sexier than any werewolf she'd ever laid eyes on, made her heart flutter.

He'd control her, tell her what to do. No way. Wouldn't happen.

She shoved the bathroom door open, kicking at stall doors to ensure she was alone.

Pushing the button to answer her call, she sucked in a breath, calming herself. "Hello."

"Jaynie?" a female whispered into the phone. "I'm scared."

"Wendy? Where are you?"

"At the bus station. My sire left when he thought the bus would leave in a minute. But it didn't leave. I'm not sure why. And Jaynie . . ." She sucked in a breath. "Are you there?"

"I'm here. What's wrong?" A quick look in the mirror had her cringing. No makeup. Her hair desperately needed brushing. And the shadows under her eyes. A seriously long nap was definitely needed.

"I think some of the Amyx den is here."

Jaynie quickly turned her back to the mirror, her stomach tensing. Wendy didn't need any more abuse from that den. The way they'd come after her, willingly taken on Perry, Wendy wouldn't stand a chance.

"Where did you say you were?"

"The bus station." Her voice quavered. "If I call my parents, they might get hurt. If I keep them out of this, the Amyx den won't go after them. It's me they want. And I can't reach Johann or his mate."

That was because they were at her den. She didn't envy Johann having to put a collar on Perry. And that is what it would take to stop him from destroying that den. Again a strange sensation fluttered through her stomach. The raw fury she'd seen in his eyes, how dangerously large his muscles had grown. Those blond curls twisting around his head, falling to his shoulders. The sensation dropped from her stomach to between her legs, a quick, hard throbbing.

Her heart went out to her cousin as well. Wendy wasn't a strong *lunewulf* yet she had such a good heart, still caring and beautiful after being treated so poorly. She deserved the best there was.

"Stay where you are. Keep close to humans. They won't come after you as quickly that way. I'll be there as soon as I can."

"Jaynie?" Wendy sounded like the little cub Jaynie had protected again and again when they were younger.

"Yes?"

"Samantha told me that Johann had an argument with his tracker, a *Cariboo lunewulf* named Perry Roth. Have you met him?"

"I've met him."

"He wants you."

Jaynie headed out of the bathroom, nerves twisting through her so violently she could hardly breathe through the intensity of smells in the shop.

"What . . . what do you mean?"

"Just something that Samantha told me before I left my parents' den. Johann told him to bring you to them."

Perry had that conversation with Johann while she'd been at Perry's den. Nothing had been said at that time. She replayed what she'd overheard of the conversation in her mind. It had been a brief phone call, Perry had simply agreed to take her to the queen bitch. Had he called Johann back?

She headed back out to the street, wondering how in the

hell she'd get across town to the bus station without a car or any money, and in broad daylight. No way could she run at full speed across Prince George in her skin or her fur with the sun up.

She glanced up and down the busy street. Telling Wendy she'd been with Perry during that conversation didn't sound like a good idea.

"Samantha told me that Johann is pissed because Perry hasn't brought you to her yet. I guess Perry doesn't want you turned over to her. He wants you for himself."

"I can't imagine that's true." She exhaled, knowing Perry hadn't brought her in yet because she'd showered and then dealt with the Amyx den. "He plans on taking me to see Samantha. He told me as much."

Wendy chuckled although her nervousness came through over the phone. "From what Samantha tells me it sounds like this Perry *Cariboo* guy is a lot like you. He plays rough, with tooth and claw bared, you know? And drifts from pack to pack. I've never understood why you never wanted a den to call your own. But he doesn't sound like someone who'd be good for you."

She wanted to ask what kind of werewolf would be good for her. Right there, on the tip of her lips; she almost argued with her cousin that Perry would be one hell of a catch.

What the hell was she thinking?

Already she had a list longer than her tail why he'd be a very bad catch.

She had a hell of a jaunt before she reached the bus station. There was only one way to get across town. She'd have to risk running.

"What makes you think the Amyx den is there?" she asked, changing the subject while darting across the street, clutching her phone to her ear.

She'd have to get off the main drag. Humans knew *lunewulf* were thick in Prince George. That didn't mean they liked a visual reminder. If she took off in a sprint in her human form, running faster than any human, more than one of them would call the police, complaining. No way did she want the pack leader pissed at her. Already more attention was focused on her than she liked having.

She took a minute to look up and down the street. There was no sensation of being followed, or watched. More than likely she'd imagined it. That or darting into the doughnut shop had thrown off her scent and she'd lost her tracker.

Now why did that leave an empty feeling inside her?

"I'm sitting next to the ticket counter. Earlier I smelled their angry stench. But I don't see the *lunewulf* that I saw earlier."

"Stay where you are. Call me back if you get scared again. I'll be there soon."

Wendy agreed, sounding more relaxed than when she'd first called. With little den left alive, Jaynie would protect her cousin with her life. Wendy's den, her aunt and uncle, were good people. Her aunt had been her mother's sister. Jaynie hadn't seen them much as a cub. But since her parents had died, they'd tried including Jaynie in den affairs. Jaynie had been the one who'd been reluctant to get close to Wendy's den. Losing her parents had been enough pain for a lifetime. She wouldn't allow her heart to suffer like that again.

Shoving her phone into her jeans pocket, she headed away from the busy street. There were miles of neighborhood to cover before she hit the industrial part of town where the bus station was. If she could hit a full run, she'd be there in less than ten minutes. But she'd have to be careful, ensure that not too many people saw her.

Maybe she should make a few phone calls, seek out help. Figure out how to call Perry.

"What the hell are you thinking?" she hissed through her teeth.

She'd made it quite a few years now on her own, enjoying

freedom, not needing or wanting another werewolf for anything. Ten years since her parents had died. Ten years that she'd made damned sure no one got too close.

Calling him would be as bad as putting the collar around her neck herself.

Half an hour later she wiped sweat from her brow, twisting her hair off her neck and taking a slow breath as she walked toward the bus station. She stopped in her tracks when she saw Wendy being escorted out of the bus station by the older *lunewulf* who'd been at her den that morning.

"Whoa. What's going on here?" She hurried toward them.

Wendy looked up, her cheeks stained with tears.

"Get in the truck." The older *lunewulf* ignored her and pulled open the passenger door, shoving Wendy forward.

"Like hell she is." Jaynie grabbed the guy's shoulder, shoving him out of the way and then took Wendy's arm. "Let's go."

"I've about had enough of you, bitch." The *lunewulf* had some foul-smelling breath.

"That makes it mutual. You have no right to her, and you damn well know it." Anger rushed through her, her bones popping while her muscles started growing.

No way could any of them allow the change while outside the human bus terminal. But a little strength wouldn't hurt anything in dealing with these lowlifes.

"You don't have your *Cariboo* here to protect you this time," the *lunewulf* sneered, glancing over her shoulder.

The little hairs on the back of her neck prickled. Anger smelling so spicy she almost sneezed filled the air around them. "I'll give the unruly one here a lesson on how much I do have a right to Wendy," someone said from behind her.

Strong hands clamped down on her shoulders. The *lunewulf* behind her reeked with so much outrage she drowned from the stench of it.

"She's my dead brother's mate. And now she's mine," he whispered in her ear. "Get both of them in the truck."

• • •

Perry glared at Johann.

"Head home, Roth," the pack leader said, a bit too calmly. "I'll call you if I need you."

"They're at the Amyx den. They've got to be. Won't take too much if you simply head over there and explain to them that our den doesn't approve of them having the bitches." Frederick Rousseau, a silver-haired *lunewulf*, hugged his mate reassuringly while addressing the pack leader.

"We've scoured the entire city. I've got pack members with the police force keeping an eye out for them. I'll head over to their den. If they're there, we'll bring them to you." Johann nodded to the older Rousseau couple.

No way would Perry simply go home, being dismissed as if his services were no longer needed.

"I'll meet you over there." He'd keep this simple.

Johann headed toward his truck, giving Perry a sideways glance. "You've known her a day, Roth. You're running on too many emotions right now. That's not what I need in a tracker."

Perry wouldn't honor the comment with a response. Storming over to his Expedition, he climbed in and stuffed the key in the ignition. Responding to Rousseau's comment would have brought a lie from him. He'd deny such emotions. And he wouldn't insult his pack leader like that. His emotions were running strong. A little *lunewulf* bitch had gotten under his skin. He needed to find her, to know where she was. Never had his protector's instinct coursed through his blood with such vengeance.

Gripping his steering wheel, he hated Rousseau for being right. The emotions that tore at him must smell worse than yesterday's trash. In as little as twenty-four hours, he'd fallen hard for a bitch who shouldn't appeal to him at all. Headstrong and disobedient, she'd run from him and then managed to disappear. He'd combed the neighborhood looking for her after she left her den. No werewolf got away from him. Yet she'd managed it. Within blocks of her house he'd lost her scent. He'd combed the area, covering well over twenty blocks of neighborhood and hadn't found her. After a couple of hours he knew that she'd obviously gone in an opposite direction from him, and had hightailed back to where he'd initially lost her scent.

His common practice when losing the scent of a werewolf he tracked would be to start questioning nearby dens, see who'd seen them last. But Johann had called him, bringing him in. He'd been forced to give up looking for her.

After watching her kick ass while taking on the Amyx den, he almost pitied the fools if they had managed to take her to their den. She'd tear the place apart.

Maybe time to clear his head would do him some good. He knew her scent still lingered on him. It had driven him nuts most of the day. Johann would have smelled her on him, would have known he'd fucked her. Not that he'd deny that. Hell, he couldn't wait to have her again.

By the time he reached his cabin, he'd convinced himself a nap was in order. Being up all night and then not enjoying his usual respite the first half of the day had to be affecting his line of thinking. No female got under his skin this fast, or this hard. And hard was an understatement. His cock had throbbed throughout the day as he thought about where Jaynie might have disappeared to and what he'd do once he found her.

After a quick shower, he collapsed on his bed, her smell wrapping around him as he closed his eyes. No way would he fall asleep any time soon.

. . .

It took a few minutes for him to register that his phone was ringing. Grumbling, he rolled onto his back, the pressure in his groin immediately bringing him fully awake.

"What?" His voice cracked, sleep leaving him groggy.

"I need your help." There was worry in Johann's tone.

Perry sat up, grabbing his hard cock, willing all the blood that had rushed there back into his body. His breath came out with a hiss. "What's wrong?"

"The two bitches, Jaynie and Wendy, have disappeared."

Perry leapt out of bed, almost sending the top drawer of his dresser flying when he pulled it open looking for underwear. He should have fought the pack leader, insisted on tracking Jaynie until he had her.

"Where are you right now?"

"Just left the Amyx den. I sent two werewolves after their scent. But I want you on this."

Perry wouldn't tell the pack leader he'd finally come to his senses. One glance toward his only window in the cabin and he realized he'd slept a hell of a lot longer than he'd thought. Darkness had settled.

"If that Amyx den hurt them . . ." He would personally hold Johann Rousseau responsible. He let his threat go unspoken.

Johann's relaxed nature grated on Perry's nerves more times than not. Now was no exception.

"That den was in an uproar over those two bitches. Sounds like Jaynie tore into a few of them, destroyed more than a few pieces of furniture and then escaped with her cousin."

"The entire Amyx den deserves their throats clawed out."

Johann ignored his comment.

"I'm more concerned for Wendy at this point. Sounds like Jaynie is more than a bit wild. I believe wicked was the term the Amyx den used for her." He chuckled at that. "Not sure what I'm going to do with her."

Perry knew exactly what *he* was going to do with her. "I'll let you know when I have them."

He hung up the phone and tied his clothes around his waist instead of dressing. He grabbed a small blanket and folded it before sliding it under his clothes. In his fur, it would look like he'd secured a saddle to his back, but he didn't give a rat's ass. Once he found the little bitch, he would take all the time needed to talk sense into her. Running away from him instead of to him wasn't her smartest move.

There were at least three males in the Amyx den that he'd had the displeasure of meeting. Jaynie had been dragged into their den, forced to protect her cousin and take all of them on as well. Damn impressive that she'd escaped.

But where had she gone? There were werewolves tracking her. Probably meant they'd chased her even farther into the wilderness. She wouldn't plan on leaving the pack.

Wherever she went, he'd find her. That hot little bitch defied every rule in the book. Running on her own, taking her cousin with her . . .

Fire burned through his veins. Muscles quivered, contorting and changing. A howl escaped him as the change ripped through his body. Jaynie had no fear of running into any situation, taking on anyone. That's how she'd entered his life.

If another werewolf got his hands on her, or God forbid, if it were a *Cariboo* . . .

His spine hardened, blood rushing through his veins while his heart pumped harder than his human body could handle. Thoughts of another male touching her, fucking her, taking what was his . . .

Perry screamed, bolting out the door that he'd yet to fix before the change had completely taken over his body.

His.

Fur spread through his hardening flesh, the prickling sensation devouring him while his face changed, his mouth and nose growing. The color of night changed, shadows fading as his vision grew more acute. He took in the night air, many scents invading him while he dug through the earth with long, extended claws.

Taking a wide curve around town, he reached the backside of the Amyx den, moving quietly through the predominantly were-wolf neighborhood until he picked up the scent of where were-wolves had recently taken off running. Years of tracking made it easier to pull out scents in the air. The only ones he focused on were those of the trackers, and the marks in the ground where they'd stampeded into the night.

He hadn't bothered to ask Johann who he'd sent off to hunt down the females. Other males stalking her, trying to bring her in, didn't sit well with him at all. Assuming Johann had called right after sending the trackers after Jaynie and Wendy, they'd have no more than a fifteen-minute lead on him. Reaching high speed in minutes, he didn't slow until well beyond the city limits of Prince George. Then, keeping his nose close to the ground, all senses on red alert, he picked up their scent, stronger than it had been at the den.

Crouching over the ground, he watched the fools Johann had sent out. Obviously he had little to worry about with these pups chasing Jaynie. She'd run them around in circles before they realized what she'd done. The noise they made was enough to send all wildlife in the area running.

Circling around them unnoticed, he focused his attention on Jaynie's scent, letting his instincts take over. Possessive instincts, raw and unleashed, tracking a female whose fire ran through her veins as hot and wild as his did. Before he'd met her, he would have denied a bitch like that would be a good mate. But now he clearly saw how she could be the only mate for him. No one else would be able to handle her.

No one else would ever touch her.

Chapter Six

S leep sounded better than anything else at the moment. It had been a good fifty-mile run to the next town where there was a bus station. After seeing Wendy off safely, knowing she'd be in Banff later that day with relatives who were excited to see her, took a load of worry off her mind. The Amyx den wouldn't mess with her cousin anymore.

The sun rested on the horizon, glaring at her. No way would she be able to run back to Prince George in broad daylight. Wendy had promised to call her parents as soon as she reached Banff and then they would know she was all right. For now, the only way she'd be fine was if she slept.

Sitting in her fur, muscles growing heavier the longer she didn't move, she stared at the undeveloped wilderness that spread out below her and stretched for miles beyond her vision. Her eyes burned.

Maybe a small cave. There were rocky cliffs scattered along the river. Just anywhere to lay her head for a few hours. Exhaustion hit so hard that nothing else mattered.

There were no caves, but after an hour's search, a back wall of hard rock with two boulders protecting her on either side looked as good a cozy bed as anything she'd ever seen. Curling up in her fur, she crashed into a deep slumber.

• • •

Hours had to have passed. Waking up so stiff she'd swear she'd slept on pure rock, she blinked several times. Oh yeah . . . she had slept on rock. She stretched, stiff muscles crying out. Yawning, she inhaled a hell of a lot more than the smells of the great outdoors.

Werewolf. And very, very close.

She jumped to her feet. Cold, fast-moving water, filled with fish that pranced without a care, tumbled over rocks several yards from her. A chilly white sky brought crisp air. A damn near perfect day, kick-ass surroundings, enough food and shelter to make the place close to paradise.

Except she wasn't alone. Whoever it was better damned well show his face, and soon. She growled, just in case the ass thought they dealt with some helpless female. Maybe she'd been an exhausted one but right now she was more than ready to take on anyone with nerve enough to come up on her while she slept.

Sniffing the air, she looked above her. The largest *Cariboo* she'd ever laid eyes on sat on the rocks above her. Tall and proud, his chest broad with muscles rippling visibly under a thick white coat. He gazed over the land, surveying it like a king. Long, thick, daggerlike canines pressed against his lower lip. The dangerous predator, confident and alert.

Jaynie's heart beat too hard to catch her breath. Slowly he lowered his head, meeting her gaze with piercing silver eyes. He returned her growl, the cocky low rumble sending hot tingles rushing through her.

She was unable to move. Her mouth went dry watching him stand, stretch slowly and begin descending the rocky terrain.

Run! Fucking run like your life depends on it!

She sat wide-eyed, heat rushing through her while roped muscles flexed under his thick, coarse hair. Never had she laid eyes on a more beautiful creature. So magnificent, with raw strength emanating from him. God. She swore his power had a scent all its own.

Perry moved over the rocks with little effort. Not even nature inhibited him. And he'd sat up there, keeping watch over her while she napped. The protector, a dominant in the purest sense. She should have known he'd be able to find her.

His scent overwhelmed her, soaking through her, demanding her submission.

She let out a low growl. *That isn't going to happen. Don't think for a second I'm going belly-up for you.*

His growl vibrated the rock underneath her. Standing over her, he was fucking tall enough that she could have darted underneath his chest, raced through his legs and jumped to her freedom. Except for the long thick cock that hung between his hind legs, hard and aimed right at her. She swallowed the thickness in her throat and lifted her gaze to his face.

He leaned down, his thick tongue tracing a damp path over her head, down her cheek, those long thick teeth scraping through her fur. Slow and meticulous, he bathed her face, wiping the sleep from her eyes, taking care of her. She closed her eyes, lifting her face to allow the warmth of his tongue to brush over her fur. When he nudged her with the side of his head she almost stumbled to the side. His cheekbone was as large as the side of her head, and harder than the rock she stood on.

The reality of the amount of power he possessed excited and terrified her at the same time. With him standing over her, there was no way she could escape him. Anything he wanted right now, he'd take. His scent dominated with satisfaction, complete control. Anytime now, he'd make her his. And in their fur, he wouldn't ask first. The tension turned to fear.

Werewolves were so damned traditional. It sucked. *Cariboo*s were more aggressive with their ways than other purebreds. And Perry was all *Cariboo*. He'd stood watch over her, like she belonged to him and he'd made sure no one disturbed her nap. No one had ever taken care of her like that before. And the security he offered her was more appealing than even the thought of that hard cock.

He nudged her again and she tripped over her paws, falling to her side. His long tongue swept over her side.

Damn it. She'd become his possession. Fucking in their fur would mate them harder and faster than any demand a pack leader could ever place on her. And the clarity that this was exactly what she'd dodged ever since her parents' death hit her harder than anything she'd taken on in her life.

No! She barked furiously, jumping to her feet. But there was nowhere to move where she could escape him. Her perfect haven of nestled boulders now served as a small prison.

You won't trap me. I won't be owned.

She lunged at him, baring her teeth, all the while knowing in the back of her head that attacking him would be futile. She did it anyway. Perry sent her rolling backward with a swift swipe of his paw.

Crumpled against a large rock, she blinked at the beautiful silver eyes that gazed down at her. Such a perfect creature. Powerful and strong, well built in either werewolf or human form. And more fucking deadly than anyone she'd ever met in her life.

His chest broadened, flattening, hair receding, while his scent quickly changed. His hindquarters grew, becoming rounder, extending, until his front paws no longer touched the ground. Hair receded on his body while he slowly straightened.

"Change," he told her in a thick rumble, speaking before his tongue had reshaped to human form.

So many smells from his emotions overwhelmed her while she embraced the metamorphosis, allowed her body to grow with his. The sweet pain plunged through her, muscles and bones altering shape while her heart slowed, altering the speed that blood pumped through her veins.

There were too many emotions. Not only the mixture of confidence and domination that she smelled from him but her own emotions too. Changing from werewolf to human, suddenly mixing deeper thought with the more carnal raw sensations that still lingered deeply in her, the sudden sensation to cry ripped at her soul.

Everything was too intense. The urge to escape him, run hard and fast, make a break for freedom while it was still within her grasp, had her mind spinning.

"You pushed me away." He stood naked before her now, magnificent, glistening skin covering corded muscle throughout his body.

"I don't like being trapped." Looking at him took too much from her, so many feelings hitting her at once, the once-closed book of a man now standing before her like a raw exposed nerve. It was damned unsettling.

Instead she searched where she'd napped, trying to remember where she'd put her clothes. Not that she was cold. It couldn't be a more perfect day.

Perry turned away from her, jumping up the rocks as easily in his human form as he had in his werewolf form, quickly reaching the perch where he'd watched over her. Muscles bulged in his legs, over his ass and up his back when he picked something up off the ground.

"And that's why you run, never staying in a pack that long, refusing to let anyone get close to you." He walked back to her with the same smooth agility, carrying a blanket bundled in his arms.

"I enjoy freedom."

"You're free with me. Had I not maintained watch, the pack would have hauled you home." He spread out the blanket, producing her clothes and his.

"Don't think I don't know what you were going to do a few minutes ago." She crossed her arms. No way would he get a thank-you out of her with that feeble comment. He wanted her to think she couldn't make it without him.

"What was I going to do?" He sat down, then leaned back and squinted up at her.

Too many muscles and one hell of an impressive-looking cock made it hard to focus on her argument.

"You were going to fuck me."

His cock stretched over his abdomen. "I still am."

She blinked, forcing herself to look away, to stare at unappealing rocks. It didn't stop the quickly building pressure inside her, the urge to climb over him, impale herself with that magnificent cock. God. Even when he wasn't bullying her, he still had the power to control her body. And not just her body. Her mind. She wanted him. With every breath, she wanted him inside her, with her. Such raw power, his calm, controlled manner, his protective strength. There would be freedom with him. No one would ever try to run her life again.

"But in our fur . . ." Her thoughts were running together, pros and cons about being with him, running at his side, having him for a mate, were all overlapping.

"We would have mated," he finished for her.

She met his gaze. His expression was intent, blue eyes devouring her. She sank into them, feeling like she was falling, rushing toward him. That's exactly what he wanted. He wanted her as a mate!

Oh shit!

Her mouth went dry, every bit of her suddenly shaking like a leaf. The thought was terrifying, absolutely terrifying.

"Mating is for a hell of a long time," she whispered.

"For life," he said, with such calm confidence that he made it sound almost appealing.

She licked her lips, her heart suddenly racing hard enough to bring on the change. His dominating manner appealed to her. Damn it. What was wrong with her? He held out his hand, reaching for her, not moving, not taking his gaze from hers.

"Come here," he whispered, a rough, raw sound.

"I don't think so." This new sensation rippling through her needed time.

He moved faster than she anticipated. His giant hand wrapped around hers, his touch rough against her skin. He tugged hard and she lost her balance. She fell onto him and he caught her, wrapping his arms around her. Muscle encased her and pure satisfaction oozed from his pores.

Dear Lord. Aggression like this had never turned her on so much. The way he took over, demanded that she be with him, made every inch of her tingle with raw energy.

"You need some serious housetraining," she whispered.

The smile that appeared on his face should have terrified her. "I'm already housebroken."

"That's a scary thought," she muttered.

Muscle closed in around her as he rolled over, taking her with him until he was on top of her, crushing her against hard, flat rock. Discomfort was the last thing on her mind.

His hands clawed through her hair, pinning her head so that she could only stare into his eyes. Holding himself off her by maybe a mere inch, he bit at her lower lip.

"You are not going to own me," she whispered, the quick pinch he gave her with his teeth shooting like currents straight through her body to her cunt.

Thick, powerful legs spread hers apart. His cock poked hard and demandingly against her heat, teasing the shit out of her since she couldn't move to do anything about it with him pinning her down like this.

"You don't think you're worthy of me?" His cockiness had a strong dominating scent to it.

She touched her lip with her tongue where he'd bitten her. Those lust-filled blue eyes of his lowered to watch the action. His blond curls fell around his face—such a fucking roguish look. God, he turned her on.

"You don't even have a den." What the hell was she thinking? She grasped at straws, and the crooked smile that crossed his face showed he saw that immediately.

"Pick any den you want, and it's yours."

Again he moved faster than she anticipated. He had her mind in such a frenzy, scraping for arguments, determined to show him that mating would make them both crazy. He scooped her off the ground, moving to his knees and bringing her up with him. With a quick, solid movement he impaled her with his cock. The damn thing split her in two.

Her nails dug into his flesh, scraping over hard muscle while she threw her head back and screamed. He had her straddling him, was holding on to her ass and lifting her, then forcing her down on him. Every movement he controlled. It was all she could do to hold on while he sent an orgasm tearing through her too hard for her to breathe.

Her come dripped down her inner thighs, soaking both of them, filling the air around them with the thick, heady smell of sex. It intoxicated her, brought out the wild craving she so often held back. He wasn't the only one who could be an animal in human form.

"Come on, wolf man," she hissed through clamped teeth that threatened to grow and puncture her lips. "Prove you're worthy."

"You little bitch," he snarled, his grin turning very dangerous.

God. Could she handle all he dished out? She sure wanted to give it a try.

Tossing her off him and then grabbing her again before she could manage to get to her hands and knees, he flipped her over onto all fours. Before she managed to move, he'd grabbed her hair, holding on to it like the leash she knew he'd love to put on her.

And then he was inside her again, fucking her doggy-style. And damn, could his cock stroke her insides better than anything she'd ever had in her life. More than that, he pushed her beyond her breaking point, building pressure in her so fast and then making her explode before she could catch her breath.

He forced her back to arch, pulling her hair so that her head stung. His primal actions had fire rushing through her. Molten heat burned her alive. And damn, if she didn't love every minute of it.

His hand on her ass was rough, kneading her soft flesh. Thick fingers teased her tight hole, spreading her cream over the incredibly sensitive skin. He impaled her ass with one finger, sending all nerve endings in her puckered flesh into a heated frenzy.

She bucked at the new sensation.

"Tell me you want me to fuck your ass." His deep baritone gave her chills.

"Beg me to give it to you," she hissed through her teeth.

His aggression made her want more. And when he slowed his movements, letting go of her hair, her head fell forward, too much blood rushing to her brain and making her dizzy.

"Perry," she whispered, her thoughts so fogged that words escaped her.

"What do you want, my little bitch?"

His cock moved so slowly in and out of her, his thick heat caressing her inner muscles. He moved his fingers expertly against her ass. And she knew he prepared her so that he could take her there. A flushed heat soared through her, anticipation making her high. She wanted it. Wanted all of him. Wanted to claim his cock in every way.

That revelation gave her clarity. No other werewolf had ever come close to giving her what Perry could give her. And not just physically. He challenged her mind. Made her feel more alive than she ever had before.

"Ask me if I will have you." She stretched to look over her shoulder.

She wanted to see his face, see his reaction to her, demanding that he humble himself enough to ask her to be his mate. Making demands was part of his nature. And something she doubted would ever change about him. But if he thought he'd train her to be some little submissive bitch who'd jump at his every bark, he could think again. She didn't belly up to any werewolf.

The way his expression hardened she wondered if she'd pushed him too far. He pulled his soaked cock out of her slowly, leaving her empty. Everything around them seemed to still, as if even the birds in the distant trees waited to hear what he would say.

Moving his cock to her soaked ass, he pressed against her. A steaming pressure surged through her, anticipation of him taking her there making her entire body shake with need. Taking control of the situation at this moment was damned near impossible.

But fuck. The *Cariboo* needed training.

Showing that *lunewulf* could move just as quickly as he'd moved on her, she collapsed underneath him, rolling over before he could slide into her again. Every inch of her tingled with need. He'd turned her into one huge throbbing nerve ending. She panted when she stared up into his rugged expression.

"Well, wolf man?" she asked, her heart pounding so hard the blood rushing through her made her muscles burn to grow. "Are you strong enough to submit?"

His fingers glided up the back of her thighs. Chills rushed over her skin. Slowly he raised her legs until he had her ankles resting on his shoulders. When he leaned into her, she swore he'd grown a foot, looking like a giant moving in for the kill. His face reddened, making his blond curls stand out more. Heat rushed through his body and burned her wherever they touched.

His cock pushed against her ass, slowly stretching the sensitive flesh. Fire ignited between them. One quick thrust, and he glided into her soaked ass with his thick cock.

She clawed at him, struggling to make words come out when all she wanted to do was scream. The intensity of the act, filling her tight hole and moving deeper inside her, burned her alive from the inside out.

"Do it!" She couldn't say any more.

Perry had never experienced emotions like this before. Not like what Jaynie had just done to him.

A growl tore through him, her demand pushing him harder than any physical aggression any werewolf had ever inflicted on him in the past.

He knew more than anything at that moment that he'd found his soul mate. Jaynie was meant to be his. Her tight ass stole his breath. So many little muscles vibrated against his cock while he took her in the most intimate way a werewolf could take another.

Clenching his teeth, he struggled to make his mind work. Giving her what she wanted, what she demanded of him, took more strength than fighting not to lose himself before he could fuck her thoroughly.

He focused on building the momentum. Heat suffocated him. Her ass gripped him so hard he knew she would take his dick, claim it for her own, without him saying a word.

But this brave little *lunewulf* demanded more of him than any werewolf had ever dared to do. Without raising her claws, she'd pushed him to the edge. His heart exploded when he realized how much that turned him on.

More than turned him on. It made her the perfect female for him.

Gliding into her heat, impaling her tight little ass. Her soft flesh, soaked with her come, padded against his balls with each thrust. The smell of her lust, of her passion, of her need to hear that he wanted her enough to beg her to be his, was a mixture of the sweetest scents he'd ever inhaled.

Her long blonde hair fanned down her front, parting over her full breasts. Her tummy was hard, moving up and down quickly as she panted underneath him. And her thin legs, muscular and perfect, were soft against his neck.

Every inch of her, inside and out, filled him with emotions that burned him alive. More than the heat of her ass, more than the physical beauty that he stared down at through blurred vision, the entire package put him over the edge. Living without her would no longer be an option.

His cock swelled, every ounce of blood in his body drained down through him. He couldn't take the heat any longer.

He exploded like he never had before. His head fell back, oxygen leaving his brain while he stared blindly at the sky and howled hard enough to burn his throat.

Muscles convulsed throughout him while he flooded her ass with his come, releasing all the heat that had built up inside him.

His arms wouldn't hold him. They were too shaky. Her small hands came up, her fingers gripping his arms, and she pulled him to her.

"Jaynie." His voice was too scratchy. "I love you."

Even though the fog that covered his brain made it impossible to focus, he didn't miss the look of surprise that swept over her face. Then the twitch of her lips, and the rich smell of happiness that filled the air.

"Damn," she whispered. "And all I wanted you to do was beg."

He frowned, managing to hold himself off her in spite of his muscles still quivering throughout his body.

"*Cariboos* don't beg," he told her.

Then she did smile, a full-fledged grin. "Maybe. But I think you're trainable."

"We'll see about that." He smelled her contentment. But, damn, what he wouldn't do to hear it.

"Yes. We will." She ran her tongue over her lips then nibbled at them, looking timid for the first time since he'd met her. "Perry?"

"Yes?"

"I love you too."

Lorie O'Clare

All my life, I've wondered at how people fall into routines. The paths we travel seem to be well-trodden by society. We go to school, fall in love, find a line of work (and hope and pray it is one we like), have children and do our best to mold them into good people who will travel the same road. This is the path so commonly referred to as the "real world."

The characters in my books are destined to stray down a different path from the one society suggests. Each story leads the reader into a world altered slightly from the one they know. For me, this is what good fiction is about—an opportunity to escape from the daily grind and wander down someone else's path.

Lorie O'Clare lives in Kansas with her three sons.

First Sharing

JORY STRONG

Chapter One

*Y*ou take a great risk, and if you fail, if your vision proves false, then you doom our line.

His father's words were a heavy weight on Laith d'Amato's shoulders as he made his way toward the transport chamber that would take him to Winseka, the Bridge City, where even now the man who had been his near constant companion since adulthood was no doubt scouring the postings in search of a job on another planet, one far from Belizair.

If time weren't so urgent, Laith would have spread the feathered wings marking him as Amato and flown to Winseka from his parents' home along the western coast of Belizair. But time was of the essence and it had taken far longer than he anticipated to accomplish the things he'd set out to do when he returned to his home world. He was anxious to return to the human woman who'd soon be his mate—and Rykken's—if he could convince his friend to cast aside his Vesti heritage and fight his Vesti nature.

A shudder went through Laith as he envisioned them both lying with Cyan, joining their bodies with hers. His cock filled and pressed against the thin loincloth favored by both Vesti and Amato males when they were on Belizair.

From the first moment he'd seen her he'd hungered as he'd never hungered for a woman of his own race. The Ylan stones, melded seamlessly into the bands he wore at his wrists, pulsed in time to the heartbeat throbbing in his penis as he thought about her, pictured sky blue eyes and the long, luxurious locks of brown hair only a few shades lighter and a few inches longer than his own.

Enchanting. Mesmerizing. Captivating.

In the brief time he'd been with Cyan it had required every ounce of self-discipline he possessed not to mate with her. He ached to possess her, to claim her and bring her back to Winseka, to the city where all those returning with human mates had to live initially. Even if the experiment failed, even if no children came from their joining, he would be content to have her as his bond-mate.

You take a great risk, and if you fail, if your vision proves false, then you doom our line.

His father's somber expression, his mother's pain-lined face as he told them of his intention to share the female he'd been matched with, made anger flash through Laith as hot as the despair that followed on its heels was cold. He cursed the Hotalings and the biogene weapon they'd unleashed on Belizair.

A few on Belizair had died when the virus was first introduced, the weak, the old, their passing painful but not the festering wound that opened later—when the true horror became known. Females early in their pregnancies miscarried, then came the devastating realization there would be no new pregnancies.

In desperation the Council's scientists had come forth with an experiment, pairing males from Belizair with human females who carried the genetic markers of the Fallon—the shared ancestor race of the Amato and Vesti.

Like some of the Amato and Vesti in older times, before laws were passed against interfering with cultures not as advanced as the one on Belizair, the Fallon had also been intrigued by the inhabitants of Earth. They'd walked among them, bred with them, though they'd also appeared to those on Earth as creatures that became a part of human legend and religion.

The Fallon could take an infinite number of forms because at their core, they were a race of winged shapeshifters. Their potential had soared without limit until arrogance and jealousy, pride and prejudice had destroyed them, ultimately splintering them into a multitude of races, all lesser than what the Fallon had once been.

With a sigh Laith entered the building housing the transport chamber. With effort he pushed away thoughts of the past and the heavy burden of his family's future.

He felt the rightness of his decision, felt an unshakable sureness. The dreams that gripped him when he slept were a vision for the future and not only erotic fantasy, though they left him writhing, waking in an eruption of hot semen.

The dreams had started only when he was on Earth, only after seeing the human female whose Fallon genes the scientists thought most compatible with his own. Cyan.

Laith wrapped his hand around his fabric-covered cock. He prayed to the Goddess for success in convincing Rykken to return to Earth with him, to the cabin where Cyan waited within walking distance from the hidden and guarded transport chamber in the Sierras—though he'd taken the car to mask his destination. There'd be no fighting against the need to make love to her the next time he was in her presence. It had taken everything he possessed to resist this long.

The Ylan stones in his wristbands warmed, pulsed, fed on the energy of those making up the transport chamber. They weren't true stones at all but almost living entities, with an infinite number of uses, but also that varied from individual to individual.

They were a power source allowing for transport between cities, for travel to Earth and back using the ancient portal in Winseka. But they were also necessary for survival on Belizair. Without the Ylan crystals worn in bands at their wrists, Amato and Vesti alike would die on their home world.

The only time they were free of the Ylan stones was at the cusp of adulthood, when the stones migrated from their parents' bands onto theirs like liquid crystal minutes after their birth melted away, allowing the new adult a choice of which stone to wear until death.

A shudder of lust rippled through Laith. The bands at his wrists were heavier now, the stones having grown denser in preparation for separating and migrating onto the bands he'd crafted for Cyan so she could be brought to Belizair.

He clenched his jaw, tightened his grip on his shaft. The transport chamber doors closed, guaranteeing him privacy. Only then did he give in to the needs of the flesh.

Laith sank to his knees. Justified the freeing of his cock by telling himself he could hardly hold an intelligent conversation with Rykken when all he could think about was lying with Cyan, thrusting his penis into her slick woman's folds.

His breath escaped in a jagged pant as he imagined what she would look like naked, open, her breasts bared, her thighs splayed. His hips bucked, forced his cock through the tight fist of his hand as he thought about positioning himself at her entrance, slowly fighting his way into her channel.

She'd be tight, or at least his size would make her so. And wet. Whenever he was with her he could smell her arousal, could see the need in her eyes, the willingness to couple with him.

It'd been so hard to keep her at arm's length until he was sure the dream of having Rykken join in a mate-bond with Cyan was a vision and not just a fantasy.

It'd been nearly impossible to pretend he wasn't ready for anything more than friendship with her when his heavy testicles and hardened penis proclaimed him a liar.

No longer. When he returned to her . . .

A moan escaped, then another as he worked his cock with his own hand. Saw in his mind's eye Cyan writhing underneath him, calling his name and pleading with him to mate with her, to fill her with his seed.

"Yes! Yes!" A hoarse shout ripped from his core as semen rushed through his penis, erupted in a heated release that coated his chest and abdomen.

"Oh Goddess, yes," Laith whispered, left weak by the orgasm even as he knew that every time he came while thinking about Cyan, the urgency to get his cock inside her became more intolerable. If Rykken couldn't be convinced, there would be no second chance.

• • •

Cyan Dupre's eyebrows drew together as dusk began settling and there was no sign of Laith. She rubbed her bare arms and shivered, told herself it was from the coolness of the early evening air in the mountains and not from being alone in the middle of nowhere.

"He'll be back," she murmured, not letting worry and uncertainty diminish the beauty surrounding her.

She'd spent the day outside photographing it, though it felt like cheating to snag images with the digital camera rather than capture them on a sketchpad. But a weekend trip didn't allow her the time she needed to draw everything that caught her attention. She loved being out of the city and when Laith suggested this trip . . .

Cyan shivered again, this time with the heated need thoughts of him always generated. He was so innately sensual she was reminded of a pagan god, a lithe, dangerous predator who defended what belonged to him with savage ferocity.

He called himself a bounty hunter. But from what he'd shared about his work, it sounded as though he and his partner Rykken did more than hunt criminals. They also guarded people and places.

Cyan nibbled on her bottom lip. Not for the first time she wondered if he'd been so careful with her because his job was dangerous and he couldn't offer a woman more than fleeting friendship and casual sex.

Maybe the emotional distance was for the best, she thought on a sigh. She was deeply attracted to him, more so than she'd ever been with any other man. It'd be easy to fall in love with him, too easy.

He was lethal grace and poetic beauty combined with tenderness and sensitivity. It was a devastating combination, especially to an artist, especially to her—and apparently unattainable, or attainable at a painful emotional cost.

But, then, didn't artists thrive on heartbreak and suffering? Didn't agony and angst fuel their creativity? She laughed. Maybe, though she'd always preferred happiness over unhappiness.

A breeze picked up, chasing her into the cabin for a sweatshirt. She couldn't resist the impulse to open the sketchpad lying on the table and page through it until she got to the first drawing she'd done of Laith, in the park, on the day they met. He was dressed in black jeans and bare-chested, the elaborate bands with the dark green stones at his wrists emphasizing his masculinity, making it raw and primitive.

She had other pictures of him, nude ones, but this one was her favorite. This one reminded her of the instant when their eyes first met and heat flashed between them with such primal intensity she'd imagined him a male animal in search of his mate and known to her core she was the female he wanted.

Cyan laughed softly. "Maybe I should have been a romance writer," she said, but couldn't stop herself from tracing the masculine lips, the flowing waves of hair.

Laith was beautiful and he responded to her physically. Either that or sporting an erection was his natural state.

She was a fool for agreeing to come here with him, for getting her hopes up. Even worse, she was a coward for not asking him why he continued to spend so much of his time with her if he wasn't going to fuck her.

There, she'd admitted it to herself. She felt so needy around him that caution and sanity fell away under an onslaught of pure animal lust. She wanted him, desperately, even though he was heartbreak waiting to happen.

She glanced at the only bed, one large enough for an orgy, and wondered if seeing it was what had prompted Laith's sudden need to take off in the car on a mysterious errand. Was the reality of being here alone with her suddenly a huge mistake in his eyes?

It hurt her to think so, sent a lance of pain through her chest. But maybe he was right, maybe coming here *was* a bad idea.

Letting things keep going the way they were without talking about it wasn't smart either. It would be easier to handle the over-whelming attraction and less confusing if Laith admitted his stay in her life was temporary and he'd decided he wanted to avoid the complications of sex.

The one time she'd tried to initiate intimacy he'd grabbed her wrists and held them away from his chest as if she'd burned him with her touch. It embarrassed her then and made heat rise to her cheeks now just thinking about it.

It was probably just as well he'd stopped her. She wasn't sure she was going to stay in California. Moving to Taos was tempt-ing, even if it'd take a huge chunk out of her savings and mean starting all over again building relationships with art dealers.

Tension settled into her shoulders as she thought about Nathan's offer to let her live cheaply in a loft above one of the gal-leries he co-owned there. He wouldn't wait forever for her answer, she knew that, just as she knew he wanted more from her than an artist-patron relationship. Getting her to New Mexico was just the first step in his plan to seduce her.

There was chemistry between them. She'd resisted it when he was in California, visiting small-town art galleries as he vaca-tioned. And then she'd met Laith a few days after Nathan left for Europe.

Intellectually she could make an argument for spreading her wings and moving to New Mexico—to grow her talent in a community where art thrived, to explore possibilities with Nathan. But her body voted against her mind, delayed her decision for one simple reason. Nathan wasn't Laith. She didn't hunger for Nathan as she did for Laith.

Cyan flipped the page of her sketchpad to one of Laith on his side, naked, his long hair unbound and draped over his shoulder and chest, his cock hard against his abdomen.

Her eyes caressed the lines of his body. Her mind wondered why he'd agreed to pose for her at all.

She didn't think she could handle the mixed signals he sent much longer. Her panties stayed wet thinking about him and being around him. Her nipples hardened to the point she found herself fighting not to bare her chest and beg him to put his mouth on them.

She ached, ached like she'd never ached before. Felt like a junkie around a drug so potent that coming into contact with it was all it took to be addicted.

A small whimper escaped as she slid her hand underneath the waistband of her shorts and panties, wet her fingers with arousal before settling them on her stiffened clit. She shouldn't give in to the need, was embarrassed to find herself looking at his picture and masturbating, but she couldn't stop herself.

It wouldn't be enough, not to relieve the deep-seated ache. But it would help her recapture some semblance of calmness.

White-hot need lanced through her as she stroked over the tiny head of her clit. A moan followed, soft, almost a mew of distress.

This is crazy, she thought, but didn't retreat from the pleasure as she imagined it was Laith's mouth between her thighs, his tongue caressing her swollen knob, his lips sucking, pulling liquid heat from her very soul.

"Laith," she panted, fingers tightening, becoming rougher as fantasies of exquisite tenderness and carnal mastery had her rushing for orgasm, shattering when it came.

"Oh God," she whispered, weak, her upper body lying across the table, tears forming at the corners of her eyes. "I need to stop seeing him if this is what it's going to do to me."

• • •

Rykken d'Vesti frowned as he studied the work postings and found nothing of interest. He'd hoped for a contract that would take him away from Belizair and keep his mind challenged so he wouldn't contemplate Laith's visit to Earth and claiming of a human mate.

They'd been like brothers, closer than brothers in many ways, their time together in dangerous situations bonding them to the point where it seemed natural to accept work together as a team. And now he felt Laith's absence keenly.

He didn't fault Laith for accepting what the Council scientists offered, a chance to claim and couple with a woman who might become heavy with child. Even if there were no guarantees it would happen, a tiny flicker of hope was better than none at all.

Still, he preferred not to remain on Belizair and witness the death of that hope, the deepening of the despair hanging like a heavy shroud over the land.

Several human women had been brought to Winseka. None of them was yet pregnant though the scientists remained convinced that all hope to avoid extinction rested with them.

Rykken rolled his shoulders in an effort to relax. He flexed the batlike wings marking him as Vesti and resumed his study of available assignments, this time with an eye toward finding something to occupy himself with, even if it was only marginally interesting.

Familiar footsteps sounded along the corridor. Rykken's eyebrows drew together in puzzlement. His attention shifted to the doorway just as Laith stepped into view and said, "I thought I might find you here."

Rykken looked closely at his friend, noted the tenseness of his features, the hardened cock impossible to conceal under the thin loin covering. "You are back with your new bond-mate?"

If anything Laith grew more coiled, a man ready to do battle. "No."

When nothing else was forthcoming, Rykken was unsure how to proceed. Of the two of them Laith had always been the more talkative, but not by much.

He thought perhaps Laith had been unable to convince the female to return with him of her own free will—a condition stipulated by the Council. That would explain his presence. And if so, then work would keep his mind off his failure.

"There are a couple of postings here to consider," Rykken said, indicating the list he'd been studying.

Laith shook his head. "That's not why I'm here. I want you to accompany me to Earth. I want you to join me in a mate-bond with Cyan."

Surprise held Rykken motionless though his cock betrayed him by hardening at the thought of taking the female who excited Laith enough to have him fully erect in public. Laith was not a man to lose control of himself.

"It's not the Vesti way," Rykken said. "We are not like the Amato to bond in whatever arrangement satisfies those in it. Vesti males claim one female and take her completely, totally, possess her in every way so that neither will crave another's touch."

"I know," Laith said. "But these are desperate times for all of us. I would not suggest it at all except I have been plagued by the same dream. You are in it. As am I. And in the end the two of us joining with Cyan are able to offer both the Vesti and the Amato what they need most, the promise of children and the hope of a lasting, deep peace between our races."

Rykken turned away from the painful plea he saw in Laith's eyes, heard the words not said, that Laith believed the dream was a vision sent by the Goddess the Amato held sacred. "So far this experiment with human women has failed to produce even a single pregnancy," he said, fighting emotion with logic.

"I know. Meet her, Rykken. At least grant me that much. Trust me that far."

"You ask much," Rykken said, shifting so he could meet Laith's gaze. "And if I take her? If the mating fever of the Vesti swamps me and I can't share her, even with you? What then?"

"It is a risk I am willing to take."

A shudder went through Rykken at the depth of Laith's belief in the rightness of this sharing of his human mate. It was not the Vesti way, but still he found himself saying, "So be it."

Chapter Two

Cyan pulled her knees up against her chest as she sat on the porch glider. She'd showered, elected to put on jeans and a sweatshirt instead of something more feminine, then gone outside to wait for Laith.

The night was pure black, the moon and stars magnificent in the velvet sky. She loved sitting underneath it, looking at it. From the time she'd held her first crayon her world had centered on color and shape, translating thoughts and feelings, impressions, into images on paper, and later onto canvas.

Study, practice, the maturity that came with getting older, knowing the pain of loss and the joy of love—they'd improved her art. But she'd never been able to capture the nighttime. It was cloaked in mystery, as deep as it was dark, unwilling to be reduced to two dimensions.

Despite the chill of the night air, Cyan's palms grew damp when she heard the rumble of a car's engine. Her labia grew flushed and heated.

She needed to get herself under control. She knew that. Her resolve to talk to Laith had strengthened in the shower, when the hot pulse of water from the handheld wand led to more fantasies, to another orgasm—to the realization that each release was only making her want him more.

Cyan stood when the car came into view. She was trapped in the headlights until it stopped in front of the cabin.

The car door opened and he emerged, filled her vision and

held her attention as moonlight bathed him, revealed him for the lithe predator he was.

Movement, a second door opening. Cyan turned her head and couldn't breathe as lust rushed through her and made her cunt spasm violently.

Oh God, she thought. It was the same first reaction she'd had to Laith, and look where that led.

She had the insane urge to flee, to get as far away from the two men as she could. That urge was matched in intensity by the desire to submit to them, to have them both.

A shudder went through her. She managed a breath, a small one because they were walking toward her and she didn't dare inhale their mingled scents.

They were like something out of an erotic fantasy. Well-matched physically, the stranger only a few shades darker than Laith, his hair equally long, straight instead of falling in waves down his back as Laith's did. And his eyes . . . They were nearly black with a hunger he was making no effort to hide.

Cyan bit her bottom lip to keep from whimpering. Arousal wet her panties as thoroughly as guilt flooded her chest. She forced her attention back to Laith, shivered when she saw his taut face and was afraid to read anything into it.

"You're back," she said, wanting to break the tension between them.

He took her hand and she closed her eyes for an instant, steeled herself against the desire coursing through her, turning her blood into molten need. It was worse now, much worse for all the hours she'd spent alone, thinking about him, waiting for him.

"Cyan," he said. "This is Rykken."

Rykken's hand claimed her free one and sent a jolt of sexual heat to her clit. Her eyes went to Rykken's face then down to the erection pressed aggressively against the front of dark sweat-pants.

She noticed the bands around his wrists. They were similar enough to Laith's that for a single shock-filled second she thought the two of them were a couple and this was Laith's way of reveal-ing it to her. But then Rykken carried her hand to his chest, pressed her palm against the tight male nipple beneath the thin mesh of his shirt and said, "I don't know how Laith has found the strength to keep his hands off you."

She shivered in reaction to the sensual promise she heard in his voice, looked to Laith and found his eyes nearly as dark with hunger as Rykken's. "Let's go inside," he said and this time she was the one who wondered if it was a good idea to be in the same room with a bed large enough to have an orgy in.

Laith took a seat on the couch and struggled to hide his satis-faction. Cyan was nervous, fighting the attraction to Rykken.

She'd curled herself into a chair, her sketchpad on her lap like a protective shield. But the scent of her arousal, the hard press of her nipples against her sweatshirt and the way she studiously avoided looking at Rykken gave her away.

In the end she would lose this fight. She wouldn't win against the desire building, heating the room.

This was meant to be. He knew it with soul-deep surety. This was what the Goddess intended when she sent the dreams.

And Rykken . . . Laith couldn't prevent the corners of his mouth from curving upward in a slight smile. Rykken struggled not to give in to the Vesti mating fever and take Cyan immedi-ately.

It would have been thoroughly entertaining if it weren't also dangerous, if his own cock didn't ache with need. Vesti males were territorial, aggressive. Their instinct was to isolate their mates completely and fuck them repeatedly until the Ylan stones split and migrated, sealing the bond and marking it permanent.

Rykken's warning on Winseka hadn't been offered lightly. But then neither had his acceptance of the risk. He trusted Rykken, believed their friendship would prove strong enough to hold against Vesti instinct, that in the end the Ylan stones at Rykken's wrists wouldn't migrate to the bands he'd yet to give Cyan until the moment his own did.

He pictured the elegant bands, imagined slipping them on her wrists. He'd crafted them himself, included the bird-of-prey device of his clan-house as well as the predatory cat of Rykken's family.

Longing filled Laith, not just the desire of the flesh but of the heart. He'd thought of nothing else but returning home with Cyan since the first moment he saw her.

Patience, it was a bounty hunter's skill, one necessary for success and it would serve him here as well. She'd been reared in a culture as restrictive as the Vesti's when it came to not only taking multiple lovers but joining with them in a lifelong bond.

A shudder of need rippled through him and he cast about for a way for them to begin. He found it in the sight of her clutched sketchpad, in the thick rug placed in front of a fireplace left ready for use.

In that moment he gained a new appreciation for the Council scientists and the bounty hunters who lived and worked on Earth, all of them focused on doing everything in their power to speed the claiming of human mates. When he'd told them of his intention to bring Cyan to this cabin only a short distance away from the building housing the transport chamber, they'd made it ready, anticipated what he might find useful.

Laith stood and pulled Cyan to her feet. He considered warning Rykken using the telepathic ability all those on Belizair possessed, then decided to enjoy Rykken's reaction instead.

"Let's start a fire and sit in front of it," Laith said. "I promised Rykken you would capture his likeness on paper."

I am only barely hanging on to my control, Rykken shot back, rising from his seat, his body protesting the thought of posing motionless even as it thrilled to the idea of being on display for Cyan.

The full heat of the Vesti mating fever was on him, had been from the moment he'd seen her in the headlights of the car. He wanted to strip her of her clothes, to fuck her until she acknowledged his dominance and accepted his protection, until she craved his touch as much as he now craved hers.

There was nothing gentle in what he felt. It was animal desire and raw hunger, tempered only by his deep friendship with Laith, his willingness to trust in Laith's vision.

He stripped off his shirt, reveled in Cyan's small whimper, in the way she fought against looking at his chest and lost. When his hands went to the sweatpants, her whispered "No" made his cock pulse in protest.

"No, leave them," Cyan said, nearly lightheaded from the lust pounding through her.

They wanted to share her. As soon as Laith had pulled her from the chair, told her of his promise to Rykken, she'd known. What she didn't know was whether she wanted to accept the pleasure they offered.

It was one thing to fantasize about having two lovers, but to actually risk her heart . . . That's what it would be for her, a risk with the potential of leaving her devastated. She knew herself well enough not to hide from the truth.

Casual lovers weren't her style. She'd never been able to separate the needs of the body from the needs of the heart, the soul. And for weeks Laith had tormented her with his closeness, his sensual appeal, the mixed signals of desire and reserve that left her aching and feeling confused. To give in now, then return to the way it had been . . . She didn't think she could handle it and yet . . . She let Laith guide her to the rug in front of the hearth.

Her cunt spasmed when Rykken lay down in front of her on his side, assumed a classical pose, the same one Laith had taken when she'd drawn the first nude of him. She forced herself to breathe deeply, to slow the wild rush of her heart, to see Rykken as an artist's subject instead of a man who wanted to cover her body with his.

It was almost impossible to do.

Laith started the fire then positioned himself behind her. She wanted to ask *why* and *why now* but fell into the rhythm of drawing, instead. She tried to keep her distance but the atmosphere in the cabin found its way into the picture—captured heat and intimacy, smoldering desire—all made more so by Laith's presence at her back. Fantasy invaded, slowed her hand as images of being held between Laith and Rykken intruded, the two of them potent masculinity, beautiful power given perfect form.

Her breath grew short. Her cunt lips were flushed and swollen beyond bearing by the time she was done sketching Rykken. She handed the tablet to him, thought to rise and escape the cabin but Laith's hands on her shoulders stopped her, his lips on her neck sent her resistance tumbling.

"Cyan," he murmured in between hypnotic kisses, the sound of her name holding such profound desire she whimpered in response, closed her eyes against the thick burn of lust.

His hands moved down her arms, stilled at her waist but only long enough to push under her sweatshirt. Sanity tried to surface but it lost against the smooth glide of his palms over her abdomen, against his whispered, "Let us have you, Cyan. Let us take care of you. I've dreamed of this from the first moment I saw you."

His words sent heat curling through her breasts and cunt. "The three of us?" she asked, wondering if this was why he hadn't touched her intimately until now.

"Yes."

"Just for the weekend?"

"No."

She wanted this, ached for it. Knew there wasn't any guarantee her heart would emerge unscathed. But she also knew she'd regret not giving in to the fantasy, not knowing what it was like to love them.

"Yes," she said, moaning as Laith's hands glided upward, unclasped her bra then settled on her breasts.

She arched into his touch, opened her eyes only to have them captured in the darkness of Rykken's gaze. Feral heat burned there. Carnal desire as he took her lips, her breath, her soul.

There was no gentleness in the kiss, no hint of seduction. It was possession, domination, a promise to cover her body with his and make her scream with the ecstasy of being claimed completely.

She struggled against it instinctively. Grew more aroused when Rykken's fingers tangled in her hair, held her in place as his tongue plundered her mouth, demanded submission.

Laith's fingers tortured her nipples. His murmured words of desire and praise had her arching, trapping his hands between her breasts and the hard wall of Rykken's chest.

Lust pooled in her cunt, so fierce and hot the feel of her panties and jeans became unbearable. She wanted them off, wanted to spread her legs, wanted relief.

"Please," she said when Rykken lifted his mouth from hers.

Satisfaction roared through Rykken, swelled his cock further and fed the flames of the mating fever.

Mine!

It echoed with savage intensity, sounded with each beat of his heart, urged him to take her, to protect her, to keep any other male away from her—including Laith.

Rykken's lips twisted in a silent snarl as he fought his instinct.

It was not the Vesti way to share a mate but if he could do it with any man, it would be with the one whose hands were even now baring Cyan's upper body, pulling the clothing away and exposing her lush curves and beautiful skin.

It took every ounce of Rykken's control not to pounce. *How have you managed to keep from taking her?* he asked as lust swamped him, made his breathing ragged.

I did what I had to do and now we both will reap the rewards of it.

Laith's hands returned to her breasts, cupped them in symbolic offering as he turned Cyan in his arms enough so he could press his mouth to hers in what Rykken knew was the first kiss Laith shared with her.

He didn't expect to find it arousing, but the intimacy of it pierced through genetic programming and cultural upbringing alike and touched the core of him. His penis jerked, leaked as Cyan whimpered softly, yielded to Laith's gentleness as thoroughly as she'd yielded to his aggressiveness.

He'd never thought to be mated to any female but a Vesti female. Now he couldn't imagine any other than Cyan. He ate her with his eyes, memorized her, inhaled her scent and imprinted her on all his senses.

Rykken remained enthralled, motionless as Laith eased her onto her back, his lips still on Cyan's, his moans joining the sweet sound of her pleasure. As soon as Cyan was stretched out on the rug, the need to see all of her became imperative.

Rykken stripped her of her shoes and socks. Groaned and was lost when his knuckles brushed against her sleek abdomen as he unfastened her jeans.

She was smooth and silky, utterly feminine, delicate. Without the wings of the Vesti or Amato she seemed fragile, in need of a strong male to care for her.

Protective urges assailed him. His mouth followed his hands, caressed her taut belly, savored the taste of her skin. He'd thought to bare her quickly but now he wanted to explore her slowly.

Rykken shed the confining Earth clothing he wore and kissed upward. Had to take himself in hand when he got to her breast and latched onto her nipple.

Desire whipped through him as he suckled. His hand slid up and down on his shaft in a pale imitation of the pleasure he would soon know.

With a groan Rykken forced his hand away from his cock, went to the waistband of her jeans and panties. He pushed underneath them, nearly came when he felt her stiffened clit and wet slit.

Hunger gripped him. His mating fangs threatened to emerge from their sheaths for the first time in his life. *I can't wait much longer,* he sent to Laith as his testicles pulled tight in warning.

Neither can I, Laith said, his mental voice husky with need, his hand joining Rykken's, making Cyan moan as they circled and teased her clit, played in her wet, silky woman's folds.

Rykken was torn by twin desires, to remain at Cyan's breast or to kiss downward and explore with his mouth what his fingers had discovered.

She was so lush, so responsive he wondered how they would ever stop making love to her long enough to get her back to Belizair. He wanted to devour her, to put his hands and mouth on every inch of her.

Her hips lifted to meet their fingers, her channel clamped down, tried to capture them and pull them deeper. Rykken's cock jerked, leaked, demanded to fill the space now occupied by his fingers and Laith's. But a more primitive need prevailed.

The thought of Laith swallowing her cries of pleasure, taking her breath, replacing it with his own, imprinting himself thoroughly on Cyan's psyche had Rykken leaving her breast, growling in warning, in a demand for Laith to yield her lips.

Chapter Three

Cyan cried out when Laith abandoned her mouth. She'd wanted, craved, fantasized about kissing him for weeks. She felt bereft even as he moved downward, latched onto a nipple that strained and ached to be sucked.

And then Rykken was there, pinning her wrists to the rug above her head, thrusting his tongue into her mouth, letting her know he saw himself as Laith's equal when it came to her body and her affections.

A small part of her was shocked at the ease with which she accepted him, needed him. But she could no more resist him than she could resist Laith.

Rykken's taste, his masculine scent mixed with Laith's, blended into a memory that would never fail to arouse her. The thrusts of Rykken's tongue were timed perfectly to Laith's suckling at her breast, to the masculine fingers sliding in and out of her slit.

Fiery hunger engulfed her, her hips jerked and her heels dug into the carpet in a desperate attempt to drive their fingers deeper into her channel, harder. She was so close to coming.

A shudder went through her when they denied her, when their fingers left her sheath as if they'd silently agreed to make her wait. She whimpered into Rykken's mouth and he settled more of his weight on her, covered her bare chest with his own as Laith rolled to the side.

Laith stripped Cyan of her jeans and panties and nearly came just looking at her. By the Goddess, she was exquisite, delicate and feminine, intoxicating. With her thighs splayed, her cunt lips parted, she was fantasy made flesh and blood.

He groaned and shed the clothing he could no longer tolerate, prayed he wouldn't disgrace himself by spewing his seed across his abdomen before getting inside her.

"You're beautiful, Cyan," he murmured as he knelt between her thighs and framed her cunt with his hands.

Her pulse throbbed against his palms, testament to the wild beat of her heart. The tiny triangle of soft down pointed toward swollen folds glistening with a sweet nectar he would forever crave the taste of.

She was his—theirs—to pleasure and protect, to claim and breed. Despite the Council's edicts, she would never escape. They would convince her to return to Belizair with them. They had to. Life without her would be intolerable.

Laith leaned forward, delayed the moment when his lips claimed her lower ones in a carnal kiss. It thrilled him to witness her response to Rykken. Drove his hunger higher.

He had shared women before with a childhood friend, had thought when the time came to settle down he'd enter into a bond that included his friend and an Amato female, or two. But now he couldn't imagine any other covering Cyan, swallowing her cries of pleasure, except for Rykken.

With a moan Laith nuzzled her, pressed his mouth to her cunt lips and licked along her slit. His cock pulsed, wet his abdomen with arousal, strained toward the heated, tight place it craved.

Cyan jerked in response, lifted into his touch, and his hands moved around to cup her buttocks, to hold her in place for his kiss. Lust burned through him, roared through his veins and left him panting, covered in a thin sheen of sweat.

He knew he was playing with fire, that he risked everything by touching her this way, claiming her first orgasm. The mating fever of the Vesti was upon Rykken and he would be driven to mount her—he'd take her first, shove his cock into her channel.

Laith didn't care. As he licked over Cyan's clit, felt the ecstasy shudder up her body, all he cared about was bringing her to completion.

He'd fought so hard to keep his distance, to hold off until he was sure about the dream. But now he didn't have to wait, didn't have to stop himself from touching her, from wallowing in her sultry heat.

He slid his tongue into her slit, fucked her with it and reveled in the way she clutched at him, tried to drive him deeper. Her scent, her taste, the silky wet feel of her, they became his reality, the only thing in either world that mattered to him.

His cock grew fuller, his testicles grew heavier. His buttocks flexed, relaxed, flexed again as the need to cover her, to thrust his penis inside her grew.

A growl sounded. He thought it was his own but it could have been Rykken's.

It didn't matter. He was like a starving man, one whose hunger wouldn't be sated until every drop of Cyan's arousal was consumed, until every ounce of pleasure had been wrung from her body and she lay limp, sprawled in utter abandon and satisfaction.

Laith took her clit in his mouth, sucked it as he'd sucked her nipple. Thrilled in the way she writhed, fought Rykken and him, fought herself. He heard her cry of release, felt it shudder through her a second before Rykken's telepathic *Move!* sounded in his mind and he yielded Cyan's cunt.

Rykken could have shifted a few inches, impaled Cyan with his cock as he kissed her. But his behavior was dictated by animal lust, by the need to cover his mate and claim her. He hooked his arm under her, easily lifted and positioned her on her hands and knees.

A nip to her buttocks and she spread her thighs, offered herself to him. And the sight of her glistening, dusky folds sent carnal hunger pounding through him.

He leaned in, tasted her. Thrust his tongue into the very place his cock would soon be, growled against her wet cleft as he found Laith's scent on her.

Mine! He wanted to punish her for accepting another's touch. Wanted to snarl and bite, thrust his cock into her until she was hoarse from screaming his name.

Raw instinct drove him to cover her, to sheath his penis into her slick heat in a single, hard thrust. It had been erotic torture knowing Laith was between her thighs. It'd pushed Rykken almost past the point of sanity to swallow Cyan's cries as another male pleasured her to orgasm.

Rykken's mating fangs descended. A growl escaped. Then another. And yet even as he felt the tight, hot, pulsing squeeze of Cyan's inner muscles, he acknowledged to himself that there was something darkly primitive in sharing her, in having Laith watch as he mounted and took her.

He could feel Laith's gaze, Laith's need. Knew Laith had his cock in hand, gripped in an attempt to stave off release, was only waiting for Rykken to fill Cyan with seed so he could do the same.

Another growl escaped. Instinct had Rykken settling more of his weight on her, reaching around to stroke her breasts, her belly, before finding her clit.

Her inherent sensuality and natural submissiveness were deeply satisfying to him. The way she softened underneath him, called out his name, begged him to allow her to come as he manipulated her clit and took her cunt, had him fighting against his own need for release.

His testicles were tight, heavy globes between his thighs. Each time his penis was fully embedded in Cyan's channel they pressed against her swollen folds, sent a jolt of ecstasy up his spine.

He'd never felt so powerful, so possessive.

The muscles along Rykken's back quivered. He ached to let the protection of the Ylan stones drop so his wings would manifest and he could take her in his true form.

Fierce pleasure coursed through him when she whimpered and pushed backward, drove him past the point of thought. He gave in to the fevered frenzy of mating with her. Thrust hard and fast. Sank his fangs into her shoulder and nearly lost consciousness as the serum of his race flowed through his fangs in the exact instant his seed spilled into Cyan.

Cyan felt boneless, lost in a sea of endorphins from Rykken's lovemaking, content until Laith slid his arm around her waist and pulled her underneath him. She moaned when he slid inside her. Her sheath tightened on his penis, trapped it in welcome as her arms wrapped around his neck.

She'd thought herself completely satisfied. But the hunger built as Laith's tongue rubbed and twined with hers, as his cock remained unmoving, lodged deep inside her like a second heartbeat.

She ran her hands over the smooth skin and sleek muscles of his back, tangled her fingers in the luxurious waves of autumn-colored hair. He was golden perfection, beautiful to her eyes and soul.

"Laith," she whispered. Meeting his eyes, melting in the rich dark gold of them, thoughts and emotions swirled inside her without definition, without taking the shape of words.

Longing filled her, the need to have him shuddering above her, calling her name as his face reflected his pleasure and jets of semen erupted from his cock and flowed into her womb. In that instant she understood her own conception, why her serious, practical mother had allowed herself to become pregnant by a man already claimed by the open road and his music.

"Cyan," Laith said, leaning in, capturing her lips. It was killing him to remain motionless as her hot core clenched and unclenched on his cock, as liquid desire burned through his veins and his heart swelled with love for her.

He gathered her closer, couldn't stop himself from lying more heavily on her. Lust rippled down his spine, tightened his balls and made his penis throb.

He wouldn't last long once he moved. He wasn't sure he could remain gentle though he desperately wanted to, was determined to show her in this first sharing that he and Rykken would take care of all her needs.

"Please," she whimpered, scraping her nails over his back.

He groaned, thrust in and out, gave them both what they needed. Slowly at first, then faster, harder, until he swallowed her cry of release as extreme pleasure exploded in every nerve ending, in every cell as she milked him of his seed.

Laith collapsed at her side, his skin pressed to as much of hers as possible, his breathing ragged. A satisfied smile curved his lips when Cyan shifted to snuggle against him, her arm draped over his abdomen, her face buried against his neck and the warm curtain of her hair spread across his chest.

He gathered her in his arms, brushed his finger across the place where Rykken's mating fangs had pierced her flesh. She trembled in reaction, moaned and pressed her hot cunt more tightly against his hip.

Laith dared a glance at Rykken's face and saw the struggle taking place there, the conflict of mind over body. *Lie with us,* he said and his words were greeted with a silent snarl, a flash of savage, primal male in Rykken's eyes. But in the end Rykken moved to position himself at Cyan's back, his mouth going immediately to the place where he'd left his mark.

What have you told her? Rykken asked, his hand on Cyan's side, gliding downward to settle on her hip, both of them shivering when the scent of her arousal intensified at being held between them.

Not much, Laith admitted. *The Council's laws are restrictive.*

No bond-mate is allowed to see our true form or know we aren't of Earth until we're in the transport chamber.

Does she have ties here?

Her father is a stranger to her. Her mother has passed from this life. But Cyan is well liked. Laith's nostrils tightened as he thought of the human male who was pursuing her.

Who is he? Rykken growled, taking the knowledge from Laith's mind.

I haven't met him. He's been away though he has contacted Cyan several times since I came here to claim her.

Rykken's lip lifted. His eyes darkened. *He will not have her. She is ours.*

Cyan stirred then, pressed a kiss to Laith's chest. "I want to draw the two of you sitting back-to-back like a pair of erotic bookends. Will you let me?"

"Of course," Laith said.

She turned, blushed under the intensity of Rykken's regard. "Will you pose for me?"

"Yes."

"Let's spend some time in the hot tub first," Laith said, cupping her breast, knowing he needed to mate with her again before he'd be able to endure having her look at him, caress him with her hungry eyes as she sketched him.

How he'd managed all the other sessions, he didn't know. But tonight he had no power to resist the scent of her arousal and the call of her body to couple.

Cyan laughed when Laith rose to his feet then swung her up into his arms. She didn't mind being carried from the cabin though she shivered as the cool night air hit her fire- and sex-warmed skin.

Rykken strode ahead of them, his sureness about the hot tub's location causing the first tendrils of doubt and pain to form in

Cyan's chest. Did they do this all the time? Invite a woman to the cabin and share her?

She was grateful when Laith released her and she slid into the water, taking shelter in velvety darkness. It was beautiful out, the stars glittering by the thousands in a way she couldn't see in the city.

Laith captured her hand in his. "What's wrong?" he asked, his sensitivity and concern deepening her feelings for him.

"Do you and Rykken come here a lot?" she asked, not able to expose her heart by putting her fear into words, that she was just one of many they'd shared.

Laith pressed her palm against his chest, whispered kisses along her neck, the corner of her mouth.

"Neither of us has been here before, nor have we ever shared a woman," he said, guessing at what was on her mind.

His tongue traced the seam of lips. "Trust us with your heart as well as your body, Cyan."

Rykken's hand stroked over her belly then lodged between her thighs possessively. "You belong to us," he said, his voice holding complete confidence along with husky desire. "No other will ever have you."

Her soul responded to Laith's gentleness. Her body responded to the sure way Rykken touched her, as if she belonged to him and it was his right.

She whimpered when Rykken began rubbing her clit, circling, pressing the hardened, sensitive knob at the same time Laith's tongue forged into her mouth, his kiss dominant, his heart racing against her palm.

The pleasure left no room for doubts or fears. The heated water and night sky enclosed them in a private world where the only reality was the intimacy they shared.

Cyan opened her thighs wider in offering, captured Rykken's cock in her hand and measured the hard, thick length of him. She loved the way his hips lifted and his breathing grew rough and fast, the way Laith's did the same when she freed her hand from his and grasped his penis.

He and Rykken were well matched. Potent masculinity packaged in breathtaking form.

Rykken endured, resisted the need to shove his cock into Cyan for long moments. Never had he felt so out of control as he did in her presence, so filled with the need to reassure himself she was his, free to pleasure as he willed and protect for all time.

We take her home with us tomorrow, he said, shifting, signaling his intention to pull Cyan onto his lap with a transmitted image.

If she agrees to return with us, Laith said.

By morning she will have no thought but to turn to us for all her needs.

Laith's laughter was like sand across Rykken's nerve endings. *By morning we will be lucky if we have a thought beyond keeping her happy.*

Rykken lifted his lip in a silent reply before sliding his arm around Cyan and repositioning so she straddled his lap, her mound pressed to the hard ridge of his erection. She moaned and rose, guided his cock head to her entrance even as she entranced him with the sight of her breasts.

Her nipples tightened under his perusal, sent a pulse of lust straight to his penis. She swayed, arched her back slightly in subtle offering and sweet temptation.

Rykken was mesmerized, felt possessiveness burn in his belly with the thought of other males seeing her bared breasts. The women on Belizair wore only thin trousers, anything more would restrict their ability to fly, and beyond that, both Vesti and Amato culture revered a female's ability to bear and nurse their young.

Cyan's dusky nipples begged to be suckled and for a long moment Rykken let himself imagine children at her breasts. Hope roared through him in a fierce wave and he sent a prayer to the wandering god of the Vesti that Laith's vision would prove true and somehow this first sharing of a human bond-mate would defeat the Hotaling virus and open a doorway to a future holding more than despair and extinction.

Tenderly he licked over first one areola and then another, nuzzled and kissed them reverently until her low moans and the whispered calling of his name, the tight grip of her sheath on his cock head, chased away thoughts of a child's hunger and replaced them with a man's.

With a low moan Rykken took a dusky nipple in his mouth and began suckling. His hands went to her hips, guided her up and down on his shaft until she cried out in release and took him with her.

Cyan laughed softly when Laith immediately pulled her into his lap. They might like sharing her, but it also made them competitive.

"What amuses you?" Laith asked, covering her breast with his hand and capturing the nipple.

She wrapped her arms around his neck, kissed him. "I was just thinking I could get used to this, having two men fighting to see who can give me the most pleasure."

His chuckle made her smile. "Both Rykken and I intend for you to get used to it."

Laith dipped his head, licked over her nipple, tugged and bit until she arched, invited him to be more aggressive.

Her hand tangled in his hair, held him to her breast. She loved the way they used their mouths on her, was coming to crave the feel of their lips and their tongues, the hunger that spiked through her with each suck, each tongue stroke.

She splayed her thighs and moaned when his hand immediately took possession of her cunt, tormented her clit until she begged for him to fuck her.

He answered her pleas with his fingers, thrust in and out of her slit while his thumb worked her hard, swollen knob as she writhed in his lap and finally shattered.

Masculine satisfaction gleamed in his eyes when he lifted his head. The sight of it challenged Cyan, made her feel unrestrained and mischievous.

She shifted position so she was straddling him though she was careful not to let him close enough to her slit to get inside. "Your turn," she whispered, kissing him, tangling her tongue with his as her hands found him underneath the water, cupped his testicles and fisted around his shaft.

He grunted, thrust, fucked through her fingers. His hands roved over her back and tried to pull her closer. She resisted, deepened the kiss until it became blatantly carnal.

"Let me love you with my mouth," she whispered when their lips parted. "Let me have you the same way you've had me."

Feminine power surged through Cyan when he lifted himself out of the water and onto the small deck built against half of the hot tub.

"Now, Cyan. Take me now," he said and she shivered, loved the command in his voice.

Laith nearly came at the first lash of her sinful tongue against his cock head. His hips jerked. A ragged plea escaped when she sucked only the very tip of him into her wet mouth.

Fire streaked up his spine. Desperate need had the testicles she was cupping in her hand pulling tight, burning, aching.

He tried to thrust deeper but her fingers prevented it. He made the mistake of demanding that she take more of him and suffered the sweet torment of her punishment for doing so.

She warned him with the press of her teeth that she was in control of his pleasure. She refused to grant him release until he was mindless, begging, completely in her power, his defeat punctuated by Rykken's low groan as he brought himself relief with his own hand.

Chapter Four

It was Rykken who carried her back into the cabin and settled her on the rug in front of the fireplace. Cyan stretched, feeling well-loved, utterly contented.

Laith retrieved her sketchpad and pencils before joining them. Cyan laughed when Rykken said, "I see she's already got you well trained."

It warmed her heart to hear him tease, to feel comfortable enough with him she could scrape her fingernails along his inner thigh, brush against his penis and say, "You're next."

His teeth flashed white against his tanned skin. He caught her hand and rubbed the knuckles along his shaft. "You won't find me as easygoing as Laith."

"I wouldn't expect to," she said, already knowing he was the more intense, the more dominant of the two, at least when it came to her.

He released her hand when she tugged it. But he crowded in, his chest touching her shoulder as he opened the sketchpad and began flipping through its pages, halted on a picture of a father hunched over his small son, their hands together on a plastic baseball bat, become absorbed in another one, this one the face of an elderly man.

"These are truly amazing," Rykken said and Cyan felt his praise all the way down to her toes.

"The ones in her studio are even better," Laith said, earning him a smile, a stroke along his naked spine.

Rykken went farther into the pad, arrived at the first picture she'd done of Laith. Moved past it.

Her sense of vulnerability grew as page after page revealed Laith drawn with her heart stripped of all protection. She gave a small sigh of relief when the blank pages began.

"I can only hope you see me in the same light as you do Laith," Rykken said, and warmth filled her chest, spiraled down through her breasts and cunt at the meaning she read in his words.

She positioned them in front of the fire, back-to-back, arm against arm, their hair draped across their chests, the leg closest to the fire bent at the knee, the other extended so the taut lines of their abdomens and the smooth perfection of their cocks was revealed.

Sensual hunger burned through her belly looking at them. Arousal coated her labia and inner thighs.

Cyan retreated to a safe distance and lost herself in her art. She rarely mixed fantasy with reality, but caught as they were in the glow of the fire, it was easy to picture them as ancient gods descended to Earth.

The firelight emphasized their golden beauty, created an illusionary space between them. Filled it with form so they were no longer back-to-back, but wing to wing in her mind's eye.

Cyan's heart raced and her hand rushed to capture what they'd become in her imagination. Only when the last line was drawn did she allow her rational mind to surface.

She bit her bottom lip then and worried what they'd think. Closed the sketchpad, but they were immediately at her side, their hands coaxing it from hers, their lips on her shoulders adding persuasion.

It was a losing battle.

They took the sketchpad from her and opened it. A knot formed in her stomach when they tensed.

"I don't know why I drew you like this," she said, seeing Laith with the feathered wings of an angel, though they were dark-veined, shaded instead of pure white. Her fingernails dug into her palm with worry over Rykken's image, a darkly handsome demon with bat-like wings.

Cyan tried to close the sketchbook but they grabbed her wrists, set it aside themselves before turning their attention to her. Her breath caught in her throat at the expressions on their faces, the lust that blazed in their eyes.

"You like it?" she whispered, needing to hear the words.

"Very much," Laith said, cupping her breast, taking possession of a nipple made tender by all the attention it'd received, his mouth going to her neck.

"It's perfect," Rykken said, his hand smoothing over her belly, his fingers sliding into her wet slit. "As perfect as the woman who created it." His lips claimed hers, his tongue dominant, demanding as it rubbed and twined with hers.

She petted them as they petted her, let her hands explore, flow over smooth skin and hard muscle, touch what her eyes had caressed as she drew them. Her heart ached at the possibility they might one day disappear from her life.

She went willingly to her hands and knees when they guided her there. Spread her thighs and shivered in anticipation when Laith's fingers gathered arousal from her slit before circling, stroking her hardened clit and sending erotic fire to her nipples.

"Please," she said and Rykken positioned himself in front of her, took her nipples between his fingers, squeezed them in perfect synch with Laith's assault on the tiny, naked head of her clit.

Rykken's cock pulsed in warning. The image he'd once believed would be impossible to endure—that of another male touching the female who belonged to him and making her respond—had become a reality that fed his hunger to mate.

The sight of Laith between Cyan's thighs, his penis hard,

glistening in anticipation of shoving into her tight channel had Rykken taking himself in hand and leaning forward, his fingers tangling in Cyan's hair, urging her to his cock head.

She wouldn't tease and torment him as she'd done Laith. He wouldn't become a slave to her mouth as Laith had become, Rykken thought as he pressed against her lips and commanded, "Take my cock, Cyan."

A pant escaped when she did as he'd ordered, rubbed her tongue over him and took him into wet heat and ecstasy.

His buttocks flexed against the need to start thrusting.

"More," he growled, pushing deeper, his chest and testicles burning.

White heat filled his mind when she whimpered, obeyed, took more of him and began sucking hard and fast.

He looked up to find Laith fucking her. Thrusting in and out, his face wreathed in pleasure, his hands alternating between holding her hips and palming the sleek curves of her buttocks.

Rykken fought to remain still. But he was helpless against the waves of sensation being pulled through him by Cyan's mouth. He tethered his cock in the tight fist of his own hand so he wouldn't hurt her in his passion.

"Cyan," he moaned, giving in to the need to fuck her mouth, knowing as he did it that he'd become enslaved. Not caring when orgasm left him weak, utterly satisfied, comfortable with the sight of Cyan gaining her release as Laith's seed filled her channel.

• • •

They took a shower later and slid into bed with Cyan between them, her face relaxed as she drifted in and out of sleep. Tenderness filled Rykken as he looked at her. He couldn't prevent himself from tracing the mouth that had given him so much pleasure, from circling the nipples that might one day nurse his young.

As soon as he'd taken her the first time, pierced her with his mating fangs, the Ylan stones at his wrists had grown heavier in preparation for binding with Cyan. *You've made bands for her wrists?* he asked.

Yes. They bear the devices of both our clan-houses.

Rykken laughed softly. *You were so sure I'd agree to share your vision?*

I had only to convince you to return to Earth with me and meet Cyan.

Rykken's hand traveled lower. His heart and soul knew complete satisfaction when her thighs parted in her sleep, welcomed his touch as he cupped her mound. *I feel hope for the first time since we learned what the Hotaling virus has done to us,* he said, letting Laith hear the fear that came with renewed hope.

Laith pressed a kiss to Cyan's forehead. *I believe there will be children from this first sharing of a human mate between Amato and Vesti, that the Goddess wants this for Belizair. But even if I am wrong, I will be happy to have Cyan as a bond-mate.*

As will I. Rykken brushed a kiss over her lips. *I don't understand how she was able to capture our true forms on paper as she did tonight, but if it means she doesn't fear us when we reveal ourselves to her, then I am glad it happened.*

The Council scientists told me it was possible. Some of the humans who have the genetic markers of the Fallon are able to pierce the veil of protection the Ylan stones provide for us while we're on Earth. They're able to see us as we are.

Cyan stirred and opened her eyes. She found both men resting on their elbows, looking at her, Laith's hand on her breast, Rykken's in possession of her cunt.

"Still up?" she asked, her laugh joining theirs when her gaze automatically strayed to their cocks.

"Perhaps not up in the way you're suggesting," Laith teased, "though I'm sure Rykken and I could rise to the occasion given the inspiration lying between us."

He leaned down and kissed her, a long, slow tangling of tongues and breath.

Cyan closed her eyes, allowed the golden, sensual lethargy to reclaim her. She felt boneless, satisfied to the core.

Rykken's mouth took hers as soon as Laith's kiss ended. She murmured appreciatively, smiled inwardly. Despite Rykken mimicking Laith's gentleness, she could easily tell the difference between the two men.

"Agree to come home with us, Cyan," Laith whispered against her hair when they'd both snuggled tightly against her.

"Live with us," Rykken said. "Commit to us."

Cyan opened her eyes and looked at them. Saw they were serious.

"I thought you lived out of a suitcase. Home is wherever the job is." At least that's the impression she'd always gotten when she managed to coax Laith into talking about himself and his work.

Laith's mouth captured her earlobe and sent heat spiraling through her. "Join permanently with us, Cyan."

She placed her hand over Laith's heart, felt its increased beat. He covered her hand with his and in the firelight the dark stones on his wristband seemed to swirl and glow with power.

Cyan blinked, cleared her vision of the illusion, looked at Rykken and saw the tension in his face before meeting Laith's eyes. "Are you saying you want me to be your wife?"

Laith carried her hand to his lips, kissed the palm. "Yes, our shared wife."

His words caused a wild fluttering in her heart and a flush of heat in her cunt. Emotion swamped her, a confusion of thoughts, hopes, dreams, all juxtaposed against reality. "I need time to think," she whispered.

"We'll talk further tomorrow," Laith said against her mouth, repositioning himself on top of her.

She spread her legs willingly. Loved the way he filled her in a single stroke, lodged himself so deeply that it felt as if his heart had invaded hers. Was lost in the way he kissed and fucked her as if she was his world. Didn't stop until she'd cried out in release.

And then Rykken took his place and did the same.

• • •

Cyan woke to sunlight on naked skin, to tangled limbs and warm masculine bodies pressed to hers. *I could definitely get used to this,* she thought, smiling, content to lie between Laith and Rykken, to feel their steady heartbeats and hear their deep, even breathing as they remained asleep.

Her thoughts returned to the night before. To the lovemaking. The conversation that followed.

Agree to come home with us, Cyan.

Live with us. Commit to us.

Join permanently with us, Cyan.

Are you saying you want me to be your wife?

Yes. Our shared wife.

She shifted onto her side and opened her eyes, lifted her hand, thinking to trace Rykken's masculine features but was immediately diverted by the sight of the bracelet on first one of her wrists and then the other.

They were so light they felt a part of her. She wasn't sure she'd have known they were there at all if she hadn't seen them.

Cyan returned to her back, brought them closer, studied the delicate craftsmanship. They were similar to the bands Rykken and Laith wore, though Rykken's contained dark red stones while Laith's contained deep green. There were no stones in the bracelets at her wrists but it looked as if there were grooved places, ready for them even if she couldn't imagine how they'd be added to the bands.

She recognized the design on her right wrist, the stylized birds of prey Laith wore. She compared the band on her left wrist to the one on Rykken's and found the same cat motif, an elongated, powerful hunter that reminded her of a sleek panther.

Cyan wasn't sure whether to be pleased or worried when she couldn't find a way to remove the bracelets from her wrists. They were significant, she knew it instinctively. They were a symbolic binding of her to them. *Like a wedding band,* an internal voice whispered.

She hadn't given the fact they both wore bands much thought beyond the first wild guess when she saw them on Rykken and wondered if he and Laith were lovers. But now . . . now the sight of them unnerved her even as she grew wet with the idea of belonging to Laith and Rykken.

Cyan touched her bands, looked again for a way to remove them and failed to find it. She thought about their asking her to return home with them without telling her where home was, thought about how comfortable Laith seemed with the idea of a shared wife, as if it was perfectly legal, an everyday occurrence.

Her imagination took over in the same way it had when she'd drawn them in front of the fireplace. It placed them in a fantastic landscape full of beautiful men who wore similar bands on their wrists.

Cyan shook her head and cleared the image. A soft laugh chased away the unsettled feeling in her chest as she eased into a sitting position, careful not to wake them.

She studied them while they slept, felt her nipples tighten and her cunt lips part just looking at their masculine faces, the long luxurious waterfall of hair spread across the pillows and over their chests—Rykken's dark brown and straight, Laith's in rippling waves of autumn gold and brown.

Was it any wonder her imagination went wild around them? They were a fantasy. And she was deeply attracted to them, physically as well as emotionally. There was no denying it.

Was she ready to live openly with two men?

A spasm of lust made her channel clench and unclench, forced arousal onto her swollen labia. Her nipples tightened in answer. Yes, she was strong enough emotionally, comfortable enough with herself to choose an alternative lifestyle.

Of course, being an artist helped. Artists were *expected* to be eccentric, to flout social norms.

She could envision a future with them, but she still needed answers—answers to questions that had a hard time forming when she was naked with them, touching them, hungry for them.

Cyan eased out of bed, stifled a satisfied laugh when they mumbled but didn't wake. They might have worn her out with lovemaking last night, sent her to sleep in a rush of orgasm, but apparently they'd exhausted themselves too. Otherwise she'd expect men who made their living as bounty hunters to jerk awake and be ready for action at the slightest movement.

She dressed and slipped into the bathroom for a few minutes before stopping in the kitchen area long enough to drink a glass of orange juice. Outside the sun beckoned and the birds sang. A walk seemed like just the thing to clear her head and gather her thoughts.

Cyan startled when her cell phone vibrated on the counter next to where she'd left her purse. She grabbed it and escaped the cabin before it switched to the ring tone.

Nathan. She recognized the number and knew he was home.

"You're back from Europe," she said, moving away from the cabin so she wouldn't wake Rykken and Laith with her conversation when she noticed the partially open window.

"Yes. I've got a surprise for you. I wanted to share it with you in person but there are too many things here needing my immediate attention."

"You didn't have to get me anything," she said, her stomach tightening as she glanced at the cabin. A touch of guilt assailed her though she'd done nothing wrong.

Nathan laughed. "It's not that kind of a surprise. It's more of an enticement to get you to move to Taos. I haven't said anything before now because I wasn't sure I could pull this off. But Pieter Van Rijn has agreed to take you on as his student."

Stunned amazement gripped Cyan. Van Rijn's work was astonishing, breathtaking, his level of mastery something she could aspire to but might never succeed in reaching.

"Pieter Van Rijn? You're serious? He's willing to accept me as a student?" Her voice was barely more than a whisper.

She'd never imagined herself the student or protégé of a man like Van Rijn. She was primarily self-taught, guided by inspiration, by the things she could learn in books and by studying the work of others.

There'd been the occasional paid-for or bartered lesson, but they'd been rare when she was growing up because money had always been tight. It had grown scarcer after her mother was diagnosed with cancer. Then at nineteen, she'd been on her own, just trying to survive and stay true to her dream of being an artist.

"He's seen your work and is impressed," Nathan said. "Move to Taos. Take the loft above the gallery and the job that comes with it. You'll have a flexible work schedule so there'll be plenty of time for your art . . . and hopefully for us to get to know one another better."

Elation gave way to sobered reality. "I've met someone, Nathan." Two someones, but there was no point in telling him that.

Silence greeted her stark declaration, expanded into awkwardness until finally she said, "I should let you get back to—"

"No. I shouldn't be surprised you've met someone. But don't be so quick to throw away this opportunity. Do you know how rare it is for Pieter to take on a student? It was my mistake for not telling you what I had in the works. Move to Taos, anyway, Cyan. If the man you've met isn't going to be supportive of your career, isn't it better to know now?"

There was confidence in Nathan's voice, anticipation, as if somehow her having a boyfriend added to the challenge. She'd wondered from time to time if her reluctance to date him because of his connection to the art world had made her more interesting to him.

And yet his question was a reasonable question. Would Rykken and Laith be willing to live in Taos with her so she could study with Van Rijn?

"If I come to Taos, I can't take the job at the gallery or the loft above it. It wouldn't be right to accept that kind of help from you, Nathan, not now." But the other . . . especially since she'd been honest about where her heart lay. "I need to discuss this with . . . him."

Cyan wiped a damp palm against her shorts and wondered what Nathan would think if she said *them* instead.

"Don't take too long."

"I won't."

She said good-bye and closed the phone. Sunlight danced off the tight bracelet on her wrist. She pocketed the cell phone, touched the band and looked again for a way to remove it. There wasn't one.

Previous conversations with Laith filtered through her thoughts. There'd been plenty featuring Rykken, enough so she'd felt as if she knew him even before meeting him. There'd been fewer about their families, none about the place they called home. It hadn't seemed all that important at the time, but now it did.

She thought about going into the cabin, waking them, telling them about the opportunity to study with Pieter Van Rijn. But worry, unnerving premonition formed a cold knot in her stomach. She decided to take a walk and give herself a chance to think about what was most important to her—in case she had to choose between living with them, committing to them, or Taos.

Chapter Five

Rykken rose from the bed, muscles rippling, possessiveness screaming from every cell. *You heard?*

Yes.

He tries to lure our mate away! Enough of this. It's time to take her home with us.

She has yet to agree.

She will when I am done with her.

Rykken snagged the sweatpants he'd worn the previous day and put them on, frowned when he saw Laith sitting on the bed, making no effort to leave it though his face was tight with worry.

You intend to do nothing? Rykken asked, disbelief in his voice.

Laith lifted his hands. *I doubt conversation is on your mind and I can't risk letting my bands touch the ones she now wears, not until we're ready to bind her to us.*

Rykken glanced down at his own wrists, felt the heaviness of the Ylan stones as they drew closer to the point of separating and migrating. *Then I will make the case for both of us and convince her she belongs to us.*

He retrieved the *bouren* tie—the restraint created to secure lawbreakers—that he'd brought with him for his hair, then left the cabin. With each step the mating fever of the Vesti burned hotter. Even without the serum he'd injected through his mating fangs, he found it easy to track Cyan.

She wouldn't escape him. Couldn't. Too much was at stake,

not just the survival of the Amato and the Vesti, but his own happiness and Laith's.

"You belong to us. You belong *with* us," Rykken said, crowding her when he caught up to her, loving the way submission filled her eyes, vibrated through her and revealed itself in the curves of her body, the heady scent of increased arousal.

He took her lips before she could challenge his statement. Thrust his tongue into her mouth as his hands made short work of ridding her of her shirt. Her soft mews of pleasure fed the fire burning inside him, acknowledged his right to dominate, to claim her so thoroughly that the thought of any other male would never enter her mind.

With a growl he raised her arms, used the *bouren* tie to tether her wrists and secure them to the tree limb above her head. He felt her shock at being restrained, felt also the tightening of her nipples where they pressed against his chest.

His hands went to her hips, to the front of her shorts, opened them and peeled them down along with her panties until they fell to the ground. Raw hunger assailed him at having her helpless, bared.

The need to taste her, to bury his face between her thighs and spear his tongue into her wet core overrode the desire to take her with his cock. He kissed his way down to her beautiful cunt. Licked and bit, told her with his actions what he'd told her with words. She belonged to them, *to him*.

He held her in position as he thrust his tongue into her opening, fucked her. Reveled in the way she panted, whimpered, tried to wrap her legs around him and hold him locked to her cunt.

"Agree to return home with us," he said, moving to her clit, rubbing the tiny head with his tongue, sucking it until she was close to orgasm, then stopping. "Agree to commit to us."

"Please," Cyan begged, her heart racing, her body screaming, needing his mouth, his cock.

She'd fantasized about a dominant lover. But no fantasy would ever match the reality of Rykken. She was a willing slave to his touch, to the desire he created in her, to the primitive need for safety and protection he satisfied.

"You will commit to us. You will return home with us," he said, making her shudder with pleasure as his tongue slid down the center of her and once again thrust into her core.

He repeated his demand each time he left her channel to claim her clit. Continued taking her to the edge of release over and over again until she was willing to agree to anything if he'd let her come.

"Yes," she finally whispered and he rewarded her by capturing her clit, sucking on it, striking it with his tongue until orgasm slammed into her and left her boneless.

Satisfaction filled Rykken as he freed Cyan from the *bouren* tie and stretched her out on the soft grass. *His!*

The word pulsed through every cell, made his cock swell further. He stripped and covered her, nearly purred when she spread her thighs, tilted her pelvis in order to coax his penis into entering her, to giving her his seed.

His! It was a chant almost impossible to ignore as he rubbed against her wet folds, bathed in heated arousal and coated himself with her scent.

He threaded his fingers through hers, held her hands to the ground, his wristbands touching hers as he took her lips.

His! It became an insistent call, repeated with each beat of his heart.

Laith's image surfaced and was growled away. Returned as Rykken's mind fought his body, as personal honor fought genetic programming.

Rykken's hips bucked. His penis throbbed. He was desperate to enter her, to finish this claiming here and now.

The Ylan stones at his wrists hummed, prepared to separate, to migrate.

Mine! his cock screamed even as he forced himself to roll off Cyan before it was too late and they were bound together without Laith's inclusion.

He took himself in hand, stroked up and down roughly until fire roared through his cock in a lava-hot release. And then Laith was there, scooping Cyan into his arms.

She agreed to return home with us, to commit to us, Rykken said, still shuddering from orgasm.

Then let's take her now, Laith said, his features and voice strained, his cock pressed hard against the front of his jeans.

Cyan wrapped her arms around Laith's neck, content to bask in the afterglow of passion for a few minutes longer.

"My clothes," she murmured.

"You won't need them where we're going," Laith said, piquing her curiosity and clearing some of the sensual haze from her mind.

Instead of returning to the cabin he continued along the path she'd been on, then turned onto one she would have sworn wasn't there the day before when she explored.

An adobe building came into view. Rykken moved ahead of them, opened the door.

Surprise made Cyan laugh in delight when Laith carried her inside. They were in an intimate, terraced garden. Above them the ceiling was clear glass to allow the sun to shine on the lush flowering plants. In the center of the room, amid an intricate pattern of stones, was a thick mattress on a frame that rested close to the ground.

Laith set her on her feet, stripped out of his pants then pulled her against him. She shivered, loved the heat of his skin, the hard press of his cock. Rykken took up a position at her back, his penis nestled against the cleft of her buttocks.

"You agreed to return home with us? To commit to us?" Laith asked.

As if Rykken made it possible to say anything but yes.

She nodded, expected Laith's lips to curve upward in a smile. Instead he grew more serious. His eyes bore into hers and uneasiness filled her.

"Rykken and I cannot live in Taos," Laith said, unable to simply take her to Belizair as he'd intended for them to do when they brought her to the transport chamber. "Our home is far from here, in a place you wouldn't have heard of, though you will be welcomed and will find yourself much sought after as an artist there."

What are you doing? Rykken growled. *She has agreed. That is all Council law requires.*

She must have a true choice, not just the illusion of one. Otherwise she might come to hate us for stealing away the chance to study with an artist she has long admired. Do you want to risk that?

No. It was accompanied by a snarl.

Laith brushed his lips over Cyan's. "Will you commit to us and return home with us?"

Somehow she'd known it would come down to this choice. She was glad now for having managed a few moments alone before Rykken caught up to her.

She'd been fifteen when her mother was diagnosed with cancer. Nineteen when her mother's death demonstrated the tenuous nature of life, showed how quickly it could end and impressed on Cyan the importance of living fully, of holding on to happiness.

Her art and her life were inextricably bound together. Her satisfaction came from creating, from capturing moments in time, translating emotion and stripping her subjects to their soul, from touching others with her work—not from gaining fame or recognition.

She still had so many questions for Laith and Rykken, but they didn't need to be answered right now. She doubted the answers would change her own.

What she'd found in their arms was the chance for a lifetime of happiness. And even for the opportunity to study with Pieter Van Rijn, she wouldn't give it up.

"I'll commit to you. I'll go home with you," she said and felt the tension drain from both men.

They hugged her before stepping away. "Then see us as we truly are," Laith said.

The air in the room seemed to vibrate with energy and the stones set in the floor and in Laith's wristbands shimmered as though they were molten liquid. Cyan's breath caught in her throat, her heartbeat sounded loud and fast in her ears as a thousand golden particles of light gathered behind Laith, took form, became the feathered wings she'd captured in her drawing.

She turned and found Rykken as she'd drawn him, the bat-winged demon to Laith's angel though she instinctively knew they were something other than what they'd been defined by religion. She reached out, touched the deep-brown suede of Rykken's wing, saw him close his eyes and felt him shudder in pleasure. "What are you?"

"Vesti."

"And I am Amato," Laith said, moving in close enough that it was Cyan who shuddered when his wing brushed across her buttock in an erotic caress.

She ran her fingers along the golden-brown edge of Laith's wing. Arousal coated her labia and inner thighs as she looked at them, as she remembered their intensely carnal reactions when they'd seen the picture she'd drawn of them together.

"Make love to me," she whispered, needing their touch more than answers. Wondering if it would always be that way when she was with them.

It was Rykken who picked her up in his arms. Rather than toss her onto the bed, he held her as Laith positioned himself on his back, his wings spread across the mattress like an exotic comforter.

Her cunt clenched. A whimper escaped.

Rykken placed her at the foot of the bed on her hands and knees but didn't release his grip on her hip. His finger trailed along the seam of her buttocks, circled the tight rosette of her anus. "This time we'll take you together, both of us inside you at once. When we are finished you will be bound to us completely, ours to pleasure and protect until this life gives way to the next." He leaned in, lightly bit her shoulder. "Do you want that, Cyan?"

Her cunt spasmed in answer. "Yes."

"Then mount Laith."

It was a command she found easy to obey. She crawled up his body, guided his cock to her opening and impaled herself on it. The feel of his wings against her thighs and legs was incredibly erotic, the sight of his face as she took him in his true form something she'd forever remember.

Laith entwined his fingers with hers so the bands at her wrists were pressed to his above their heads. She moaned when Rykken joined them, gasped when his fingers danced over her dark opening, coated the tight rosette with something that warmed, made her pant and writhe with the heightened need to feel him inside her.

"Please," she whispered, lifting, sliding along Laith's cock as she pushed against Rykken's fingers.

Beneath her Laith's breathing grew fast. His hips jerked, sent his penis back into her and made her gasp as whatever Rykken was using for lubricant found its way into her channel.

"Hurry," Laith said, bucking, his mouth capturing Cyan's.

Rykken's cock head pressed against the tight rosette he'd prepared and she pushed against him as she'd done to his fingers. Pain and pleasure blended, became an addiction she would never choose to fight.

Sensation, heat, ecstasy. All of them pulsed through her, left her begging for more.

Rykken's wings spread, covered and trapped them in a sensual cocoon. His hands joined with hers and Laith's, bands touching, symbolic, intimate.

They began thrusting then, in perfect sync, building the hunger, adding to it with their kisses, their moans, their whispered words of a future together, their promises to always be there for her.

Cyan gave herself over to their care, accepted what they offered, matched it with her own words of commitment. Their thrusting increased in pace, shook the bed and made the room hum with energy, with a light show fed by the cries of pleasure, the wild energy of orgasm.

• • •

For long moments afterward they lay in a tangled heap of arms and legs, wings and silky hair, their bodies pressed together. "I liked that," Cyan murmured, freeing her hands, intending to explore soft wings and breathtaking masculine features, but distracted instead by the blend of green and red now present in the bracelets they'd placed on her, as if the stones on Rykken's and Laith's bands had merged onto her own.

You have guessed and found the truth, Cyan. The Ylan stones separated and migrated. For us this is what it means to commit, to bind ourselves to another, Laith said, kissing her, delaying for a second the realization he'd spoken in her mind.

When she stiffened, Rykken laughed, kissed her shoulder. *Perhaps it would be better for us to leave the transport chamber and get to the living quarters assigned us. There we can spend the day answering your questions as well as making love.*

Shock shot through Cyan. She rose on her elbow, felt confused. The room they were in was the same.

Laith caressed her cheek with the back of his hand. "We aren't of Earth, Cyan." He indicated the door with the tilt of his head. "A new world waits for you to explore and capture in your art."

Fear settled in her chest. "And my old world?"

"Your things will be brought here by the bounty hunters who serve the Council," Laith said. "Your disappearance will be handled by them as well, in a way that will minimize worries and fears for your safety."

"But I can't go back?"

"I don't know. Not many humans have been brought here and none of them has asked to be returned."

"Why me?" she asked, almost dreading the answer.

Rykken moved then, made her shiver with renewed need as his wing brushed against her leg. His hand cupped her breast possessively. "Don't think to leave us, Cyan," he growled, his dominance making her feel secure.

Laith speared his fingers through her hair, reassured her with his kiss. "You are our hope, Cyan. Our future."

From his thoughts she learned of the Hotaling virus and its devastation. Saw the dreams he'd had of sharing her with Rykken, felt the depth of his belief—that the Goddess he held sacred intended this first sharing of a human mate between Amato and Vesti to light the way for others.

Laith's sureness became hers. And just as she'd captured their wings in her drawing, an image rose of her swelling with their children, answering their prayers and their dreams.

Her cunt lips parted and grew slick. Need rose and she rubbed herself against them, melted under the onslaught of their emotion and need, felt it more intensely, as if the bands in her wrists captured it, amplified it.

They do, Rykken said and she clung to them as they chased away any lingering fear with heated kisses and intimate touches, with masculine confidence and the erotic brush of feathers and suede, made love again before coming full circle, lying together in a tangled heap of arms and legs, wings and silky hair.

Ready? Laith and Rykken asked, united in their desire to introduce her to their world.

And this time she was. *I'm ready.*

Jory Strong

Jory has been writing since childhood and has never outgrown being a daydreamer. When she's not hunched over her computer, lost in the muse and conjuring up new heroes and heroines, she can usually be found reading, riding her horses, or hiking with her dogs.